LUNATICS

LUNATICS

A Novel by Bradley Denton

ST. MARTIN'S PRESS ❧ NEW YORK

LUNATICS. Copyright © 1996 by Bradley Denton. All rights reserved. Printed in the United States of America. No part of this book may be used or reproduced in any manner whatsoever without written permission except in the case of brief quotations embodied in critical articles or reviews. For information, address St. Martin's Press, 175 Fifth Avenue, New York, N.Y. 10010.

Design by Pei Loi Koay
Edited by Gordon Van Gelder

Library of Congress Cataloging-in-Publication Data

Denton, Bradley.
    Lunatics : a novel / by Bradley Denton ; [edited by Gordon
Van Gelder].—1st ed.
        p.   c.m.
    ISBN 0–312–14363–X (hardcover)
        1. Young men—Texas—Austin—Fiction. 2. Goddesses—
Fiction. I. Van Gelder, Gordon. II. Title.
PS3554.E588L86   1996
813'.54—dc20   96–1366
                                                            CIP

First edition: June 1996

10   9   8   7   6   5   4   3   2   1

for the owls

CONTENTS

◆

PART I

WOLF MOON

Friday, January 8, 1993

◆

I

❖

Jack Was Naked

Jack was naked, and it was night, and cold. The Moon shone full in a purple sky, but the trees and clouds tried to hide it. To be sure that its light fell on him, Jack closed his apartment door and went down to the street. He stepped gingerly on the concrete and gravel. When he reached the street and looked up, he had to squint to see past the glare of the streetlamps. But it was all right. A cloud moved away from the face of the Moon so that its light became as bright as the streetlamps'. Jack was sure that Lily would be able to spot him, so he sat down on the curb between two parked cars to wait. He yelped as his bare ass touched the concrete, then gritted his teeth until the coldness faded. The things a man would do for love.

He remembered a TV commercial that had aired back when the media had first realized that AIDS wasn't going to limit itself to gay men. The commercial, in an effort to promote the use of condoms, had featured a beautiful young woman speaking with solemn sincerity: "I'll do a lot of things for love," she had said. "But I won't die for it."

The first time that Jack had seen it, he had gone apeshit. "Well then, it's not *love*, is it?" he had yelled. "It's only *screwing*, isn't it? I mean, if it's *love*, dying's one of the *easier* things you'll do for it! If it's *love*, you'll crawl naked across a Wal-Mart parking lot covered with broken Coke bottles! If it's *love*, you'll starve yourself for a month and break the fast with a washtub full of horseshit! If it's *love*, you'll do a jig on a bed of nails while juggling hand grenades! If it's *love*, you'll run a razor across your arm and write poetry with the blood! If it's *love*, you'll—"

He had stopped upon realizing that everyone else in the bar was staring at him.

Now, gazing up at the Moon, waiting, he finished the sentence he had started a few years before. "—sit naked on the curb in January."

He knew that he should be freezing, but he didn't feel cold. Chilly, yes, but not so much so that he couldn't keep himself from shivering. His skin wasn't even goose pimpled. The one thing that did bother him was that his genitals had shrunk up tight against his body. Lily might be less than impressed. But Jack knew that the condition wouldn't last long. Lily's effect on him was incredible.

This would be only the third time that they had seen each other, but she was already the motivation behind everything he thought and did. He was grateful. For almost nine months before meeting her, Jack had cared about nothing. He hadn't been cynical or depressed. He just hadn't cared. With Natalie gone, he had been unable to work up any emotion of any kind over anything at all. He had remembered yelling at the TV in the bar as if it were a scene from a movie starring someone he didn't recognize.

Even the presidential campaign and election had left him unmoved. When one of his friends had asked him why he hadn't voted, he couldn't even explain his apathy by saying that the candidates were all bastards anyway. The truth, he had admitted, was that he didn't care if one of them *wasn't* a bastard, or that one of them might even make a positive difference in the course of national events.

He just didn't care.

On an intellectual level, he had been concerned about this emotional flatness, because he knew that it meant something was wrong with him. Whatever it was hadn't always been wrong, and despite what his friends thought, it hadn't gone wrong all at once. Once upon a time, Jack had been laughing, crying, and raging with the best of

4

them. He had protested injustice, howled at comedians, yelled at the TV, and fallen in and out of love. But it seemed to him that somewhere along the line he had contracted a slow, chronic virus that had drained the juice from him at a trickle—and then Natalie had wrecked her car in the rain, and the trickle had become a torrent, leaving him empty and dry.

But one week after Election Day, on the night of the first full Moon after Halloween, he had met Lily at the Avenue B Grocery. She had commented on the weather, and they had continued talking as they walked out of the store. They had wound up standing outside his apartment building, and after less than an hour of conversation, Jack had not only remembered everything that he had yelled at the TV in the bar, but had wanted to do all of those things and more to prove his love for Lily. He had told her so. She had laughed and asked him how he could be willing to crawl over broken glass for her when they had only just met and she hadn't done so much as kiss him on the cheek.

Jack hadn't had a good answer, so instead he'd said, "I'm a time traveler. In the future we're lovers. That's why I'll do anything you want—because in the future I'm already crazy about you."

"So how did we meet?" Lily had asked.

"Just like this," Jack had answered. "I came back to make sure it happened."

Lily had smiled. "What a coincidence. I came here just to make sure I met you, too. But I'm not from the future. I'm a goddess from the Moon."

After that, she had gone into his apartment with him, spent the night, and then disappeared for a month. Jack had tried everything he could think of to find her, including putting an ad in the notorious Personals section of the *Austin Chronicle*. But nothing had worked.

Then, on the night of December 9, she had appeared at his door. She'd had a hell of a time finding him, she'd said. Not only had he failed to wait naked in the light of the full Moon—standard procedure, she'd said—but there happened to be a lunar eclipse that night that had disoriented her. She had been half blind and lost while the Earth's shadow had covered the Moon, and she wasn't happy about it.

But she'd let him make it up to her.

Tonight Jack wasn't taking any chances. If he could see Lily only once a month, it was doubly important to avoid the risk of blowing it. So, cold or not, shrunken gonads or not, he was waiting outside on the curb in the light of the full Moon. He felt a little stupid, but he figured that love was supposed to make you feel stupid. At the very least.

A car went by, moving slowly. Jack cringed as it passed. A man and a woman were inside the car, and Jack thought he saw the woman look right at him. When the car was past, he told himself that he was being paranoid. The woman's expression had not been one of shock at seeing a naked man on the curb. It had just been a dull, bored stare out the window. There would not be any trouble. There couldn't be, at least not until after Lily had come to him and gone away again.

As Jack worried about the woman in the car, a shadow passed over him. He looked up but saw only the streetlamps and the Moon. Then he heard a rustle, and he looked down again. Lily had come. She stood in the street, smiling. She was wearing a blue dress and a white scarf, and she had let her black hair down so that it cascaded over her shoulders.

"Jack," she said. Her voice told him that she was happy with him. "Look what you've done for me. You'll catch your death."

She came toward him then, her clawed bird-feet clicking against the asphalt. She had worn shoes when they had first met, but there were no secrets between them now.

Jack stood. He had forgotten all about the cold, all about the car that had passed, all about everything except Lily.

"This is nothing," he said. "You should see the way I climb rivers and swim mountains."

Lily laughed and came into his arms. They kissed, and Jack felt dizzy. The scent of her hair, the soft pressure of her lips, and the firm resilience of her body charged and overloaded his senses. As Lily broke the kiss, Jack toppled backward and landed on his rump on the sidewalk.

He groaned. "You're going to kill me," he said.

"If you're lucky," Lily said. She tilted her head and cast a wry look down his body. "But you seem to be all right so far."

It was true. The base of Jack's spine ached, but everything else felt great. He stood, ignoring the popping sounds, and said, "Want to go inside?"

Lily shrugged her shoulders, teasing him. "Oh, I don't know. I'm more of an outdoor type. Wouldn't you like an open-air experience?"

"I've been having an open-air experience for the past half hour," Jack said. "I'd like an indoor one now, with a bed. And warm air from the wall vent."

Lily sighed. "You're so conventional. I'll race you." She bolted for the stairs on the outside of Jack's building. As she passed Jack, she trailed a fingernail across his chest.

"Yow!" Jack cried. He started after her, but she was already up the stairs and inside the apartment before he'd made it halfway. She was as fast as a falcon. Her clawed feet hadn't even seemed to touch the ground.

Jack ran after her, but he didn't make it to the stairs. A cop tackled him from behind, and he landed facedown in the dormant flower bed at the edge of the parking lot.

The cop cuffed Jack's hands behind his back, hauled him to his feet, and shoved him toward the patrol car while reciting his rights.

Jack was stunned. He hadn't heard a siren or even the patrol car's engine. But then, he had been preoccupied. He spat the dirt out of his mouth and then looked down to see if what he feared was true. Sure enough, he was still what one of his old girlfriends had called "perky." He suspected that this would not look good on the arrest report.

He tried to convince the cop to let him go upstairs to put on a pair of jeans and a T-shirt, but the cop was having none of it. The cop had a blanket in the car, he said, and Jack could cover himself with that. The cop would then have the blanket burned.

Another patrol car arrived then, its siren silent but lights flashing. The cop who emerged from this car was more sympathetic to Jack's plight, albeit amused.

"Let's get some pants on this guy before that thing goes off," the second cop said.

So the cops took Jack up to his apartment. Lily was not there, and Jack didn't think that either of the cops had seen her, so he didn't mention her. No sense in getting them both in trouble.

He discovered that it was difficult to pull on a pair of jeans with his hands cuffed behind his back. The cops wouldn't help. They were busy searching the place for evidence that Jack was a criminal of some kind—or, rather, of another kind than they already knew he was. They didn't find any, and they seemed disappointed.

"Not even a *Playboy* or *Penthouse*," the first cop grumbled. "What are you, strictly an exhibitionist?"

"Actually," Jack said, struggling with his jeans, "I'm an engineer. Or I was, anyway."

"Perverts associate trains with sex," the second cop murmured to the first.

"Not that kind of engineer," Jack said. His jeans were stuck at crotch level because he was even now exhibiting perkiness. It was beginning to be embarrassing. "Could one of you guys give me a hand?"

"In your dreams, pervo," the first cop said. The second cop applauded.

2

❖

Carolyn's Orgasm

Gave Her Hiccups

Carolyn's orgasm gave her hiccups, so she got up after Artie fell asleep and went into the bathroom to hold her nose and drink a glass of water. It didn't work, so she sat on the toilet, put her head between her knees, and hyperventilated. That didn't work either, but she got a slight rush when she stood up again, so it was almost worth it. For just a moment the buzzing in her ears and the pulsing darkness at the edge of her vision reminded her of some of her old drug experiences. A few of those days had been happy ones, although they'd almost killed her.

The hiccups were now stronger than ever, sending her entire upper body into quick convulsions. She had no idea why this happened so often with Artie. It had never happened with any of the other men she'd been with. But then, she hadn't come with most of them anyway. With Artie, coming was almost frighteningly easy, as if she were under the spell of some dark magic whenever they made love—except that half the time, the magic turned to hiccups as soon as they were finished. Carolyn couldn't help but think that it was a punishment for enjoying herself.

Artie appeared in the bathroom doorway, still naked, rubbing his sleep-sagged face. "You okay?" he asked blearily.

Carolyn nodded, but took a step back from him. Artie still had the thick vanilla smell of his semen about him. It was a smell that Carolyn liked during the moment, but not afterward. "Yeah, I'm—*hurp*—fine," she said. "It's just these goddamn mother—*hurp*—fucking hiccups again." She gave him a sharp look. "Sometimes I think you do it to me on—*hurp*—purpose."

Artie gave her a sleepy smile. "How could I do that?"

It pissed Carolyn off. She was being racked by spasms of near-epileptic proportions, and here the smug little prick who had done it to her was laughing about it.

"You think it's funny?" she said. "You think it's fucking—*hurp*—funny?"

Artie's smile disappeared. "No, babe, I just—"

Carolyn was having none of it. "You can just keep your—*hurp*—penis to yourself for a week or two, that's what you can—*hurp*—do. See how funny you think that—*hurp*—is."

Artie looked at the floor, avoiding the direct glare of Carolyn's anger. "Have you tried swallowing a teaspoon of dry sugar?" he asked.

Carolyn didn't bother answering. She hadn't tried it this time, but she'd tried it before, and it never worked. Artie knew that. Or maybe he was just too stupid to remember from one night to the next.

She looked at him standing there in the doorway. He was twenty-three years old with a golden, muscled body and a smooth, boyish face that only needed shaving every three days. And for someone so young, he was an amazing lover. When they weren't in bed, though, he irritated the living shit out of her.

That wasn't always his fault, and Carolyn knew it, and felt guilty about it. But she couldn't help herself. There was just something about him that got on her nerves and wouldn't get off.

It didn't help that she was thirty-seven, and that she didn't think she would be able to hold his interest forever. She knew that she was still physically beautiful—she had long legs, amber hair, blue eyes, good skin—but she also knew that with their age difference, Artie was going to stay beautiful longer than she was.

"Just go on back to—*hurp*—sleep," Carolyn said. She wasn't angry now, just tired of having to deal with the hiccups and Artie at the same time. "I'll come back to—*hurp*—bed as soon as this is over."

Artie nodded. "Okay." He started to turn away, then paused. "Say, did you see that owl outside our window while we were screwing? Biggest one I ever saw."

Carolyn was getting a headache. "No, I—*hurp*—didn't. When we're making love, I'm paying attention to—*hurp*—you."

Artie reddened. "Well, I was paying attention to you too, babe. But I mean, I heard this owl fly up, and when I checked it out it was like it was looking at us between the blinds, and then it flew off, and it—"

Carolyn just stared at Artie and hiccupped twice.

"Well, it was big," Artie said, turning away.

Carolyn watched the muscles of his back and butt as he left and knew that many women would envy her. But those women didn't know how much work a guy like this could be. He was never mean or deliberately hurtful, but he was unsocialized and naive. Sometimes she even thought that he was flat-out dumb.

Still, there were compensations. He could be awfully sweet. And he would do anything that Carolyn told him to do. Although that in itself was irritating too, sometimes.

Carolyn tightened the belt of her robe, which had come loose during the past few hiccups, and headed for the kitchen to make a cup of tea with honey. It never cured her hiccups, but it gave her something to do while she waited for them to go away.

The telephone rang just as the teapot started whistling, and Carolyn was startled. The glowing blue numerals on the microwave oven said that it was 11:43 P.M. No one called her this late. Her friends all knew better. So that meant that this was either an emergency or one of Artie's idiot pals. Or one of his ex-girlfriends calling him for comfort because the new guy wasn't being nice to her.

Let it ring, let the machine get it. She had tea to make.

Carolyn was pouring the hot water into a mug when Jack's voice blared from the answering-machine speaker. "Carolyn!" he bellowed. "Hi! It's Jack! How ya doin'? Hope everything's great! Uh, let's see, why'd I call? Oh yeah! I'm in jail!"

Boiling water splashed onto the kitchen counter, and Carolyn yelped, dropping the teapot and jumping away to avoid being scalded. The teapot knocked over the mug, which rolled off the counter and broke on the floor. Water and bits of ceramic sprayed everywhere.

Carolyn scrambled around the mess to the phone, picking up the receiver with one hand and punching off the answering machine with the other.

"Jack?" she yelled. "Jack? What do you mean, you're in jail?"

There was a brief silence, then Jack's voice again. "Hey, you're there," he said. "I'm sorry to bother you, but I wanted to let you know that I'm in jail."

Carolyn couldn't stand it. She had no idea why all of the men she'd had in her life were as stupid as stumps. "You already said that. I want to know why you're there."

"Well, I was outside my apartment, naked," Jack said, "and a police officer saw me."

"What the fuck were you doing outside naked?"

Jack sighed. "It was a misunderstanding."

Carolyn was willing to bet that was the biggest understatement she'd heard all week, but she decided to let it go for now. Jack was a friend, and he was in trouble. She could get the details later.

"I guess I'd better come down and bail you out," she said.

"Oh, you don't have to do that," Jack said. He sounded surprised that Carolyn would even think of such a thing.

"Then why'd you call me?" she asked. "Don't you need to be bailed out?"

There was another brief silence. "Well, I—I guess I don't really know," Jack said. "They just told me that I could call someone, so I did."

Carolyn's attitude softened. Jack sounded like a child. In fact, ever since Natalie's death, he had seemed like nothing so much as a confused little boy. Carolyn began to feel sorry for being annoyed with him, and then had a sudden memory of the first time she had made love with him back in college. He had been clumsy and quick, and she had been annoyed with him then, too. Afterward, he had confessed that she was his first. That had stunned her. At nineteen, she had already lost track of how many other partners she'd had, but she knew that she hadn't been the first time for any of them. And Jack had seemed so cool and world-weary when she'd met him in the cafeteria that she'd never dreamed he'd turn out to be a goofy kid in bed.

Later she had realized that it had actually made her like him.

That had been eighteen years ago, and now she found herself feeling the same way about him again. He was a goofy kid who had gotten himself into something he couldn't handle, and she wanted to take care of him.

"Okay," Carolyn said. "I'll be there as soon as I can."

"You don't have to—"

"I said I'll be there, all right?" Carolyn paused, remembering, amazed that she and Jack were still friends after so many years. After Halle and Katy and Natalie and everything else. "And listen, I'm—I'm glad you thought to call me. I would've figured you'd call Steve and Katy."

"Well, I tried to," Jack said, "but I got their answering machine. They go out on Fridays sometimes, though, so I'm sure they're okay."

Carolyn's irritation returned. "Yeah, I'm sure."

"And then I tried to call Halle, but a babysitter answered. Halle has a date tonight. Isn't that great?"

Carolyn squatted and began picking up the broken pieces of ceramic. The water on the floor was still warm, but not hot enough to burn. "Yeah. Great."

"So then I called you."

"Gee," Carolyn said dryly, "I'm so flattered to be on your list somewhere."

Another silence. "I don't understand," Jack said then.

"Never mind. You're downtown, right? Municipal Court building, second floor?"

"Yup. I've got black ink all over my fingers. I can't figure it out. I mean, why fingerprint me? My hands are *always* naked. It's the rest of me that the arresting officer will have to identify, isn't it?"

Carolyn didn't respond to that. Instead, she said, "Don't worry. I've bailed out people before." Most of them had been her boyfriends. The most recent one, in fact, had been Artie, on a drunk and disorderly not long after she'd met him.

Jack had waited longer, but he had finally proven himself to be like all the others—in this one respect, at least. The realization made Carolyn angry.

"But just what the hell were you doing naked out in public?" she asked again. "I mean, Jesus, Jack, what was going through your head?"

Jack answered without hesitation. "I was waiting on a goddess from the Moon," he said. "Her name is Lily."

"Lily," Carolyn repeated. She was having trouble processing the information.

"Lilith, to be accurate," Jack said. "But I like to call her Lily. You know that old Who song 'Pictures of Lily'? She makes me think of that song."

Carolyn stood and dropped the broken bits of the mug into the wastebasket beside the refrigerator. "Better hang up now, Jack," she said. "I'll be right there."

"Okay. You're a pal. Bye." There was a click, and the line was dead.

Carolyn stared at the receiver for a few seconds, then slapped it into its cradle. She was Jack's "pal." Seventeen years ago she'd aborted his baby, and now she was his "pal."

She couldn't think of anyone who had a weirder and more fucked-up life than she had. Maybe Halle or Natalie. Except that Natalie didn't have any life at all anymore.

"Whozzat onna phone?" Artie shuffled into the kitchen. He was wearing his pajama bottoms now, but they were riding low and exposing the golden curls of his pubic hair. Carolyn felt a quick rush of lust, but suppressed it.

"That was my friend Jack."

Artie squinted at her through a fog of sleep. "Jack? Dude whose wife got killed on Valentine's Day?"

"That's the one." Carolyn pushed past Artie and went down the hall into their bedroom. She shrugged out of her robe and began pulling on jeans and a sweatshirt.

Artie followed her. "Whazz goin' on? Where you goin'?"

"Jack's in trouble. I'm going down to the city jail to see if I can help."

Artie seemed to snap awake. He pulled off his pajama bottoms and began getting dressed too.

Carolyn looked at him sidelong as she sat on the edge of the bed and tied her shoes. "What do you think you're doing?"

"I thought I'd go with you," Artie said.

"Why? You don't know Jack."

Artie looked puzzled. "Sure I do. I met him at what's-their-faces' New Year's party."

Carolyn rolled her eyes. "Yeah, but you don't *know* him."

Artie shrugged, then sat down beside Carolyn and pulled on the pointy-toed blue cowboy boots that she hated. "Well, I know he's an old friend of yours. And at the party he seemed pretty cool for a guy whose wife just got creamed."

"It's been almost a year."

"Well," Artie said, looking thoughtful, "I don't think I'd be cool if you'd gotten creamed a year ago."

Carolyn couldn't believe the crap that came out of Artie's mouth sometimes. They hadn't even known each other a year ago. "I'm overwhelmed," she said. Then she stood, grabbed her keys from the dresser, and started out. She wasn't going to waste any time waiting for Artie. Her little house off Rundberg Lane was twenty minutes from downtown if traffic cooperated, and it probably wouldn't. If Artie really wanted to go with her, he could get his ass in gear and catch up with her before she reached the car.

He did.

❖

Carolyn had a terrible time finding a place to park. The city lot under the interstate overpass across from the Municipal Court building was full. Carolyn was annoyed but not surprised. It was Friday night, and the Sixth Street club crowd would have every space within five blocks parked up.

"Dude I work with at the restaurant says his band's playing down here tonight," Artie said as Carolyn drove past Sixth on the interstate access road. "After we spring your friend, you want to check it out?"

Carolyn gave him a look that had withered a lot of other men. But Artie just looked back at her with a benign, uncomprehending expression. Sometimes Carolyn supposed that was why they were still together after seven months: He just wasn't bright enough to know when she was pissed off, so he never got pissed off in turn.

Sometimes she found it endearing. But this wasn't one of those times.

"No, I do not want to check out your friend's excuse for a band,"

Carolyn said, clipping each word off short. "In the first place, I don't know how long it's going to take to find one single goddamn parking spot, let alone get Jack out of jail. And in the second place, I was coming down here back when they had real bands with real music, so I'm not much interested in hearing the kind of cover-band shit you dragged me to last time."

Artie gave a pouty frown. "Jeez, babe, I'm sorry."

Carolyn felt guilty then, but her mood didn't soften. "Yeah, yeah. Help me look for a space."

"There's one," Artie said.

To Carolyn's further irritation, he was right. She swerved her Accord into the spot and was already starting to walk the four blocks back to the Municipal Court building before Artie was out of his seat belt. She heard him shut his door and run to catch her.

"Whoa, wait up," he said. His breath came out as soft, crystalline fog. "You don't want to take off down here without me."

"Why's that?"

"Well, jeez, there are a lot of drunks and jerks around. You might get, I dunno, bothered. Or assaulted. Or something." Artie's voice trailed off.

"So I need you to protect me, is that it?" Carolyn asked.

Artie's eyes darted about as if he were looking for someplace to hide. "That's not what I meant, babe," he said.

"I'm not your 'babe,'" Carolyn said. "I'm not anyone's 'babe.' All right?"

Artie was quiet for the rest of the walk to the Municipal Court.

As they crossed Seventh Street to the brown-brick building, Carolyn saw Katy and Stephen Corman coming out. She and Artie met them on the sidewalk below the smoked-glass doors.

"Let me guess," Carolyn said before either Stephen or Katy could speak. "You got Jack's message."

Stephen nodded. His thin, pale face looked even more pinched than usual, and his thick glasses were fogging up. Even in a down coat, he seemed skinny. "We didn't even take off our coats when we got home. Just turned around and came down here."

"Running to take care of Jack," Katy said, pulling her wool scarf away from her mouth. "The way we always do. The way that you do too, apparently. It's virtually a Pavlovian response, isn't it?"

She sounded bitter, which surprised Carolyn. Katy had always seemed willing to do anything for Jack. In fact, he was the only person that Katy had *ever* seemed willing to do anything for. Carolyn wondered how that made Stephen feel—and whether he even knew that Katy had lived with Jack for several months before Stephen came into the picture.

Carolyn had been horribly jealous when Katy and Jack had been together. And she'd been confused because Katy was short and chubby, which she didn't think was Jack's type. But then Carolyn had come to realize that Katy was also smart as hell, which explained Jack's attraction to her. It also explained why Carolyn hadn't been able to help liking her.

Stephen, though, Carolyn couldn't quite figure out. He wasn't particularly tall, but he was thin, and that made him look like he towered over his wife. He had a semi-permanent stoop that Carolyn thought might be an attempt to correct that. And she knew that he was probably bright—he taught American literature at the University of Texas—but he always seemed rather dim in comparison to Katy.

Carolyn didn't know what kept them together. But she doubted that people who looked at her and Artie had a clue as to what kept them together, either. She wasn't too sure herself.

Artie scuffed his shoe against one of the concrete steps—to get everyone's attention, Carolyn knew. He hated feeling left out. "Uh, what's a Pavlovian response?" he asked.

Stephen and Katy both looked at him as if he had just popped into their space from another dimension. Carolyn wished that she could just make him invisible unless she wanted him around. Sometimes he was an embarrassment.

"A bell rings," Katy said. "A dog drools."

Carolyn leaned close to Artie. "You know, like in the Rolling Stones song," she muttered. " 'Bitch.' "

Artie shrugged. "Well, you know, I like the Stones okay, but I guess that one must be before my time."

An awkward silence followed.

Stephen coughed. "Um, anyway, it turns out that there's nothing to be done until morning. They're holding him overnight. Something about a judge not being able to set bail until then. And they said they explained that to Jack before he called, but—"

"But Jack doesn't seem to be receiving messages transmitted from this particular planet these days," Katy said, interrupting. "So he called us anyway, and, obviously, you as well. If we stay here long enough, I have no doubt that everyone we know will show up. But I think I'd like to go home instead."

"Not much else to do right now," Stephen said.

"That's a drag," Artie said brightly.

"Shut up, Artie," Carolyn said. She tried to mutter it under her breath, but it came out louder than she intended. Stephen and Katy pretended not to have heard, and Artie gave her another pouty frown.

"By the way, Carolyn," Katy said, "when Jack called you, did he tell you why he's here?"

Carolyn nodded, grateful to have her attention drawn away from Artie. "Yeah, he did."

Katy shook her head and gave an exasperated sigh. *"We* had to hear it from the police."

For a moment then, Carolyn found that she and Katy were smiling at each other. She knew what it was: Both of them had seen Jack naked—although it had been a long time ago in each case—and each of them could imagine what he had looked like tonight as he stood outside his apartment building. He had probably, Carolyn thought, looked pretty good. He had always looked pretty good. And she was sure that Katy was thinking the same thing.

Stephen coughed again, and Katy's smile vanished. Carolyn made hers vanish too.

"I heard what you said when you were on the phone, babe," Artie said. "Dude was buck naked, right?"

"I believe that the legal term is public indecency," Katy said. "Or something of that nature."

Artie grinned. "Yeah, well, it still means buck naked, doesn't it?"

Stephen was looking at Carolyn. It was clear that he was avoiding looking at Artie. "Katy and I have already said that we'll take care of the bail tomorrow. We'll call to let you know what happens."

Carolyn nodded. "I'd appreciate that. And I'd be happy to chip in on the bail."

Stephen shook his head. "No need. We'll be getting it back anyway. I don't think Jack will skip town."

"Of course not," Katy said. "He's already skipped the planet Earth."

"You can't really blame him," Artie said. "I mean, the dude's wife got creamed."

"Talk to you tomorrow, then," Stephen said to Carolyn. She could tell that he was pretending to be oblivious to Artie's existence. "Good night."

"Sure," Carolyn said. "Thanks." She thought about giving him and Katy each a quick hug, then decided not to. She had never hugged either of them before, except at New Year's Eve parties, and she wasn't sure this was the time to start.

Katy said good night as well, and then she and Stephen headed eastward down the sidewalk and crossed the interstate access road to the city parking lot.

"Hey, how'd they find a space there?" Artie asked, too loudly.

Carolyn turned away from him and jaywalked back across Seventh Street. The night was cold and she was embarrassed and angry, so she walked fast again.

And again, Artie caught up with her. "Did you notice that ever since this Jack dude called, you don't have the hiccups?" he asked.

Carolyn looked at his face. It wasn't fair to be annoyed with him. He wasn't stupid, really—just young. If she should be annoyed with anyone, she thought, it should be with herself. After all, she was old enough to know better than to be involved with someone with whom she had so little in common.

She had the sudden awful realization that he'd been two years old when she'd lost her virginity.

"Shut up, Artie," she said again.

3

◆

The Woman Had Wings

The woman had wings. Stephen was sure of it. He was pulling the Toyota out of the city lot onto the northbound I-35 access ramp, and he saw her atop a parked car. The car was parked beside one of the support pillars of the overpass, and the pillar blocked her from view until he was already on the ramp and accelerating. So he had only a glimpse of her.

But a glimpse was all he needed. Some things, Stephen thought, could be taken in quickly.

She was squatting on the roof of a seventies-era Chevy Nova. It was too dark to see the color of the car, but the woman herself was illuminated by a shaft of moonlight. She was looking westward toward the municipal building and police station. Her skin was as pale as skim milk. Her hair was long, thick, and black. She was nude.

Also, she had dark-feathered wings sprouting from her shoulder blades. As the Toyota drove past her, Stephen saw the wings spread out and shudder. Most of the feathers were as black as the woman's hair, but those near the wing tips were streaked with white.

Stephen tried to look back over his shoulder at her, and the Toyota almost swerved into the guardrail of the access ramp.

"Stephen!" Katy yelped. "Watch what you're doing!"

Stephen straightened out the wheels, then checked the rearview mirrors. The roadway behind them was clear. He stopped the Toyota, put it into reverse, and began backing down the ramp.

"Honey, you're going to kill us!" Katy shouted, and then gurgled something incoherent.

Stephen found that he rather liked it. Katy was never incoherent. It was a refreshing change.

"Didn't you see her?" he asked. "On top of that car?"

He brought the Toyota to a lurching stop at the parking lot entrance, put it into Drive, and pulled back into the lot. He switched the headlights to high beams and pointed the Toyota at the Nova beside the support pillar.

The Nova was still there, but the winged woman was gone.

Stephen looked at his wife. She was wide-eyed and shaken.

"I'm sorry," Stephen said. "I thought I saw something. But it's gone now."

Katy took a deep, shuddering breath. When she let it out, Stephen could see from the look in her eyes that she was back to her normal articulate self. He could also see that he was in trouble.

"I'm curious," Katy said, "as to just what you might have seen that would warrant a backward plunge down an interstate access ramp."

Stephen considered for a second. Katy would know if he lied, but he didn't want to tell the whole truth. "I thought I saw a naked woman," he said.

Katy raised her eyebrows, opened her mouth, and nodded in mock understanding. "Ah, I see. At age thirty-four, you still find yourself so unfamiliar with the particulars of the female anatomy that you find it necessary to behave like a lunatic at even the imagined sight of bare breasts."

"I guess so," Stephen said. He turned the car around and returned to the interstate ramp.

"Maybe I should drive," Katy said. "Unlike you, I find that I'm able to function in the presence of nudity, whether real or fantasized."

"I'm fine," Stephen said, looking over his shoulder to check his blind spot. "Don't worry about it."

"I'm not worried. I'm in fear for my life."

Stephen said nothing. Katy would have a cutting response for anything. He would have to wait out her mood.

No matter what, though, he couldn't tell her that he thought he'd seen not only a naked woman, but a naked woman with wings sprouting from her back. Katy was so contemptuous of the irrational that she didn't even acknowledge the existence of dreams. She claimed to have never had one. Once she was asleep, she said, her brain was a black void until the alarm clock went off.

Maybe it hadn't been wings anyway, Stephen thought. Maybe the moonlight had made a long coat or poncho look winglike.

A coat or a poncho with feathers.

He turned west onto 2222 to cut across town, and a battered pickup truck with no lights blasted out from under the overpass and nearly hit the Toyota. The pickup blared its horn, swerved across three lanes and through a red light, and then disappeared down Highway 290 East.

As the pickup's horn blared, Katy screamed. When the truck was gone and the Toyota was headed west on 2222, she took a deep breath and said, "Pull over and let me drive."

Stephen didn't look at her. He gripped the wheel tight with both hands. "That wasn't my fault," he said. His voice quavered. "The guy ran a red light. He didn't even have his headlights on."

"Pull over and let me drive."

Stephen pulled into a Circle K convenience store parking lot, put the car into Park, and shut off the engine. He took his keys out of the ignition switch.

"You didn't have to turn it off," Katy said. "We could just switch seats."

Stephen looked at her and decided that yes, he still loved her, but he sure didn't like her much.

"Why?" he asked. "Don't you have your keys?"

Katy gave him a pointed stare. "Yes, I have my keys. I have my keys in my purse. I always have my purse with me." She hefted her black leather purse and shook it. It jingled. "See? I have my purse; therefore I also have my keys. Whether or not I have my keys, however, is irrelevant to what I said. My point was that you did not have to turn off the engine, since we'll only be here for fifteen seconds while we trade places."

"We've already been here more than fifteen seconds," Stephen said. He had resolved to stay pissed off for a while.

"That," Katy said, "is because you're being a jerk."

"Wanting you to use your own keys doesn't make me a jerk."

Katy's eyes widened, and her nostrils flared. They did the same thing when she was turned on. Stephen thought it was weird that she looked the same way when she was angry as she did when she was aroused. Sometimes it made him feel as if she was angry at him for making love to her.

Not that there'd been much of that lately.

"I have to disagree," Katy said. "My opinion is that behaving like an unreasonable, infantile, childishly possessive motherfucker does indeed make you a jerk."

Stephen felt a warm flush of impending victory. Katy almost always won their arguments, but on those rare occasions when she resorted to obscenity, he knew she was vulnerable.

"The last time you used my keys," he said, "you put them in your purse, and I was stranded the next day. I had to call a colleague for a ride to campus."

Katy's nostrils flared wider. She looked scary. "I told you that I was borrowing your keys. I didn't have any choice. Mine were lost."

"Ah-hah!" Stephen said, and then paused. He was behaving like a bastard, and he knew it. But he pressed the attack anyway, trying to sound as much like Katy as he could. "You've just said that you *always* have your keys because they're *always* in your purse, which is *always* with you. But how can that be true if, as you now admit, you on at least one occasion *lost* them?"

Katy glared at him for a long, blistering moment, then turned away and stared through the windshield toward the fluorescent glow of the Circle K.

"Well?" Stephen said.

"Take me home," Katy said. Her voice was a monotone.

Stephen put his key back into the ignition switch, started the car, and drove them home. When he pulled into the carport of their red-brick house in Allandale, Katy opened the door and got out before the Toyota came to a full stop. She was in the house and had slammed the front door behind her before Stephen had turned off the engine.

"Shit," Stephen said.

After eight years of marriage, and seven months of living together before that, he hadn't learned a thing. Not that he didn't know Katy.

On the contrary; he *knew* everything he needed to know about getting along with his wife. He just hadn't managed to *learn* any of it. The difference between knowing something and learning it, he thought, was like the difference between reading a play and staging it—or between understanding the concept of a zone defense and actually playing full-court basketball. Knowledge didn't count for much if you couldn't execute.

That was his problem. For a long time now, he and Katy just hadn't been able to . . . execute.

He got out of the car and went to the front door. It was locked, so he reached into his coat pocket for his keys. They weren't there, so he checked his other coat pocket and then his pants pockets. No keys.

He trudged back to the car. His keys hung from the ignition switch on the steering column, still swaying. They caught the moonlight and glinted at him. All four of the Toyota's doors were, of course, locked.

Stephen looked up at the Moon. Just to look. Just to put off what he had to do next. The night was clear and cold, and the Moon shone so bright that he could hardly make out any of its features. The pure white light made his eyes water. He wiped them on his coat sleeve.

"Shit," he said again. The word came out loud, and he worried for a second that some of his neighbors might have heard. But the surrounding houses stayed dark and quiet. He trudged to his own front door and rang the bell.

He stood and waited and looked at the Moon. After a while he rang again. This time Katy opened the door, handed him her keys, and slammed the door in his face.

Stephen trudged back to the car and retrieved his keys, then made sure that he had both sets of keys in hand before he locked the car again. Then he trudged back to the front door, unlocked it, and went inside. He was careful to relock the door behind him. Katy hated unlocked doors.

The light was on in the kitchen, so Stephen went there first. Katy's purse sat open on the table. He dropped her keys into it, then turned off the light and groped his way down the hall to the master bedroom. A yellow line of light shone underneath the door to the connecting bathroom.

Stephen stripped in the dark and got into bed naked. He put his glasses on the nightstand beside him, then lay on his side staring at the fuzzy, oblong light under the bathroom door. After what seemed like a long time, he heard the toilet flush and the faucet run. The pipes shuddered as the faucet was shut off. Then the fuzzy line under the door disappeared, and all was dark. Stephen heard the bathroom door open. Then he heard Katy pad around the foot of the bed to her side.

She slid under the covers beside him and pressed up against his back. She was naked too. Her breasts and belly were warm. He slid his right hand up over her hip and down and found that her bottom was cool. Her bottom was always cool. He had never been able to figure that out. Every other spot on Katy's skin always seemed abnormally warm—except her bottom, which in the winter felt as if she had just run outside and exposed it for a minute or two. In the summer it felt the same way. As if it were winter, and she had run out and exposed it.

Stephen liked it. He didn't know why. Maybe it was because it was something he knew about her that not many other people did.

They lay there together without speaking for a while, skin touching skin, until Stephen's left arm started to fall asleep. Then he had to turn onto his back, and when he did, Katy scooted away.

"What do you think of that Artie person?" Katy asked then. "Carolyn's boyfriend."

"I knew who you meant," Stephen said, and then regretted it. It had sounded combative, and he was tired of that.

But Katy's question had surprised him. Instead of continuing their fight or making further comments about the pitiful situation that Jack had gotten himself into, she was trying to gossip about someone else's relationship. Stephen had been mentally preparing himself for several contingencies—including just falling asleep—but this hadn't been one of them.

"Okay, then," Katy said, "so what do you think?"

"I guess I don't know what you mean."

"I mean, do you think that he's unsocialized—poor toilet training or whatever—or is he merely egregiously stupid?"

Stephen shrugged, and the bottom sheet wrinkled under his shoulders. "I haven't given the guy that much thought," he said, squirming to try to straighten out the wrinkle. "I've only seen him at parties, and now tonight. Never talked to him. Never cared to. So I have no opinion."

Katy turned onto her right side, with her back to him. "I vacillate between thinking he's just so much younger that he *seems* stupid," she said, "and thinking that he's just so stupid that he seems like an idiot child."

Stephen turned onto his right side too and snuggled up against Katy. As he came into contact with her cool bottom, he began to get aroused. He was pleased. Getting aroused hadn't been so easy for a few weeks.

"Speaking of children," he murmured, "would you like to try again?"

"No," Katy said. The word snapped out.

Stephen moved back so that they weren't touching anymore. His arousal died.

"I mean," Katy said, a hint of exasperation in her voice, "we just had a fight, and I'm still angry. And one of our best friends is in jail. I don't mean that I don't want to try again. Just not right now, all right?"

"Sure," Stephen said. He wrapped his arm around his pillow, bunching it into a compact wad, and closed his eyes.

The hell with it. He didn't want her right now anyway. And she was right, after all. Tonight just wasn't a good time.

But for too long it had been a real trick figuring out just when *was* a good time. Katy only seemed to want him when he was exhausted or had a mountain of essays to grade, and he only seemed to want her when she was pissed off at him. It was almost as if they each wanted to risk rejection—as if they had taken sex for granted for so long that they had come to a silent agreement to make it a challenge again.

As Stephen began to doze off, Katy jolted him awake with another question: "What could she have been thinking, anyway?"

Stephen rose up on his elbow. He was cotton-headed and alarmed in the way that only the almost-asleep-but-startled-awake can be alarmed.

"Who?" he asked. "What? What happened?"

Katy turned to face him. Without his glasses, Stephen could just make out her face in the moonlight that filtered through the bedroom-window curtains.

"What do you mean, who?" Katy said. "Who have I just been talking about?"

Stephen tried to search his foggy brain, but didn't get far. "I dunno," he said.

"Carolyn," Katy said, exasperated. "Carolyn Jessup and her embryonic boyfriend. I was wondering what she could possibly have been thinking when she decided to shack up with him."

Stephen let his head fall back to his wadded pillow. "I dunno," he said again. "What would *you* have been thinking?"

Katy was silent for a long moment. When she spoke again, her voice was cold. "What was *that* supposed to mean?"

Stephen knew that he was in trouble again, but he was too sleepy to care. "It meant," he slurred, his mouth half buried in his pillow, "that you sure seem to have taken a lot of notice of this guy."

"Because he's a moron!" Katy shouted.

"So he's not worth noticing, then, is he?" Stephen said as he pushed his face even deeper into his pillow. "Ignore him and go to sleep."

Katy was silent again for a few seconds. Then she said "Fine," and turned away from him.

When Katy said "Fine," it meant that the conversation was over. It was the only one-word sentence she ever uttered.

It was odd that their night had ended in yet another stupid argument, and over a stupid person at that. Not that it was odd that they'd had a stupid argument—they had plenty of those—but it just seemed that tonight they would be thinking more about poor Jack, stuck in jail overnight for the crime of being naked.

Jack had been Katy's friend for almost fifteen years, since well before Stephen had met either of them, so she ought to be expressing more concern instead of complaining about Carolyn's boyfriend. Who gave a shit about the head-banging yutz? Why should she care? One of her best friends had lost his wife just last year and was now skirting ever closer to a nervous breakdown, with a stop or two in police custody on the way. And here she was going on and on about some peabrain just because he was Carolyn's boyfriend. Carolyn had terrible taste in men and terrible luck with them as a result. So what was the big surprise? True, this one had lasted longer than most of the others, but maybe that was just because he was younger and Carolyn thought she still had time to change him.

Stephen opened his eyes, angry with himself now. Katy had gotten him to thinking about Carolyn and her goddamn boy-toy, and now he couldn't sleep.

"Maybe," he said loudly, "she thinks she can change him."

Katy said nothing, so Stephen rose up on his elbow again and leaned over her. Her eyes were closed and her mouth was slack. Her breathing was slow and regular, with a faint snore.

Stephen was annoyed, but he didn't wake her. He knew he would only regret it if he did.

And the thing was, he thought as he leaned closer, she really looked sweet. He loved her face when she was asleep. All of the hard edges that she set up during the day disappeared when she slept. In the moonlight, her skin looked pale and smooth. An elongated shadow of her nose fell across her cheek. Her cheeks were a little chubby, but it was noticeable only when she was like this. It made her look vulnerable, and Stephen liked it—again, because it was something about her that almost no one else ever saw.

As he watched her sleep, something outside blocked the moonlight. Stephen looked up at the window, and through the white curtains he saw the blurry silhouette of something on the backyard privacy fence. Whatever it was, it was big.

He rolled away from Katy and fumbled for his glasses on the nightstand, knocking his reading lamp and a stack of mystery novels onto the floor. But he found his glasses, put them on, and went to the window.

The bedclothes rustled behind him. "What's going on?" Katy asked, her voice thick. "What happened?"

Stephen pushed the curtains apart and saw the black-haired, naked woman as she spread her wings, flapped them twice, and then flew up from the fence and out of sight. He stared after her, but once she was gone, there was nothing left to see but the Moon. He let the curtains fall over the window again.

"What was it?" Katy asked as he got back into bed.

Stephen took off his glasses and replaced them on the nightstand.

"Nothing," he said. "I thought I heard something, but it was nothing. I'm sorry I woke you."

They lay in silence for a few minutes. Stephen could tell from the sound of her breathing that Katy wasn't falling back asleep. And neither was he.

"I've been thinking," he said at last, "about what you asked about Carolyn and Artie. About why she's with him. And I think that maybe she just likes to fuck him."

Katy giggled, and Stephen was surprised. Katy hardly ever giggled.

"I was kind of thinking the same thing," she said.

They lay still and quiet for a few more minutes.

Then Katy whispered, "Yes, I'd like to try again. If you would."

Stephen slid over to Katy and held her so that her cool bottom pressed tight against his stomach.

"I would," he said.

4

❖

The Kids Made Fart Noises

Т he kids made fart noises when Halle brought her date home. Both Cleo and Tony kept leaning over the railing at the top of the stairs with their cheeks pooched out, forcing the air out between pursed wet lips and then running back to their rooms, giggling.

Yelling at them wouldn't do any good, and going up to their rooms and giving them each a lecture wouldn't do any good either. The only thing that ever worked was revoking their Nintendo privileges, and Halle hated doing that because the whining that ensued over the course of the Nintendo shutdown was always worse than the initial offense.

She wanted to be angry at the babysitter for not getting the kids to sleep on time, but she couldn't be. The poor girl had looked like a war refugee by the time that Halle and Marvin—how had she wound up dating a guy named Marvin, anyway?—had arrived. The teenager had probably tried everything short of smacking the kids upside the head with a hammer, and Halle almost wished that she'd given permission for that.

"Sometimes," Halle told Marvin as they sat at the kitchen table drinking coffee, "I wish I'd lived in the 1800s. Parents could give kids laudanum to drug them into a quiet stupor. Talk about the good old days."

Marvin chuckled for, Halle figured, the two hundred and ninety-seventh time that evening. Marvin didn't have much to say, but he seemed to find plenty to chuckle about. So she wasn't sure whether she wanted to go to bed with him or not. He was nice enough, and better looking than anyone named Marvin had a right to be, but she kept imagining what it would be like to do it with a guy who kept chuckling every thirty seconds. She was afraid she would wonder what the hell he was laughing at.

But then again, he had great hands. She caught herself staring at them wrapped around his coffee cup. The fingers were slender and tanned, and they looked strong. She knew they would feel nice fluffing up her short brown hair.

Cleo, Halle's blond eight-year-old daughter by her ex-husband Bill, appeared at the top of the stairs and made another fart noise. Then she dashed away again.

"Ah-huh-huh-huh-huh-huh," Marvin chuckled.

Halle looked up from his great hands at his not-quite-so-great-but-not-half-bad face. "I don't know how long it'll take them to get sleepy," she said. "You don't have to stay if you don't want to. I mean, I understand."

"Ah-huh-huh-huh," Marvin said. "No, not at all. I'm having a great time. Ah-huh-huh. It's been a great evening. Ah-huh. I think your kids are great. Huh."

"Great," Halle said, and then had the sudden wish that a meteor would come crashing through the roof and kill both of them where they sat.

Her six-year-old, Tony—the dark-haired result of an adulterous one-night stand with an Italian truck driver from Waco—appeared at the stair railing and cut loose with a long, moist noise that was even more impressive than his sister's had been. Then he disappeared again too.

"Don't take it personally," Halle said. "They're just competing with each other. It doesn't have anything to do with you."

Or maybe it did. Marvin had passed gas just as they were coming into her South Austin duplex, and they had both pretended that it hadn't happened. But if one or both of the kids had been hiding on the stairs, they had no doubt heard it, and this was their response. Of course, it wouldn't be polite to tell Marvin that.

"Oh, I, ah-huh-huh, didn't think it did, ah-huh," Marvin said, and then took a sip of coffee. He smiled at her as he swallowed.

Maybe if she just kept his mouth busy while they were in bed, it would be all right. Except for the chuckle and being a little inarticulate, he seemed like a pretty good guy. And he had a decent smile. And terrific earlobes. Absolutely terrific earlobes.

Halle hadn't been with anyone in five weeks, so she was willing to overlook minor faults. Marvin seemed to be a better deal than maybe sixty-five percent of the men she'd ever been with, so using his chuckle as a reason not to sleep with him didn't seem reasonable.

"Have you been HIV tested?" Halle asked.

Marvin made a noise that Halle thought at first was a new kind of chuckle, but then she realized that some of his coffee had gone down the wrong pipe.

"I'm sorry," she said. "Was that a rude question?"

Marvin shook his head. His face was turning red, and he didn't seem to be breathing.

"Are you all right?" Halle asked, starting up from her chair. "Is there anything I can do?"

Both kids appeared at the top of the stairs and made a big fart noise in unison.

"Get back in your beds right this second and stay there or there's no Nintendo for a week!" Halle yelled. "I mean it! A solid week! Starting tomorrow! And tomorrow's a *Saturday!*"

The kids vanished, and Halle grimaced. Now if they reappeared, she'd have to make good on the punishment. And it really would hurt her more than it would them.

Marvin was still choking on his coffee, so Halle went around and thumped him on the back. She didn't think the Heimlich maneuver worked with liquids. She doubted that thumping the back worked either, but all she really wanted to accomplish was to let Marvin know that she didn't want him to die.

As she thumped his back, she smelled musk in his hair. She hadn't been this close to him before, and this was the first time she'd noticed it. She loved musk, and Marvin's chestnut hair was wavy and thick. She imagined burying her face in it and breathing deep. Then moving down and tasting salt on his neck.

At that moment Marvin gagged, leaned forward, and spit something into his coffee cup. Halle tried not to look. She didn't want anything to spoil her mood.

"Are you okay now?" she asked.

Marvin sat up and nodded. He didn't seem to be choking anymore, so Halle stopped thumping his back and went back to her chair. As she sat down, Marvin wiped his face with one of the cloth napkins she'd set out with the coffee. He was sweating, and his face was still red. Halle sighed. That was just the way she wanted him to be. Only naked.

"I'm sorry I blurted it out like that," she said. "But it doesn't make sense to be coy. I mean, you seem like a great guy—"

Well, she thought, he seems like an *okay* guy with great hair, hands, and earlobes. But telling him that he himself seemed great was more appropriate, considering that she was pretty sure she wanted to spend the night with him.

"—and we seem to be getting along," she continued, "so why wait until things have already reached a certain level before asking the important questions? You know?"

Marvin lowered the napkin and nodded. The red in his face was draining fast.

Halle waited a few seconds, but Marvin didn't say anything. He was just staring at her. She hoped that meant he was enraptured. But it didn't seem likely after the kids had done their fart bit and he'd nearly choked to death.

"Well, then," Halle said, "I'll go first. I've had myself tested every six months for the past three years. I just had a test last month, in fact. They've all been negative. I wouldn't even be dating if they weren't."

She waited again, but still Marvin said nothing. All he did was shift his stare from her to his coffee cup, apparently fascinated by whatever he'd hawked into it.

"Marvin?" Halle asked. "Excuse me? Is something wrong? Are we still having a conversation?"

"Ah-huh-huh," Marvin chuckled weakly. "I, uh, was just wondering . . . why you had those tests."

Halle was surprised. Marvin hadn't seemed like the hippest guy in the world, but he hadn't seemed stupid either.

"Well, gee," Halle said, "mainly so I could find out whether I had any retroviruses swimming around my bloodstream waiting to infect someone I cared about. Why else?"

"Ah-huh," Marvin said, and it was more of a throat-clearing than a chuckle. He looked up again, and now his face was pale. "What I meant was, why would you think those tests were necessary? After all, you're the mother of two children, and I wouldn't think that you—"

Marvin finished his sentence with an odd gesture from one of his beautiful hands.

Halle was beginning to get the picture. The picture was of her alone in bed with a slice of cold pizza in one hand and her Hitachi Magic Wand in the other.

"You mean you wouldn't think that I'd be getting laid much," she said. She was torqued. Marvin's hair and earlobes weren't so damn great after all.

His hands still looked pretty good, but fuck it.

Marvin flinched as if she'd slapped him. "That's not what I meant at all," he said. "Ah-huh."

Halle stood. "No, that's exactly what you meant, along with the implication that if I *am* getting laid, I really *shouldn't* be."

Marvin glanced from side to side as if evaluating escape routes.

"But I'll have you know," Halle said as she started to clear the table, "that I'm a fully functioning, healthy woman, despite the fact that I've reproduced. Contrary to popular male opinion, babies don't wreck your body." She picked up Marvin's coffee cup, looked into it, and made a face. "I can't believe I was going to do it with a guy whose body produced *that.*"

"Ah-huh," Marvin said, standing. "I should be going."

"Also," Halle said, "I want to point out that everybody knows you broke wind." She made a noise like the kids had made, then dumped the coffee cups, saucers, and milk pitcher into the sink with a loud clatter. "So thanks for a rotten evening, Marv. Don't let the door hit you in the ass on your way out."

He didn't. In fact, he left the door open. Halle stomped after him to slam it, but stopped when she saw a woman with long black hair outside. The woman was coming around the garage as if from the other half of the duplex, and she passed Marvin on the sidewalk. Then she paused and stood looking after him for a moment. She was tall and pale-skinned, and her hair gleamed in the moonlight. She wore a dark blue coat that was so long it hid her feet.

"Are you looking for someone?" Halle asked.

The tall woman turned away from Marvin and stepped closer to Halle. Her unseen feet made a strange clicking sound as she walked. Halle started to close her door, but then the tall woman smiled. It was such a nice, nonthreatening smile that Halle let the door stay open.

"Yes, I am," the tall woman said. "I tried the other apartment first, but no one was home. Am I too late?"

Halle frowned. "I don't know. For what?"

"Why, for you and—" The tall woman looked over her shoulder at Marvin's car backing out of the driveway. "What's-His-Name."

"His name's Marvin," Halle said. "If you want him, he's yours. Have a ball." She started to close the door again.

The tall woman frowned in obvious frustration. "Oh, dear," she said. "I really am too late. I'm so sorry."

Halle paused with the door half closed. She looked around it at the tall woman. "Excuse me?"

The tall woman sighed and shook her head. Her hair swirled as if it were liquid.

"Well, you'll have other nights," she said. "Better nights. I promise. I won't let you down again. But you're on your own for the next month."

Halle laughed. "Honey, I'm on my own *every* month."

The tall woman smiled again. "I know. But everyone can use some help now and then." She started to turn away, then looked back at Halle.

"By the way, Jack needs you," she said.

Then she strode away, click-click-click-click, and went back around the garage the way she had come.

"Hey!" Halle yelled. She opened the door wide and ran after the woman. "What are you talking about? How do you know Jack? What's happened to him? Damn it, wait up!"

As she rounded the corner of the garage, she stepped on the tall woman's coat. It was lying in the driveway. Halle stopped and picked it up. It was warm.

She looked down the street, but all she saw were the two shrinking red lights that were Marvin driving away. The tall woman with the glossy black hair was gone.

Something fell from the coat and fluttered down. Halle bent to look at it and saw that it was a long black feather with a white tip.

A shadow fell over her then, and she looked up just in time to see something fly across the face of the full Moon. She caught a glimpse of large wings, and then whatever it was vanished into the night sky.

Halle took the coat into the duplex and closed and locked the door behind her. She laid the coat on the kitchen table, then went to the wall phone to call Jack. It was late, but he wouldn't mind. She had to know that he was all right, that the weird tall woman hadn't done something to him. Jack was her only former lover who was still a friend, and she cherished him.

As she reached for the phone, she saw a note from the babysitter taped to the wall: *Jack called 11:06 P.M.*, the note said. *He is in jail.*

Upstairs, Tony started crying. He was having nightmares of late because Cleo kept telling him stories about boogeymen biting off kids' faces . . . if the kids were dark-haired boys.

Halle rubbed her eyes. She was usually wide awake until at least two in the morning, but here it was just after midnight and she was tired enough to sleep for a week.

Jack needed her help, but he would have to wait for it a while longer. The kids had priority. The little shits. Even if Marvin hadn't been a jerk, she would have had to kick him out before they woke up for Saturday morning cartoons.

She read the note again. *He is in jail.*

"Ain't we all," she whispered, and then went upstairs to comfort her son.

PART II

SNOW MOON

Saturday, February 6, 1993

◆

5

❖

Marriage Was Like Eating Tuna

Marriage was like eating tuna, Katy thought as she and Stephen walked into the Zilker Clubhouse. Just when you got used to the taste, and were maybe even enjoying it a little, you came across a stray bit of slaughtered dolphin.

At least that was what it was like being married to Stephen. The smallest thing would anger or hurt him, and she was never able to predict what it would be. It was frustrating because Katy prided herself on being smarter than average—and among other things, that meant being able to figure out what made people tick. What their buttons were. How they could be mollified or manipulated.

She was usually successful at discovering those things, except with her husband. She wondered sometimes if that was why she had married him. For the challenge.

He was in a blue funk tonight, and she had no idea why. All she was sure of was that it was something she had done or said. It almost always was. She hated knowing that she hurt him so often, but she didn't know how she could avoid it. She couldn't decipher the pattern of his weak points, and she doubted that she would ever be able to change herself enough to avoid those points anyway.

Stephen paused inside the clubhouse doorway and leaned down to whisper to her. "See anybody we know?"

Even his whisper sounded petulant. Almost surly. He was miserable. It was clear that he didn't want to be here. Or it might be that he didn't want to be here with *her*.

Katy hoped that wasn't true, because she still wanted to be with him.

She squinted in the yellow light to survey the people clustered across the room at the coffee urn. There were fewer than twenty of them. Not much of a turnout for Jack's first class.

"No," she said. "I don't even see Jack."

Stephen grunted. "Be just like him not to show up."

Katy studied Stephen's face, trying again to see through to whatever had upset him. But she couldn't even see his eyes because his glasses had fogged up the way they always did in cold weather.

"He'll show up," Katy said. "Jack is only unreliable if the event in question has nothing to do with him. When he's the main attraction, he always manages to make it."

Stephen grunted again, unzipped his coat, and headed for the rows of metal folding chairs that had been set up facing the limestone fireplace on the north wall. He sat down in a chair at the end of the last row.

Katy stayed at the doorway to watch him walk and to study his posture as he sat. Body language was important in reading a person's mood and attitude. But Stephen's body language always defeated her—except in bed, where she always knew what he wanted. Or didn't want.

Or wanted, but couldn't do anything about. Like last night and this morning.

Katy wondered if what was bothering him was nothing more than that. But if that was the case—if he really wanted her, but couldn't achieve an erection—why didn't he go to his doctor? There was no shame in admitting that there was something physically wrong.

Or if it was because he just didn't feel like making love, then why did it seem to trouble him so much? Surely he knew that it wasn't that important to her. Yes, she loved him; and yes, she would like to have a child. But she didn't need sex every day, or even every week or month, to maintain her self-image or to feel loved. And Stephen knew that. She'd told him so.

So what was going on with him?

He made no sense to her sometimes.

Stephen looked back at her and frowned, so she went to join him. "Why the last row?" she asked, squeezing past to sit beside him.

"I like the last row."

She gave him a smile. "Yet I'll wager that in your literature classes, you suspect those who sit in the last row of being behind in their assigned reading. And so you call on them more often than those in the front row."

Stephen looked at her over the tops of his fogged lenses. "Yup," he said. And that was all.

It was a bad sign. Usually Stephen would at least have asked what her point was.

"Jeez, I guess they'll let anyone in here," a voice said behind them.

Katy turned and saw Halle Stone grinning down at her. Behind Halle, at the clubhouse's south wall, Halle's two children were making lip and nose prints on one of the tall, hinged windows. It seemed to be some sort of contest.

"It's great to see you, Halle," Stephen said. "I don't think we've had a chance to talk since New Year's Eve."

Katy gave him a glance. He sounded in a much better mood than he had thirty seconds ago. She wondered if the change was deliberate. Maybe he was trying to make her jealous so she would be sorry for whatever it was that she had said or done to him.

Well, if that was the case, it wouldn't work. Katy didn't believe in jealousy. It had always seemed to her to be the least productive of all emotional states.

If she *was* going to be jealous of someone, though, she had to admit that it would be Halle. Halle wasn't as physically beautiful as some women—as, say, Natalie had been, or as Carolyn Jessup was—but Halle carried an aura of mingled playfulness and lust that men found attractive. Tonight she was wearing old jeans and a dingy brown jacket, but the gleam in her eyes made it clear to Katy that Halle didn't have to dress well to be alluring.

"It's good to see you guys too," Halle said. "And thanks again for the New Year's party. It was great. I mean, hey, I almost got laid."

Halle's voice was low and smoky. Katy didn't think it was a calculated tone, though. It was just Halle's voice. Men seemed to like that too.

"Oh, yeah?" Stephen asked. He sounded intensely interested. "Who with?"

Halle rolled her eyes and made a whistling sound. "Oh, one of those guys Katy works with. I won't say which one."

"Halle, all of my male coworkers are married," Katy said.

Halle grinned again. "That's why I won't say which one."

Katy forced a grin in response, but she felt a little sad. Halle attracted men like no other woman she knew (with the possible exception of Carolyn), but few of those men had ever stayed with Halle longer than it took to get her pregnant. And most hadn't stayed that long. Katy didn't know enough about Halle's private life to speculate on just what the problem might be, but she did know that attracting someone was an entirely different matter from living with him.

She looked at Stephen. An entirely different matter.

"I'll bet I know," Stephen said. "It was Randal, the bald guy, right? With the drunk wife?"

Halle rolled her eyes and whistled again.

Katy decided that it was time to change the subject. "So," she said, "have you seen Jack since his court date, or did you just receive one of his bizarre little invitations?"

"Bizarre invitation," Halle said. She reached into her purse and pulled out a white circle of paper.

It was like the one Katy and Stephen had gotten. THIS IS THE FULL MOON, it said in electric blue letters. DISCOVER THE POWER OF HER LIGHT.

"I take it this is some free-university class he's doing?" Halle asked.

Katy nodded. "It's part of his community service sentence, although he seemed so delighted about it when I spoke with him on the phone that it hardly seems like punishment. Apparently the judge found out that Jack was an astronomy major before switching to engineering, and so he thought that Jack could best pay his debt to society by sharing some of his special knowledge."

"Weird," Halle said.

"Yeah, but it beats seeing him go to jail," Stephen said. He looked at Katy. "And he has to see a therapist every two weeks for four months. Sounds like plenty of punishment to me, honey. Especially for the minor crime of being naked in Austin."

Katy had noticed that Stephen called her "honey" only when he was irritated with her but was pretending not to be. She didn't like it.

"I think the judge would have been more lenient," Katy said, "were it not for the fact that Jack was, um, aroused throughout the arrest procedure. My impression was that the officers who brought him in felt that he was threatening them."

Halle laughed. "Oh, those sissies. I mean, I've seen Jack's erect penis, and threatening isn't the word I'd use to describe it. Perky, maybe."

Katy felt her face reddening, so she looked away from Stephen and Halle and watched Halle's kids continue their window-smearing contest. She couldn't believe the things that Halle said sometimes. Of course everyone knew that Halle and Jack had slept together back in the Pleistocene, but that didn't make it appropriate for her to talk about his penis.

After all, Katy had slept with Jack, too, but she didn't go around discussing his anatomy. Or anything else that she knew about him, either. In fact, she was careful about discussing Jack in general, because Stephen didn't know about her former relationship with him. It had all happened before she'd started seeing Stephen, so it shouldn't matter one way or the other . . . but men could be funny about these things.

Halle and Stephen were still chatting, but since Katy no longer felt comfortable with the direction of the conversation, she concentrated on Cleo and Tony. The two children looked nothing like each other. Both were cute, though. "Cute" was a concept that Katy didn't often understand, but these children were an exception. It bothered her a little that in this regard she was as much a slave to her genetic imperatives as anyone else. All she had to do was look at those kids, and she wanted to hug them. It was especially odd because she thought that, behaviorally, Cleo and Tony were brats.

As if to confirm that opinion, Cleo grabbed Tony's hair and rapped his forehead against the window. Tony screamed, and everyone in the room turned to stare.

"Oh, piss," Halle muttered, starting toward the kids.

Katy put a hand on her arm. "Would it be all right if I tried to deal with them?" She hesitated, not sure that had come out right. "What I mean is, I'd enjoy looking after them for a little while."

Halle looked at the kids, both of whom were screaming now. Apparently Tony had done something invisible in retaliation. Halle winced.

"I couldn't do that to you," she said. "You'd have to take them outside until they cooled down, and you might miss Jack's talk. I was just hoping for a chance to say hi to him before having to haul them out of here."

Katy stood and pushed her chair back so she could get out without having to squeeze past Stephen again. "Here, you sit down," she said to Halle. "I've heard Jack talk on numerous occasions, and he's never made sense."

Besides, after Halle's "perky" comment, she didn't think that she would be able to look at Jack tonight without mentally seeing him in another context. She headed for the kids before Halle or Stephen could say anything in response.

Tony and Cleo kept screaming as Katy took their hands and led them out to the limestone-and-concrete patio. They didn't struggle against her, though. She thought that she could handle this.

She took them across to the edge of the patio, where a metal double railing marked the beginning of a sharp drop down a tree-and-brush-choked hillside. The night was clear, and the view eastward across the MoPac expressway to the downtown skyline was perfect. The office buildings were outlined in red, blue, and gold lights, and the dome of the state capitol reflected a white radiance. Above it all, the full Moon shone in a clear sky.

"Look at all the lights," Katy said. "Aren't they pretty?"

Cleo looked up at Katy and shrieked, "He *bit* me!" She dug her fingernails into Katy's left palm.

Katy resisted the impulse to jerk her hand away. Instead, she managed to say, "Why do you think he did that?"

Cleo shot Tony a look of pure hatred. "Because he's not a human being!" she yelled. "He's a *swamp rat!*"

"No, you are!" Tony shrieked, yanking hard on Katy's right hand.

"No, you!" Cleo retorted.

"No, *you!*"

This went on for several more exchanges while Katy tried to think of a way to break the stalemate. Then she looked up at the Moon.

"Maybe you're both swamp rats," she said, loud enough for the children to hear her over their own shrieking. She squeezed their hands to make sure she had their attention. "Maybe you're *were*–swamp rats."

Cleo and Tony stopped shrieking and stared up at her. "What's that?" Cleo asked.

Katy nodded toward the Moon. "Old stories say that when the Moon is full, it can turn people into animals. The stories say that some grown-ups turn into werewolves or werebears—so maybe children turn into something smaller. Like, say, weregophers, or werefrogs." She paused and bent down close to them. "Or maybe . . ." She pulled them to her and shouted, "WERE–SWAMP RATS!"

The kids squealed, and for a moment Katy wasn't sure she'd been successful. But then she heard that the squeals were laughter. Cleo and Tony had forgotten their fight with each other and were happy.

It had been easily accomplished, too. Being a mother wasn't all that difficult. All you had to do was pay attention to what was going on in their little minds and then apply a bit of good sense along with some minor psychological manipulation. Halle, she was afraid, simply didn't possess the right stuff for the job. Having skill at making kids didn't guarantee skill at taking care of them.

And as Katy had that thought, Tony pulled his hand from hers, darted under the bottom rail, and tumbled into the darkness below.

Katy stood frozen in shock for a moment, and then Cleo's scream jolted her. She dropped Cleo's hand and started climbing over the railing. But she hadn't hitched up her shin-length skirt, so she fell back. She hitched up the skirt and started to try again.

"Excuse me," a woman's voice said behind her. "I caught him."

Katy, now straddling the top rail, looked back to the patio and saw a tall woman with glossy black hair. The woman was wearing a long blue cloak that looked as if it belonged in the nineteenth century.

The woman was holding Tony's hand. Tony was gazing up at her with his mouth wide open.

Katy stared too, and then she remembered that she was halfway over the fence. She swung her leg back and dropped to the patio with as much grace as she could muster.

"Thank you," she said to the tall woman. She was incredibly relieved that Tony was safe.

But then the scene seemed strange to her, and her relief gave way to surprise. "How on earth," she asked, "did you manage to catch him and bring him back here so quickly?"

The tall woman smiled. "Oh, I happened to be coming up the hill. There's a path. I was just lucky to be in the right place at the right time. I'm sorry to have popped up behind you like this, but the best way up is over there." She nodded toward a spot near the northern edge of the patio. The drop-off and the fence curved inward there, and the hillside's trees and brush were thinner.

Katy could believe that she might not have seen the woman come up there with Tony. What amazed her was that it had been done in a matter of seconds . . . unless Katy's time sense had been thrown off by the shock of seeing Tony fall. How long had she stood there stunned?

"Well, however you did it," she said, "I'm very grateful. I don't know how I would have explained it to Tony's mother if anything had happened to him."

The tall woman smiled and extended the hand that held Tony's. "I'm sure that Halle would have understood that it wasn't your fault. After all, they really should put up a better fence here. Electrified chicken wire, perhaps. Something to discourage children from plunging to their deaths."

Katy smiled and took Tony's hand. Her fingers brushed the tall woman's wrist, which was slender and cool. At that touch, Katy experienced a sudden surge of envy, and she didn't like it. Envy, like jealousy, was a useless emotion. But she couldn't help it in this case. Next to this tall, beautiful, and obviously competent woman, she felt short, chunky, and clumsy. Clumsy was the worst. After all, she had let Tony fall down the hill, and this other person had come along to save the day for her. She didn't like depending on other people for anything. Even something as random as this.

"I'll write a letter to the city parks department," she said. "Some kind of fence will be put up here, I can assure you."

The tall woman smiled back at her. "I'm sure it will. You sound determined." She glanced back at the clubhouse. "Shall we go in for Jack's presentation now? I think he must be about to start."

Katy tried not to frown. She didn't like this situation at all. The tall woman seemed too perfect, and she also seemed to know both Halle and Jack. But Katy had never seen her before and had no idea who she was.

"Well, I'm not sure that Jack has even shown up," Katy said, more snappishly than she'd intended. "And Halle doesn't want me to bring the kids back inside while they're misbehaving, so—"

"They seem to have calmed down," the tall woman said.

Katy looked at them and saw that it was true. Both Cleo and Tony were staring up in awe at the tall woman as if she were Barney the Dinosaur.

It irked Katy, then saddened her. They hadn't looked at *her* like that.

"By the way," the tall woman said, "I'm Lily. Jack's friend."

It sounded as if Lily expected Jack to have mentioned her to Katy, but he hadn't. On the other hand, Katy hadn't really talked with Jack much in the past few months.

She hadn't really talked to him much, she realized, since Natalie had been killed. Natalie's death had changed everything for everybody, and Katy resented it. She resented it not only because it had brought changes, but because those changes emphasized what a warm, supportive person Natalie had been.

Katy doubted that anyone had ever described *her* as warm or supportive. But then, she also doubted that anyone had ever described Natalie as smart.

Not that being smart was doing as much for Katy as it once had. She couldn't figure out how to make her husband happy, and she wasn't having any luck conceiving a child.

But Natalie, she was sure, could have handled both of those things.

Katy forced herself to hold out her stubby-fingered hand to shake Lily's long, slender one. "I'm happy to meet you, Lily, and I'd like to thank you again for snagging Tony. I'm Katy Corman."

Lily nodded, and her black hair shimmered in the moonlight. It made Katy aware of the static nature of her own hair—a curly, dirty-blond mass that she kept cut short in order to maintain some measure of control over it.

"I knew who you were right away," Lily said. "Jack's told me all about you. He thinks so very highly of you. In his opinion, you're one of the most important people on the face of the Earth. His exact words."

Katy was surprised. Years ago she had thought she was in love with Jack, but she had never believed that she had made much of an impression on him. She had always assumed that they had remained friends because—well, because Jack remained friends with everybody.

She was surprised now to find that she was embarrassed.

What was it about this Lily, anyway? Since she had shown up, Katy had bounced from one emotion to another and then another. And none of them were emotions that Katy normally let herself feel. Love, anger, and joy could be useful, but jealousy, envy, and embarrassment were just too pointless to allow them to exist. And Lily had managed to make her feel all three in the span of two minutes.

Katy decided that this was reason enough to dislike Lily. "Thank you for passing that on," she said.

Lily raised an eyebrow. "You're welcome."

An awkward silence followed, and then Katy said, "Well, since the children are behaving, I suppose we might as well see if Jack has made it here from Venus or wherever it is he's living these days."

Lily looked amused. "Nowhere so unpleasant as Venus, I don't think," she said. Then she turned toward the clubhouse. Her cloak billowed, and as she walked away her steps made clicking sounds.

Katy looked down at Cleo and Tony and saw that they were still staring in awe at Lily.

"She's a nice lady, isn't she?" Katy asked, hoping that they would stick out their tongues and make retching noises.

But Cleo nodded and whispered, "She's the most beautiful lady I've ever seen."

"Maybe you need to get out more," Katy said, and then hated herself for it.

Self-hate was yet another of those useless emotions. Lily was really doing a number on her.

Cleo looked up at her with a puzzled expression. "Huh?"

Katy shook her head. "Nothing. Come on, let's go see what kind of show your uncle Jack has cooked up for us."

She was holding both children's hands, and Cleo came with her as she started for the clubhouse. But Tony tried to hang back.

Katy paused. "What's wrong, Tony?"

Tony was gazing after Lily, who was now silhouetted in the yellow light of the clubhouse doorway.

"That lady," Tony said in absolute wonder, "is a where-bird."

Katy was confused. "I'm sorry," she said, leaning down. "She's a what?"

"A where-bird."

Cleo rolled her eyes and slapped Tony's arm. "Not a where-bird, doofus. You mean a *were*-bird. Right, Aunt Katy? There's no such thing as a *where*-bird, is there?"

Katy looked back toward the clubhouse and saw that Lily had disappeared from the doorway.

"I don't have any idea, guys," she said. "But maybe Aunt Lily will know." She was pretty sure that Jack must be sleeping with Lily, and since he was Cleo and Tony's Uncle Jack, that meant that Lily was Aunt Lily. Katy didn't like the sound of it. "Let's go ask her, okay?"

They went back into the clubhouse then, but they couldn't find Lily anywhere.

6

❖

Her Presence Was Warm Breath in His Ear

Her presence was warm breath in his ear. Lily was here somewhere. Jack was sure of it. He hadn't gotten naked yet, but somehow she had found him.

He became aware of her as he was chalking sketches to illustrate various theories of the Moon's origin to the people in the Zilker Clubhouse. He didn't see her, but he felt a puff of air from her wings, and then her breath. It distracted him, and as he lost his train of thought, he turned away from the chalkboard to face his audience.

They looked at him dully. He didn't know most of them, so he was glad that a few of his friends had shown up. Stephen and Halle were in the back row, and Katy was coming in from the patio with Halle's children in tow. Jack didn't see Carolyn or her boyfriend anywhere, but that didn't surprise him. Carolyn was probably still mad at him for not calling her first when he was arrested.

"Um, where was I?" he asked.

The audience shifted in their seats. No one answered him.

Jack's face began itching. In jail a month ago, he had decided to grow a beard again. It was still looking pretty scraggly, and patches on both sides of his chin were coming in gray. He hoped that

Lily liked beards, particularly beards with gray in them. If not, he had his rechargeable electric razor out in the car.

"Well then," he said, scratching his jaw, "stop me if I repeat myself too much." He turned back to the chalkboard, which he had found in the clubhouse's storage room. He would have preferred to use a slide projector with some nifty illustrations, but he hadn't gotten the necessary materials together in time. In fact, he had forgotten that he was supposed to do this at all until an hour ago.

He had left a note for Lily on the refrigerator, but he was still surprised that she had been able to find him without the usual moonlight-on-naked-flesh requirement. Now that he knew she was here, though, he felt much better. He knew she would wait for him until he was finished with his presentation. She would like the fact that he was teaching people about her home.

He took a deep breath and plunged ahead.

"What I've sketched out here are three old attempts to explain how the Earth and the Moon came to be together," he said. "First there's the simultaneous creation idea, which is a load of crap because the Moon is iron poor and the Earth is iron rich, mainly in its core. The Earth also has a lot of volatiles, like water, and the Moon has none. If they'd formed from the same cloud of primordial glop, they'd be more similar in composition.

"Next there's the mitosis notion, which suggests that a goopy Earth spun faster and faster until a blob broke off to become the Moon. This hypothesis is also a load of crap, because if it were true, the Earth would still be spinning fast enough to fling us all through the ceiling."

A few people in the audience chuckled at this, which startled Jack and made him pause for a few seconds. What in holy hell, he wondered, would be funny about being flung through the ceiling?

"Third," he said then, shaking off the disruption, "is the capture hypothesis, which claims that the Moon was just wandering through space and happened to be grabbed by the Earth's gravitational field. This idea isn't entirely crap, but the odds against it are incredible. It's far more likely that such a big stray chunk would either escape the field or plow right into the planet."

Jack took a chalkboard eraser from the tray and wiped out his three sketches. Then he looked back at the audience and grinned. This was going to be the best part. Lily would really like this.

"So," he said, "how, then, did the Moon come into being? Anybody?"

The audience was silent. Most of them looked pretty bored. Even his friends. He guessed that almost everyone was here for extra credit of some kind. They didn't really give a shit about the Moon at all.

But he would make them see the error of their attitudes.

"The true solution to the problem," he said, facing the chalkboard, "is obvious. Think about it: The Moon can be thought of as the child of the Earth, right? And where do children come from? The answer, of course, is—"

In huge letters, with the chalk squealing, he wrote:

SEX

He heard a collective gasp behind him.

"That's right," he said as he started to sketch a diagram beside SEX. "Coitus. Congress. Boinking. Schtupping, romping, thumping, banging, whanging, porking. In other words, aardvarking. Coming together in a mindless, passionate embrace and—" He dropped the chalk, snatched up another eraser, and slapped it against the first, creating a huge cloud of white dust. "Blammo! Changing your life forever with one momentary intoxicated act of all-consuming lust."

He paused and coughed, then wiped his forehead with the back of his hand before turning to face his audience again.

"Whew!" he said. "Anybody else getting tumescent?"

The audience stared. His friends looked pale.

"Oh, come on," Jack said, exasperated. "We're all adults here." As he spoke, he caught sight of Halle's kids in the back of the room. "Well, most of us are, anyway. And those of us who aren't will be growing up soon enough."

He turned back to the board. "See, what we've got here is the Earth, which I will henceforth refer to as Mom. Whizzing through space over here is a randy, maybe Mars-sized planetoid we can call Dad." He drew a series of arrows from Dad to Mom. "Now, what happens when you get a randy guy wandering through the cosmos, and he comes across this buxom, fertile, and—this is crucial—*lonely* babe doing nothing but spending her life going around and around in the same tired circle? Why, he zeroes in on her, seduces her, and—"

Jack threw his head back and gave an imitation of some of the sounds he himself often made while achieving orgasm. Then he glanced at his audience again and saw that a few people had left their chairs and were going outside. No doubt they wanted to take a good look at the Moon as he spoke. He began shouting so that they could still hear him.

"But Dad makes a fatal mistake!" Jack bellowed, taking up the chalk again and drawing a cluster of rays emanating from the point of Dad's impact with Mom. "Rather than just using Mom for his own hedonistic pleasure and then moving on, he *falls in love* with her. But, alas, Mom doesn't love *him,* and he's devastated. In fact, he blows up into a zillion pieces, with the heat of his tragic death boiling away all of the volatiles from his remains. And Mom, realizing once it's too late that she *did* love the jerk, a little, loses some of her own outer crust in that same hot mingling of sex and self-destruction. But her core, her true heart of iron, remains unviolated and strong. You see, she's a survivor."

He began tapping the chalk around Mom in a circular pattern, leaving a ring of jumbled dots. "So what Mom winds up with," he said, "is a spread-out embryo consisting of bits of herself mingled with bits of Dad, a diffuse zygote of sorts, circling around and around her. Eventually most of these bits come together, and they grow into a beautiful daughter."

He left the chalkboard and walked across to the tall windows on the east side of the room. The full Moon was high over the city now, and its pure light made him shiver in anticipation. "And there she is. Her mother named her Luna. She goes through phases, and she jerks us around a lot—but you shouldn't blame either her or her mother for the way she was raised. Remember how tough it is to be a single parent, or the child of one."

He admired the daughter's beauty for a long moment, then sighed and turned to his audience. A significant number of people seemed to have left. But his friends were still there.

As he winked at them, a whisper told him that Lily was waiting in a shaft of moonlight in the grove of trees north of the clubhouse.

"Any questions?" he asked his audience.

There didn't seem to be any, so he thanked them for coming, pushed open a window, and jumped outside. Once on the patio, he headed for the trees. As he walked, he stripped off his sweater and started to work on the buttons of his shirt.

Then someone grasped his arm from behind and stopped him. He turned and saw that it was Stephen. Stephen's eyes looked big and worried behind the thick lenses of his glasses.

Jack was concerned. "Hey, man, what's the matter?" he asked, putting a hand on Stephen's shoulder. "You look like you've just lost your best friend."

Stephen took a breath as if he were about to speak, but then let it out and shook his head.

Katy came up beside Stephen, looked at Jack, and gasped. "Jack, button your shirt! You're going to freeze."

Jack smiled. His friends were sweet, but there were things that they just didn't get.

"No, I'm fine," he said, "but Steve seems to be upset about something. Would you take care of him, please? I'll come back later to make sure he's okay, but right now I really have to go. I have an urgent appointment that I can't miss. See, I had to miss it last month because of being arrested and all, and if I miss it again—well, she might think I'm blowing her off." His throat tightened as he thought of that awful possibility. "And I can't let that happen. So if you'll look after Steve for now—"

"I don't need looking after," Stephen said. His voice quavered. "But you do, Jack. Something's gone wrong, and your friends want to help you make it right again."

Jack was discombobulated. What, had his friends all become so static and dull that they didn't understand the concept of a hot date?

"Here," Katy said, reaching for him. "Let's button up your shirt and—"

A high-pitched scream interrupted Katy, and Jack looked past her and saw that Halle's children were racing around the patio throwing punches at each other while Halle tried to catch them. Stephen and Katy both turned toward the commotion, and Stephen's hand fell away from Jack's arm.

Jack took two steps backward, then turned and ran into the grove.

He pulled off his shirt and dropped it, zigzagged around several trees, and searched for a shaft of moonlight. He heard Katy shout his name, but he didn't stop. He would explain things to his friends later. Right now he didn't have the time. Right now he had priorities . . .

And there she was, caught in a moonbeam, standing beside the trunk of a live oak. She was wearing a long blue cloak, and as Jack ran up to her, she opened it and let it fall to the ground.

Jack stumbled at the sight of her smooth, pale skin, and he dropped to his knees at her feet. His chest was thundering, and he was out of breath. Lily touched his forehead with a fingertip, and an electric shiver rippled over his skin.

"Nice speech back there," Lily said. "You left out a lot of things, though."

Jack caught her hand in both of his and kissed it. He loved her hands. They were strong. "I was in a hurry," he said into her palm. "I wanted to see you."

Lily looked past him, toward the clubhouse. "Your friend Stephen is heading this way. We can't stay here."

Jack looked over his shoulder. He didn't see Stephen, but he knew that Lily had terrific night vision, so he took her word for it.

"Where can we go?" he asked, looking back up at her.

She smiled. "Do you trust me?"

Jack rolled his eyes. "Does a fish trust water?"

"Then take hold of my ankles," Lily said, "and don't let go."

Jack did as she said, grasping her where her claws ended and the white flesh of her calves began.

Then Lily spread her wings, and they rose into the sky.

As Lily picked up speed, the cold air rushed past and stung Jack's face and chest. He didn't mind. They flew high above the trees, high above the stream of red and white lights on MoPac, and high above the downtown buildings outlined in red, blue, and gold.

"By the way," Lily called down to him, "I like the beard."

Jack's heart leapt.

As Lily turned south and they crossed the Colorado River, Jack looked down and saw the face of the full Moon shining up from the rippled water. The Earth's beautiful daughter was laughing in delight, so Jack laughed with her.

PART III

WORM MOON

Monday, March 8, 1993

❖

7

◆

Sex in the Woods Would Be Cool

Sex in the woods would be cool, Artie thought as Carolyn steered the Honda up the winding gravel driveway. The live oaks and cedars were thick on either side of the gravel, and Artie imagined taking Carolyn and a blanket in among them. The weather was chilly, especially now that dusk was falling, but that would make it even better. A cold breeze on naked flesh might be exciting. He looked at Carolyn and imagined her on the ground nude, with goose bumps and hard nipples, her hair loose and wild.

"What?" Carolyn asked without turning toward him. "What is it?"

She had taken off her sunglasses, and Artie could see that her eyes were focused on the driveway. But he knew he'd been caught. If you were going to look at Carolyn, even for a few seconds, she expected you to say something.

"Uh, nothing," Artie said. Then, remembering that she never believed that, he said, "I mean, I forgot."

That, she would believe. He knew that she thought he was dumb. He guessed that he was, too, compared with her and her friends. But he was smart enough to know what Carolyn needed when they were alone together.

They weren't alone together now, though. Her old friend Jack Thomson was snoozing in the backseat. Artie glanced over his shoulder and grinned at how goofy the guy looked. Jack's head lolled, his mouth was open wide, and he had drooled into his beard. He was in decent physical shape for an older dude, Artie supposed, but he was also nuts.

The driveway ended in a loop near the top of the hill. As the car came around the cluster of trees inside the loop, Artie saw Halle's cabin—two cabins, really, with a roofed breezeway connecting them. They were constructed of rough timbers and limestone blocks, and they looked as if they must be a hundred years old. Artie wondered if they even had indoor plumbing. He hoped so. Sex in the woods was one thing, but taking a squat out there was something else.

Jack came awake as Carolyn stopped the car. "Are we there?" he asked, wiping his face on his sleeve. "Is Lily here?"

"Yes, we're there," Carolyn said. "It looks like we beat everyone else." She opened her door, and the motorized shoulder belt hummed forward. "And no, Lily's not here."

Artie was surprised that she didn't sound sarcastic. Carolyn didn't believe that Lily even existed, but she had answered Jack's question as if she did.

Weird, Artie thought. She sure hadn't answered him like that yesterday when they'd been watching the news and he'd asked how they could be sure that David Koresh *wasn't* Jesus Christ.

He pulled on his black leather jacket as he got out of the car and then realized that he had to pee like crazy. He ran to the cabin ahead of Carolyn and tried the doors, but they were locked.

"Take it easy," Carolyn said, coming up beside him. "Halle should be here soon. I called her as we were leaving, and she said that she was heading out too."

Artie shook his head. "Can't wait." He ran into the woods west of the cabin.

In among the trees, the remaining daylight dimmed so that the air itself seemed to turn dark gray. It was even chillier than he'd expected. As Artie unzipped his jeans and began whizzing against a cedar trunk, he shivered. Not only was it cold, but he thought that he heard things scrabbling in the dead leaves behind him. Maybe sex out here would be fun, he decided, but not at night. He finished in a hurry and zipped up.

As he headed back toward the cabin, he encountered Jack coming into the woods.

"Nature calling you too?" Artie asked.

Jack smiled. "You could say that."

"Okay, well, catch you back at the ranch."

"Wait." Jack gripped Artie's arm. "You didn't see Lily, did you? Black hair, dark eyes, perfect legs, impressive wings?"

Artie resisted the urge to pry Jack's fingers from his arm. He wanted to get out of the woods and back to Carolyn, but he couldn't act like a wuss. "I didn't see anybody," he said.

Jack sighed. "I hope she can find me. The Moon's risen, so she should be here soon. If she's coming at all." He looked past Artie into the depths of the forest.

"Well, if she makes it," Artie said, "she should come have a beer. I got a cooler of Shiner Bock in the trunk."

Artie doubted that Jack really knew anybody named Lily, and if Jack did, why would she show up only at full Moons? But suggesting that they could offer her a beer was the only polite thing he could think of to say.

"I don't know if she likes bock," Jack said, releasing Artie's arm, "but I'll ask." He continued into the woods.

"Later," Artie called after him, and then hurried back to the cabin. There was a little more light when he was clear of the woods, but the sky had turned a deep purple. Some stars had come out. And Jack had been right about the Moon having risen. Artie could see its white glow through the trees to the east.

Carolyn came out of the cabin's breezeway to meet him. "Where's Jack?" she asked.

Artie jerked a thumb over his shoulder. "Taking a leak. Or something."

Carolyn stared at him. "You let him go off into the woods by himself?"

Artie had the feeling that he was in trouble again. "Well, I mean," he said, "I went by myself, right? So I guess I figured he could too, you know?"

As Carolyn began to respond, the sound of tires on gravel drowned her out. Artie was glad. Headlight beams swept over them and the cabin, and then a pale blue Toyota pulled up behind Carolyn's Honda.

Katy Corman emerged from the Toyota's passenger side as the engine stopped, and she made immediate eye contact with Artie. He gave her a smile. He had noticed her looking at him at the New Year's party, and also at the police station the night that Jack had been arrested. She was shorter, plumper, and a little grayer than the women he was usually drawn to, but he thought he might make an exception for her . . . especially if Carolyn wasn't nice to him on this trip. Also, Katy was smart—smarter than Carolyn, even—and he liked knowing that someone with brains wanted him. He hoped that Carolyn picked up on it.

"I take it that we've all managed to beat Halle here," Katy said, coming up to Carolyn and giving her a perfunctory hug. "Not a big surprise, I suppose, since the kids always slow her down."

The Toyota's lights cut off, and Stephen stepped out of the car. "Can't we get into the cabin yet?" he asked.

Artie shook his head. "Locked up tight as a snake's asshole. Guess we could bust a window. I pissed in the woods myself."

Carolyn gave him one of her shut-up-Artie looks, then turned back to Katy and Stephen. "It gets worse," she said. "Genius boy here let Jack go off into the woods alone."

Katy rolled her eyes. "Already? How long have you been here?"

Artie's throat tightened, and his face felt hot. He wasn't sure what those sensations meant at first, but then he realized that he was angry at Carolyn. It startled him. He had known she could be bitchy from the moment that they'd started seeing each other, and it had never bothered him before. But up to this point she had mostly griped at him in private. Now, though, she'd made him look bad to Katy.

He nudged Carolyn's shoulder. "Hey," he said, "I didn't notice you keeping a real close eye on him either."

Carolyn's back stiffened. She was getting seriously annoyed now, but that was fine with him. Sometimes Carolyn was a better lay when she was mad.

Stephen came around the car to join them. "How long ago did he wander off?"

"Couple minutes," Artie said. "But maybe he'll be right back. Maybe he just went to take a whiz."

"I doubt it," Katy said. "The last time he ran off to frolic among the trees, all we found was his shirt. He disappeared for a day and a half, Artie, and then he turned up on our doorstep with scratches all over his chest and back."

Artie couldn't help grinning. This was the first time that Katy had called him by name. It always meant something if a woman used your name when she didn't have to.

"What are you smirking about?" Carolyn snapped.

"Uh, I'm just happy that he showed up okay," Artie said.

Stephen was looking off into the woods. "He might not show up okay this time. The Hill Country is a little rougher than the stuff around MoPac. Besides, it's getting dark, and considering Jack's tendency to be oblivious to his surroundings, he could get hurt." He cupped his hands around his mouth and shouted. "Jaaaack! Jack Thomson! Come on back, it's suppertime!"

There was no answer.

"Really, Stephen," Katy said. "Come on back, it's suppertime? He's not a hungry dog."

Stephen shrugged. "So what should I say instead? That his Moon goddess is serving tea in the living room?"

"Might work better to say she's buck naked in the bedroom," Artie said, and waited for the others to laugh.

None of them did.

Carolyn cupped her hands around her mouth too and yelled, "Jack! Come back to the cabin! We're worried about you! Can you hear me?"

There was still no answer. Katy went to the Toyota, opened the trunk, and brought out two flashlights. She handed one to Carolyn.

"The next logical step," Katy said, "is to tramp around the woods in the dark, bellowing like idiots."

Carolyn switched on the flashlight that Katy had given her. It cast a weak yellow circle on the gravel.

"Its batteries are almost croaked," Artie pointed out.

"So are yours," Carolyn said. "Which way was he going when you last saw him?"

Artie pointed. "Straight west, pretty much."

Stephen started heading in that direction, but Katy caught his arm. "Halle will be here any minute. Someone ought to stay by the cabin to let her know what's happened. Otherwise she'll wonder where we've gone."

"You want me to stay?" Stephen asked.

Katy nodded. "If Jack's in mental distress, there's a better chance that he'll come to me than to you. He's known me a lot longer."

Stephen looked puzzled, but he said, "All right," and gave Katy a kiss on the cheek.

At that moment Katy glanced at Artie, and he looked away so that no one would see him grin again. Katy just wanted an excuse to be close to him in the dark without Stephen around. Even if Carolyn was along.

"Why don't you stay here too?" Carolyn said then, touching Artie's arm. "Keep Steve company."

Artie didn't like that suggestion. Stephen was a geek. But Carolyn's tone told him that there would be more trouble if he tried to object.

"Sure," he said. "But if you're not back real soon, we'll have to go looking for you too, you know?"

"Don't worry," Katy said, flicking on her flashlight. Its beam was stronger than the other one's. "I was a Girl Scout."

"You never told me that," Stephen said.

"I haven't told you a lot of things," Katy said. "And actually, I was only a Brownie. But I remember how to tie knots and treat snakebite."

"Just the skills you'll need to find Jack," Stephen said.

Artie leaned against the Honda's fender. "Hey, man, think about it. If he's snakebit, she can suck out the poison and then tie him up so he doesn't run off again."

No one laughed this time, either. Carolyn's friends might be smart, or think that they were, but they sure as shit didn't have a sense of humor.

Carolyn and Katy walked into the darkening forest, calling Jack's name. The white and yellow circles cast by their flashlights danced before them like giant fireflies. Artie watched the lights and was surprised at how soon they vanished among the trees. He could still hear

Carolyn and Katy calling for Jack then, but their voices sounded distant.

"I don't like this," Stephen muttered. He was standing a few feet away from Artie, his arms crossed over his chest.

"Don't worry," Artie said. "Carolyn can kick ass better than most guys, and Katie was in that scout thing. They'll be okay. Probably find Jack humping a log or something."

Stephen made a noise in his throat and looked up at the sky. Artie looked up, too, and saw that more stars had come out. He decided to try to make conversation.

"Hey, you know the constellations and crap like that?" he asked.

"I used to," Stephen said. "That one straight up is Orion, the Hunter. I think. The three stars in a straight line are his belt."

Artie tried to see what Stephen was talking about, then gave up and shook his head. "I never could learn any of that. They all just look mixed up to me, you know? Like you drop a bottle or something, and it busts, and the stars are all the little bits of glass."

"You mean like the pitcher you dropped at our New Year's party?" Stephen asked.

"Yeah, like that. Totally random, you know? Except that with the stars, there's no margarita puddle."

Stephen made another noise in his throat.

"I was kinda plowed that night," Artie said.

"Don't worry about it."

"Thanks, man. I sure did hate to waste good tequila."

They were both quiet for a few minutes then, looking at the stars, and Artie listened to Katy and Carolyn's faraway voices calling for Jack. They sounded artificial, as if they were coming from a tape player hidden in the woods.

"We've baited a trap with women," Artie said.

"Excuse me?"

"I mean," Artie said, "if we were hunting a mouse, we'd bait a trap with cheese, right? Or if we were hunting a bear, we'd bait a trap with, I don't know, bear food. Like, Yogi Bear always liked pick-a-nick baskets, remember? They have Yogi Bear when you were a kid?"

"Uh-huh."

"Well, you know, so it's the same thing with Jack. He had a woman but he doesn't anymore. But he wants one. I mean, jeez, he wants one so bad that he's made one up in his head. He's even run off into the woods to look for her, I guess. So we send a couple of babes after him, right? And Jack's out there alone, looking for this imaginary honey from Venus—"

"The Moon," Stephen said. "He thinks she's from the Moon."

Artie gave a nod but didn't take his eyes off the stars. He had just managed to make some of them form the shape of a tapped beer keg. "Right, the Moon. But anyway, he's out there in the woods, and he can't find the Moon girl on account of she doesn't exist, and then he hears two real women calling his name. And you know what I'm thinking if I'm Jack? I'm thinking, time for a Jack sandwich, is what I'm thinking."

He looked down at Stephen and laughed. But Stephen didn't seem to get the joke this time either.

"Your point being?" Stephen asked.

Artie decided that he and this dude weren't destined to be buds. "I just mean that we did the right thing sending the women after him," he said. "They'll find him, and everything'll be cool."

Stephen looked off into the woods again. "I hope so," he said. "But I still don't like it."

The guy sounded so morose that Artie couldn't stand it, so he looked up to try to locate the Beer Keg constellation again. As he found it, something huge and silent moved across the stars that formed the tap. Artie couldn't make out a shape, but whatever it was seemed to be flying only a few feet above the treetops.

"Holy fuck!" he yelled. "Did you see that?"

Stephen might have been about to answer, but he didn't get a chance because a car came barreling up the driveway. Another set of headlight beams swept over the trees and the cabin as a dented, rust-pocked Plymouth roared around the circle. Gravel sprayed as it came to a sliding stop a few inches from the rear bumper of Stephen and Katy's Toyota. The headlights went dark, and then the engine rattled and knocked for half a minute before dying.

The Plymouth's right rear door flew open, and Halle Stone's two kids exploded out like rocket-propelled grenades. The boy was screaming, and the girl was swinging something at his head. They disappeared into the woods at about the same point that Jack, and then Katy and Carolyn, had disappeared.

Halle got out of the car just as the engine gave one last clank and fell silent. She walked around the Plymouth and faced Stephen.

"I hate spring break," she said.

Stephen gave Halle a hug, but Artie noticed that it was quick and that Stephen seemed nervous. Artie figured that meant that Stephen was hot for Halle, but didn't want her to know it. She might know it anyway, though. Some women could see what a guy was thinking even if his brain was encased in lead, and that was usually reflected in the women's faces. But it was too dark now for him to get a good look at Halle's expression. Her body language was tense, but that might be because of her kids.

"Uh, is it okay for the yard apes to be out there in the dark?" Artie asked.

"It's sure okay with me," Halle said. "I hope they run into a tribe of intelligent squirrels who drag them underground and use them for acorn-storage experiments."

Artie was shocked. "Really?"

Halle started for the trees. "No, of course not. I've just been running after them all day and didn't get a lick of work done, that's all. I've got three programs to debug, but my children don't care. And they were horrible on the drive up here. I wish it were legal to make them ride in the trunk." She took a deep breath and shouted, "Cleo! Tony! Get back here this minute, or—" She stopped and looked back at Stephen and Artie. "What am I going to threaten them with? There's no TV or Nintendo out here to take away."

Stephen went to stand beside her. "Katy and I brought marshmallows to toast in the fireplace. Maybe we can bribe them with those."

"Good idea," Halle said, then yelled, "Tony! Cleo! Uncle Steve's going to stick marshmallows into a disfiguring fire so that they turn into shriveled horrors like Freddy Krueger! And if you don't get back here, you can't watch!"

Artie was intrigued. "Freddy Krueger?" he asked.

Neither Halle nor Stephen answered him. And there was no clear response from the children, although there were distant squeals.

"Guess I'd better go look for the little bastards," Halle said. She pulled a key chain from her coat pocket and flicked on a tiny flash-light attached to it. "Want to help me round them up?" she asked Stephen.

"Sure," Stephen said. He sounded hoarse, and that clinched it. Artie was now positive that Stephen had a hard-on for Halle. He still couldn't tell whether Halle was aware of it, but he was willing to bet that Katy was. And that might make Katy more . . . accessible. If things came to that.

"I'll stay here," Artie said. "You know, in case Jack or the Moon chick or Batman or somebody shows up."

Halle and Stephen didn't seem to hear him. They walked into the woods calling for the children, leaving Artie alone.

Artie leaned back against the Honda and listened to Katy and Car-olyn calling for Jack, and to Stephen and Halle calling for Tony and Cleo. He thought about putting a scratch down the Toyota's fender with a piece of gravel. Then he thought about his discovery of the Beer Keg constellation and looked up again to find that it had disin-tegrated. The stars were all random again, like bits of glass from a busted margarita pitcher.

He hoped that Carolyn would come back soon so that they could go off into a room by themselves and make love. It was about the only thing he felt like doing right now.

It bugged him that they had all left him here by himself.

When he looked down from the mess of stars, he saw that a light was glowing inside the cabin. Firelight, in fact. It shone from a window in the west wing, casting an elongated, flickering orange rectangle on the gravel. A set of deer antlers was propped on the windowsill, and its wavering shadow seemed to reach for Artie's feet.

He took a breath to call for the others, but then he let it out silently. They were all out there yelling, and they wouldn't pay any attention to him even if they heard him. So instead he went to the window and looked inside.

What he saw was Jack and a dark-haired woman he didn't recog-nize. They were on their knees on a big multicolored rag rug, illu-minated by a blaze in the fireplace. The woman seemed to be wear-ing only a dark robe that was pushed back to expose her breasts and shoulders. She was kissing Jack's neck. Jack, Artie noticed, wasn't wearing anything at all.

Artie didn't like the idea of disturbing a guy who was getting some, but this was a special case. He rapped on the window. "Hey! How'd you get in there? Open up, man!"

Jack and the woman turned to look at him. They didn't seem upset that he had interrupted them. Jack said something to the woman, stood, and headed for the door.

Artie met him there as the door opened, and then he wondered if he should have. It was obvious that Jack's mind, or a large part of it, was still concentrating on the woman on the rug.

"Artie!" Jack said. Despite his condition, he sounded happy that Artie was there. "Come on in!"

Artie hesitated. "Uh, how'd you get in? Halle has the key, and she's off in the woods."

Jack chuckled. "Oh, Lily jimmied a back window or something. I'm not sure, really. Come on, I know she'd love to meet you." He grabbed Artie's wrist and pulled him inside.

Artie stumbled to the edge of the rug and stared at the woman who knelt in its center. She was backlit by the fire, so he couldn't see her as clearly as he would have liked—but he could see her well enough to know that she was an absolute babe.

"Uh, I'm Artie," Artie said, extending his hand.

The woman smiled and extended her hand as well. But her fingertips were still several inches from his, and he found that he was afraid to move any closer.

"Hello," she said. Her voice flowed over him like warm honey. "I'm Lily. But I'll bet you've already figured that out."

Jack went to kneel beside her. "Isn't she something?" he asked. He gazed at Lily with a rapturous expression.

"Yeah, she—yeah, sure," Artie said. He felt that he was intruding, but he also felt that Jack owed him and the others an explanation. "But see, man, we all took tomorrow off work so we could come up here tonight. Like, Carolyn closed up her shop, and I got someone to take my shift at the restaurant. And then you run off into the woods like Tarzan. Everybody's out looking for you. Not cool, dude."

Jack looked up at Artie as if for forgiveness. "I'm sorry," he said. "It's sweet of Halle to offer this place, and great of all of you to come here to be with me. But I still have to do what I have to do. Just like Gary Cooper."

"Who?" Artie asked.

"Never mind," Lily said. "But believe me when I promise you that everyone who's out in the woods tonight will be fine. I'll see to it. For now, though, Jack and I need to spend some time together. Do you understand?"

Artie blinked. Lily's hand was still extended toward him, and he found himself fascinated with her fingertips. "Yeah, I guess so . . . but how are you gonna be sure they're okay?"

"Trust her," Jack said. "She saw to it that I came back here safe, didn't she?"

"You see, Artie," Lily said, "although you know a few things about sexual attraction and pleasure, there are a lot of other things you don't have a clue about. So just shake my hand, and we'll be friends. Then you can relax, and you'll know that everything's going to be all right."

Artie began to take a step back. There was something weird about this babe. Her shoulder blades were too high.

But on her it worked.

"What the hey," he said, and stepped forward to take Lily's hand. As her fingers touched his, her shoulders shifted and spread out to become a huge pair of black-and-white wings. An electric tingle ran up Artie's hand and arm, and it felt pretty good.

When he awoke, he found himself on a couch beside the rag rug. He was wrapped in a beige afghan. Stephen, Katy, Tony, and Cleo were squatting before the fireplace toasting marshmallows, and the other adults were sitting at a card table sipping from ceramic mugs. The table was covered with used paper plates. Jack was wearing clothes.

"Thank God you've stopped snoring," Carolyn said, getting up from the card table and coming over to the couch. "It was like a chain saw cutting a concrete block. Oh, gross, and you've drooled down your chin."

Artie struggled up to a sitting position and wiped his chin with his shirt sleeve. He saw that his jacket was draped over the back of the couch.

"How long have you guys been back?" he asked, giving Jack a sidelong look. Jack winked at him.

"An hour or so," Carolyn said. "Katy and I came across the kids, and then Steve and Halle found all four of us. Then we heard Jack calling for us from here, which made it clear that we'd been wasting our time. Especially when we found you warm and cozy with a fire and everything. And now that you're rested, I'm worn out and want to go to bed." She looked at Halle. "I put our things in the back bedroom in the other wing. Is that okay?"

Halle gave them a sly smile. "Good choice. It has the newest bed with the quietest springs."

Carolyn blushed, which surprised Artie. He'd never seen her embarrassed before. He wondered if it was because of what Halle had said, or if it was because Halle was the one who'd said it.

He unwrapped himself from the afghan, stood, and took Carolyn's hand. "Let's go," he said.

"Do you want to eat first?" Carolyn asked. "There are some hot dogs and potato salad left."

"Let's go," he said again.

Carolyn said good night to the others, and then she and Artie went out and across the breezeway into the east wing of the cabin. Their bedroom was chilly, but there were plenty of blankets and a thick quilt on the double bed. The room smelled of cedar and dust, and the water in the bathroom across the hall had a faint brown tinge as it sputtered from the faucet. Halle had said that she'd inherited this place three years ago and used it only once every month or two. Artie could tell.

When he and Carolyn had each taken a turn in the bathroom, they stripped quickly and put on sweatshirts and sweatpants. Then they got into bed and burrowed under the covers. A minute later, Carolyn untied the drawstring on Artie's sweatpants and put her hand inside.

"Is this all right?" she asked. She asked it in the voice that he liked, the voice that she used only in bed. It was the voice that said that all she wanted in the world was to touch him all over and have him do the same for her.

"Always is," Artie said, and after that neither of them spoke again for several minutes.

Then Artie drew back. He'd had a thought. Maybe he should tell Carolyn that he had found Jack naked with a woman who called herself Lily. But if he did tell her, should he leave out the part about the wings?

"What is it?" Carolyn asked. "What's wrong?" She sounded worried.

He knew why. Once he and Carolyn started making love, they didn't stop. He had never gotten distracted before.

So now he had to say something. She was expecting it. He considered starting to make love again without answering her, but he knew that she wouldn't let him get away with that.

"I was just wondering," he said, "why you're so mad at me all the time."

He was shocked at himself. Of all the dumbass questions. Where had that come from?

"I'm not mad at you all the time," Carolyn said.

Artie's arm tingled, so he rose up on his elbow. "Yes, you are," he said. "Except when we're screwing, you're pissed off at me almost every minute."

He was shocked at himself all over again. He wanted to take off his tube socks and stuff them into his mouth. What was making him say these things? Maybe he was dumb, but not this dumb.

Carolyn was quiet for a long moment, and Artie thought he was as good as dead. But then she put her hand on his chest and moved it in a slow circle.

"I'm never really pissed off at you," she whispered. "Mainly, I'm pissed off at me."

This explanation had never occurred to Artie. He couldn't get his head around it. How could a woman as smart, tough, blue-eyed, long-legged, and tight-assed as Carolyn be unhappy with herself?

"What for?" he asked.

Carolyn put her other hand on his chest too. "I don't want to talk about it," she said. She took a shuddering breath. "God, you're gorgeous."

Artie lay down again and slid his hands up her rib cage until he was touching her as she was touching him. "So are you, babe," he said. "So why be pissed off at yourself?"

Carolyn gave a soft laugh. It sounded sad.

"Artie," she said, "shut the fuck up." She covered his mouth with hers.

Okay, Artie thought. I can do that.

Later, when Carolyn was asleep, he heard something rustle in the brush outside their window. He put his head under the covers so there was no chance he would be tempted to look out and see what it was. He didn't want to know.

PART IV

PINK MOON

Tuesday, April 6, 1993

◆

8

◆

Bologna Was Comfort Food

Bologna was comfort food for Stephen. In the summer that he'd turned eight, when his father had been at work and his mother had been too depressed to make lunch, bologna and white bread with Miracle Whip had been his solution. He had always made two sandwiches, one for himself and one for his Heinz 57 dog, Champ. He and Champ had eaten in the shade of the elm tree outside his parents' bedroom window and watched the big diesel trucks blast by on the highway. Stephen had discovered that if you raised your fist and pulled it down as if you were yanking something, the truckers would blow their air horns in response. He had done it for fun at first, and then to see if the noise might rouse his mother. Sometimes it had. For years, even after she'd moved to the nursing home, she would complain about those damn noisy trucks blowing their horns. She had never figured out that Stephen had been responsible. After she'd died, Stephen had felt guilty for never telling her. But then he'd eaten a bologna sandwich and felt better.

He remembered that as he unwrapped one of the sandwiches that Jack had brought and discovered that, yes, it was bologna on white bread with Miracle Whip. He was glad for the comfort because he was a passenger in Jack's latest vehicle, an ancient postal jeep, on a twisting state highway en route to Halle's cabin. Jack's driving in any car was dicey enough to make Stephen nervous, but Jack's driving in a jeep with the steering wheel on the wrong side took Stephen to the verge of bladder-voiding panic. He clenched the sandwich in both hands and took a huge bite.

It tasted just the way he remembered it, and for a moment he forgot that he was about to die.

Then Jack took a curve too fast, and the jeep tipped up on its left wheels. Stephen saw the asphalt rushing toward him and tried to yell, but his mouth was full of bologna and white bread. He swallowed hard as the jeep slammed back onto all four wheels and rocked on its decrepit suspension.

"Whoops!" Jack said. "Sorry about that. You okay?"

Stephen wasn't sure. He'd swallowed the chunk of bologna sandwich without chewing, and it felt as if it were stuck in his heart. But he nodded and wheezed something that was almost "Yes."

"Good," Jack said. He looked thoughtful. "If you died on me, Katy would come after my ass with a garden weasel. She's always put on a show of being unemotional, but down inside she's got big-time passion—anger, angst, the works. But I guess that isn't news to you."

Stephen frowned. It *was* news to him. One of the reasons he'd married Katy was because he thought her cool reserve would make a good balance for his irrational moodiness. She had feelings, sure, and maybe some of them were relatively strong . . . but he didn't think it was accurate to describe them as big-time.

"She'd be upset if you killed me in a car wreck, if that's what you mean," Stephen said. "But she'd get over it."

He wanted to take back the words as soon as he'd said them. Natalie had been killed in a car wreck, and Jack had *not* gotten over it. That was, after all, why Stephen was going to Halle's cabin again— to keep an eye on Jack while he had his monthly bout of naked insanity.

Jack didn't seem to have heard him. Instead of responding or paying attention to his driving, Jack was looking at his watch.

"Hoo boy, gotta hurry," Jack said. "The Moon's up in six minutes. I tell you, daylight saving time throws me off every year. Is that the driveway up there?"

Stephen shook his head. "It's another mile."

"Then I'd better stomp on it," Jack said. He jammed the gas pedal to the floorboard.

The engine roared, and the jeep sped up another two or three miles per hour. Stephen guessed from looking at the speedometer that they were now barreling along at about forty-eight. It was hard to tell because the needle kept jumping back and forth between zero and sixty.

Stephen wished that this full Moon wasn't falling on a Tuesday. He didn't like the thought of being the only one responsible for Jack tonight. Katy had wanted to come, but she had a project at work that had to be done by noon the next day. And none of Jack's other friends could make it either. So because Stephen had no classes to teach tomorrow, and because everyone knew that academics with no classes to teach had nothing to do, here he was. He hoped that Jack would have his nude episode as soon as they reached the cabin. He'd brought essays to grade, and the sooner he could get to them, the better.

There was a slim chance that Halle would be at the cabin tonight too, but she'd said it would depend on whether she could find a sitter who was willing to stay the night at her duplex and get Cleo and Tony ready for school in the morning. That didn't seem likely, which was just as well as far as Stephen was concerned. He would never get any papers graded if she showed up. She made him uncomfortable.

Not that he didn't enjoy her company. On the contrary— whenever she was around, she was all he could think about. He hadn't felt that way about anyone since he was nineteen. Not even about Katy. He did love Katy, but he'd never had trouble getting work done in her presence.

The mouth of the cabin's long driveway appeared on the right in a cluster of brush and cedar. Jack, however, was looking back over his shoulder.

"Look," he said, "the Moon's rising."

"Watch what you're doing!" Stephen yelled. "You're going to miss the—"

Jack cranked the wheel before Stephen could finish. The jeep went up on its left wheels again, and this time Stephen saw gravel rushing past his nose. Then the jeep whumped back down and fishtailed its way up the winding drive.

"I just realized that this must be the first time you've ridden in this car," Jack said. "It's great, isn't it? You wouldn't believe the deal I got on it."

Stephen rubbed his face and found that it was slick with sweat. "Yes," he said, "I would."

He resisted the urge to leap out and kiss the ground when the jeep stopped in front of the cabin. Instead, he managed to pick up his overnight bag and Jack's cooler, get out, and walk to the west wing's front door without running, screaming, or falling over. He put down the cooler, fumbled in his pockets until he found the key that Halle had given him, and opened the door. Then he looked back and saw that Jack was bracing himself with one hand on the jeep's left front fender while taking off his shoes and socks.

"Uh, Jack," Stephen said, "wouldn't you rather do that inside?"

Jack gave him a you-must-be-kidding look. "Lily's coming from the Moon, Steve, and she navigates by sight. If I'm not outside where she can see me, she'll have a hell of a time." He tossed his shoes and socks into the jeep and unbuckled his belt.

"Was she here last month?" Stephen asked.

"You bet." Jack shucked his jeans and kicked them away. "She met Artie, but the rest of you guys were out hiking."

"Well, if she was here last month," Stephen said, "can't she find her way back without, uh, help?"

Jack pulled off his sweatshirt. Now he was wearing only a T-shirt and briefs. "I don't want to take any chances."

Stephen hesitated. Short of putting Jack in a headlock and dragging him into the cabin, he couldn't think of any way to get him inside.

"All right, then," Stephen said. "Will you at least promise that you'll wait for her right here? That you won't go off into the woods like last time?"

Jack smiled. "Sure. But once she shows up, I'll do whatever she wants." He stripped off his briefs.

Stephen tried not to be disgusted. He found male bodies, including his own, rather ugly. "Fine," he said. "But if she's not here in half an hour, come inside anyway, okay? You don't want to catch cold."

"I might have to wait an hour," Jack said. "Even a goddess can be late."

It seemed like the best compromise Stephen could make. "Good enough," he said. "Halle said there were makings for tea in the kitchen, so I'll brew some and bring you a mug. Lily won't mind if I wait with you, will she?"

Jack sat on the jeep's fender and looked up at the sky. "I don't know. I've always been alone before. But she's never said I had to be. So I guess it'd be all right. If she doesn't show up in an hour, though, I'll have to ask you to let me wait alone some more. Okay?"

"No problem," Stephen said. He picked up the cooler and went inside, leaving the door open behind him.

He turned on a lamp in the living room before taking his overnight bag to the front bedroom where he and Katy had slept on their previous visit. Then he went back through the living room to the kitchen and transferred the contents of the cooler to the refrigerator. He liked the refrigerator. It was a big, rounded-corner Kelvinator that reminded him of the refrigerator his family had owned when he was a child. It even had the same four-inch-thick rime of ice in the freezer compartment. These were refrigerators that looked as if they were built by the same people who made hardened bomb shelters. These were refrigerators that were worthy to house your bologna. These were refrigerators that made you feel safe.

After contemplating the refrigerator for a few moments, Stephen found an aluminum teakettle on the counter, filled it with water from rattling pipes, and set it on a stove burner. He had been disappointed last time to find that the stove was electric. A cabin in the Hill Country with a Kelvinator, he thought, ought to have a stove fired by wood or propane.

When he saw that the burner was turning red, he went to the bathroom adjacent to the kitchen and urinated. While he was doing that, he heard the front door close. He wondered if that meant that Jack had given up on Lily already, or if he was just coming inside for a sandwich to take back to the jeep.

Stephen came out of the bathroom while zipping up and stepped into the kitchen to find Halle looking inside the refrigerator.

"White bread," she said. "Yuck." Then she looked up at Stephen.

Stephen finished zipping with a quick tug.

Halle grinned. "Don't get all dressed up on my account."

Stephen hoped that his face wasn't turning red.

"Boy, you sure embarrass easy," Halle said.

Stephen went to the stove and pretended to watch the teakettle heat up. He hadn't heard Halle's Plymouth drive up, so he guessed that she had arrived as he'd flushed the toilet. The plumbing here was loud. "I take it you got a sitter," he said. He was appalled at how squeaky his voice sounded.

"Yeah, my ex-mother-in-law lives in Round Rock, and she volunteered," Halle said, looking into the refrigerator again. "The old bat hates my guts, but she loves the kids. She even thinks that Tony is her son's child. She's a firm believer in recessive genes, I guess." She closed the refrigerator door and frowned. "Didn't you guys bring anything besides bologna sandwiches? That stuff turns your shit to cement in your bowels, you know."

"Uh, no, I didn't," Stephen said. "Jack planned the menu and made the sandwiches. He says he doesn't want to be a burden."

Halle rolled her eyes. "Jesus, we're *all* burdens."

Stephen was trying not to stare at her. She was wearing a baggy blue sweater and rumpled black painter's pants. Her short brown hair was sticking up at odd angles at odd places. Her mouth looked wet.

"You're not," he said.

Halle blinked. "Who, me? Not a burden?"

Stephen's clothes began to irritate him. He shrugged in an attempt to camouflage his squirming. "Well, this is your place. You can't be a burden in your own place."

Halle laughed. "You don't know me very well, do you?"

Stephen considered. "I guess I don't," he said.

Halle's expression changed to one of concern. "Hey, what's the matter?"

It took him by surprise. "I don't know what you mean."

She took a step toward him. "You just sounded so sad there for a second. I thought maybe——"

The teakettle began whistling then, and Stephen was grateful. But as he lifted the kettle from the burner, the steam fogged his glasses. He tried to carry the kettle across the room to the counter, but he was half blind, and he stumbled on a curled linoleum tile.

Halle caught his arm. "Something *is* wrong," she said, guiding him to the counter.

"No, really," he said. "My glasses are fogged up, that's all."

"Yeah. Sure." She released his arm. "Here's a hot pad."

Stephen set the kettle on the pad, then took off his glasses and wiped them on his shirt. He paid close attention to the process so that he wouldn't have to look at Halle again. He wished that she had stayed in Austin. He would never get any work done now.

While he looked down at his glasses, he heard ceramic mugs clinking together. Then came a rustle of cellophane and the pop of a small box being opened. He caught the mingled scents of herbs, flowers, and coffee, and he closed his eyes. This smelled just like Halle's duplex had smelled every time he had been there. This smelled just like Halle.

"You have your choice of several healthy teas or unhealthy coffees," Halle said. "If you prefer tea, you may select blackberry, peppermint, hibiscus, lemon peel, or sloe gin."

At that, Stephen looked up at her again. He couldn't help it. But he wasn't wearing his glasses, so now she was a little fuzzy around the edges.

"Excuse me?" he said.

"Just checking to see if you're paying attention," Halle said. She put a tea bag into a mug and poured hot water over it. "Which room is Jack in? I'll see if he wants some."

Stephen put on his glasses again. "Wasn't he out by the jeep? He promised he'd stay there unless his Moon goddess showed up."

Halle groaned and set the teakettle back on the pad. "She must have showed up, then, because he wasn't there."

They went outside, and Jack was nowhere in sight. Stephen looked inside the jeep just in case, but only Jack's clothes were there.

"So do we start yelling and go after him like last time?" Stephen asked. "Or should we just wait and hope he turns up all right again?"

Halle crossed her arms, looked around at the woods, and shivered. "Choice two, I think. We're in the middle of sixty acres of nothing but live oaks, cedars, and poison ivy, and it's getting dark. The odds that the two of us would just run across him aren't too good."

Stephen looked at her. She was illuminated by the lamplight that spilled out from the cabin windows, and Stephen noticed for the first time that she had a mole just under her right ear. He had the sudden urge to kiss it.

He didn't do it, but neither did he stop looking at her the way he usually did whenever he had such thoughts. Even though they were standing in the light from the cabin and the Moon was shining down on them, he felt protected by the gathering darkness. He had the sense that she couldn't read his face so long as that darkness was there.

Halle yelled for Jack several times, and then Stephen did the same. There was no response.

"Hell with it," Halle said. "I'm going back inside before my tea's stone cold." She started toward the door, then paused and looked back at Stephen. "You coming, or are you still thinking about tromping around out there?"

Stephen had been watching her walk. "No, I'm, I'm coming with you," he said. He felt ashamed, and he was reluctant to leave the darkness that had helped him hide. But if Halle wasn't going to be there anymore, there was nothing to hide from. So he might as well go back inside with her and try to keep his thoughts buried under thick layers of bewilderment where they belonged.

They drank their tea in the living room. Halle curled up on the couch under an afghan, and Stephen sat in a metal folding chair across the rag rug from her. His mug of tea rested on the chair between his thighs. It warmed him. A little too much, he thought, glancing at Halle. He was trying not to look at her any more than good manners demanded.

"Did I tell you," Halle said, "that I'm not so sure Jack's Lily doesn't exist?"

Stephen looked back down at his tea. "Uh, no," he said. "You haven't mentioned that."

Halle laughed again. Stephen liked the sound of it. He wished he could lean in while she was doing it so that her lips brushed his ear.

"I don't mean that I believe in some winged Moon goddess," Halle said. "But I think there's a real woman who has become that goddess in Jack's mind. Her name could even be Lily. After all, there was that woman who came to my house the night that Jack got arrested, and she sounds like the woman Katy met outside the clubhouse on the night of Jack's spectacular lecture."

Stephen forgot the way he was feeling about Halle for a moment. He looked up and stared at her. "What are you talking about?"

Halle sipped her tea. "You know," she said. "The woman with black hair. Katy said that she even called herself Lily—although Katy thinks that might have been a joke at Jack's expense. We figure that whoever she is, Jack met her sometime after Natalie died and projected all kinds of wonderful goddesslike qualities onto her. And she might not know that he's doing it. She probably thinks he's just a sweet, slightly fucked-up guy that she met at the laundromat or wherever."

Stephen picked up his mug, stood, and went over to the fireplace. "Katy didn't tell me about that," he said, staring at the ashes from last month's fire.

"Oh," Halle said, and then was quiet for a few seconds before speaking again. "You mean she didn't tell you about the woman who came to my house, or the one she met at Zilker?"

"Either one."

"Well, I'm sure she meant to."

Stephen took a sip of tea, found that it had gone lukewarm, and emptied the mug onto the ashes. "I'm sure she did," he said. "But she's been working a lot lately, and whenever she does manage to be home in the evenings, I have a class to teach or an exam to give or a visiting writer to babysit. So we haven't been talking as much as we used to." He picked up a poker from the rack on the hearth and stabbed the wet ashes. "I'm just surprised that she had time to tell you. I don't mean that badly. But I didn't know that you and she talked all that much."

"We have for the last month or two," Halle said. "See, Katy and I were pretty close in college, but then we sort of . . . I don't know, got busy with real life. This whole business with Jack has sort of thrown us back together, I guess."

"When do you talk?" Stephen asked. "She's never home."

"During the workday, on the phone."

"Mmm. Whenever I try to call her, I wind up getting her voice mail."

"You sound bitter."

Stephen decided that he ought to shut up, so he muttered, "No, not at all," and then pretended to drink from his empty mug. He stared down at the ashes.

Then he felt Halle come up beside him. His heart quickened.

"That fire was dead a month ago," Halle said, "and I saw you pour out your tea. Yet here you are poking cold ashes and drinking from an empty cup. What's wrong?"

Stephen replaced the poker in the rack and started for the kitchen. "I just need a refill," he said.

He wanted to get away from her. He was angry at Katy, and Halle was being nice to him, and it was a rotten shitty uncomfortable situation. Jack was lost in the woods, and he had a pile of sophomore essays on "The Horse Dealer's Daughter" to read. Too much was going on, or ought to be going on, for him to be wanting to kiss Halle. It wasn't as if she would want to kiss *him* anyway, was it?

Halle followed him into the kitchen. "Yeah, sure, you need a refill," she said. "But unless you want it tepid, we'd better reheat the water." She turned the stove on again and replaced the kettle on the burner. "Which gives us time for you to tell me what's going on."

Stephen went to the sink and ran water to rinse his mug. "I'm just worried about Jack."

"We're all worried about Jack. Whatever's bugging you is in addition to that. And you might as well tell me about it, because I can pester the living shit out of anyone if I put my mind to it. Ask Katy or Carolyn or any of the old gang."

Oh, sure, Stephen thought. I'm going to tell you that I want to kiss you all over starting at your toes and ending at the nape of your neck just below that soft fringe of brown hair. And that then I'd kiss your ears and eyes and mouth and throat and breasts. That's just the sort of thing I tell people, right in between giving my corporate engineer genius wife a quick peck on her chilly lips at seven A.M. and trying to explain D. H. Lawrence to a slack-jawed pack of nineteen-year-olds at eight-thirty. Fits right in with my self-image, this notion of opening up the stupid adolescent corners of my soul to you, Halle Stone. You bet.

"The old gang," he said. "I never could figure out how the lot of you became lifelong pals, anyway."

Halle came up beside him at the sink and gave him a narrow-eyed glare. "Don't dick around with me, Corman. You're just trying to change the subject. I don't put up with that crap."

Stephen turned off the water and set the mug upside down on the counter beside the sink. "No, this *is* the subject," he said. "Katy, Jack, Carolyn, and you have all known each other since the age of dinosaurs. The four of you and some of the others who pop up every now and then, like David McIlhenney or Bruce Foster or Susan

What's-Her-Name. You're like this clique of old war buddies, and I've always felt like an intruder."

Halle nodded. "I get it. So when I told you about something that Katy told me, but that she neglected to tell you, you felt excluded. Is that it?"

"That's it." It was as close as he would let her get, anyway. "And to tell you the truth, I've never really figured out what brought you people together, anyway. It's not as if you all protested against Vietnam together or anything like that."

Halle grinned. "It'd be nice if we had that excuse, wouldn't it? But that had been over for a couple of years by the time all the yahoos you mentioned started hanging out. It's kind of depressing, really. I mean, people a few years older than we are have Vietnam and the sixties as a unifying late-adolescent-early-adult trauma, and people a few years younger than us have all that cool, alienated Generation X stuff. But people like you and me, people born between maybe 1956 and 1964, don't have a damn thing." She paused. "Well, that's not entirely true. The men, at least, all share a universal fear of commitment."

"I beg your pardon."

"Present company excepted, of course."

Halle sighed then, and Stephen felt a twinge in his chest.

"I guess that the sad truth," Halle said, "is that all of the people you mentioned, plus four or five others that you didn't, were originally brought together by one or both of two very stupid things: They happened to meet just as they began having actual sex lives, and/or they happened to meet because they were engineering-school geeks at UT. You may recall that the late seventies were weak in the areas of popular music and social conscience, but strong in sex and engineering."

"I remember," Stephen said. "I didn't actually participate in either one, but I heard about them."

Halle shook her head and made tsk-tsk noises. "No wonder you don't fit in," she said. "You celibate, artsy-fartsy freak."

She was giving him a look that could melt aluminum, and he felt his face getting hot. He was grateful when a knock at the front door made her look away from him.

"Sounds like Jack's finished his monthly romp," he said as they both went into the living room.

"Maybe," Halle said.

Then she opened the door, and Stephen saw a tall, granite-faced man with hairy forearms. He was wearing tight jeans and a Gold's Gym T-shirt. He had a slight paunch, but the rest of his body looked as if he spent five hours a day lifting weights.

"Tommy!" Halle said. She sounded happy. "You made it!" She glanced back at Stephen. "This is my friend Steve Corman. Steve, this is Tommy, uh, Morton. A fellow Austinite and new part-time Hill Country landowner."

"Morrison," Tommy said, coming inside and extending a beefy hand. "Glad to know you. I just bought the cabin a quarter mile west, so I thought I'd walk over and say howdy."

Stephen had no choice but to shake hands. And, just as he expected, Tommy tried to crush his knuckles into powder.

"Likewise, Mr. Moribund," Stephen said. He couldn't help it. It was out before he thought about it.

But Tommy didn't seem to notice. Instead, he turned to Halle and said, "Did you know there's a guy out there swinging his pecker around?"

"Sounds like Jack," Halle said. "Where'd you see him?"

Tommy grunted. "Down the hill a ways, next to the driveway. He was hanging from a branch trying to do gymnastics or some such shit."

Halle started outside. "We'd better see if we can coax him in."

"Wait," Stephen said. "I'll go. He might freak out if we gang up on him. Besides, you have company."

Halle stopped at the threshold and looked back at him. "You're sure?"

"Absolutely." He looked down at Tommy's hand, which was still crushing his. "That is . . ."

"Oh, sorry," Tommy said, releasing him.

"No problem." Stephen squeezed past him and was about to squeeze past Halle too, but she put a hand on his shoulder to stop him.

"Are you okay?" she asked. "You look funny."

"It's the glasses," he said. "They distort my face like a fun-house mirror."

Halle frowned. "I'm not joking."

Stephen pulled away from her. "Me neither. Look, I'm going to go find Jack, okay?"

He turned his back on Halle and the cabin and went down the driveway as fast as he could without breaking into a run.

"Don't you want a flashlight?" Halle called after him.

He didn't answer her. He didn't want a flashlight. He didn't want light of any kind. Even the moonlight was too much. He wanted darkness. He wanted to hide.

The white gravel stood out like neon. It crunched under his shoes. He didn't like it, so he stepped into the trees and tried to make his way down the hill by struggling through the brush and weeds. He didn't like this, either, but at least it was darker.

In two months he would be thirty-five years old. In three months he and Katy would have their eighth wedding anniversary. He felt old. Worse, he felt stupid. He had a Ph.D. that he had earned by studying great writers for seven years, but it was clear that he hadn't learned a goddamn thing from what they'd written. He had just put in the time and accepted his hood. Oh, and he had also written a 342-page dissertation on Katherine Mansfield that had never been published and that no one would ever read. He didn't even think that his committee had read it, given the moronic questions they'd asked him during his defense.

Pushing thirty-five meant pushing forty. An eighth anniversary meant that the tenth and the fifteenth were just around the corner.

He knew nothing. He didn't know his wife, and he didn't know what he was going to do with himself or with her for the next thirty years or so. They were trying to make a baby, but that seemed almost an end in and of itself. They hadn't talked about what would happen afterward.

It bothered him that he felt so little passion for Katy anymore.

What bothered him even more was that he knew he would feel it for Halle, if he let himself. And he hated the fact that he had experienced an instant stab of jealous pain the moment that Tommy Moribund had appeared at the cabin door.

He came to a stop and listened. He thought that he had heard a moan. Then he heard it again, and again. And then the words "Oh, God," almost shouted.

The voice came from deeper in the woods, and it definitely belonged to Jack. Stephen changed direction and thrashed his way toward the ongoing moans, which kept getting louder.

Then he broke through a clump of brush into a small clearing and stopped short. Twenty feet away, Jack was hanging by his hands from a branch of a live oak. The full Moon was visible beside him for a moment, but then was obscured by an enormous dark wing. Then that wing and another enfolded Jack, who shouted "Oh, God" again.

Stephen was horrified.

Jack was fucking an owl.

Then Jack and the owl twisted, and moonlight gleamed from long black tresses and bare white shoulders . . . where the wings were attached.

Stephen recognized her now. She wasn't an owl. She was the woman he had seen three months ago under the I-35 overpass and on his backyard fence. He had thought he'd dreamed her.

He *still* thought he'd dreamed her. He thought he was dreaming her right now. He had been listening to Jack too much, and was thinking too much about a woman who wasn't his wife. So he had gone off into the woods to sulk, had fallen asleep, and now was dreaming this. Instead of grading essays, he was wasting his time with sleep and hallucinations.

When he woke up, Jack was squatting beside him.

"Steve, are you all right?" Jack sounded worried.

Stephen sat up and looked around. He was in the clearing in the woods near Halle's cabin. He had lain down and fallen asleep right on the ground, among the dead leaves and sticks and snakes and God only knew what else. He wondered if maybe this was an indication that he was entering his midlife crisis a few years ahead of schedule.

"Yeah, I'm fine," he said, and then noticed that Jack was still naked. "Are you about ready to head back, or hasn't Lily shown up yet?"

Jack smiled. His teeth gleamed. "Oh, she showed up. We had a nice time. She would have stayed the night, but she has to help somebody in Guatemala with an impotence problem. She says she likes you, by the way."

Stephen stood and brushed himself off. "I'm glad," he said. "Do you want me to bring you your shoes, at least?"

"No, I'm fine. My feet are tough. I could use a cup of tea, though."

They walked back to the cabin. Halle was waiting for them in the doorway of the west wing.

"Well, this is a relief," she said, walking out to meet them. "I wasn't sure you were coming back."

"Where would we go?" Jack asked. He stopped at the jeep and began putting his clothes back on.

Halle took Stephen's arm and pulled him a few more steps toward the cabin, then leaned close and whispered in his ear. "What was he doing when you found him?" she asked.

Stephen considered for a moment and decided not to tell her what he'd thought he'd seen. After all, it had only been a dream.

"Nothing," he said. "Just being naked."

Halle glanced at Jack, who was pulling on his pants, and then shook her head. "Well," she whispered, "either he's just had sex, or he's been jerking off."

Stephen was startled. He looked back at Jack and then at Halle again. "How can you tell?"

"I used to sleep with the guy. I can tell."

Stephen decided that he didn't want to know any more, so he said nothing. Jack finished dressing and joined them, and they all went inside. The teakettle started whistling as they entered the kitchen.

"Great!" Jack said, delighted. "We're just in time."

Stephen was confused. "How long was I gone?" he asked Halle.

"Maybe two minutes. Tommy's still here, if that's what you're wondering. He's washing up in the east wing."

"That wasn't what I was wondering."

"See, none of the utilities in his cabin have been turned on yet," Halle said. "So I told him he could stay here tonight. If that's okay with you guys."

Stephen could hear something in her voice that he didn't like, and it made him angry at himself because he didn't have any right not to like it, or to feel anything at all about it. It was none of his business what she did with Mr. Moribund.

"It's your place," Jack said, pouring hot water into a mug. "Why should we mind?"

"Exactly," Stephen muttered.

"By the way, Halle," Jack said, "Lily says hi."

Hours later, deep in the night, Stephen lay awake in his room with a bologna sandwich beside him. Jack was asleep on the couch in the living room. Jack had been snoring earlier, but Stephen had gone out and nudged him until he turned onto his side. Now all was quiet.

Almost all. Stephen heard occasional soft sounds coming from the east wing. He nibbled on the sandwich and told himself that he was imagining what he was hearing.

But he knew. He knew.

He finished the sandwich and went to the kitchen for another one. On the way back through the living room, he paused and looked at Jack sleeping. Jack had built a fire after having his tea, and the embers were still red. They cast a soft glow over Jack's face.

Jack's grief over Natalie's death had driven him crazy, but it was a craziness that had made him happy. Right now, asleep before the fire, he looked like the most contented man on earth.

"Lucky son of a bitch," Stephen whispered. Then he went back to his room, ate the sandwich, and tried to sleep. But the soft sounds from the east wing wouldn't let him. So after a while he sat up, turned on the bedside lamp, and began grading essays.

They all sucked. Nothing better than a C– in the bunch. These kids wouldn't recognize "The Horse Dealer's Daughter" if she came up to them in her wet clothes and smelly hair and bit them on their callow asses.

Stephen tasted bologna and Miracle Whip at the back of his throat, and for the first time in his life, he hated it.

9

◆

Something Was Wrong
with His Eyes

Something was wrong with his eyes, Halle thought as she looked at Stephen across the card table. She had always thought he had abnormally large eyes, but that might be— as he'd suggested yesterday—because of the bulletproof-thick lenses in his glasses. Whatever was wrong this morning, though, was something else. An unusual dilation of the pupils, perhaps, coupled with a vague redness in the whites. Halle couldn't be sure. She had never studied Stephen's face this closely before.

"Are the eggs okay?" she asked, yawning. She had gotten up at six and scrambled some eggs and fried a few potatoes. Stephen and Jack had both come into the kitchen and offered to help, but she'd shooed them out. She liked cooking breakfast, and she liked doing it alone. At home, she made it a point to get up before Cleo and Tony awoke so that she could make breakfast and have some time alone and in control. It made her feel as if she would be in control of the rest of the day, too.

That feeling never seemed to pan out, but it was nice while it lasted.

"They're very good, thank you," Stephen said. He looked down at his plate.

"Great chow!" Jack said around a mouthful.

Halle looked away from Stephen and watched Jack eat for a few minutes. She was now more convinced than ever that he had done something sexual the night before. It had been a long time since she'd slept with him, but she remembered that he had always been ravenous the morning after.

And Jack had never liked masturbation. So she was betting that somehow he had found a partner in the woods last night. She suspected the strange woman who had shown up at her duplex on the night that Jack had been arrested. Halle still had the long blue coat that the woman had dropped in the driveway. It was hanging in the duplex's hall closet.

Jack polished off his potatoes and eggs, leaned back, and grinned at Halle. She felt a twinge. Years before, that grin had told her that she was doomed to fall into bed with him.

"Any more?" Jack asked.

Halle was relieved to find that her twinge was already gone. She still cared about Jack, but there were some things it was better not to revisit. She couldn't imagine sleeping with Jack again without seeing the ghost of Natalie wedged between them.

"On the stove," Halle said. "Help yourself."

Jack scooted his chair back from the table, stood, and picked up his plate. "That's what I've been doing," he said, "but my friends keep pitching in anyway. Not that I'm complaining, mind you, but I wish that y'all didn't feel so all-fired responsible for me."

"We don't feel responsible for you," Halle said. "But we do feel a duty to our fellow citizens to protect them from the sight of your penis. Think of the car wrecks that would result from all those cases of hysterical blindness."

Jack chuckled and took his plate into the kitchen. Halle smiled, then took a bite of eggs. She had spiced them with Creole seasoning. The flavor bit into her tongue and made her lips feel as if they were on fire. Licking them only made them feel hotter. She liked it.

She glanced up at Stephen and caught him staring at her. She was sure of it because he looked away so quickly. People didn't look away quickly unless they were staring to begin with. She wondered if Stephen might be pissed off at her about something. He'd never

seemed entirely comfortable around her, but this morning he was acting downright uneasy.

"Are you sure your eggs are okay?" she asked. "You're picking at
them."

Stephen picked at them some more, scratching his fork across the
paper plate. "They're delicious," he said. He sounded nervous. "It's
just that I don't usually eat breakfast. Not this early, anyway."

"I'll bet it's the spices," Halle said. "I'll bet I made 'em too hot for
you."

Stephen scooped a forkful into his mouth and shook his head.

Something was definitely wrong with his eyes. Halle was determined to find out what it was.

"Did you sleep all right?" she asked. "Were you too warm or cold
or anything?"

He swallowed and said, "I slept just fine, thanks."

"You're sure? I stepped out for some fresh air in the middle of the
night, and I saw your light on. And your eyes look just the tiniest bit
bloodshot."

Stephen didn't seem to be able to look at her at all now. His eyes
kept shifting. "I was up for a while grading papers."

"Ah-ha, so you couldn't sleep."

Now he looked at her. Yes, he was pissed off. He thought she was
a jerk for prying. She had done it last night, and she was doing it now,
and he wanted her to leave him alone. Maybe.

"I could have slept," he said. "But I had to grade papers."

Halle decided to cut through the bullshit. She and Stephen were
supposed to be friends, and she was tired of trying to figure out what
was going on with him by dancing around the real question.

"So what's your problem, anyway?" she asked.

In an instant, he no longer looked pissed. Now he looked as if she'd
slugged him. "I, uh, I— What?"

"No, you tried to pull that yesterday too," she said. "I'm not letting you get away with it today. There's something bugging you, and
it's not just that you feel left out of the gang. You've been part of the
gang for almost nine years. So spill."

Stephen now had the look of a trapped animal searching for a way
to escape. Halle found that she rather enjoyed it. She wasn't sure why,

but she liked the fact that she could make staid, quiet, thick-spectacled Stephen Corman squirm.

"I'm just not quite awake, that's all," he said. His voice was not convincing. "The sun's not even up yet."

Halle pressed the attack. "You're up almost this early every morning. Katy told me that you get up when she does, and she gets up at six-thirty. Right about now."

"But it's really only five-thirty," Stephen pointed out. "I need more than three days to adjust to daylight saving time."

"Oh," Halle said. But she knew there was something else going on with him. She just knew it. Trouble with Katy, maybe? "So why didn't you stay in bed another hour or two?"

"I smelled breakfast."

"Yet you're hardly eating."

"I'm enjoying the smell."

Halle sighed. "Okay, Steve, you win. But if there's something you want to talk about, I can listen. Okay?"

Stephen looked either pained or puzzled. Halle couldn't tell which. Those big, weird eyes kept throwing her off.

Those eyes were staring at her again now. But she was staring right back at them, and they weren't flinching away.

"Okay," Stephen said. His voice was hoarse. He sounded sad. But sadness was only part of it.

And in that moment, Halle recognized the tone. She had heard it in the voices of a lot of other men too, and it had always gotten her into trouble. She began to have a queasy feeling in her stomach that she hoped was just the Creole seasoning. She didn't want it to be what she was afraid it might be.

The front door banged open then, and Halle turned toward it, relieved, as Tommy clomped in. She was glad to see him. His hair was mussed, his bare belly pooched out below his T-shirt, and he was wearing boxer shorts and cowboy boots. His eyes were heavy-lidded, his jaw was slack, and he looked like shit that needed a shave. He was a beautiful sight. He gave Halle something else to think about.

"Well, good morning, bedhead," she said, standing up to give Tommy a hug. "I thought you'd be zonked for another two hours."

Tommy grunted as she hugged him, then mumbled, "Coffee."

"It's in the kitchen," she said. "I'll get it."

Tommy grunted again, then sat down heavily in the chair that Halle had just vacated. He looked across at Stephen and said, "Mornin'."

Halle risked a glance at Stephen and saw an expression that said he wouldn't mind too much if someone plunged knitting needles through his eyes and into his brain.

"Mornin'," Stephen said. It was an almost perfect reproduction of Tommy's voice.

Halle escaped into the kitchen and found Jack leaning out the open window over the sink. In order to do this, he was kneeling in the sink itself. Coming closer, Halle saw that the sink also contained two inches of water and the skillet that she'd used to cook breakfast.

"Mind telling me what you're doing?" she asked.

"Not at all," Jack said without looking back inside. "I'm watching the most important event of the morning."

"Sunrise is in the other direction."

"Sunrise?" Jack said. "Sunrise happens *every* morning, day in, day out. Booo-ring. No, I'm watching the Moon set."

Halle looked past him. "How can you see it through the trees?"

"I can see the light. And I can smell the perfume."

"Perfume?"

"Lily's perfume."

Halle couldn't help responding to that. "Let me guess," she said. "Moonflowers, right?"

Jack looked over his shoulder at her. "How'd you know?"

"Shot in the dark."

Jack turned back toward the trees. "You might think about planting some moonflowers in front of the cabin, by the way. The ones that look like white trumpets. We had some when I was a kid, in a flower bed bordering the front porch. Some nights my mother would let me stay up late enough to watch them open."

"They don't open all that late, do they?"

"Just after dusk," Jack said. "But I was a little kid, and my folks made me go to bed at eight." He paused. "Something about the way those flowers opened so slowly and deliberately was incredibly sensual. Sexy, even. Of course I didn't realize that at age six. Not consciously, anyway. Didn't you come in here for coffee?"

"How'd you know that?"

"Sound carries." He made a throat-clearing noise. "So, do you think Steve's okay? I mean, considering that you fucked Tommy last night?"

Halle couldn't believe it. Jack's insanity had left him with all the social tact of a swamp rat. "Shh!" she hissed. "Didn't you say yourself that sound carries?"

"Steve can't hear us," Jack said. "I just now heard him go to his room. Maybe to sleep some more, but probably to pack up his stuff. He doesn't like Tommy, and he wants to get away."

"Well, then," Halle whispered, "you don't want Tommy to hear you, either."

"He won't. He's asleep with his head on the card table. I heard a thunk."

Halle went to the kitchen door and looked into the living room. Sure enough, Stephen was gone and his bedroom door was shut. And Tommy was zonked. He was even snoring. He had also done that during the few hours that they'd actually slept in the night. It had woken her up, but she had liked it anyway. It had been a long time since she'd spent an entire night with someone who snored. She'd missed it.

"So," Jack's voice said behind her. "How was he?"

"I don't know that it's any of your business," Halle said, crossing back to the sink.

"Oh, come on." He looked back at her again. "I'll tell you how Lily was."

"I'm sure I don't care."

"Liar. You've always wanted to know everything about everybody. So I'll go ahead and tell you that Lily was wonderful. She always is. How was Tommy?"

"He was okay," Halle said before she could stop herself. It was even the truth. Tommy had been okay. He hadn't provided any carnal epiphanies or skull-shattering orgasms, but he'd done nothing that had made her want to retch, either. They'd had comfortable, ordinary sex. Better than a kick in the head any day. But maybe not as good as a truly fine Boston cream pie.

Jack looked thoughtful. "Just okay, huh? You should tell Steve that.

He might feel better if he knew that Tommy didn't exactly put a crack in your Liberty Bell."

Halle laughed. "Put a what in my what?" she said when she could talk. "Jack, that's the stupidest metaphor I've ever heard in my life."

"Well, then, you need to get out more," Jack said. "There are lots of stupider metaphors. Particularly metaphors having to do with sex. Stupid metaphorical terms for breasts and penises alone could take hours to recite. Besides which, attacking my metaphor is just your way of avoiding responding to what I said about Steve."

Halle was quiet for a moment. Jack was right. She didn't want to deal with what she—and obviously, Jack—now feared was going on with Steve. "I came out here to get some coffee to help Tommy wake up," she said. "I should do that and leave you to your sink-kneeling."

"At this point, the only way that coffee will help Tommy wake up," Jack said, "is if you throw it in his face. And Steve might come out of the bedroom and see you do it, and it could get his hopes up. That would be cruel."

Halle put her elbows on the counter beside the sink and cupped her chin in her hands. "I don't get it," she said. "Steve's married to the greatest woman on earth. Why would he be interested in me? And what makes you think he is, anyway?"

Jack grinned at her again. "Answer to question one: Beats me. Answer to question two: Lily told me. It surprised me too, believe me."

"Thanks a lot, asshole."

"You're welcome. But Lily knows about these things. It's her area of specialization. So it must be true: Associate Professor of Literature Stephen Corman, devoted husband of Katy the Amazing Four-Point-Oh Engineer, has a major case of primal lust for you."

And Halle knew it was true. Lily or no Lily, she knew it. She had felt it in her stomach at the card table. Stephen had looked at her with those huge confused and confusing eyes, and she had known. And then Tommy had walked in—

Shit. She and Tommy hadn't exactly been quiet in the night. And the bedroom they'd used was right across the breezeway from the bedroom that Stephen had been in. And Stephen's light had been on when she'd gone outside to let the night air dry the sweat from her skin.

Stephen had heard her with Tommy. It must have been awful for him, feeling the way he felt, knowing what she was doing, having to listen to it . . .

Halle took her chin from her hands, stood up straight, and shook her head. What was she thinking? So what if Steve had a crush on her? Was she supposed to factor *that* into the decisions she made about her life? What business was it of his if she slept with Tommy or anybody else?

"Steve's an idiot," she said. "If he has to want someone besides Katy, he ought to be wanting someone who's a better person than she is. Or at least gorgeous. I'm neither one. And don't say that I am, because you and I both know I'm not."

"I didn't say a thing," Jack said.

Halle raised her voice, almost hoping that Stephen would hear her. "I mean, why doesn't he make goo-goo eyes at Carolyn, for example? She's beautiful, at least."

Jack nodded. "Yes, she is. As we males say, a fabulous babe. And she has other qualities, too. So do you. Not the same ones as she does, of course. But different qualities appeal to different people." Jack's eyebrows rose in mock surprise. "Gee, I wonder if maybe that's why Steve's attracted to you instead of her. Ya think?"

Halle grimaced. "Yeah, well, you were attracted to both of us."

Jack looked westward again. "But not at the same time. Quiet, now: The Moon's setting. I have to say good-bye until next month."

Halle turned away from him and went to the stove. The coffee was still more or less warm, so she took the pot out to the card table and poured a cup for Tommy, who came awake at the sound. He gave her a groggy, lopsided smile—his face looked a little flattened on one side—and grunted a thank-you. He drank the coffee without complaining that it wasn't hot.

He looked cute, and he was being sweet. Maybe, Halle thought, he had been better than okay. Maybe he had been pretty good.

The door to Stephen's bedroom opened, and Stephen emerged with his overnight bag. He looked at Tommy, and then at Halle, and then at nothing at all as far as Halle could tell.

It made her angry. It wasn't her fault that he was feeling whatever he was feeling. Maybe she shouldn't have flaunted Tommy in front of him, but Jesus, she'd thought she was among adults. She always had to be painfully careful with men around Cleo and Tony, so coming up to the cabin to have a night with Tommy had felt like freedom. And Jack and Stephen were her friends. They should be happy for her. Not weird. Not jealous. Not like head-butting, hormone-driven adolescents.

Mr. Moribund, indeed. She had caught that crack the night before and had chosen to ignore it. But she'd caught it, all right. What did Stephen think she was, stupid?

Or maybe he didn't. Maybe he'd expected her to catch it. Maybe it was his way of telling her something without having to put himself on the line to do it.

"Thanks for breakfast," Stephen said.

"Are you leaving already?" Halle asked. She tried to put a deliberate note of disingenuousness into her voice.

Stephen nodded. He was looking at the floor now. "If Jack's ready. I thought we'd have to stay the day for his sake, but he said something a little while ago about having to go back to being mundane once the Moon had set. And the Moon's setting just about now. So if he wants to go home, I'm all for it. I have a lot of work to do."

"I see," Halle said. She paused, trying to decide how much double meaning she wanted her next words to carry. "I take it that you didn't get your papers graded even though you were up most of the night. I can relate. I didn't get anything done, either . . . even though I was up most of the night, too."

Tommy, sipping his coffee, gave her a puzzled look.

Stephen didn't look at her at all. He did start to say something, but then Jack came into the room and interrupted him.

"Moon's set," Jack said. "I'm done. Let's blow this Popsicle stand. No offense, Halle, but what would Steve and I do out here all day?"

"Same thing I do," Halle said. She gave Stephen what she hoped was a piercing stare. "Whatever I feel like."

But Stephen still wasn't looking at her. "Uh, Jack," he said, "your jeans are wet."

"He's been in the sink," Halle said.

"What for?" Tommy asked.

"Never mind," Halle and Stephen said in unison.

At that, Stephen looked at Halle and smiled.

She knew why. It was because they had just shared something that she couldn't share with Tommy. It was because she and Stephen had known each other for years, and had known Jack for years. Halle and Stephen had never been the closest of friends—most of the time Halle had just thought of him as Katy's husband—but nine years of interpersonal osmosis meant that there were things between them that Tommy just wasn't in on. And never would be, because even though she'd met him only a week ago, Halle was already pretty sure that she would never see him as anything more than a casual lay.

"Thanks again," Stephen said. His eyes didn't flinch from hers now. "I had a good time."

It was a lie, and Halle knew it, and she was sure that he knew she knew it. And in a weird but real sense, that meant they were more intimate than she had ever realized before. More intimate, in a way, than she had been with Tommy last night.

Jack went back into the kitchen and returned with his cooler. "Saddle up!" he yelled. "The left-handed chariot awaits!" He gave Halle a kiss on the cheek, nodded to Tommy, and went outside.

Stephen rolled his eyes. With eyes as big as his, it was impressive. "Pray for me," he said. "I'm convinced that Jack's jeep is possessed by the spirit of a dead but still disgruntled ex–postal worker."

Halle laughed. Stephen could be funny. She'd never noticed before. It made her want to hug him, so she did.

"It was sweet of you to come up here with Jack," she said into his ear. "You're a good friend."

When she released him from the hug, he seemed to be trembling. And his glasses looked smeared. Or fogged.

"Are you okay?" Halle asked.

He nodded. "Just in fear for my life," he said. "I have to ride back to Austin with Jack."

Tommy stood and shook Stephen's hand. "Y'all be careful on the road," he said. "There's lunatics everywhere."

"Sure," Stephen said. He pulled his hand away from Tommy's and then looked at Halle again. "Bye."

"Bye," Halle said. "Tell Katy I'll call her tomorrow."

"You bet," Stephen said. Then he went outside. He seemed to be in a hurry.

Halle followed him to the doorway, then leaned against the jamb as the jeep clattered to life and Stephen climbed inside.

"Tallyho!" Jack bellowed, and popped the clutch.

The jeep lurched once, then twice, and then roared off down the driveway at a speed far slower than the noise and spraying gravel suggested. Stephen and Jack both waved, and then they were gone.

Halle smiled. They were all such kids still. Jack wouldn't be flat-out crazy again for another month, but even when he wasn't crazy, he was still just a boy in a man's body. And Stephen, to her surprise, had proven that he wasn't much past puberty himself. Even she had reacted like a child when she'd gotten angry at Stephen for his behavior . . . which hadn't been all that bad, really.

Tommy came up beside her and put a hand on her back. It felt good.

"You want me to leave too?" he asked.

Halle thought about it while she looked around at the trees and the brightening sky. The sun was coming up, birds were singing, and the air was crisp. A hundred and ten miles away, her children were being readied for school by their grandmother. And she was giving herself the day off. Her clients could wait until tomorrow for their code to be debugged.

So Stephen liked her a little. She didn't mind that. Katy wouldn't mind either. Katy would probably even approve of it. Katy had told her more than once that she wished Stephen wasn't such a hermit.

Halle turned to face Tommy.

"You're not going anywhere," she said, "until I give you written permission. You hear?"

"Yes, ma'am," he said.

Halle pushed him back inside and kicked the door closed behind her.

PART V

FLOWER MOON

Wednesday, May 5, 1993

10

❖

The Tent Was Hot,

and It Shuddered

The tent was hot, and it shuddered as Carolyn unzipped the panels covering the screen windows. The breeze came through then, and the blue dome rattled. Carolyn sat down on the lumpy floor, wiped the sweat from her eyes, and hated Artie. He had helped her pound in the tent stakes, but then he'd dashed off to the river with Halle's kids and Jack. There was some crazy talk about going swimming. Sure, the temperature was in the upper eighties, but the river would still be too cold this early in May. Artie, Jack, and the kids would find out if they were stupid enough to try it.

And of course they would. Artie had no more sense than a kid himself, and Jack was due for his monthly bout of bat's-ass insanity. Carolyn couldn't believe that Halle trusted those two to look after Cleo and Tony. But then, Halle probably figured that Jack would be fine until the Moon rose, and she didn't know Artie the way Carolyn did.

"Knock-knock," Halle's voice said outside the flap, and then she came inside without waiting for an answer. She was lugging two fat, rolled-up sleeping bags. "Hey, this is great," she said, standing hunched over while glancing around the tent. "It was swell of you to bring it. The kids'll be thrilled."

"What the kids'll be," Carolyn said, scooting back against the southernmost screen window, "is freezing their heinies off. Doesn't it get cold out here at night?"

Halle dropped the sleeping bags. "Cold enough. But the little apes made me promise to let them camp. If I don't, they'll throw tantrums tonight that'll wake the dead—and I have to get up early to drive them back for school, so I don't want that. Steve says he'll keep them company, and I figure that if they get too chilly, he'll bring them in."

Carolyn frowned. "Both kids plus Steve and Katy in this little space? I don't think so."

"Neither does Katy. She's going to be inside in a bed, like the rest of us with any sense."

The crunch of tires on gravel came from the driveway. Carolyn looked out through the screen and fifty yards of forest and was just able to see the Cormans' Toyota pull into the circle in front of the cabin.

"And here they are now," Carolyn said. She felt a twinge as she watched Stephen and Katy get out of their car. She had always envied them. They were the perfect married couple, in love forever, devoted to each other, sensitive to each other's needs, and all that other greeting-card horseshit. Her only consolation was that she doubted their sex life was as good as her and Artie's. Probably nobody else on the planet had as good a sex life as she and Artie did. Well, maybe Jack did—but Jack's was all in his imagination.

Halle untied one of the sleeping bags, unrolled it, and flopped down on it with her chin in her hands. "I guess I ought to go greet them," she said. "But it's kind of awkward."

Carolyn's curiosity was piqued. "Oh? Why's that?"

"It's no big deal," Halle said, but the tone of her voice suggested that maybe it was. "I found out Steve has a crush on me, so I'm afraid he'll feel embarrassed. I haven't even laid eyes on him since he and Jack were up here last month. I've talked to him on the phone a few times, though, and he seemed nervous. Once he just said hi and handed the phone to Katy. And the next time, when Katy wasn't home, he made me do all the talking." She sighed. "I get the feeling that he knows I found out, and that's got him spooked."

Carolyn didn't know what to say. Usually, if there was an attached male of her acquaintance who had a crush on someone, that crush was on her. Not that she had ever wanted or expected any attention of that sort from Stephen Corman. It was just that it was weird to think of him lusting after anyone besides Katy . . . unless it was her. Because that was the way things usually went, and she usually wound up with a woman friend angry at her as a result.

Not that Halle was unattractive. Halle was a terrific person, and she'd had more than her share of men. But if Stephen was going to want anyone besides Katy, it ought to be . . .

Carolyn wanted to slap herself. Where did this ego the size of Big Bend come from, anyway? Okay, so she was physically beautiful. Like she'd had anything to do with that. All it meant was that she could draw gorgeous young dipshits like Artie to her like gnats to buttermilk.

"Wow," Carolyn said.

"Yeah."

"How'd you find out? I mean, he didn't tell you himself, did he?" Carolyn supposed that she could imagine Stephen wanting Halle, but she couldn't imagine him ever saying so.

"No, of course not," Halle said. "But I got some signals last month. I had a guy here with me, and it seemed to get Steve's back up. And then Jack—well, Jack just came right out and told me that Steve had it bad for me."

"Did Steve tell him that?"

"I don't think so." Halle gave Carolyn a look that implied shared knowledge. "But crazy or not, there are things that Jack understands."

Carolyn flashed on a memory of when she had been Jack's first serious girlfriend. They had been walking on campus together, and had passed a bunch of guys playing Frisbee. The Frisbee had flown wild and skittered to a stop on the sidewalk at Carolyn's feet. She had picked it up to throw it back, but one of the guys had run over to take it from her instead.

The guy had been stunning—an Artie prototype, in fact, only beefier—and a sexual spark had passed between them when she'd returned the Frisbee. Except for his "Thanks," though, neither of them had said a word.

But as she and Jack had walked on, Jack had said, "Make him be good to you."

And Carolyn had looked at him and said, "What the *fuck* are you talking about?"

A week later, she'd started sleeping with the Frisbee guy, whose name had turned out to be David McIlhenney and whose major had turned out to be chemical engineering, and with whom she would live for the next eight months.

Jack had been nineteen; she had been twenty.

"Okay," Carolyn said. "If Jack says Steve has a thing for you, he probably does. So what are you going to do about it?"

Halle rolled her eyes. "Jesus, what do you think? I mean, Steve's great, but Katy's my friend. And even if she weren't—would *you* want Katy Corman torqued off at you?"

Carolyn tried to imagine that. She knew that most of her friends thought of her as the vicious she-devil in their circle, but that was mostly an act. Katy, on the other hand, was cool, rational, and potentially deadly. Carolyn wouldn't cross her for all of the money and insatiable Artie clones in the world.

"Not on a bet," Carolyn said. She heard footsteps on dry leaves and looked out through the screen again. "Oh, God!" she whispered, turning back to Halle. "Here she comes. You don't think she heard us, do you?"

Halle shook her head, then rolled over and sat up as Katy pulled back the tent flap and came inside.

"Is this the estrogen ward?" Katy asked, smiling.

Carolyn was surprised. Katy almost never smiled.

"All of us except my daughter," Halle said. "And the way she's been behaving lately, I think she might be mostly testosterone. She'll probably grow up to be a bull dyke who's disgusted that her mother does it with men."

"Oh, well, I'm sure you'll love her anyway," Katy said.

Halle grinned. "You bet. More men for me."

Carolyn didn't know why, but she found this remark irritating. "How many do you want?"

Halle gave her a sharp glance. "How many you got?"

"Just the one," Carolyn said, "and you'd better keep your mitts off." She tried to make it sound like a joke, but as she spoke she had a vision of Artie and Halle making love. It made her stomach knot up.

"No problem," Halle said. "I have my hands full at the moment, anyway. And I do mean full."

"Oh, are you still seeing Tommy?" Katy asked.

"Maybe, if the big doofus shows up. He didn't know if he could get out of Austin on a Wednesday."

"What did you mean by 'And I do mean full'?" Carolyn asked. It was her opinion that anybody bold enough to hint at certain things ought to be bold enough to come right out and say them, goddamn it.

"I mean he's hung like a Clydesdale," Halle said.

Well, if Halle was going to come right out and say it, Carolyn was going to come right out and ask the next thing that came into her head. "Don't you find that uncomfortable?" she asked.

"No, but I imagine that he does," Halle said. "He wears tight jeans, and it's gotta be cramped in there." She looked thoughtful. "On the other hand, I've never seen him when he wasn't perky, so maybe he's not cramped at all."

Katy gave a dry laugh. "You realize, of course," she said, "that if we continue this discussion we'll be acting out every man's stereotypical fear of what women sit around talking about."

"What's that?" Carolyn asked.

"Penis size," Katy said.

"Speaking of your husband," Halle said, "where is he?"

Katy raised an eyebrow. "Am I to understand that if you hear the words *penis size,* you immediately think of my husband? I shall have to have you killed."

"Don't bother," Halle said. "My children will do me in long before you could raise the money for a hit. No, I was just wondering if he might be in earshot. We wouldn't want to give him a heart attack with our gutter talk."

Katy's smile became a thin, knowing line. Almost a smirk, Carolyn thought. "You might be surprised," Katy said.

Carolyn couldn't stand it. "By what?" she asked.

"Oh, nothing."

Halle looked at Carolyn. "Are we gonna let her get away with that?"

Carolyn glanced from Halle to Katy. Halle looked mischievous, and Katy's knowing smirk was still there. Carolyn began to wonder if she might be out of her depth. It occurred to her that she'd spent a lot of time with Halle and Katy as part of a larger group of friends, but that this was only the second or third time since college that the three of them had been together without anyone else present. The dynamics were different, and she hadn't figured them out yet. But she had the feeling that if Halle and Katy wanted to, they could gang up on her and tear her soul into little psychic shreds. Katy was so mentally strong that it was scary, and Halle didn't seem to be fazed by anything. And from the way the conversation had gone so far, they both seemed more secure in their sexuality than she had ever been in hers.

She supposed that the men she knew would find that strange. Men always seemed to think that because Carolyn was attractive and dirty-minded, she must be the Sex Goddess of Central Texas. But there were a lot of things about her that none of the men she knew had ever figured out. Artie sure as hell hadn't . . . but then, Artie had trouble figuring out a can opener.

"I think," Carolyn said, "that I'll let Katy get away with whatever Katy wants to get away with."

Halle shrugged. "Well, not me." She turned back to Katy. "Confess: You and your old man tore off a big one just before driving up here."

"I admit nothing."

"Hah!" Halle said. "I knew it. And it was great, too, wasn't it? I always guessed that Steve had hidden depths."

Carolyn couldn't believe it. Five minutes before, Halle had been telling her that Stephen was attracted to her, and now she was teasing Katy about whether Stephen was good in bed. It seemed a little—well, not two-faced, exactly, but dancing close to that edge.

"They aren't all that hidden," Katy said. "But from what he's told me, I gather that no one else ever—" She stopped short.

Carolyn was so curious she felt as if she were about to split open like a ripe melon. "What? What's he told you?"

Katy fidgeted with one of the strings holding the sleeping bag in a roll. "If either of you repeats a word of this to anyone," she said, "I truly will have you both killed."

"Not a word," Carolyn said. She was embarrassed at how eager she was. She wasn't even sure why she *was* so eager. She had never had any sexual curiosity about Stephen . . . until now.

"Who am I gonna tell?" Halle asked. "Outside of my business, you're the only adults I ever talk to."

Katy smiled again. "What about Tommy?"

"Oh, we don't talk. I generally see to it that his mouth is full."

They all laughed, but then there was a silence until Carolyn couldn't stand it anymore. "So, Katy . . . "

"All right," Katy said. "I suppose I have to go ahead and tell you now, or be accused of being a gossip tease." She took a deep breath. "It's nothing mind-blowing. It's only that Stephen was a virgin when we met. I'm the only woman he's ever been with."

"You're kidding," Halle said.

"Tell *no one*," Katy said.

Carolyn was a little disappointed. "That's it?" She thought about it for a few seconds, remembering when she'd found out that she was Jack's first. "Actually, that's sweet. It's sort of like the myth of the unicorn, or Jack's goddess from the Moon. You know, it's nice to imagine, but it never occurs to you that it might actually exist."

"I agree that it's sweet," Halle said, "but it's also bizarre. I mean, Katy, how old was Steve when y'all met?"

"Twenty-five."

"Don't you think that's weird?" Halle asked Carolyn. "Can you imagine a twenty-five-year-old guy who's never done it?"

"Sure," Carolyn said. "I can imagine fifty-year-old guys who've never done it. I see guys every day who I'll bet have never done it. Or at least who won't ever do it with me."

Halle shook her head. "You're talking about the creepy, the freaky, the pathetic, and the pathologically shy. Steve's not in those categories. He's a nice guy—and pretty cute, too."

"I am most definitely going to have you killed," Katy said.

"I don't care what you say," Carolyn said to Halle. "The fact that he *is* a desirable man is the very thing that makes it sweet." She looked at Katy. "I think you're pretty lucky."

Katy looked down at the sleeping-bag string. "Well, things aren't perfect," she said. "But overall, we're a good match."

Carolyn couldn't miss the note of sadness in Katy's voice. It scared her a little, and she found herself wanting to fix whatever had caused it.

"Things are never perfect," she said. "But you and Steve sure come closer to it than most."

Halle shook her head. "I still can't get past the virgin thing. I guess it just seems odd to me because I've never been with someone who had no experience at all."

"I have," Carolyn said, blurting it out before thinking.

Halle's eyes lit up. "Get out. Who?"

"You wouldn't believe it." Carolyn was feeling a little mischievous herself now.

"It must have been someone we know, or you wouldn't have said that," Katy said.

"I'm guessing David McIlhenney," Halle said.

Carolyn cringed. "Please," she said. "I think Dave must have been screwing before he could walk."

Katy had a sour look on her face. "Yes," she said, "in every sense of the word."

Carolyn was astonished. "You too?"

"Hell, me too," Halle said.

"Well, I knew that," Carolyn said, not caring how it sounded. She felt a little peeved at Halle. "But jeez, Katy, I thought you had sense."

"Meaning that I don't?" Halle asked.

"Not back then, you didn't," Carolyn said. In fact, she wasn't sure that Halle had a whole lot of sense now, either. But she wasn't going to say that.

"It was a long time ago," Katy said. Her voice was somber. "The motherfucker."

Carolyn was startled for a moment because Katy almost never swore. But then she remembered that they were talking about David McIlhenney.

"He should die screaming," Carolyn offered.

"I don't care if he screams or not," Halle said, "just so he dies." She touched Katy's knee. "Not that it matters now, but I knew about you and Dave. It was while you were still living with Jack, right?"

Katy nodded.

"It was okay with me by then," Halle said. "Really. I was already in recovery from the McIlhenney treatment. I should have warned you, though."

Katy said nothing.

Carolyn thought she should try to change the subject. "What is this, Halle, do you know everybody who's slept with everybody?"

Halle got up from her sleeping bag. "As a matter of fact, I do," she said. "Don't go anywhere." She left the tent, and Carolyn watched through the screen as she jogged off through the trees.

"How could intelligent people like us have been so stupid?" Katy asked.

Carolyn looked at Katy's face and realized for the first time that Katy might not be the invulnerable intellectual rock she'd always seemed to be.

"We weren't stupid," Carolyn said. "We were lied to and jerked around by a camouflaged asshole." She hesitated then, wondering if she should tell Katy the next thing that came to mind. "I saw him at Whole Foods last week. He looks like shit."

Katy nodded. "I know. I almost wish that he didn't, because every time I see him now, I remember that I went insane for him—but I have no idea why."

Carolyn was having trouble remembering what *she* had liked about McIlhenney, too. "He had the power to cloud women's minds, I guess. But now he's lost it, and he's miserable. That's his punishment."

Katy looked up. She was smiling again. "Good," she said.

Halle came back into the tent carrying a soft-sided briefcase. "I brought some work with me," she said, flopping down on the opened sleeping bag again, "in case Tommy doesn't show up. And along with it I find that I have the current version of what I call the Big Ol' Fanfold of, um, Friends." She reached into the briefcase and pulled out a huge sheet of paper folded like a highway map. "It's not complete, because I don't know everything. But I know a lot."

She unfolded the sheet on the floor of the tent, and Carolyn saw that it was crisscrossed with red and blue lines that had numerous intersections at three-digit numbers. It reminded her of a drawing toy she'd had as a child. The thing had been called a Spirograph, and it had produced geometric patterns almost as complicated as this one.

"Well, I don't know what the hell this is," Carolyn said, getting on her hands and knees for a closer look, "but there's no doubt that it was done by an engineer."

Halle looked at Katy. "How about you, genius? Do you know what this is?"

Katy looked at the chart for several seconds before answering. "Given what prompted you to bring it to us," she said then, "and given the fact that the numbers are connected by lines—some with more connections than others—I'd have to guess that you've put together a chart of which friends of yours have slept with whom."

"No wonder you had a 4.0 GPA," Halle said. "But not all of these people are now, or ever were, my friends. I did the first version while we were still at UT, and I've expanded it periodically ever since."

Carolyn stared at her. "Why, for God's sake?"

Halle stared right back. "You know exactly why. You of all people. I'm surprised you haven't made up a chart like this yourself."

Carolyn thought about it and realized that, in a way, she had. She just hadn't put it down on paper.

"So what do the red and blue lines mean?" she asked.

"Blue lines," Halle said, "are extended relationships. Boyfriends, girlfriends, husbands, wives. Red lines are short affairs, brief mistakes, and one-night stands. The numbers are to protect the anonymity of the guilty. Women are even numbers . . . and men, of course, are odd."

"Of course," Carolyn said. She was beginning to like this.

"Numbers starting with 1 are people I first met at UT between 1976 and 1980," Halle said. "Numbers starting with 2 are people who became connected with that original group through sexual liaisons. Numbers starting with 3 are people who became connected with the extended group through liaisons with 2's. I started counting some 4's and 5's too, but then gave up and called all of them 3's. Middle and third digits give the order in which I first heard about the activities of each individual—keeping in mind that females have to be even, and men have to be odd."

Carolyn gazed at the chart. It was amazing. There were lines everywhere, and more than a hundred numbers. It looked as if any one of those numbers could be linked up with any other number just by tracing the right zigzag of red and blue lines.

She pointed at number 100 on the chart, which had so many red and blue lines converging on it that it was surrounded by a solid purple ring. "My God," she said, "who's the slut?"

Halle made a throat-clearing noise. "Actually," she said, "that's me."

Carolyn bit her lip. Whoops. She should have been able to figure that out from Halle's explanation of the numbering system.

"I apologize," Carolyn said as contritely as she knew how. "What I meant to say was, Who's this really *popular* girl?"

There was an uncomfortable silence for a moment, but then Halle and Katy both convulsed with laughter. Carolyn tried to hold it in, but with the other two cracking up—particularly Katy, who seldom laughed and was now making up for it—she couldn't. As she rolled onto her side, gasping for breath, she hoped that Halle wouldn't hold it against her.

"Hoo boy," Halle said after a while. "Popular. I like that. I want that on my tombstone. Just that one word. Promise me that y'all will see to it."

Katy, who seemed almost recovered now, nodded. "Very well. But only if you tell me my number."

Halle leaned over to Katy and whispered into her ear.

Carolyn heard the number. It was 106. She examined the chart. Now that she knew both Halle's and Katy's numbers, she could figure out all kinds of things—

"Do you want yours?" Halle asked her.

Carolyn shook her head. She was tracing lines. And within moments she knew that she was number 112. She knew that because of where blue lines from Katy and Halle converged.

"Jack," she said, "is number 111."

Halle's eyes widened. "How did you know that?"

Carolyn didn't want to admit that she had overheard Katy's number. But she didn't have to. She had realized that there was another way to figure out Jack's number.

"Because of the lines," she said. "Number 111 only has four. And they're all blue." She looked up at Katy and Halle. "That's you, you, me, and—" She paused and looked at the chart again. Her finger went to number 208. Number 208 only had one blue line, connected to 111.

"Yes," Halle said. "Natalie."

Carolyn felt a pang and realized that she missed Natalie even though she had never really liked her when she'd been alive. Natalie had been too young, too pretty, too bright—and worst of all, too *good*.

She had made Carolyn feel like an evil skank, and Carolyn hadn't liked it.

They were all quiet again for a few moments, and then Katy spoke. "So the chart isn't quite up-to-date," she said.

"Why do you say that?" Halle asked. "You know something I don't?"

"No," Katy said. "I'm just thinking that we ought to add a line and a number for Jack's Moon goddess. For Lilith. Or Lily, as he calls her."

"Jesus, Katy," Carolyn said. This notion seemed a little sick to her.

"I don't mean to suggest that Jack's really sleeping with a supernatural being," Katy said. "But I do think there's a woman who calls herself Lily who's seduced him, and whom he thinks is a goddess. I met her at his Zilker lecture a few months ago."

"I met the same woman in January, when he was arrested," Halle said. "At least I think it was her. She didn't tell me her name."

This was all news to Carolyn. It irritated her.

"So how come neither of you has mentioned this person to me before now?" she asked. She didn't try to hide her annoyance.

Halle shrugged, but Katy looked taken aback. "I just assumed that you knew about her," Katy said. "It's the same woman, I believe, that Artie saw up here a few months ago."

Carolyn felt a hot pressure behind her eyes. "What are you talking about?"

Katy frowned. "Why, I'm talking about the woman Artie said he found with Jack in the cabin. Two months ago, when we all came up here and went looking for Jack in the woods while he was back at the cabin the whole time. Artie told me that he found Jack with Lily in the living room, but that she left before we came back inside."

Carolyn was boiling. In addition to her anger at being left out of the information loop, she was experiencing a hot flash of jealousy. It was all she could do to keep from shouting. "He didn't say anything to me about anything like that," she said. "And I'm wondering when he talked to *you*."

Katy's eyes narrowed. "Some colleagues and I had lunch at Terrazo several weeks ago, and Artie was our waiter. We spoke then."

"Oh," Carolyn said. And as her anger and jealousy began to wane, she saw that Katy looked a little irritated herself. That was not good. She did not want to mess with Katy.

Halle took an audible breath. "Yikes," she said. "Is it my imagination, or is there a sudden tension in here that's thick enough to cut with a chain saw?"

"It's not your imagination," Katy said. Her voice was flat, and her facial expression looked as hard as granite.

Carolyn was scared. "I'm sorry," she said, trying to sound contrite again. "I didn't mean to grill you like that. I'm just upset because Artie didn't tell me about that woman. He should have."

Katy's expression softened. "Yes," she said. "He should have."

Carolyn looked back at the chart and had a thought. "Halle, is there a number here for Artie yet?"

"Uh, no. Not yet."

"Why not? I'm just curious."

"Well, to be honest," Halle said, "I haven't been sure whether he's a red line or a blue line."

"We've been together almost a year," Carolyn said. "I'd guess he's blue, wouldn't you?"

"I hadn't realized it had been that long," Halle said. She rummaged in her briefcase. "Time seems to be compressing on me as I get older. I'll scribble him in immediately."

"Don't," Carolyn said.

Halle looked up from the briefcase. "Why not?"

Carolyn glanced at Katy. "I'll bet Katy can tell you."

Katy looked thoughtful. "Yes. The first thing I did when you told me my number was to see if I could tell which was Stephen's. And I knew which it was because it had only one line, connected to me. If it had been otherwise, I would have been upset."

"I see," Halle said. She sounded uncomfortable.

Carolyn was glad; she thought that Halle *should* feel uncomfortable about now. "So I'd be grateful," she said, "if you just wouldn't put Artie on there at all."

Halle began folding the chart. "I guess this is pretty sick," she said. "All I can say in my defense is that it seemed like a good idea at the time."

"Oh, it's terrific," Carolyn said. "Just so long as you don't include Artie."

"Or draw any more lines that connect to Stephen," Katy said. "And it occurs to me that we ought to agree on one additional thing: None of the men who appear on that chart must ever know about it."

"God, no," Carolyn said. "McIlhenney would probably make a copy and frame it."

"I take it that you guessed his number," Halle said, returning the chart to her briefcase.

"No guessing about it," Carolyn said.

"No," Katy said, "it rather advertises itself." Her voice became quiet. "And I wouldn't want Stephen to start tracing some of those lines."

"Or Artie," Carolyn said. "Sometimes he suffers from what I guess you'd call retroactive jealousy."

"It probably wouldn't do Jack much good if he got a look at this, either," Halle said. "So we're agreed: The men must never know. In unison, now."

Together, they chanted, *"The men must never know."*

They laughed again, but then Halle stopped them with a finger against her lips. "Did you hear that?" she whispered.

Carolyn listened. She heard a faint rustle outside. She looked out through the screen again but saw nothing she could be sure of. The shadows were long now, and it was hard to tell just what among the trees was real and what was a trick of the light.

"What is it?" Katy whispered.

"Male infiltration," Halle murmured. "I don't know who, but definitely male."

Carolyn looked back at her. "What, can you smell them or something?"

"Yes," Halle whispered. Then she spoke in a loud voice. "Absolutely—anything less than nine inches is unsatisfying."

"Are you referring to length or circumference?" Katy asked.

"Diameter," Halle said.

"Like they're gonna fall for that," Carolyn muttered. She turned to look through the screen, yelped, and fell backward. A big man with a chiseled face and a lot of hair poking up from the collar of his T-shirt was peering in at her. She had never seen him before.

"Nine inches in diameter," the man said, his voice a low rumble, "is about the size of one of them really big coffee cans."

"Tommy!" Halle said. She sounded happy. "So what's your point?"

"I'm just wondering if y'all have thought this through," Tommy said. "That's a lot of coffee." He glanced at Katy and then at Carolyn, who was still sprawled on the tent floor looking up at him. "Gonna introduce me?"

"Like they give a shit who you are," Halle said. "But just in case. Katy Corman, Carolyn Jessup, this is Tommy, uh, Morrison. Friend of mine. And apparently a peeper and eavesdropper."

"Hi," Carolyn said. She was still a little shaken.

"Number 243, I presume," Katy said.

This amused Carolyn and made her feel much less shaken. "I was thinking 257," she said.

Tommy looked puzzled. "Beg your pardon?"

"Never mind," Halle said. She left the tent then, taking her briefcase with her, and walked around to join Tommy.

"Whatcha got there?" Tommy asked.

"Never mind," Halle said again, taking his arm and pulling him toward the cabin.

Carolyn snickered.

"Oh, shut up," Halle called back. "Supper's in thirty minutes, or as soon as Tommy and I get back from the Mexican joint in Kerrville. Enchiladas, tamales, rice, and plenty of beans and cheese. Be sure to sleep with someone who already loves you."

Carolyn watched Halle and Tommy until they blended with the trees and disappeared. A few moments later, she heard Halle's Plymouth rattle down the driveway.

She looked at Katy. The light in the tent was growing dim. "I guess we'd better go see if the men and the kids made it back alive."

Katy nodded, but made no move to get up from the rolled-up sleeping bag. She looked as if she were about to say something, but was afraid to. She didn't look at all like the Katy that Carolyn was used to seeing.

"Is there . . . something on your mind?" Carolyn asked.

"There's always something on my mind," Katy said. "Right now I suppose I just want to tell you that I already knew about Halle's chart. I'd never seen it before, but she told me about it a long time ago."

Carolyn was hurt. It was as if all of the others were closer to each other than they were to her. Jack had called the others first when he'd been arrested; Halle had told Katy about her stupid chart. "Why did you want to tell me that?"

"Because I felt false," Katy said. "When she pulled out the chart, I pretended to be surprised even though I wasn't. But I don't want to be false to you. You're my friend."

"Yes," Carolyn said. She thought of what Halle had told her about Stephen and wondered which would be worse: to betray Halle's confidence, or to keep that information from Katy. "Yes, I am."

Now Katy stood. "And I'm glad of that," she said, "because I'd be terrified if you were my enemy. Are you ready to head back?"

Carolyn said "Sure," and they left the tent together. But they said nothing on the walk back through the woods to the cabin. Carolyn was trying to get her head around the idea that Katy found her as formidable as she found Katy. And it was strange that Katy was worried about being false to her. They'd known each other for years. Why was Katy having a concern like that now?

It made Carolyn nervous.

❖

Later, after the Mexican food feast, Artie behaved like an idiot in the west wing's living room in front of everybody. He stuck the corn husks from the tamales onto his fingers and tongue and chased Cleo and Tony around the room while snorting and drooling. The other adults pretended to be amused, but Carolyn was mortified. She walked out of the cabin and down the driveway to cool off.

The sun had gone down, but the Moon had not yet risen. Artie had wondered aloud at dinner why Jack hadn't gotten naked yet, and Jack had explained that the Moon wouldn't rise tonight until 9:08. As Carolyn tramped down the hill and out of sight of the cabin, she checked her watch. The dim light in the watch face illuminated the numerals 9:06. Terrific. She would probably run into Jack when he came outside. The last time she had seen him naked had been, what? Seventeen years ago, give or take a few months. He had looked great, she remembered. He probably hadn't looked quite as great in reality as he did in her memory, but even so, he had no doubt looked pretty good. And she didn't want to know if that was no longer true.

It was strange. She had seen him bare-chested and bare-legged any number of times since then. But there was something about that last bit of clothing that was important. Removing it changed the shape of the whole body. That had been true for every man she'd ever been with.

"It's true for women, too," a female voice said behind her. "At least that's what men tell me."

Carolyn didn't recognize the voice. She stopped and turned. No one was there.

This pissed her off. She hadn't realized that she'd been thinking out loud, and now someone was messing with her mind. That was one thing she didn't appreciate.

"Lily, I presume?" she asked sarcastically.

"Over here," the voice said.

Carolyn turned eastward and saw a woman silhouetted against the trees. The Moon shone through the branches behind her. The woman seemed to be wearing a cloak or cape, but Carolyn couldn't be sure. All she could see was the woman's outline and a gleam of moonlight from long dark hair.

Carolyn was not intimidated. She was too angry for that. "If you're the person who's been fucking up my friend Jack," she said, "you and I are gonna have problems."

"I'm not fucking him *up,*" the woman said. Her voice was rich and sensual, and Carolyn hated her for it. "I'm giving him what he needs."

"Implying what?" Carolyn said, taking a step toward the woman. "That the rest of us have failed at that?"

"It's not your fault."

"Oh, well, thank you very goddamn much."

"You're welcome," the woman said. "And I'd like to chat with you more, but I hear Jack looking for me now. He'll think I've forgotten him. You and I can talk another time."

The woman took a step to one side, and Carolyn blinked as the moonlight caught her in the eyes. And then the silhouetted woman was gone.

Carolyn's hands curled into fists. Something had just happened that she didn't understand and didn't like. It was something over which she had no control but thought that she should. She was furious.

"Bitch!" she yelled. The word echoed among the trees.

Carolyn stood there watching the Moon and despising it until she heard Artie call her name. She headed back to the cabin then, and she and Artie had a big fight. Who did he think he was, yelling for her like she was his dog or something?

She felt better afterward, though, so she let Artie make love to her. It was wonderful. It always was, even when he gave her hiccups. She was glad she'd kept his number off the chart.

PART VI

STRAWBERRY

MOON

Friday, June 4, 1993

◆

❖

11

She Tried to Scrub
Away His Scent

She tried to scrub away his scent, but it was no use. Artie smelled of salt and sun and leather and she didn't know what all else. Maybe vanilla. He smelled like no other man she had been with. Not that she had many data points for reference. There was the boy at Methodist Youth summer camp when she was sixteen, then nothing until the two sequential boyfriends her sophomore year in college, then David McIlhenney, then Jack, and then Stephen. But she was certain that even if she'd been with a hundred or more, none of them would have been anything like Artie.

A knock at the bathroom door made her drop the showerhead. It clattered against the tub and then dangled, spraying wildly. Katy stared at it and at the hot spray that swept back and forth across her thighs. She had no idea what to do about it.

"Are you okay?" Artie called. "Can I come in?"

Katy didn't know. Could he come in? She looked down at her breasts, which suddenly seemed inadequate, and then at her belly, which seemed to be a grotesque protrusion, and then at her legs, which seemed fat and stubby. No, she didn't think that Artie could come in. She had just spent two hours naked with him, but she didn't want him to see her in the shower. She had washed off her makeup, and her hair was wet. She would look terrible. He would take one look at her short, fat, grub-white body and flattened hair and ask himself what on earth he had been thinking.

The shower door slid open, and Katy yelped. She grabbed the showerhead hose to keep from falling, and then she saw Artie. He was standing just outside the tub enclosure, framed by the open shower door. He was nude. He had put his clothes on after they had finished on the couch, but now he was naked again. She had fled into her bathroom and shut the door and tried to wash him away, and here he was naked again.

He was beautiful.

She had never touched anyone this beautiful before.

"I thought you were just going to the bathroom," he said. "But then I heard the shower."

"That's because I turned it on," Katy said. She realized then that she was gripping the flexible metal shower hose so hard that it was cutting diagonal lines into her palms. She let go of it, then pulled up the showerhead and replaced it in its bracket. Its spray caught Artie in the face.

Artie grinned. "Hey, I'm already wet now," he said, "so can I join you?"

"No," Katy said. She slid the door shut, but it slammed and bounced back, the noise echoing from the tile. So she shut it again and held it there. "No, no, no." She was astonished at herself. She was intelligent and articulate, but she couldn't think of any other word to say. "No," she said again. She felt as if she were two years old, determined that her will would be contrary to the will of the rest of the world, and that her will and her will alone would prevail. "No, no, no, no, no."

"Are you sure?" Artie asked.

Katy remembered then what she had forgotten for a few hours: Artie wasn't particularly bright. And she only liked bright men. Men like Stephen. But she could still think of only one word to say.

"No," she said, and let go of the door.

She didn't think he would hear her over the roar of the water. But the door slid open again, and he stepped inside.

◆

"*I hate teaching* summer session," Stephen said. "The classes are too long, the rooms are hot, and none of the students are paying attention to anything except each other. I mean, just try teaching *Walden* to a bunch of twenty-year-olds in June. They could give a shit about Thoreau's bean patch, you know? All they're thinking about is how much longer they have to listen to me yammer before they can get back to their air-conditioned apartments and rip each other's clothes off."

Katy almost dropped the pickle relish. Rip each other's clothes off. Did Stephen know? Was he trying to get a reaction out of her? She watched his face as he tossed his briefcase onto the kitchen table, and then she saw that he didn't have a clue. That made her angry. How dare he not know? Didn't he even consider the possibility? Did he find her so unattractive now that it didn't occur to him that someone else might like her just fine?

"Need a hand with that?" he asked.

"What?" Katy asked. "A hand with what? It's just potato salad. I think I can make potato salad on my own, thank you very much. I've made potato salad any number of times in the past, and I expect that I'll continue to be able to make potato salad well into my twilight years."

Stephen looked as if she had just thrown a glassful of cold water into his face. "Well, okay," he said. "I just thought you might like me to open that jar."

Katy looked down at her hands and saw that she was trying to twist the lid from the jar of pickle relish without success. The jar was cold and slick, and her hands were trembling. Just a little. Not enough so that Stephen would notice. They had been trembling for the past twenty-five minutes, ever since Artie had given her one last terrific orgasm.

"Well, actually," she said, "yes, I do. Come to think of it. Make yourself useful." She held out the jar.

Stephen took the jar with one hand and untucked his shirt with the other. He used his shirttail to get a grip on the lid, which came off with a pop. Relish spilled out onto his shirt and the floor.

"Oops," he said.

Katy was furious. Even as she felt the rage well up, she knew that it was overblown and ridiculous. But she couldn't stop it.

"You did that on purpose," she said.

Stephen's face paled. "Oh-oh," he said.

Katy glared. "What do you mean, oh-oh?"

Stephen set the jar on the counter and opened the pantry door. "I mean," he said, pulling a wad of paper towels from the roll attached to the door, "that you only sound like you sounded just now when you're really pissed."

"That's because I am."

"I can see that." Stephen got down on his knees and began wiping up the mess from the tile. "But it's only a little pickle relish."

She knew he was right, and the fact that he was right only made her angrier.

"It's not a little pickle relish," she said. "It's a lot of pickle relish. And I think you spilled it on purpose to sabotage my potato salad."

Stephen looked up at her. "Excuse me?"

"You heard me. We're supposed to take potato salad to the cabin tonight, and that was my only jar of relish."

"I doubt that anyone will notice if you only use half a jar."

"Half a jar isn't enough. I always use a whole jar."

"I really don't think—"

"I *always* use a whole jar. Twelve ounces. So did my mother. Probably her mother did, too. And now I'm going to be the first in three generations to make substandard potato salad, thanks to you. But will you get the blame? No, I will. Because I made it. Because I always make it. Because the only thing you've ever cooked outside of the microwave is blackened marshmallow. You'll probably do it again tonight and give us all cancer."

Katy hated herself. She sounded like a moron, and she wasn't used to it. It was awful. Other people were supposed to sound like morons. Not her.

Stephen stood up, a dripping green mass in his right hand. "Tell you what," he said. "I'll run down to H.E.B. and get a fresh jar."

Katy stared at the mess in Stephen's hand. "You shouldn't be using paper towels for that. It's wasteful. You should use a dishrag."

"It's a little late now," Stephen said, stuffing the clumped towels into the garbage can under the sink. "But I'll keep it in mind the next time I deliberately ruin your third-generation potato salad."

Now Katy didn't know whether she hated herself or her husband more. "Was that supposed to be funny?" she asked.

"I'm not laughing, am I?" Stephen said, heading toward the living room. "I'll be back in fifteen minutes with your goddamn pickle relish."

"Dill," Katy shouted after him. "Not sweet. In a twelve-ounce jar. Are you listening?"

The front door slammed, and the house shuddered.

Katy stared down at the bowl of cold boiled potatoes on the counter. They had been at a full boil when Artie had come over. Then as she and Artie had kissed in the living room, she had heard the hiss of the overflow hitting the electric burner. She had pulled away and run out to turn off the burner, and Artie had followed her. Where Stephen had knelt to mop up the pickle relish, she had knelt before Artie just a few hours earlier.

She hadn't thought Artie would really come over. She'd taken the afternoon off work to do some shopping and get ready for this month's trip to Halle's cabin, but then had decided to skip the shopping and just come home for a nap. And there had been a message from Artie on the answering machine, asking if the trip to the cabin was this weekend or next.

It was a stupid question. The trips to the cabin would always be at the full Moon until Jack lost his habit of stripping naked in its light. Artie knew that. And if he didn't, Carolyn would tell him so. So why had he called Katy?

She had her suspicions.

So when she'd called him back, she had flirted with him. She didn't think she had done a good job of it, because flirting wasn't one of her skills. But she doubted that Artie was enough of a flirting connoisseur, or enough of an anything connoisseur, to know the difference. And it had been fun.

"How come you're home in the middle of the day?" he'd asked.

"I'm entertaining my numerous lovers," she'd answered.

"Cool," Artie had said. "I'll be right over."

Katy had laughed. She had thought he was joking.

She had even thought *she* was joking.

But then he'd shown up at the door, motorcycle helmet in hand

and a V of sweat darkening his T-shirt, and before long it became clear that neither of them had been joking at all, not even a little bit.

Katy thought now that she must have imagined the whole thing. It had seemed real enough at the time, and perfectly right and natural, but now she was convinced that it had all been nothing more than a fevered daydream. She must have fallen asleep on the couch with the thermostat still set up at 86 degrees, the way Stephen set it every day when he left to teach summer session.

She shouldn't have gotten after him for spilling the relish. She knew that it hadn't been deliberate. What she and Artie had done, though, *had* been deliberate. And she wasn't sorry for it. She was horrified, mystified, confused, angry, surprised, frightened, and a little sore, but she wasn't sorry.

Artie had been wonderful.

Imagine that.

But it couldn't happen again. Yes, it had been wonderful, and no, she wasn't sorry, but it couldn't, shouldn't, wouldn't happen again. There was Stephen, and there was Carolyn, and there were all sorts of other reasons too—such as that she would leave someone like Stephen for someone like Artie on the same day that Jack really and truly went to live on the Moon. It just wasn't going to happen.

But did Artie know that? She should have told him before he left. She didn't know whether he expected anything more than what had already happened, but to be on the safe side, she should have told him before he left. He definitely had to be told before they saw each other at the cabin tonight.

Katy picked up the kitchen phone and punched the speed dial for Carolyn's house. It was number five, after her office, Stephen's office, Halle, and Jack. She didn't use it much. There were a lot of people she called a lot more than Carolyn. She and Carolyn really weren't very close anymore. So maybe she hadn't really betrayed her. If you weren't close with someone, betrayal didn't enter into the equation, did it?

"Hello?" It was Carolyn's voice.

Katy hung up and looked at the microwave oven clock. It was four-thirty. What was Carolyn doing home so early? She had thought that only Artie would be there.

Then she realized that Carolyn would be wanting some extra time to get ready for the trip to the cabin. Maybe she would even make love to Artie before they left.

Katy hoped that she had worn Artie out that afternoon. She hoped that Carolyn would try to make love to him, and that he would have no interest whatsoever.

But Carolyn was beautiful, and Artie was twenty-three.

The clock on the microwave changed its display to 4:31, and Katy sat down on the floor. She was horrible. She had betrayed her husband, her friend, and—since she had always maintained that she liked only intelligent men—herself. And given half a chance, she would do it again. She loved Stephen, but being with Artie had done something to her. She felt it riding low in her belly, heavy and warm.

In one afternoon, she had gone from smart to stupid. Stephen was the most important thing in her life. They had been having some problems this year, but so what? Every marriage had problems.

But the one that had been bothering her most was that Stephen no longer seemed to find her desirable. He claimed that he was just having some temporary problems, but he wouldn't go to his doctor to find out if there was something physically wrong. She knew there wasn't, anyway, because sometimes he became aroused in his sleep. And often he started making love to her at those moments, but then woke up and lost the erection.

So maybe he really didn't want her anymore. Maybe she was already too gray and tubby for him.

But she had found out today that she wasn't too gray and tubby for everyone. She wasn't too gray and tubby for Artie. Young, golden, energetic Artie.

She wiped her eyes with her fingers and wiped her fingers on her jeans. Then she put her left hand on the floor and felt something cold. She lifted her hand and saw that a bit of pickle relish was stuck to her palm. It was dirty. A wisp of dark fuzz clung to the tiny square of pickle skin. The kitchen hadn't been mopped in three or four months.

Katy stood, shook the green bit into the bowl with the cold potatoes, added the remaining half jar of relish, and proceeded to stir in mustard, mayonnaise, chopped celery, and spices. No one would know that she'd added floor grunge as a special ingredient. It made her feel evil. And feeling evil, for a change, felt pretty good.

The phone rang, and she resented it. She was trying to make

potato salad. Stephen and the phone and maybe even the whole world were conspiring to keep her from doing this job right. She tried to answer the phone with one hand and keep stirring with the other, but it was no use. The bowl wanted to spin away across the counter.

"Yes, hello, what is it?" She normally made it a point to sound cool and polite when answering the phone no matter what her mood really was, but right now she didn't care. She was beyond even her own rules today. Today was Fuck a Greek God and Make Dirty Potato Salad Day, and she was allowed to do whatever she wanted.

"Katy, I'm glad I caught you." The voice in the receiver was a woman's, but one that Katy didn't recognize.

She knew that its owner had to be beautiful, though—maybe even as beautiful as Carolyn—and therefore disliked her instantly.

"Why, so am I," Katy said. "It's been far too long since we've talked, but I'm afraid that I'm rather busy right now. So if you could call back later this evening, say about eight o'clock, I'd appreciate it."

At eight o'clock, Katy would be driving her Toyota up the driveway at Halle's cabin, and the telephone at home would ring and ring. She would be sure to shut off the answering machine before leaving.

"Oh, I only need a minute of your time," the voice said. "This is Jack's friend Lily. We met at the Zilker Clubhouse when Tony fell down the hill, remember?"

Katy thought for a moment then that it was Halle playing a joke. But the voice was nothing like Halle's.

"Yes, I remember," Katy said, using her polite telephone voice now. "What can I do for you?"

"Actually," Lily said, "I'm calling because I'm wondering whether I can do something for *you.*"

"I beg your pardon?"

An electric hum blurred Lily's next words, and Katy couldn't make them out. From the hum emerged the sound of a man speaking in Arabic. Then the hum faded away, and Lily's voice was back.

"—depending upon whom you desire," Lily said.

Katy said nothing. She had heard only the last five words of whatever this Lily person had said to her. But she didn't like any of the possible meanings those five words might have.

It occurred to her that she didn't really know Artie at all. She didn't know whether he could be trusted. Maybe he was already telling his friends that he had done her. Maybe Lily was one of those friends.

"I'm afraid that I don't understand," Katy said. She tried to sound aloof.

"Oh, dear," Lily said. "Were we cut off? I apologize. I don't understand these satellites very well. But this is the only way I could talk with you before moonrise."

Katy was confused. "Why are you talking with me at all?"

"Because you're a friend of Jack's," Lily said, "and I know he'll be worried about you."

Katy began to experience a growing paranoia, cold and clutching. "Why would Jack worry about me?"

Lily sighed. "You don't want me to say it. Not that it's necessarily a bad thing, you understand. Good or bad, though, I feel responsible. My presence with Jack each of these past several months has been bound to have an influence on the rest of you. Besides, I confess that out of my own selfish curiosity I've looked in on all of you at one time or another. So if you'd like any help, I'd be more than happy to oblige. I'll be spending most of my time tonight with Jack—we only have one night a month together, after all—but I'm sure he'd spare me for a few minutes."

Katy's hands shook. "Listen, I don't know who you are or why you've called me. I don't even think you're the woman I met at Zilker. But whoever you are, if you bother me again, I'll call the police."

"I live a little out of their jurisdiction, Katy."

Katy slammed the receiver into its cradle, then stood there breathing hard, waiting for it to ring again. It didn't.

She heard the front door open and close then, and a moment later Stephen came into the kitchen with a jar held high.

"Ta-da," he said. "Pickle relish. Dill, not sweet. Twelve ounces. Go wild."

Katy took the jar from him and set it on the counter. Then she put her arms around Stephen's waist and squeezed hard.

Stephen grunted. "Ungh, what's this for?"

"Because I'm sorry."

He put his hand on the back of her neck. "It was just a dumb argument."

She pressed her face into his chest until her nose hurt. She wasn't crying, and she didn't feel like crying, but she still didn't want him to see her eyes just yet. In a half minute she would break the embrace and finish the potato salad. She would use all of the jar that Stephen had bought, to mask any potential taste of gray fuzz. And then she and Stephen would throw some clothes into a bag and drive out to the Hill Country for this month's full Moon. And things would happen. Things always seemed to happen.

But for right now, for just this moment, she was home in her kitchen with her husband. For now she wasn't thinking of anything or anyone else.

"I know," she said. "But I'm still sorry."

She could smell his skin through his shirt. He smelled of pickle relish.

"I think I'll make some bologna sandwiches," Stephen said.

Katy hated bologna. She wrinkled her nose, but kept her face against Stephen's chest.

"Whatever you like," she said.

PART VII

BUCK MOON

Saturday, July 3, 1993

◆

12

◆

Blowing Stuff Up Would Be
a Positive Step

Blowing stuff up would be a positive step, Artie thought as he stepped out of the cabin. He had stashed a few hundred dollars' worth of firecrackers, bottle rockets, Roman candles, and other fireworks in the trunk of Carolyn's Honda when she wasn't looking, and now he was waiting for his opportunity. He had opened a package of firecrackers and set off a few in the restaurant parking lot yesterday, and his appetite was whetted.

Carolyn, however, thought that fireworks were dangerous and a waste of money. She had told him so more times than he could count over the past few weeks. She would no doubt be pissed as hell that he had brought an arsenal to Halle's cabin, but screw it. She had been a ball-busting bitch lately, and he was tired of trying to accommodate her and always falling short.

Besides, during last month's full Moon weekend, he had promised Cleo and Tony that he would bring explosives for the Fourth. Neither of the kids had ever set off a firecracker—much less set off a firecracker inside a pop can, Artie's personal favorite—and it was high time that they scratched that itch.

Artie paused at the rear of the Honda and looked back at the cabin. Cleo and Tony were watching him through the screen door. None of the other adults seemed to be paying attention, so Artie waved to the kids to come on out.

"Yay!" Tony yelled, pushing the door open so hard that it slammed against the cabin wall.

Artie cringed and put a finger to his lips. Cleo grabbed Tony and clamped a hand over his mouth, then propelled him outside and across the gravel to Artie. The other adults remained inside the cabin, oblivious. They all seemed to be caught up in doing the supper dishes or getting ready to play cards. Good. Artie opened the Honda's trunk and pulled away the blanket covering the fireworks.

Cleo gasped and took her hand away from Tony's mouth. Then Tony gasped too. Artie had crammed the fireworks into two shallow cardboard boxes, and the jumble of red-papered firecrackers and multicolored mortar tubes was impressive.

Artie grinned. This was going to be great. Watching stuff explode would take his mind off things. It would help him forget what a pain Carolyn was being, and how difficult it was to find time to be with Katy. Katy worked every weekday doing whatever genius-type engineering stuff she did, and Artie worked most evenings at the restaurant. That only left weekends, and on weekends Carolyn and Stephen were always around. Artie and Katy had managed to be together only four times in the month since they'd started. It wasn't enough.

And that was weird. Artie hadn't thought he'd want to have a long, drawn-out affair with Katy. In the first place, he had a pretty good deal going with Carolyn, despite her bitchiness. And in the second place, he had thought that his attraction to Katy was strictly an I'd-sure-like-to-fuck-her feeling. He'd had that feeling plenty in the past, and had acted on it plenty. Once or twice was usually enough to take care of it, and he had thought that would be the case with Katy. It wasn't like she was a babe. Not a babe like Carolyn, anyway.

But after being with Katy once, Artie had found that his desire for her hadn't waned. It had increased. And that had happened again the next time, and the next, and the next. He couldn't figure it out. But there it was, so he had to act on it. And it was frustrating to have to wait so long each time—just as it was frustrating to be here at the cabin in Katy's presence and not even be able to touch her hand. But Katy had told him that if he ever did anything like that where anyone else might see, he would never touch her again. And she would never forgive him.

That mattered to him. And that was weird, too.

He took one of the boxes of fireworks out of the trunk and handed it to Tony, who held it in his arms as if it were the most precious thing in the universe. Then Artie took the other box under one arm, closed the trunk, and started down the driveway with the kids close behind him.

Yeah. Blowing stuff up was a great idea. The best movies he had ever seen had a lot of stuff blowing up in them. And he wasn't much of a reader, but last week he'd found a novel in the gutter by the restaurant's Dumpster that had turned out to be something he could relate to. It had skateboarding in it, and at the end, the guy had blown up everything. Artie had thought it was pretty cool.

As he thought of the guy in the novel blowing up everything, he remembered that he needed some empty cans. "Cleo, you want to blow stuff up?" he asked.

Cleo gave him a sardonic look. "Well, duh," she said.

"Okay, then run back and get us some soda cans," Artie said. "And a bottle to launch the bottle rockets."

Cleo's eyes narrowed. "Why do I have to do it?"

"Because you're the only one not carrying anything."

Cleo looked suspicious. "Are you going to light stuff before I get back?"

Artie shook his head. "It's not dark enough yet."

"Just don't start without me," Cleo said, turning back toward the cabin.

"We'll be down the hill a little way," Artie said. When Cleo was gone, he winked at Tony. "We can maybe light some firecrackers if she's not back real quick," he whispered. "It doesn't have to be dark for firecrackers."

"I want to light a *lot* of firecrackers," Tony said.

"You and me both, man."

They stopped at a curve in the driveway, out of sight of both the cabin and the highway, and set their boxes down on the gravel. Then Artie removed the rubber band from a bundle of punks.

"What's that?" Tony asked.

"You are one deprived kid," Artie said, fishing a Bic lighter from his jeans. He lit two of the punks and handed one to Tony. "See how it stays lit, like charcoal? If it starts to go out, blow on it. Like this." He blew on the tip of his punk, and it glowed bright orange.

Tony tried it but somehow managed to get smoke up his nose. He coughed and dropped his punk, and it landed in one of the fireworks boxes.

"Shit!" Artie said, dropping his own punk. He squatted and rooted Tony's punk out of the box, then looked at the packages to see if any fuses had been lit. None had. Artie was relieved. He wanted to blow stuff up, but on his own terms.

"Artie," Tony said, still coughing, "look."

Artie looked. The punk that *he* had dropped had fallen into the other box. Just as he reached for it, the central fuse on the pack of firecrackers he'd opened yesterday began sizzling.

"Shit!" Artie yelled. He tried to grab the firecrackers and throw them up the driveway, but they started going off as he touched them. He yelped, jumped back, and then stared as everything in the box began exploding, whistling, and spraying showers of sparks.

After a few seconds of staring at the erupting chaos, Artie remembered that he ought to look after Tony. But then he discovered that Tony had already run a safe distance back up the driveway. As a pair of bottle rockets bounced off Artie's shoulder, he decided that maybe he ought to retreat a few yards too.

Cleo came running down the driveway with a Perrier bottle and two Dr Pepper cans as Artie joined Tony. She stopped beside them, dropped the bottle and cans, and glared at Artie.

"You promised you'd wait, you fucker," she said.

Artie was taken aback. This was the first time that he had been called a fucker by an eight-year-old. He guessed that Cleo was going to grow up to be a lot like Carolyn. Halle was probably encouraging it.

"I'm sorry," Artie said. "It was an accident."

"You're an accident," Cleo said.

Artie was about to say "No, *you* are," because he was pretty sure it was the truth—but then a fireworks helicopter came buzzing straight at him and the kids. They all yelled and dropped to the gravel. Artie looked up in time to see the helicopter veer into the woods and explode among the trees.

"Hey, watch it!" a woman's voice yelled from the vicinity of the helicopter explosion.

Artie was surprised that he was able to hear the voice over the whistling, rat-a-tat-tatting, and ka-powing of the fireworks. It was as if it were being transmitted directly to his brain.

And with that thought, he knew who it was.

"Wait here," he said to Tony. He ignored Cleo because he was pissed at her. "I'm gonna go check something out."

Tony didn't seem to have heard him. The boy was lying on his belly with his chin propped in his hands, staring at the explosions and fountain sprays. His eyes reflected green and gold light.

"Are you running away so you don't get in trouble?" Cleo asked, sneering.

Artie understood now why he felt no attraction toward Halle even though she was a semi-babe. Anybody who got Halle would get her kids as well—and the girl, at least, was a pain in the ass.

"No, I'm not running away," Artie said, sneering back. He stood up and headed into the woods.

"Chickenshit!" Cleo yelled after him.

Artie wished that Cleo were ten years older and male so that he could pop her in the mouth. As it was, he had to try to pretend that he wasn't bothered. He had something else to deal with now, anyway. He had heard the voice of Lily, and he wanted to get a look at her again to see whether she really did have wings. It had been bugging him for four months.

He stumbled through brush and over rocks and roots, and within twenty steps the woods seemed to close up behind him. He could still hear the fireworks going off, but it was as if someone had pushed a MUTE button on a remote control. He paused and looked back, but all he could see of the sparks and flashes were diffuse reflections from leaves and tree trunks.

Artie didn't like it. He remembered now that he hadn't liked being in the woods on his previous trips here, either. The shadows and the noises inside them gave him the creeps. So the hell with Lily. He was going back to the driveway where things were exploding and he knew what was what.

"Does this belong to you?" a voice asked.

Artie froze. The voice was Lily's again, but now he couldn't tell where it was coming from. It seemed to be everywhere, all around him. He tried not to breathe.

Something dropped past his face and landed on the mulch at his feet.

"I asked if that belongs to you," Lily said.

Artie still couldn't tell where her voice was coming from. It scared him, and that made him angry. So he forced himself to stoop and pick up what had fallen at his feet. He couldn't see it well, but he could feel the plastic rotor and charred cardboard of the fireworks helicopter. It was still warm.

"Yeah," he said. "It's mine."

"Got away from you, didn't it?"

"Guess so." Artie looked to the right and left and behind him. He couldn't see anything but trees illuminated by fireworks flashes. "Look, you're freaking me out. Just show yourself, okay?"

Lily laughed. "I'm not hiding, Artie. Why do you suppose the helicopter dropped right in front of you? I swear, of all of Jack's friends, you have the least grasp of the obvious. But I find that rather sweet. People who cling to the obvious tend to be dull. I'm up here."

Artie looked up. Lily, bathed in moonlight, was sitting on a tree branch right over his head. Her clawed feet almost brushed his hair. She was naked, and she was looking down at him and smiling. He couldn't see any wings, though. Maybe he had imagined them before.

Then he noticed her feet.

"You don't have regular toes," he said.

Lily grinned. "They're regular for me." Her talons waggled.

Artie's stomach lurched. He had been right to dislike the woods. He was getting out of them right away.

But Lily dropped in front of him before he could take a step. "Wait a second," she said. Her wings spread out for a moment, then folded back down again. Artie hadn't imagined them after all. "I think we should talk."

She sounded perturbed. Artie didn't want that. There was no telling what she might do. She was some kind of mutant monster chick. If he pissed *her* off, it would be a lot worse than when he pissed off Carolyn. Carolyn just bitched at him. Lily, on the other hand, might claw his eyes out of their sockets and pop them into her mouth.

"I'm sorry about the fireworks," he blurted. "I'll put them out."

Lily shook her head, and her glossy black hair flowed over her shoulders and down to cover her breasts. "That's not what I want to talk to you about. It's bad enough, of course, because everything's dry and you're likely to start a fire. But what I'm wondering about is the fire you've already started, and whether you can handle it. If you can't, I'll try to help. I feel partly responsible."

In an instant, Artie forgot his fear and found himself staring at the hair that had fallen over Lily's breasts. He wanted to feel its texture, to brush it aside.

"Are you paying attention?" Lily asked. "I'm talking about you and Katy. You've been sleeping with her for a month now, and I'm wondering whether you've considered the possible consequences. Not that it isn't wonderful, I know, but you ought to take the personalities of your respective mates into account. What will happen if you're discovered?"

Artie managed to look up from her breasts. "How do you know about me and Katy?"

Lily rolled her eyes. "Artie, check it out." Her wings spread again and flapped twice, and then she was hovering with her talons at the level of Artie's nose. "I'm a *goddess*. I know things that you wingless types never find out without hiding in closets or hiring private detectives. And what drew you to Katy, and her to you, is my particular province. Understand?"

Artie blinked. Lily's talons looked awfully sharp. He wondered if she was more woman or more owl, and whether she ate mice and spit up neat little bundles of bone and fur afterward.

Or whether mice were too small for her . . .

He decided not to take that chance. "Yes," he said, "I understand."

Lily's wings flapped again, and she returned to the branch over Artie's head. "You're a lying sack of shit," she said, "but you're a pretty one. Go on, then. Maybe I'll talk to Katy instead. I tried to last month, though, and she wouldn't listen."

Artie started back toward the driveway, then hesitated and looked up again. Lily was still there.

"You won't say anything to Steve or Carolyn, will you?" he asked. "I mean, about . . . you know."

Lily looked sad. "No, that's not something I would do. But they'll find out anyway."

Artie felt a sudden knot in his chest. "How do you know?"

Lily sighed. "Because you're clumsy, Artie. Katy is careful because she doesn't want to hurt Stephen. But you're not careful, partly because you *do* want to hurt Carolyn, a little. But mainly because you're clumsy."

Artie was offended. "The fuck I am," he said. "I was a gymnast in high school. And I know that's not what you meant. See, I'm not as stupid as everyone thinks."

"Well, Grace," Lily said, "you have a fire to put out. Good luck." She spread her wings again, rose up through the branches and moonlight, and was gone.

Artie stared after her. He was caught between his fear of Lily and his indignation at what a snooty bitch she had turned out to be. Who was she, goddess or not—he wasn't religious, anyway—to tell him that he wanted to hurt Carolyn? He was ass-over-head crazy about Carolyn. This thing with Katy would resolve itself in time. These things always did.

"Fire, my hairy butt," he said.

"Fire!" Cleo screamed behind him.

Artie spun around and saw Cleo and Tony running through the woods toward him. Behind them was the bright orange glare of burning brush.

"Two whole packs of bottle rockets went off at the same time!" Tony shouted, grabbing Artie's arm.

Artie was surprised. "Really?" he asked. "When?"

"Just now," Cleo said. "Didn't you see them? Didn't you *hear* them?"

He hadn't. While Lily had been talking, he hadn't heard anything except her voice.

"What do we do?" Tony asked, shaking Artie's arm. He sounded frightened.

Artie was frightened too. The brushfire was growing fast.

"Run back to the cabin," he said. It was the only thing he could think of.

But the fire had spread between them and the driveway now, so they had to crash through the woods for a few dozen yards before they could cut over to the gravel. When they did, Artie saw Carolyn and Stephen running down the driveway with fire extinguishers. He was glad to see them.

"Jesus H. Christ on a fucking crutch!" Carolyn yelled as she stopped beside Artie. "What did you do, set them all off at once?"

"It wasn't on purpose," Artie said.

"He was supposed to wait for me," Cleo said.

Stephen stopped long enough to say, "You take the brush, I'll take the fireworks." Then he ran on down the driveway to where the blazing boxes were still whistling, spraying sparks, and erupting in explosions of various magnitudes.

"Where'd you get the fire extinguisher?" Artie asked Carolyn.

"From my car trunk," Carolyn said, heading into the woods toward the brush fire. "Right next to where you hid your toys."

Artie followed her. "How did you know about them?"

"Because you're about as stealthy as a dump truck." They had reached one end of the fire, which was now spread out in a crooked line fifteen yards long. Carolyn began spraying along that line, and the flames began winking out inside white clouds.

"I'm sorry," Artie said.

Someone nudged his shoulder. He looked around and saw that it was Halle.

"Don't be sorry," Halle said. She pushed a shovel into his hands. "Just cover everything with dirt, and maybe I won't have to call the volunteer fire department."

"Where'd the kids go?" Carolyn asked.

"I turned them over to Jack," Halle said. "But if you guys think you have this under control, I'm going to go keep an eye on them. The Moon's up, so Jack's no doubt approaching his usual ultra-weird phase. I mean, he's cute naked, but I don't really want my kids exposed to quite that much cuteness just yet."

Artie scooped up some dirt and mulch and tossed it onto the charred brush that Carolyn had just extinguished. "Don't worry, we can handle it," he said. He was feeling better. The fire hadn't been his fault, really, and it was turning out to be no big deal. He and Carolyn would have it out in no time.

But Carolyn was shaking her head. "I think that shovel might have done more good in the long run," she said to Halle, "if you'd bashed him upside the head with it."

Artie didn't let that bother him. Carolyn was pissed at him, that was all. So what else was new? Maybe she even almost had a reason this time.

"Well, I'll leave that to you," Halle said, and then turned and headed back toward the driveway.

Artie followed along behind Carolyn, smothering the burnt brush just after she sprayed it. "So how much trouble am I in?" he asked.

Carolyn didn't look at him. "I don't know yet," she said. "Let's see if we can put this out, and I'll get back to you."

Artie scooped a few more shovelfuls of dirt and then decided that if he was in deep shit anyway, he probably couldn't say anything that would make it much worse.

"I saw Lily," he said.

Carolyn didn't respond, so Artie thought that maybe she hadn't heard him.

"I saw Lily," he said again, louder. "You know, Jack's girlfriend?"

"I heard you the first time," Carolyn said, shouting over the whoosh of the fire extinguisher. But she still didn't look at him.

"She was naked," Artie said.

"How nice."

"She had wings. Her feet were claws."

Carolyn had reached the end of the crooked line of fire. She squeezed the fire-extinguisher handle, but this time nothing came out. She lowered the extinguisher and pointed at the last patch of flame. "Could you put that out, please?" she asked.

Artie stepped up and smacked the flames with the shovel until they were gone, then covered the spot with dirt.

Now that the fire was out, Artie and Carolyn were in the dark. There was just enough filtered moonlight for Artie to see Carolyn's face.

"I don't hear any fireworks," he said. "I guess Steve put them out."

"I guess so."

Carolyn was making no move to leave the woods. She was just standing there, still not looking at him.

"If you're going to chew my ass out," he said, "go ahead and do it."

Now she looked at him. "You don't decide when I'm going to chew your ass out," she said. "I decide that. And you'll deserve it. Right now, though, I want to ask you about this Lily."

Artie suppressed a grin. Carolyn sounded jealous. "I already told you," he said, leaning on Halle's shovel. "She was naked, and she had wings and claws. I saw her once before, too. But I didn't tell you."

"Why not?"

"Seemed like a bad idea."

"So why tell me now?"

Artie shrugged. "I don't know. I guess I just decided, what the fuck."

"I see," Carolyn said. "Well, then, what the fuck. I saw her two months ago myself. I didn't see any wings, but I did see that she's insane. I think she roams around in these woods waiting to meet Jack when he goes meshugga. Maybe she even puts on a bird costume."

Artie shivered. "We should get out of the woods, then." He started toward the driveway.

"Not yet." Carolyn grasped Artie's arm and stopped him. "You're going to make love to me first."

Artie was confused. "Right here?"

Carolyn's eyes gleamed. "Right here. Right now. Haven't you ever wanted to do it outside?"

She had him there. "Yeah, sure," he said, "but . . . we don't have a blanket or anything. And what if some of the others come looking for us, or the kids—"

"We'll be quiet," Carolyn said. She dropped the fire extinguisher and began unbuttoning her blouse. "We'll be fast. It's dark. They won't find us."

Carolyn, like Lily, had gone insane. This was not like her. This was not something she would do. Artie didn't like it. He didn't like the woods, he didn't like the dark, and he didn't like Carolyn behaving like someone else.

But Artie never turned down sex with Carolyn. Maybe she could behave like someone else, but he had to remain true to himself.

He had just pushed down his jeans when Stephen and Katy appeared in a patch of moonlight behind Carolyn.

"Hey, we've got the fireworks under—whoops," Stephen said. He turned around as he said "whoops" and started back the way he had come.

But Katy didn't. She stood there in the moonlight staring past Carolyn's shoulder and into Artie's eyes.

Artie's eyes stung.

So far, this evening sucked.

13

◆

The Branch Would Leave

Bark Patterns

The branch would leave bark patterns on his butt, but Jack didn't think Lily would mind. The bark was also making him itch a little, but he would put up with it. He was sitting halfway up a live oak just west of Halle's cabin, waiting. He was naked except for his wristwatch, and he kept turning on the blue glow of the display to check the time. It was 9:30 P.M. Moonrise had been more than half an hour ago, and Lily hadn't come to him yet.

Jack was worried. There had been a lunar eclipse last month, and even that had delayed Lily by only a few minutes. He had never thought to ask how long it took to make the trip from the Moon to Texas, but he knew that she was overdue. He wondered if Artie's fireworks debacle had anything to do with her tardiness. Maybe the glare and noise and everyone clustering together afterward had scared her off. Lily seemed to like darkness and quiet, and the intimacy of just herself and Jack. Jack liked that, too.

Below the tree, a rectangle of yellow light from the kitchen window stretched out along the ground to touch the live oak's trunk. The window was open, and Jack could hear someone banging around with a teapot or saucepan. There was no sound of conversation, though. That was odd. His friends usually talked all the time.

Everyone was acting weird this weekend. At first Jack had been glad to see that they'd all seemed to stop worrying so much about him—but then, after the fireworks, he had realized that it wasn't because they thought he was all right. It was because they had problems of their own.

Jack knew what some of them were. For one thing, Stephen was still smitten with Halle. That was obvious, and it wasn't likely that Halle had forgotten about it, either. Jack didn't know if it was obvious to Katy, but it was clear that something was bothering her. Jack hadn't heard her say a word since the fireworks. She hadn't even risen to the bait when Halle's friend Tommy—who had arrived just after the fires had been put out—had said that Clinton had done the right thing last month in withdrawing Lani Guinier as a Justice Department nominee. That was normally the sort of thing that would get Katy going on a verbal tear, but she hadn't even seemed to notice.

Things, to say the least, were uncomfortable. Carolyn was angry with Artie; the kids were in trouble with Halle; Katy was silent and sullen; and Stephen was pining for someone he couldn't have. Tommy seemed to be fine, but why shouldn't he be? He had shown up after the fireworks, so nobody was mad at him. The worst that Tommy had to worry about was Stephen's jealousy, and Jack was pretty sure that Tommy was oblivious to that.

So Tommy, at least, was happy. But Tommy was also temporary. Halle would continue to go through men like a hyperactive kid through SweeTarts until she found one she could live with. And Tommy, though he was nice enough, wasn't that man. He seemed to know it, too, so at least he was emotionally healthy.

Everyone else, though, was a mess. Jack was just beginning to realize the extent to which that was true.

"And they think *I'm* the crazy one," he muttered.

He felt a puff of air on his cheek, turned toward it, and saw Lily settling onto the branch beside him. Her wings folded, and she smiled.

"You *are* the crazy one," she said. "I don't see anyone else sitting out here in the nude."

Jack was exhilarated. Lily hadn't forgotten him.

"Well," he said, "you're naked too, aren't you?"

Lily licked her lips. "I'm supposed to be naked. For me, it's wearing clothes that's abnormal."

"Yet I've seen you wear clothes," Jack pointed out.

"Yes," Lily said. "To get to you."

Jack spread his hands. "Hence my nudity."

"How gallant." Lily looked at his crotch. "How very gallant."

Jack squirmed. "I'm glad you're here. What took you so long?"

Lily didn't stop smiling, but her brow furrowed. "I was contemplating a problem."

"Anything I can help with?" Jack realized the absurdity of that even as he said it, and he laughed at himself. "Like a goddess needs any help from me."

Lily reached out and caressed his cheek where the puff of air from her wings had touched him a few moments before. "You might be surprised," she said.

Jack shuddered. Lily's fingertips were electric.

"God, I've missed you," he said.

Lily's index finger traced a ticklish line around his lips. "I've missed you too," she said. "You think it's any fun waiting around in the cold and gray for four weeks before I can come down and mess up your mind some more?" She leaned close and kissed him, her lips just brushing his. "But it's not only to mess up your mind, Jack. It's also because . . ." She hesitated, looking chagrined. "You've done something to me."

Jack was nonplussed. "Like what?"

Lily closed her eyes. "I don't know. But I don't feel the same anymore."

She sounded unhappy, and Jack was alarmed. "I'm sorry," he said.

"Don't be," Lily said. "Whatever it is, at least it's different." She opened her eyes. "But I think I may have fucked up as a result. You have to understand, Jack, that while I have on occasion fucked people up, I have never myself fucked up. Do you understand the difference?"

Jack chuckled. "Sure. I could write a book."

Lily squeezed his hand. "Good. Because I now seem to have fucked up. You see, ever since I started coming down to be with you, I've been paying visits to your friends. I thought I'd do some nice things for them, as a favor to you . . . but it's all taken off in ways I didn't expect."

Jack nodded. "I can see that. They're acting a few bubbles off true, if you know what I mean."

Lily gave him a puzzled look. "I'm afraid I don't."

"A few bricks shy of a load."

Lily, still looking puzzled, shook her head.

"Not playing with a full deck," Jack said. "You know, failing to fire on all eight cylinders. Hitting the ball with the skinny end of the bat. Two quarts low. Driving on underinflated tires. Not enough yeast in the dough. The stairs don't go all the way up. Running with your shoes on backwards. Eating pudding with a fork."

"Jack," Lily said.

"Drinking a potato. Spitting out a rolled-up window. No lights on in the attic. Playing horseshoes with hand grenades. Hammering the pointy end of the nail. Missing some primary colors from your Crayolas. One burrito short of a combination plate. Dribbling without a basketball—"

"Jack," Lily said, "let's just stick with 'fucked up,' okay?"

Jack took a deep breath. He was dizzy. "Sorry about that," he said. "I get carried away."

Lily took his hand in hers. "That's one of the things I like about you. And it seems to have rubbed off on me a little." She looked down at the cabin. "So the answer to your question 'Anything I can help with?' turns out to be yes. You know more about fucking up than I do."

Jack touched Lily's shoulder and let his fingers trail down to the feathers. "Just tell me what you need," he said.

Lily sighed. "That's part of my problem. I don't know what's needed. You see, Jack, my domain is limited to Desire. I know what people want, and when and how they want it."

"Well then," Jack said, "I think that maybe you know pretty much everything."

Lily spread her wings, rose into the air, and wrapped her legs around Jack's waist. "Do you have your balance?" she asked.

Jack's breath quickened. "I think so."

"All right, then." She settled onto his lap and enfolded him in her wings.

Jack gasped. "I get the feeling," he said, "that we're not talking about your problem anymore."

Lily kissed his nose. "Yes, we are. But I don't want you to think I'm only interested in your mind."

"No chance of that," Jack said.

"The thing is," Lily whispered into his ear, "that you're wrong. I've just now become aware of the fact that knowing what people desire *doesn't* mean that I know everything. What I don't comprehend at all is what happens to you and your kind after you *get* what you desire."

"Huh?" Jack said. He was confused. And it was no wonder. He hardly had any blood left in his brain.

Lily's breath was hot on Jack's neck. "I'm here once a month," she said, "for one night. But what happens the next morning, when I'm gone? And the day after that, and the day after that? What do you feel like, what do you do, all those days and nights when I'm not here?"

"Wait for you," Jack said. "Ache for you. Try to remember the taste of you."

"But surely there's more."

Jack thought about it for a few seconds. "No," he said.

Lily pulled away and hovered before him. "That can't be true."

Jack reached out for her. "Okay. Here's the rest: My life is what most people would call easy. I'm living off my retirement fund, my savings, and some . . . insurance money. So mainly I goof off. I read, I go to movies, I take long walks, I watch late-night TV, and I eat lunch with friends and sometimes with total strangers." He stared into Lily's eyes. "But even when I'm doing all of those things, I'm thinking about *you*. About what you were like the last time. About what we'll do the next time."

"Don't lean forward any more, Jack," Lily said. "You'll fall."

"Then don't fly any farther away, goddamn it!" Jack was angry, and it startled him. He had never been angry with Lily before. He had never thought that he could be. "Don't breathe on my neck and then fly *away* from me!"

Lily's eyes flashed with white light, and in that moment Jack was terrified that he had enraged her. But then she returned to sit on the branch beside him, so close that her hip was touching his. Her left wing lay across his back. The feathers were soft against his skin. Jack wanted Lily so much then that he was pretty sure he could pull the live oak up by its roots if she asked him to.

"Now we're getting somewhere," Lily said. "So part of what you feel while I'm gone isn't longing, but anger. Anger at me for not being here."

Jack started to deny it, but then wondered if that would be a lie. He didn't want to lie to Lily.

"And I realize now," Lily continued, "that part of what brought me to you in the first place must have been that same anger. The flavor of your desire was particularly intense. Dangerous, even, if I were mortal."

Jack wanted her. He didn't want to talk anymore, to think anymore. He just wanted her.

."How could I have been angry with you before I ever knew you?" he said, putting his arm around her waist. Her skin was warm.

"You weren't angry with me," Lily said. "But you were angry with someone you desired."

Jack closed his eyes. He wished Lily would stop talking. He wished they would just make love.

"All right," Lily said. "I'll stop now, because you've given me my first clue: anger. I've always known about jealousy, of course, because desire and jealousy are essentially the same thing. But I see now that there are other things linked to desire as well. That will help me understand you and your friends—and where I've made my mistake. Thank you."

"You're welcome," Jack said, not entirely sincere. He still wanted her, but he was feeling petulant. Lily had jerked him around tonight. She had never done that before, and he didn't like it. And then there was the fact that she was spending time and energy on his friends. He cared about them too, but Lily was supposed to be here to pay attention to *him*.

"Oh, Jack, I'm sorry," Lily said. She sounded as if she meant it. "I hate seeing you unhappy—and that's a new thing for me too. In the past, I haven't given a rat's ass if what I did made anyone unhappy. In fact, that was sort of the point." She sighed again. "You've done something to me that no one else—certainly no mortal—has ever done. I wish I knew what to call it."

She rose into the air and wrapped her legs around his waist again. Her talons raked across the small of his back.

Jack drew in a sharp breath. Lily had scratched deeper than usual, and the wounds burned like fire.

"Damn," Lily said. "I've drawn blood. I just can't seem to keep from fucking up tonight."

Jack looked into her eyes, saw her concern, and smiled.

"But I liked it," he whispered.

Lily's eyes widened. "I should have known that. Why didn't I?"

Jack pulled her close. "I can't answer that. I don't even know my *own* mind, so how can I hope to figure out a goddess?"

"Shit," Lily said.

Jack kissed her neck. She tasted like honeysuckle and coffee.

"Funny," he murmured. "I heard Artie yell the same word when he almost burned down the woods. Speaking of fucking up."

Lily enfolded him in her wings and traced lines down his chest with her fingernails. "I thought you didn't want to talk anymore," she said.

And until the Moon set the next morning, they didn't.

PART VIII

CORN MOON

Monday, August 2, 1993

◆

14

◆

Like a Ballpeen Hammer
to the Temple

Like a ballpeen hammer to the temple, it hit Stephen that Katy was having an affair.

It happened while he was teaching. Professor Lesley was off having her baby, and Stephen had volunteered to babysit her course on seventeenth-century British literature. The material was a few centuries removed from his area of expertise, but it was the end of the second summer session, and Lesley had told him that she'd already covered everything that would be on the final. He could let the students direct their own review session, or he could talk about whatever he wanted.

The class was filled with dullards, so he wound up talking about whatever he wanted. And with eleven minutes left before the end of the period, he was reading "To His Coy Mistress" aloud and stopped dead.

He had just remembered the laundry.

That morning he had switched laundry from the washing machine to the dryer because Katy had forgotten to do it before leaving for work. In fact, the load in the washer seemed to have been left from the evening before, when he'd been on campus giving an exam.

Stephen had discovered that the washer needed to be emptied only because he was out of clean shirts.

But the forgotten laundry wasn't shirts. It had turned out to be sheets and underwear. So Stephen had made the switch, washed his shirts, and then switched the loads again. His shirts had still been damp when he'd grabbed one and dashed out the door. He had just made Lesley's class.

Now, reading "To His Coy Mistress," he realized that the sheets he had found in the dryer had been stuffed away in the linen closet for as long as he could remember. They shouldn't have needed washing. They were never used.

And clinging to one of those sheets when he pulled it from the dryer had been a pair of Katy's panties. The panties were white, lacy, and sheer. There wasn't much to them, and Stephen hadn't seen them in a long time. He had forgotten that his wife even owned underwear like that.

At this moment of realization, a girl in the front row of Lesley's class—Stephen couldn't think of her as a woman; she was too young—coughed and recrossed her legs. She was wearing one of the short denim skirts that seemed to have come back in style. Her thighs were muscled and tanned. Stephen caught a glimpse of purple lace, and it struck him that denim and purple lace looked stupid together. This girl was trying to be erotic but didn't have a clue. She was a child playing at being a grown-up.

Stephen looked out at all the young, alien faces. They were all children playing at being grown-ups.

He looked back down at the poem. He had no idea of where he'd left off, and that fact reminded him of Jack's disastrous "lecture" at the Zilker Clubhouse back in February. Jack had forgotten his place too, and then he had climbed out a window. Maybe Stephen should consider climbing out of a window as well.

He closed the book and glanced at the windows to his left. The day was sunny, and he could see blue sky and treetops. The room was on the eighth floor. He wondered if that was far enough to pulp his skull, or if he would only get a concussion.

"Unless there are any questions," he said, "we'll call it quits."

When he turned to look at the students again, they were gone. He hadn't heard them leave. He stuffed his books and papers into his briefcase, then headed home for lunch.

He never went home for lunch. His usual habit was to buy a sandwich at the Union and eat it in his office while making lecture notes. Today, though, he wanted to go home. He didn't want to be anywhere near children who pretended to be adults. Or near anyone at all, for that matter.

But then he saw Katy's Toyota in their driveway when he turned onto their street. And it occurred to him that she never went home for lunch either.

He drove on past the house, then cruised up one street and down another until he hit MoPac and headed south. He didn't know where he was going. Just south. Maybe south and then west, all the way out to Halle's cabin. Jack would be there sometime today. It was a full Moon tonight, but Jack was the only one who would be at the cabin. Halle had given him the keys and made him promise that he would be all right by himself. Everyone else had too much to do to go with him this month. Stephen, for one, was supposed to be grading exams and reading term papers.

But going to the cabin sounded like more fun.

Except that Stephen would feel obligated to keep an eye on Jack. To take care of him. And Stephen didn't want to take care of anyone right now. He wanted someone to take care of *him*. Either that, or just leave him alone.

The lunch rush on MoPac was a congested mess, and it was stop and go, stop and go. Just north of the 360 interchange, where everything had come to a halt, Stephen found himself screaming. Every other driver on the road was a moron who drove like there was no one else who had to get anywhere. Their fathers were pinheaded geeks and their mothers were bearded, foul-smelling goats.

At that, a woman in the car next to him gave him the finger.

It startled him and shut him up. This was a petite, attractive woman in a business suit who had just flipped him the bird. He gave her a weak smile and mouthed, "I'm sorry," but she simply flipped him off again.

Traffic started moving then, and Stephen edged his way over to the right lane. The enormous Barton Creek Mall squatted just off the interchange, and he had decided that it was his destination. He didn't want to shop, but he didn't want to drive anymore either. And this was a mall big enough to get lost in. Getting lost sounded like as good a plan as he was going to come up with.

He parked his Escort—a bad-handling piece of shit; Katy had gotten the good car—and walked across the hot asphalt to the mall entrance. The asphalt felt soft enough to lie down on. That appealed to him. He would like to lie down on something hot, black, and oily, and then go home and soil those sheets that Katy had washed for no good reason.

No good reason unless she was putting them on the fold-out couch, or even on their own bed, and screwing someone passionately enough to leave wet spots the size of Idaho.

The mall was considerably cooler than the parking lot. Downright cold, in fact. Stephen hadn't been aware that he'd been sweating so much until the mall's nuclear-powered air-conditioning hit his shirt and plastered it to his skin like a wet washcloth on a fevered forehead. Like his mother had done for him when he was sick—those few times that she hadn't been sick herself, anyway.

Great, he thought. He suspected his wife of doing it with someone else, and that had led him directly to thoughts of his dead mother. Just swell.

He bought a chocolate chip cookie for the price of an entire meal, then walked around the perimeter of the mall's lower level. When he had done that twice, he took an escalator to the upper level and did it there too. He checked his watch then and saw that he had twenty-five minutes before he would be late for his penultimate Thoreau/Emerson summer-session class.

Screw it.

He found himself watching girls a lot. The mall was full of them. It was bleeding girls from the walls. Not women: girls. Not a one over nineteen. And they all looked like the girl in the front row of Lesley's BritLit class. They were toying with sensuality, goofing around at adulthood. Not having any notion of the consequences, because for them, there weren't any. They were invincible.

Stephen found them all so unappealing as to border on the repulsive. He craved the sight of someone who looked like a woman. Someone with hips and breasts and a few lines around her eyes to prove that she knew a thing or two.

Someone who looked like Halle.

And there it was. He was freaked because he thought Katy was having an affair, but what had him downright despondent was that he *wasn't* having an affair with Halle.

"What an idiot," he said.

Two girls walking the other way gave him dirty looks, and one of them flipped him the bird.

Stephen was beginning to notice a trend.

He looked at his watch again. He had fifteen minutes before it became obvious to the world that he had abrogated all responsibility. And it was at least twenty minutes from the mall to campus, then another ten before he could get to his classroom. It was hopeless.

So he turned and ran like a madman to the nearest exit, passing the two girls again and flipping them the double bird as he did so. Flipping the double bird wasn't something that he was wont to do— but he was in a hurry, and they had flipped him off first. He ran to his rotten little Ford, jumped inside, burned his hands on the steering wheel, and started the engine. The car rattled to life like the crapmobile that it was, and Stephen drove it as fast as it would go back up MoPac.

He burst into his classroom nine minutes late, with no books or lecture materials, his shirt drenched, his hair wild, and his glasses askew. His students were waiting for him, and he took a weird satisfaction in seeing their hairless jaws drop and their callow eyes bug out. Professor Corman did not have the reputation of showing up for class like he was strung out on angel dust.

Stephen stood at the lectern, panting hard, silently daring any one of his students to ask him what was wrong. None of them did.

"All right, then," he said at last. "We've been talking about Thoreau and Emerson for half the summer. So." He paused and glared. "Just what the *fuck* do you still need to know about these guys?"

❖

He didn't stay for the Graduate Committee meeting or for his office hours. Immediately after his class—which had gone surprisingly well, he thought, considering that he had twice referred to Henry David Thoreau as a civilly disobedient cocksucker—he went to his car and drove to Jack's apartment. But Jack didn't answer his knock, and the postal jeep was gone. Jack had already left for the cabin.

For a moment Stephen thought again about going there too. But it was late enough now that by the time he got there, Jack would already be traipsing around naked. And Stephen didn't have the stomach for that this month, even if there were bologna sandwiches available.

He drove to a Circle K store on Guadalupe Street, bought a frozen Coke, and slurped at it while sitting in his car in the tiny parking lot. It was almost six o'clock now, and the crush of after-work traffic on Guadalupe was noisy and reeked of exhaust. Somehow that made Stephen feel more isolated than if no one else had been around. There were cars and people everywhere, but everybody was in a foul mood and a hurry, and no one paid any attention to him. He was as alone in the middle of Austin as he would have been on the Moon.

Assuming, of course, that Lily had already left the Moon for her monthly tryst with Jack.

Stephen drained the last of the frozen Coke with one long, oxygen-deprived suck on the straw, and in the process gave himself a terrific icy headache behind his eyes. He appreciated it. It woke him up and made him notice that he was rumpled and smelled bad.

He supposed that Katy had gone back to work after her lunchtime visit home, which meant that she wouldn't be home right now. She never made it home from work before seven-thirty. So he could go to the house, shower, and change, and be gone again before she showed up.

Because regardless of whatever else he did tonight, he was sure of one thing: He didn't want to see Katy at all. If and when he did come home for the night, he would sleep on the couch in the living room.

But thinking of the couch, and of how it folded out into a double bed, made him think of the sheets and the underwear.

And so he told himself that he was ridiculous. He had no proof of anything. As for the sheets and underwear . . . well, so what? Maybe Katy had decided she wanted to use them again, and they'd been gathering dust for so long that they needed to be washed first.

Except that Katy had never done anything like that in all the time he'd known her. Normally he was the one who changed the linen and did the laundry. The closest that Katy ever got to being domestic was an occasional attempt to re-create her family's ancestral potato salad.

Stephen noticed that the icy headache behind his eyes wasn't going away the way those things usually did.

He got out of the car, stuffed the empty Coke cup into an overflowing trash barrel at the Circle K's entrance, and then went to the pay phones at the corner of the building. Halle worked at home, and she was there for her children in the evening. So she was there for him to call, too, if he felt like it.

She might think it was strange, though. They were friends, but Stephen almost never called her—because until now he had been afraid that she might figure out how he felt about her. But now he hoped that she *did* know. And if she didn't, maybe he would go ahead and tell her.

Halle answered on the third ring. "Hello, yeah, yeah, what is it?" She sounded perturbed.

Stephen stood there stunned, unable to speak, suddenly aware that the six o'clock Texas sun was beating a hot tattoo on his pale neck.

"If this is an obscene phone call," Halle said, "you'd better call back later. I've got one kid with a bloody knee and another kid who tried to bandage it with a poultice of Play-Doh and boogers. So unless you're a premature ejaculator, I don't have the time."

Stephen managed to find his voice. "Uh, no, it's just Stephen. I'll call back."

"Steve?" Halle said. "You sound funny. What's the heavy breathing about?"

"Am I breathing heavily?"

"It sure sounds that way."

Stephen hadn't been aware of it, but he didn't doubt it. "There's a lot of noise on the line," he said. "I'm at a pay phone."

"What, did you have a breakdown? Do you need help?"

Have I had a breakdown? Stephen wondered. Do I need help?

He felt like the king of self-pity, and he didn't mind it too much.

"No, I was just running some errands," he said, "and I—wondered if I could pick up anything for you. I know you've been busy, so I thought you might . . . need something."

It was lame, and he knew it. The line was silent for a long moment.

"Well, that's sweet of you," Halle said at last. She sounded dubious. "But I made it out to H.E.B. this morning, believe it or not. It was the highlight of my day, which gives you some idea of what my days are— Cleo! Get your fingers out of there! Now!"

"You're busy," Stephen said. He felt like turds on stale toast. "I'll let you go."

There was a clatter on the other end of the line as something was dropped or thrown. Then Halle was back, sighing in exasperation.

"Look, Steve, I'm sorry," she said. "Can I call you back?"

"I'm not home."

"Oh, right. It's just that the kids are acting up, and Tony might have an infected knee. And the microwave's not working, so I'm having to cook on the stove. Dinner just boiled over."

Instantly Stephen said, "I could bring you something, if you like. Chinese? Pizza?"

Of course. He would bring supper to Halle and her children. He would eat with them and stay all evening, then help put Cleo and Tony to bed. After that, he and Halle would talk through the night.

Katy? he would say. Katy who?

"Oh, no, really," Halle said. "I couldn't ask you to do that."

"It would be my pleasure."

Deep inside the onioned layers of Stephen's brain, a muffled voice screamed, *You're making a pathetic fool of yourself!*

Stephen told the voice to go piss up a rope.

"Seriously, Steve," Halle said. Her voice had a strain of self-conscious kindness in it. "I've got it covered. But thank you for asking, and for calling. I do want to talk to you—but this is a crazy time right now. I'll call you later at home, okay?"

See? the voice asked.

"I don't think I'm going home," Stephen said, and then was furious at himself. Why had he told her that? Now she would wonder and speculate and maybe come up with the right idea. And he had just now decided that he didn't want that, after all. He felt stupid enough as it was. The voice was right.

"Not going home?" Halle sounded worried now. "Why not?"

"Because—" Stephen scrambled for an idea and told the first almost-truth that came to mind. "I thought I might go up to your cabin to keep an eye on Jack."

Halle didn't respond for a few seconds. When she did, she said, "That's great of you, but I don't think it's necessary. Jack seems to have gotten a lot better these past few months. That's why I was willing to let him go up there by himself. And I think it might do him some good to know that we trust him to be okay."

Stephen was relieved. Now he wouldn't have to drive all the way out to the cabin just to avoid having lied to Halle.

"Well, I guess I won't go, then," he said. "And you sound as if you're in chaos over there, so I'll call you later, all right?"

"I'd like that," Halle said. "Just give me a few hours to get the kids fed and sedated."

"Sure," he said. He ached for her. He was miserable.

"Bye, Steve," Halle said. "I— Tony! I swear, I'm gonna sell you as a circus geek if you don't stop eating your own—"

There was a rattle and a thump, and then the line was dead.

Stephen hung up the receiver. He had been able to picture everything: Halle's kitchen, her two hell-on-wheels children, the spaghetti (or whatever) boiling over, and Halle herself. On a hot day like today she would be wearing shorts and a tank top, and her short brown hair was no doubt mussed up. And she wouldn't be wearing makeup.

She was beautiful.

He couldn't avoid it any longer: He was in love with her.

Okay, so you're in love, the voice inside his brain said. *And, clearly, Ph.D. stands for Phucking Dickhead.*

"Shut up," Stephen said as he walked back to his car.

An overweight, sweating man going into the store glared at him. "You talkin' to me, asshole?"

Stephen shook his head, and the fat man sneered and went inside.

He's right, you know, the voice said. *You're an asshole.*

Stephen got into the Escort. He still didn't want to spend his evening at home, so he decided to buy himself dinner out and then hit a bookstore or two. But first he would go by the house and clean up a little. Quickly, before Katy got home.

You're also a married *asshole.*

"Yeah, well," Stephen said, pulling out onto Guadalupe, "so's my wife."

169

He went home and found the driveway empty.

Good.

Before showering, he snooped in Katy's closet and found another rarely used set of sheets wadded up in the corner. He picked them up and smelled them, and they stank of sex. Katy must have been in a big hurry to get back to work this afternoon. She could have at least put them in the washer the way she had yesterday.

Stephen felt strangely calm. And as he took his shower, he realized that he had an odd sense of freedom.

Katy had broken faith first, so he could do as he wanted. If he chose, he could even tell Halle that he loved her. He doubted that he would, really, because she didn't seem to think of him in that way at all. But that was the only thing holding him back now.

He toweled off, dressed in jeans and a blue T-shirt, and left. It was twenty minutes after seven. Katy might be home in ten minutes, or she might not. Usually, if she wasn't home by seven thirty-five, Stephen called her at work to ask how things were going and whether he should eat dinner without her. Tonight, though, she would just have to wonder about *him* for a change.

Or maybe she wouldn't. Maybe she wouldn't even notice that he hadn't called. Or maybe she would notice and be glad that he hadn't. Maybe she would come home, find that he wasn't there, and instead of wondering where he was, see it as a lunch-hour-type opportunity.

He ate a huge chicken-fried steak at Threadgill's and had a booth all to himself except for the poster of Janis Joplin laughing down at him. In addition to the steak, he ate two rolls, three pieces of cornbread, mashed potatoes, broccoli-rice casserole, and buttermilk pie. He also drank four Shiner Bock beers, a personal record. Stephen was not a beer drinker, but it occurred to him that Shiner Bock was the official beer of Austin—which didn't make any sense, but nothing did right now—and that it was probably considered unpatriotic not to slam some down now and then. By the time he waddled away from the booth, Stephen was dizzy, grinning, and stuffed. For the first time in eight years, he felt like he belonged in this town.

It was a quarter to nine. Night was falling, the Moon was up, and he had waited long enough. He had told Halle that he would call her back tonight, but that seemed inadequate. So he would drive south of the river and go see her instead. It was the sort of thing that a man who drank four Shiner Bocks with a chicken-fried steak supper would do.

As he turned onto her street, he saw that a new blue Chevy pickup was parked in the duplex driveway behind Halle's beat-up Plymouth. So he parked his Escort along the curb across the street and stared at the pickup for a while.

What the hell.

Maybe Halle had just bought it.

Yeah.

He heard a noise from the duplex, and when he turned to look, he saw Tommy Moribund, or whatever the jerk's name was, stepping outside. Halle was right behind him, but she stopped at the threshold. Tommy turned back to face her, and she put her arms around him. She said something into his ear, then kissed him on the mouth for far too long.

"Shit," Stephen said, scrunching down in his seat. "Shit piss crap." As he slunk down as far as he could, he became aware of the fact that his bladder was full to the point of pain.

Weirdly, he thought of sixteenth-century astronomer Tycho Brahe, whose bladder had burst and who had subsequently died, all because he was too polite to leave a banquet after the royalty arrived. That, Stephen thought, had been a stupid way to go. Having your bladder burst while you were parked across the street from the house of a woman you were smitten with, on the other hand, made a lot more sense.

At least, it did if she was with someone else. *Something* ought to be bursting in that situation, anyway.

Stephen could still see the doorway, could still see Halle kissing Mr. Moribund. He couldn't stop watching. He supposed that if anyone spotted him, he would look like one of the Kilroy figures he had drawn on his desk in grade school. Nothing showing but the nose and eyes.

Halle finally broke the kiss and went back into the duplex, closing the door behind her. Mr. Moribund then came down the sidewalk alongside the garage, but stopped at the Chevy pickup's front bumper.

He was looking straight across the street at Stephen's car.

No: He was looking straight across the street at Stephen's eyes.

"Shit," Stephen said again.

Tommy Moribund was coming across the street now. Stephen considered starting the car and tearing out of there, but he was slouched down so that his knees were jammed up behind the steering wheel. By the time he had struggled up to driving position again, Mr. Moribund was tapping on his window.

"Yo, Steve?" Mr. Moribund said, his voice muffled by the glass. "That you?"

Stephen rolled the window down a few inches. He had no choice now but to behave as though nothing were out of the ordinary. And maybe he would get lucky. Maybe Mr. Moribund would place his hands on the window's top edge—and then Stephen could roll it up real fast and sever his fingers.

But Mr. Moribund put his hands in his pockets. "How's it goin'?" he asked, giving Stephen a self-confident grin.

What Stephen wanted to say was *How the bleeding fuck do you think it's going, you grinning piece of dung?*

What he said instead was "Okay."

Mr. Moribund glanced across at Halle's duplex. "You here to see Halle?"

No, Stephen thought. I'm here to ram a tire tool sideways up your ass.

But what he said was "Uh-huh."

Moribund shook his head. "Well, I just got my walking papers. But at least she blew a joint with me first. So good luck, bud." He started to walk away.

Stephen rolled the window down farther and stammered, "Wait, wait, what was that?"

Moribund paused and looked back over his shoulder. "She just dumped me, so you've got a clear shot."

Something in Moribund's tone made Stephen angry. He forgot about his full bladder, opened the car door, and stepped out.

"Excuse me," he said. To his own ears, his voice sounded like it had an edge of blue steel. "I'm married, and Ms. Stone is simply my good friend."

Mr. Moribund's eyebrows rose. He looked amused. "Right," he said. "I guess that's why every time I've seen you, you've been staring at her like a redbone hound at a pork chop."

The Shiner Bock in Stephen's veins began to boil. "Did you just refer to her as a piece of meat?" he asked, stepping toward Moribund with his hands balled into fists.

"That was just a metaphor," Moribund said, backpedaling into the street. "I thought you were an English professor. Haven't you ever heard of a metaphor?"

Stephen kept on walking toward him. "Dipshit," he said. "That wasn't a metaphor; it was a simile."

Moribund continued backward across the street. "I thought a simile was a kind of metaphor. But maybe I'm just stoned and don't know what I'm saying. Jesus, take it easy."

"I'll take off your goddamn head, is what I'll take," Stephen said. He was surprised at and delighted with himself. He felt like killing Tommy Moribund, and he was confident that he could do it with his bare hands, or perhaps with just one of them. No wonder Shiner Bock was such a popular drink around here.

Moribund took his hands out of his pockets and held them up, palms out, as if to ward off the blows that Stephen was about to let fly.

"Look, man," Moribund said, "I've obviously pissed you off, and I apologize."

Stephen's adrenaline surged. Moribund was afraid of him. The big hairy weightlifter was in fear of the weak-chinned literature professor.

Cool.

"Stop backing off," Stephen said, "you corn-holing puss."

Abruptly, Moribund did just that. He stopped at the mouth of Halle's driveway, just behind the tailgate of the Chevy pickup. The pupils of his eyes reflected the full Moon.

"What I have to ask myself now, Steve," Moribund said, "is whether I consider that particular insult to be worth a parole violation."

And it was at that moment that Stephen remembered how much he had to urinate.

"Pardon me just one moment, Mr. Moribund," he said, unzipping his jeans and stepping around to the pickup's right rear wheel, "while I whiz on your candy-ass excuse for a pickup truck."

Things got blurry then, and when they came back into focus, Stephen was sitting in the grass beside the driveway with his pants unzipped. The Chevy pickup was driving off down the street, its engine roaring like a dinosaur.

A bare leg brushed Stephen's shoulder then, and Stephen recognized it. It was Halle's.

"That was entertaining," Halle said.

Stephen looked up at her. "Did he hit me?" he asked.

Halle looked surprised. "Of course not. Tommy wouldn't hurt a fly." She bent down, put her hands in Stephen's armpits, and helped him to his feet. "Because if he did, he'd go back to the big house."

Stephen was standing so close to Halle now that he could feel her breath on his face. In fact, her breath was *all* that he could feel. Or smell. She'd been drinking something herbal. Or maybe that was her hair. Whatever it was, he liked it.

"So how'd I wind up on the ground?" he asked. He asked only because he was afraid that if he didn't keep his mouth busy talking, he might try to kiss her. And then he might wind up on the ground again.

"That's a puzzler," Halle said. "I heard you guys having words, so I came out to see what was going on—just in time to see your butt hit the dirt. But Tommy was a good seven or eight feet away."

Stephen was mortified. He wanted to flee, but as he started to pull away from Halle he realized that if he didn't relieve his bladder in thirty seconds or less, it was going to take care of its problem without his consent.

"Could I please—" he began, wishing that a lightning bolt would strike him.

"Sure," Halle said. "Come on in."

She put her arm around his shoulders as they went inside, and he wished that she hadn't. By the time he got to the bathroom, he had another problem to complicate the one he already had.

Eventually, though, he managed. As he returned to the front door,

Halle came down from upstairs and stepped in front of him.

"Unbelievably," she said, "the kids are still asleep. Lucky for you, because if Tony was awake, I was gonna make you read his *Aladdin* book to him for the umpty-zillionth time. It's all he wants to hear. No *Wrinkle in Time,* no *Phantom Tollbooth,* just freaking *Aladdin.* I curse Disney and all their minions, including Tony's wicked-witch paternal grandmother for giving him the evil thing. As if bringing her pissant son into the world wasn't a big enough sin for one lifetime. You want coffee?"

Stephen shook his head. He had made a fool of himself in front of Halle, and he wanted to get out of her sight. "I should be heading home."

But that wasn't where he would go. He didn't have a destination in mind, but he knew that it wouldn't be home.

"I don't think so," Halle said. "Not just yet. I smell beer. Shiner Bock, right?" She went into the kitchen and gestured for Stephen to follow.

Stephen followed, then sat at the table when Halle told him to. He didn't really want to get out of her sight. What he really wanted was for her to take his hand, tell him that he didn't have to say anything, that she felt the same way, and that she wanted him so bad her teeth hurt. He watched her make coffee and became so aroused that he couldn't sit completely upright without hurting himself.

That morning he had watched Katy dress and undress four times as she tried to decide what to wear to work, and all he had felt at the repetitive exposure of her body was annoyance that she was wasting so much time. But here was Halle, dressed in baggy shorts and a baggier T-shirt, taking her own sweet time making coffee, and all he wanted to do was watch her forever. Well, not just watch her. But he would settle for that.

After a while she brought two cups of coffee to the table and sat down across from him. "Feeling sober yet?" she asked, sliding a cup toward him.

"I never felt otherwise," Stephen said. He accepted the cup and took a sip. It was terrible. But he would drink it all. Slowly.

"Well, you acted otherwise," Halle said. "Starting a ruckus and trying to pee on somebody's truck are not the actions of the Stephen Corman we've all come to know and love."

Stephen winced—not from shame, but from hearing Halle use the word *love* without meaning anything close to what he wanted the word to mean.

"Sorry," he said. "I guess maybe Jack's full-Moon insanity has rubbed off after all these months."

Halle smiled. "Well, you haven't gotten naked in public yet. Although part of you almost did."

Stephen could feel himself blushing. It was as if his face had been dunked in hot water. Or as if a cup of Halle's terrible coffee had been dumped over his head.

"Look," Halle said, "I know that it's none of my business, but are you and Katy doing okay?"

Stephen considered telling her the truth, but rejected that notion. Telling Halle that Katy was being unfaithful would sound like a pity ploy. Besides, he already felt sorry enough for himself. He didn't need it from anyone else—least of all from Halle.

Pity was not the emotion he desired from her.

"We're fine," he lied. "But I was wondering about you and, uh, Tommy."

"Oh, the guy whose truck you almost took a squirt on?" Halle asked.

"That's the one."

Halle pursed her lips and looked up at the ceiling. "Well," she said, "we broke up. We put my kids to bed, got stoned, and broke up. Not that we were all that serious to begin with. But it was time to stop."

Stephen took a mouthful of bad coffee to bolster himself. He swallowed hard, and it burned all the way down. "Why's that?" he asked.

Halle looked at Stephen's eyes. "Because there's someone else I'm interested in," she said.

Stephen wanted to take another big gulp of coffee, but his hands were shaking and he didn't think he could bring the cup to his lips without spilling most of its contents into his lap.

"Who?" he asked. He was appalled at the sound of his voice. It was a squeak. He sounded like a goddamn rubber duckie.

Halle looked toward the staircase. "He's . . . nobody you know. A software engineer. I met him at a seminar a few weeks ago, and we hit it off."

Stephen didn't want to look at her face now, so he stared down at his coffee. If he smashed the cup, would there be a shard sharp enough to jab into his jugular vein?

"His name's Carl Sugarman," Halle said.

"Carl Stygian," Stephen muttered.

"Stop that!" Halle snapped.

Stephen had to look up at her again, and he was horrified to see that she was truly angry. "I'm sorry," he said, trying to think of an excuse. "It's just a reflex."

"You haven't even met him," she said.

Stephen downed the rest of his coffee and stood. "It was only a joke," he said. He was desperate to get out of there. He had a horrible burning sensation in his throat and eyes. "Thank you for the coffee. I'm sober now, and Katy will be wondering where I am."

Halle stood too. "You can call her from here so she won't worry."

Stephen started toward the door. If he didn't make it outside in another ten seconds, he was going to fall down in a fetal heap. "No, really, that's okay," he said. "Thank you for the coffee."

"You already thanked me for the coffee, Steve," Halle said, moving ahead of him to open the door. "And you're very welcome. But it was awful. I don't know what happened. Bad filter, maybe."

"It was fine," Stephen said. The burning sensation in his throat and eyes was getting worse, and his frozen-Coke headache of several hours earlier was back. He wanted to rush out into the night, but Halle was standing in the doorway, blocking him.

"You're upset," she said.

Yeah, he thought, and Krakatoa was a little pop.

"I just ought to be getting home," he said.

Halle stepped aside. "Call me when you get there, all right? I'm worried about you."

"No need," he said, and went out. Behind him, Halle said goodbye, but he just waved without looking back.

He did look back when he reached his car, but Halle's door was already closed.

So he got into the Escort, put the key into the ignition, and then saw that someone was sitting in the passenger seat.

He was too startled to scramble back outside. Instead, he stared at the car's uninvited occupant. She was a dark-haired, fair-skinned woman, her face illuminated by the moonlight that shone in through the windshield. She was wearing something filmy and white that exposed the tops of her breasts.

"Don't freak out," she said. Her voice was mellifluous, like honey pouring over an apple. "It's only me. You've seen me before, but we haven't actually met until now." She extended a pale, slender hand. "I'm Lily."

Stephen shrank back against the driver's-side door. "How did you get in here?" he asked.

Lily gave him a wry smile. "You left it unlocked."

Okay, Stephen thought, it had been a stupid question. But it was better than the others he might ask:

Did I see you naked under an overpass along I-35?

Did you sit on my back fence and then fly away?

Did I see you having sex with Jack in a live oak tree, or was that an owl?

"I recognize you," he said.

Lily laughed. It sounded like crystal wind chimes. "Well, that was a non sequitur. But it's nice to know that I'm memorable. You aren't freaking out, are you?"

Stephen considered. A strange woman had gotten into his car. She called herself Lily, which was the name that Jack had given to his Moon goddess. Furthermore, Stephen thought that he had seen this woman before, only naked, and with huge feathered wings.

"Not at all," he said.

"That's good," Lily said. "Because I'm not here to freak you out. I'm here to see that you're all right. You're a friend of Jack's, and the well-being of his friends has become important to me."

Stephen studied her. She was beautiful and smelled wonderful, like a white flower. He could feel himself becoming sexually excited just from being this close to her.

But that only depressed him. She wasn't who he really wanted.

"I'm fine," Stephen said. "Thank you for your concern."

Lily opened the passenger door. "You're not fine at all," she said. "But now you know that someone cares." She stepped outside, then leaned down and looked in at him. "I'm going to talk to Halle now. She'll be feeling bad for having broken your heart. And you should go talk to Katy."

Stephen became angry again. What gave Lily the right to talk to him like this? "I haven't had my heart broken since I was sixteen," he said. "And I don't need a total stranger telling me when to talk with my wife."

Lily sighed. "Actually," she said, "yes, you do."

Then she stood up, closed the door, and walked across the street to Halle's duplex. Stephen watched her go. The filmy white dress was sleeveless, and her bare shoulders and arms caught the moonlight. The dress was too full and puffy across the back, but the hem swirled around her knees the way it was supposed to. Below that she was wearing dark stockings and high heels, which seemed weird for an August night in Austin. Especially with a white dress.

But Stephen guessed that weird was this woman's middle name.

The high heels clicked all the way across the street and up Halle's driveway and sidewalk.

Stephen didn't wait to see whether Halle opened the door. As Lily rang the bell, he started the Escort, put it into Drive, and got away as fast as he could.

He didn't know who Lily was, and he didn't care. All he cared about right now was that both of the people he loved the most seemed lost to him.

Katy, whom he loved despite everything, was sleeping with someone else.

And Halle had made it clear that she had no interest in him. She wanted someone named Stygian.

So Stephen was a low-paid, weak-chinned, four-eyed English professor—no, *associate* professor—with a receding hairline. He was on a fast track to becoming a solitary forty-year-old pasty-faced geeb who went back to his office and jerked off after teaching classes full of dewy twenty-year-old girls about T. S. Eliot. J. Fucking Alfred Prufrock, indeed.

He didn't want to go home. And the bookstores were closed. So instead, he went to a blues club and tried to drink another Shiner Bock while watching a beautiful red-haired woman play a pink paisley Telecaster. She played like she'd been to hell and back with a stop at every smoky bar in between, but she looked like a teenage girl who might just have gotten her first kiss. There was no way she'd seen twenty-five yet.

But she wasn't a girl. She was a woman. She knew some things. He could hear it in her playing. And she gazed down toward him as she played, and looked right through him.

Stephen stood it as long as he could, then left two-thirds of his beer on the bar and went outside. Bats were swooping and diving everywhere, snapping up the bugs dancing in the streetlight halos. Stephen stopped on the sidewalk, looked up at the Moon, and stayed perfectly still with his mouth open wide. He was hoping for a bat to come close enough for him to bite off its head.

15

◆

The Weird Babe Was Back

The weird babe was back, Halle saw as she opened the door. This time the woman was wearing a gauzy white dress that Halle wouldn't have been caught dead in. But on the weird babe, it worked. The long black hair against the white fabric made it.

"I thought I'd retrieve my coat," the woman said in her smooth, musical voice. "I dropped it in your driveway several months ago." She hesitated. "I'd also like to talk with you, if I may."

"Certainly," Halle said, crossing her arms and leaning against the doorjamb. She was still feeling a residual buzz from the pot that she and Tommy had smoked, and nothing was going to faze her. "Whatcha been up to?"

The woman smiled. "Oh, I've been around."

Halle smiled right back. "No, honey, *I've* been around. I'll tell you one thing you've done, though: You've worked up a big-ass reputation with very little actual ass. Jack only sees you once a month, he says—yet for most of this year it's been Lily this, Lily that, Lily makes Jack's willy fat. Your name *is* Lily, isn't it?"

"Lilith, actually," Lily said. "I'm a goddess."

It seemed to Halle that this chick had a mighty high opinion of herself. Maybe it was time that someone took her down a peg or two.

"A goddess?" Halle said, feigning puzzlement. "That's odd. See, I'd always heard that Lilith was a succubus. That's more like a demon than a goddess, isn't it? I mean, a goddess has charms that make men fall in love with her, whereas a succubus merely fucks them stupid."

Lily scowled, and Halle thought she looked comical. That pale, flawless face wasn't made for scowling. Clearly, Lily wasn't used to being challenged, disappointed, or buffaloed. Halle was glad for the chance to rectify that.

"I think," Lily said, "that I've just been insulted."

"You're not sure?" Halle asked. "Then let me make it obvious: I suspect that you might possibly be a manipulative bitch. The way I see it, you've been skulking in the shadows like a vampire avoiding sunlight, showing up only to cock-tease Jack or to bait his friends. I know for a fact that you've pulled this now-you-see-her-now-you-don't horseshit not only on me, but on Artie and Carolyn, too."

"Did Carolyn tell you that?" Lily asked.

"Not in those words," Halle said. "But close enough. And my kids told me about a lady who could change into a bird. I suggested that they shouldn't be telling me fibs—but now I have a feeling that it was a fib *you* told them. And if that's the case, you're a sick woman."

Lily's eyes flashed white light.

"I'm not a woman at all," she said. Her voice was no longer musical.

Halle looked her over. "Sure you are," she said. "No cross-dresser in the world is that good, especially not with the boobs. And I should know. I once went to bed with a transvestite so skilled that he made the one in *The Crying Game* look like a gorilla. He thought he'd give me a shock when he revealed his secret, but I knew he was male from the moment he stepped within smelling distance."

"Smelling distance?" Lily asked disdainfully.

"Don't scoff." Halle took a long, deep breath. "In your case, it's not what I smell, but what I don't. I can smell men. It's a gift I've had since puberty."

"How is such a gift given?" Lily asked.

Halle couldn't tell whether Lily was mocking her. But she didn't care. The truth was the truth.

"I was running laps in gym class," she said, "and as I passed the boys' locker room, I got a lungful of something that knocked me out. Literally. The gym teacher brought me around with ammonia, but even that couldn't clear away what I'd caught a whiff of."

She paused then, remembering.

"What had you smelled?" Lily asked.

Halle was surprised at Lily's tone now. She sounded interested. Like a friend would be.

"Boys, naturally," Halle said. "But like I never had before. Until that moment, boys had only reeked of peanut butter and Band-Aids, Pixy Stix and baseball gloves, boogers and bubble gum. What I smelled in the gym that day, however, was something new. What I smelled that day was just-barely-post-pubescent, newly hairy, sexually frustrated teenage males, dozens of them, their sweaty, sticky stinks all mingling together and boiling up like steam from a hot stew." She chuckled. "The teacher took me to the girls' locker room then, and that's when I discovered that I was having my first period. Two weeks later, I lost my virginity. Or, more accurately, I threw it away in a Kleenex."

Halle looked past Lily's shoulder at the full Moon, remembering her first skinny boy and how the two of them had taken turns treating each other like dirt for most of the ninth grade.

"How old were you?" Lily asked.

"Fourteen," Halle said. "But so was he. I know most girls have older guys the first time, but I didn't want someone who thought he was teaching me something. I wanted someone I could learn with, not from."

She looked back at Lily's face and saw that Lily still seemed interested. Compassionate, even.

"Fourteen is awfully young, isn't it?" Lily asked.

Halle snorted. "Of course it is. If my daughter does it at fourteen, I'll kill not only the guy who nailed her, but every human male in a twelve-mile radius. How'd we get onto this, anyway? You want to come inside?"

Lily looked startled. Her face didn't seem used to that expression, either. "Are you sure that you want me in your home?" she asked. "I had the impression that you disliked me."

Halle considered. "I thought I did," she said then. "But I just now told you my how-I-lost-my-cherry story, so my subconscious must think you're okay even if you are missing a few lug nuts." She stepped back from the doorway and gestured for Lily to come inside.

Lily hesitated, but then crossed over the threshold. Her high heels clicked on the tiles in the entryway. Halle looked down at Lily's black shoes and stockings and wondered what the deal was.

"I don't often come into people's homes," Lily said. She sounded nervous. "At least, not women's homes."

Halle went into the kitchen, waving for Lily to follow. "Ah-hah, I knew it. You only visit men, which no doubt means you *are* a succubus. No offense."

"None taken," Lily said uncertainly. She followed Halle into the kitchen, her heels clicking all the way.

Halle stopped, turned, and looked at Lily's feet. "You don't actually enjoy wearing heels, do you?"

Lily gave Halle a thin smile. "It depends on what you mean by enjoy. I find them uncomfortable. But my feet are unattractive, in human terms, and the shoes compensate."

"You mean you wear them to please Jack?" Halle asked. She was appalled at the thought. Not that pleasing Jack was necessarily a bad thing—she had done some of that herself, once upon a time—but there were limits, and physical discomfort was one of them.

Lily shook her head, and her black hair swirled. Halle hated her for just a second then. No one ought to be allowed to have hair that good.

"I don't wear them for Jack," Lily said. "With Jack, I'm—well, barefoot. The shoes are only for when I'm out in public. Which isn't often."

"Well, you're not in public now," Halle said. "Feel free to kick them off. In fact, I'm kicking my own off." She pushed off her Reeboks without untying them, then wiggled her toes against the tile floor. "See? My knotty old feet aren't exactly what you'd call beautimous, either."

Lily laughed. It sounded like silver bells. "But at least they're human," she said.

"I'm sorry, I'd forgotten," Halle said, gently sarcastic. "You're a goddess."

Lily's expression turned so solemn then that her face looked like white marble with two dark stones set into it.

"No," she said. "I think that perhaps you were right. I'm a succubus. A demon."

Halle felt a little irritated by this. "Oh, stop it," she said. "I was just yanking your chain." She turned toward the cabinets over the stove. "You want coffee or tea? Or something else?"

"Nothing, thank you." Lily's voice was low. It sounded sad, and Halle didn't like it. She didn't know Lily well enough to deal with any sadness.

"Then let's move to the living room," she said. "If we talk out here for long, our voices will go up the stairs and wake the kids. You don't want that, trust me." She went into the living room then and heard Lily clicking behind her from the tile to the hardwood. It was a little creepy.

Halle flopped down in her overstuffed, ugly green easy chair, and Lily sat on the edge of the futon couch. So much on the edge, in fact, that she looked as if she were perched there.

"Thank you for taking the time to see me," Lily said. "It's more than your friends have done. Katy and Carolyn both seem to hate me, and Artie is afraid of me."

"What about Steve?" Halle asked. "I saw you get out of his car just now."

Lily's eyebrows rose. "You were watching?"

Halle shrugged. "So sue me. I was worried about him, so I peeked through the kitchen curtains to see if he drove away all right. Call me Gladys Kravitz."

Lily frowned. "Who?"

Halle was amused. "Deprived childhood, huh? Didn't have a television?"

"Not where I lived."

"Sorry, I forgot again." Halle's sarcasm was less gentle this time. "You grew up on the Moon."

Lily was still frowning. "I didn't grow up at all. When I came into being, I was just as I am now."

"I see," Halle said. She stretched out her legs, crossed her ankles, and folded her hands on her stomach. "Well then, let me ask you this: Why would an eternally mature—and therefore eternally wise—goddess want to talk to the likes of an immature idjit like me?"

Lily hesitated, then looked down at the floor and licked her lips.

"Because I'm feeling some strange things. Strange to me, anyway. Things about Jack and his friends and his life and this city, and—" She looked up at Halle. "I was hoping that talking to you might help me begin to understand some of it. That hearing what a mortal—and a friend of Jack's—had to say about these things might make my own reactions clearer to me."

Halle decided to play along. "Are you saying you wanted to talk to me in particular?" she asked. "Or to the entire gang of suspects that Jack hangs out with? Because what you hear from me isn't going to be what you hear from anyone else."

"I've been wanting to speak with all of you," Lily said, "but especially the women. Artie and Stephen are interesting, and I suppose that if I were without prejudice I might learn as much from them as from you. But I find myself thinking of them the way I've always thought of men: as simple-minded. Their desires are too obvious and too easily satisfied for me to value their opinions too highly."

Halle laughed. "You're not a goddess, Lily. You're just enlightened."

"Except that I'm feeling something different for Jack," Lily said. "Hence my problem."

Halle didn't have to think long to come up with a reason for that. "Well, shit," she said. "What it sounds like to me is you're in love with the guy. And it's only natural not to understand or like what that does to you. In fact, that's the one thing that a woman of your obvious adulthood ought to know by now: Loving a man isn't a thing to be understood at all. It's a thing to put up with and suffer through. It's a thing to be endured." She paused for a moment, thinking back on some of the relationships that she herself had endured. "And if you're lucky," she continued, "you just might manage to enjoy yourself a little in the process."

Lily looked thoughtful. "So you're telling me," she said, "that if I can survive this, it will pass and I'll be as I was before?"

"Good Lord, no!" Halle said. "It may well pass, but you for damn sure won't be as you were before. If you love somebody, it changes you. And even if it ends, and you get over it, then one day you'll look in the mirror and see that you don't even look like the same person anymore. And I'm not talking about just getting older, either."

Lily stood and walked across to the window that looked out on the duplex's tiny backyard. She seemed to be staring out at the kids' swing set—but then Halle realized that Lily was in fact looking at her own reflection. She was looking for that change already.

"Does that sort of thing happen to men, too?" Lily asked.

"I suppose so," Halle said. "The ones who really do fall in love, anyway. The ones who aren't assholes."

Lily continued to stare at her own reflection. "Jack isn't an asshole, is he?"

Halle thought she knew now what Lily was really worried about. Lily was afraid of losing Jack.

"No," Halle said. "Jack is not an asshole. When I was with him, he loved me as much as I was willing to let him. And I think Katy and Carolyn would say the same thing. He never broke our hearts. And we didn't break his heart, either. At least, I didn't."

Halle uncrossed her legs, sat forward, and put her elbows on her knees and her chin in her hands. "But Natalie did. I mean, Jack loved Carolyn, me, and Katy with a perfectly sweet and thoroughly normal kind of love. But he loved Natalie like Romeo loved Juliet and Popeye loved Olive Oyl. You know, with passion, fire, and utter slavish devotion."

"She was his wife?" Lily whispered.

Halle nodded. "Yeah, for a little while. Until she got herself killed. And not just killed, but killed in a moment of dumbass stupidity. She turned left on a red light in a thunderstorm and was pulverized by a cement mixer. I swear to God, a fucking cement mixer. It'd be funny if it wasn't so awful."

Lily turned away from the window. "I hate her," she said.

Halle grimaced. "Yeah, well, I'm kinda pissed off at her myself."

"No, you don't understand," Lily said. "I truly hate her."

Halle gave Lily a narrow-eyed stare. "Sorry, honey, but you didn't even know her. You don't have the right to hate her."

"The hell I don't," Lily snapped. "He was asking for her."

Halle winced. "Ouch. You mean, he was making love to you, and he said her name?"

"No," Lily said. She sounded furious. "I mean that his longing was so strong that I was drawn irresistibly to him—but what he was really asking for was her." Lily's voice turned bitter. "Instead, he got me."

Halle was worried now. She had almost forgotten that Lily wasn't wrapped too tight. It might be a good idea to try to soothe her a little . . .

"Well, I know he's happy that you're in his life," Halle said. "After all, it's not every man who gets to sleep with a goddess."

"But he wanted *her*," Lily said. "His Natalie. A mortal woman. Not—not *this*."

And then Lily kicked off her high heels, and her feet uncurled, and her talons tore through the black stockings and dug white scratches into Halle's hardwood floor.

"Jesus Christ!" Halle yelled, jumping up backward onto her chair.

Lily glared. "Please don't mention that name. There was one man who was no fun at all." Her talons curled and uncurled, leaving more scratches on the floor. "But at least he didn't do what Jack's done. At least he didn't want somebody else more than he wanted me."

Halle stood frozen on her overstuffed chair. This was deeply weird. It was also deeply real. Tommy had shared a pretty good joint with her, but it wasn't that good. No pot in the world was that good.

"You—you—you—" Halle said.

Lily scowled again. She appeared to be in a foul mood. Halle didn't like seeing it as much as she had before.

"What?" Lily asked.

Halle sank down so that she was sitting with her knees tucked up under her chin. Her shock was starting to subside and be replaced by wonder.

"You really are a goddess," Halle said.

Lily looked down at her feet. "Yes. But maybe that's just another word for freak." She started for the kitchen, her talons scratching across the wood. "Thank you for talking with me, Halle," she said. "I have to go now."

She entered the kitchen and clicked across the tile. Halle got up and hurried after her.

"You don't have to leave on my account," Halle said. "I can handle this. If you'd like to stay and talk some more, that would be fine with me."

Lily went on through the kitchen and past the stairs, then paused at the front door. "I'm not leaving on your account," she said. "I'm leaving on Jack's account. He's waiting for me at your cabin, remember? And I can't make him wait all night. He needs me." She sighed. "And it seems that I need him too. This annoys me to no end—but at least my desire isn't entirely unrequited." She gave Halle a piercing look. "Stephen, on the other hand, isn't so lucky."

Halle was taken aback. She hadn't been expecting that.

"Are you suggesting that just because he's attracted to me, I should do something about it?" she asked.

"No," Lily said. "I just wondered if you were fully aware of the situation."

"Aware, yes," Halle said. "But fully aware? No. No one's ever fully aware of anything." She gave Lily a piercing look of her own. "Apparently, not even a goddess."

Lily sighed again. "Apparently not." She opened the door and stepped outside.

"Oh!" Halle said then. "Wait! You forgot your coat."

Lily looked back over her shoulder. "Keep it. It's August, and I don't need it. Now, would you mind killing your porch light for a moment? I don't want to dazzle your neighbors if any of them are Kravitzing."

Halle flipped the switch, and as her eyes adjusted to the moonlight, she could see Lily stepping out of her dress and stripping off her stockings. She could also see black-and-white wings unfolding from Lily's upper back.

"Hoo boy," Halle breathed.

Lily laughed her silver laugh. "I thought you said I didn't smell anything like a boy."

Then her wings flapped twice, and Lily rose above the garage and was gone.

Halle turned the porch light back on, stepped outside, and picked up the dress and stockings. As she brought them into the duplex, she decided that she would indeed keep the blue coat in her closet. She had tried it on, and it looked good on her. It would come in handy this winter.

The dress, though, was going to Goodwill. And the stockings were just plain ruined.

"Mommy!" Tony cried from upstairs. "Why'd you yell for Jesus?"

Halle tossed the dress and stockings into the hall closet, then went up to Tony's room.

"I'm sorry, sweetie," she said, leaning over him. "I got overexcited and woke you up for no good reason. What can I do to fix it?"

"Read *Aladdin*," Tony said.

Halle groaned. "Sugar, I've read *Aladdin* to you twice today, and three times yesterday."

"I like it," Tony explained.

So Halle turned on Tony's nightstand lamp, sat on the edge of the bed, and picked up *Aladdin*. But as she opened it to the first page, she had an idea.

"Tony, I'll make you a deal," she said. "I'll read *Aladdin* if you'll do something for me first."

Tony looked suspicious. "Like what?"

Halle thought about the scratches in her living-room floor.

"Tell me again about the where-bird," she said.

PART IX

STURGEON

MOON

Tuesday, August 31, 1993

❖

16

◆

Retaliation Was Her Right

Retaliation was her right, Carolyn told herself as she turned the OPEN sign on the shop's front door to CLOSED. If she'd had sex with Stephen just because she'd wanted him, without any crime having been committed against her, then she would have a reason to feel guilty. But that wasn't what had happened.

She went behind the jewelry case and began counting the day's receipts. No, that wasn't what had happened at all. She would never have done anything that might hurt Katy just because she felt like it. Katy was her friend.

"Ha!" she shouted. It was so loud bouncing off the walls of the shop that she startled herself and had to start counting all over again.

Some friend Katy was. Friends didn't pretend to be one thing and then turn out to be another. Katy had only pretended to be happily married and to have no interest in Artie. She had only pretended to be someone that Artie would never find attractive.

But that lie had been exposed for what it was three weeks ago.

Carolyn had been driving to the shop on a Monday morning when she'd realized that she'd left a stack of invoices at home. So she had gone back, parked on the street, and let herself into the house as quietly as possible so she wouldn't wake Artie.

Then, after finding the invoices on the kitchen counter, she had picked up the phone to call Time and Temperature. It had seemed unseasonably cool outside to her. But instead of a dial tone, she had heard Artie on the extension in the bedroom. And the things he was saying made it clear that he was talking to a lover.

Then the lover had responded. It had been Katy.

Carolyn had stood there listening for a few minutes, and then she had left the house as quietly as she'd come in. She had been so dazed that she hadn't even been able to work up the fury that would have been appropriate.

Because the betrayal had not been just that of an unfaithful mate—Carolyn had, after all, almost expected that of Artie—but a betrayal of reality itself. The world was not what she had believed it to be. A woman like Katy was not supposed to be able to lure someone like Artie away from a woman like Carolyn.

Just as Carolyn was not supposed to be the sort of woman who would deliberately seduce a married man. But then she had picked up the phone, the paradigm had shifted, and a new reality had taken over. It hadn't been her choice. It had been forced upon her.

She bore no responsibility in the matter.

Carolyn's Crafts had not had a good sales day. Customers had been few and far between, and they had bought only a handful of loose beads, one silver ring, and a flawed vase that Carolyn had been forced to discount. But Tuesdays and Wednesdays were always slow. In fact, Carolyn would have preferred to just close down on Tuesdays and Wednesdays, but she was afraid. As long as the shop was open all week, she told herself, it was still in business. If she started taking days off because she didn't think it was worth it to stay open—well, then she might as well admit failure, put on a business suit, and take an office job.

But she had been there and done that, and she had hated it. She had hated giving up control over her life to a boss for eight hours a day. She would be thirty-eight next month, and she didn't feel like going back and doing any of it again. Things might be different if she had gotten her chemical engineering degree . . . but she hadn't, and it was too late to go back for it now.

She finished counting the receipts, checked her total against the register total, and locked up the cash drawer. She could go home now if she liked. She could go home to Artie and do whatever she wanted with him. Make love to him or snub him or murder him. He had worked the lunch and happy-hour shifts at Terrazo and had the evening off, so he would be home waiting for her.

No, not just waiting: expecting.

It pissed Carolyn off mightily. He was there at her home *expecting* her.

Maybe only because he thought he had to.

Maybe he would rather be with Katy. Why else would he have said those things to her?

Well, he wouldn't have either one of them tonight, Carolyn thought as she unplugged the telephone. She had told him she would be home by eight, but he could just sit there on his cute little butt and wonder where she was. It was already almost eight-thirty. If Artie was smart, he would figure out that he was in trouble, and he would come down to the shop to try to make things right.

But Artie wasn't smart. That had been established. So if anything was going to be made right, Carolyn would have to do it herself.

She sat down on the stool behind the counter and put her face in her hands. Yeah. She would do it herself.

She already had.

It really was her right. The dirt had been done to her first. She bore no responsibility in the matter.

The bells on the door jangled as it was pushed open and someone stepped inside. Carolyn gritted her teeth and cursed. She had turned the OPEN sign to CLOSED, but she had forgotten to lock the door. Normally she locked the storefront, counted receipts, and then left the building through the workroom in back. Tonight, though, she had screwed up.

She pushed her hair back from her face and stood. "I'm sorry," she said, "but we're—"

Carolyn didn't finish the sentence. She had never seen the woman this clearly before, but she recognized her anyway. She was the one who called herself Lily. The one with pale skin and long dark hair. The one who had been playing hide-and-seek all year, and messing with Jack's mind. The one who had taunted Carolyn in the woods near Halle's cabin. The one whose guts Carolyn hated on principle.

That hatred now jumped up a notch or two. Lily was wearing a baggy purple blouse, tight black jeans, and cross-training sneakers. They were exactly like the clothes that Carolyn was wearing.

"The door wasn't locked," Lily said. "I hope you don't mind."

Carolyn looked her over with what she hoped Lily would read as an expression of utter disgust.

"Mind?" Carolyn asked. "Why should I mind? My door has a sign that says CLOSED, and a person I have every reason to dislike waltzes in dressed like she thinks she's my evil twin. Which means she's been spying on me. Why should I mind?" She reached behind her and picked up the telephone receiver. "And since you've been spying on me, I have to assume that means you've been casing the joint for a robbery. You have ten seconds to hit the bricks, or I'm dialing 911."

Lily gave her a sad smile. It infuriated Carolyn. It was the same kind of smile her freshman-year roommate had given her whenever she had come in after sunrise with a headache, burning nasal passages, and no memory of what had happened to her underwear.

"You'll have to plug your telephone back in first," Lily said.

Carolyn slammed down the receiver. "Just go, then. Go far away. Far away from me, from Jack, and especially from Artie. Just *go.*"

Lily tilted her head, and her thick hair fell over half her face. She regarded Carolyn with one huge eye that seemed to keep changing colors.

"Why especially from Artie?" Lily asked. "I've done nothing with Artie."

"And you're not going to, either," Carolyn said. "Now I'm counting to three, and then I really am plugging in the phone and calling the cops."

"But I came to talk with you," Lily said.

Carolyn wanted to leap across the counter and wrap her fingers around the bitch's neck.

"You came here dressed like me," Carolyn said, "to weird me out."

Lily shook her head. "No. I came here dressed like you because I'm your sister."

Carolyn came around the counter, went past Lily, and opened the door. The bells clanged against the glass.

"I'm an only child," Carolyn said.

Lily's eyebrows rose. "Perhaps that's why you're so selfish."

Carolyn couldn't believe it. This woman had no right to talk to her like that.

"Fuck you," Carolyn said. "Fuck you and get out. There's Burnet Road right outside this door, so why don't you go jump in the middle of it and see if someone out *there* wants to be your sister."

Lily sighed. "This isn't going well."

"No shit?" Carolyn asked, wide-eyed.

Lily pushed her hair back from her face and glared. She looked enraged. Carolyn was glad to see it. She had never liked being pissed off alone.

"Please close the door so we can talk," Lily said. Her voice had a dangerous edge.

Carolyn considered that a challenge.

"Fuck you twice," she said. "Fuck you up the ass with a red-hot fireplace poker."

Lily did something then that Carolyn didn't expect: She pulled off her baggy purple blouse and dropped it on the floor.

This made Carolyn almost as amused as she was angry. What, did Lily think that exposing her breasts was going to win the argument?

Lily said nothing, but gave Carolyn another glare.

Then a pair of enormous black-and-white wings unfolded from Lily's shoulders, spread out, and swept downward. The rush of air jerked the door from Carolyn's hand and slammed it shut. The bells bounced off their hook and clattered to the floor. Two vases blew off their shelves and broke into fragments that scattered everywhere. Handmade greeting cards flew from the rack beside the cash register and fluttered down like wounded birds.

"Now," Lily said, "perhaps we can talk."

Carolyn was stunned for a few seconds, but only for a few seconds . . . because she was still angry. And in any confrontation, no matter what else she might be feeling, anger was dominant. Anger gave her strength.

It was something she had cultivated. It was her best survival skill. Anger had gotten her through a rotten childhood with a beer-soaked father, adolescent poverty with a clinically depressed mother, a sexual assault when she was seventeen, and dozens of horrid relationships and assorted disasters in the twenty years since then. It had also gotten her through the condescension of the eight bank officers she'd had to hack her way through before she'd finally secured the loan she'd needed to open the shop.

So if anger could sustain her through all of that, it could sustain her through this. Compared to everything she had already faced in her life, a half-naked freak of nature ought to be a piece of cake.

She made herself take a step toward Lily. "Okay, we can talk," she said in a low voice. "But first let me make one thing clear: You're cleaning this crap up."

Lily blinked, then lowered her wings. "It's a deal."

That made Carolyn feel bolder, and she decided that it wasn't enough. "And you're paying for the vases you broke."

Lily looked a little worried now. "I'm afraid that I don't have any money."

"Then you'll have to work it off," Carolyn said. "So after you've cleaned up the mess that *you've* made, you can go into the workroom and clean up the messes that *I've* made. And since those were twenty-dollar vases and I pay part-time help six bucks an hour, you can expect to work most of the night."

Lily glanced toward the door. "I can't stay that long. I have to meet Jack."

Carolyn held her ground. "I don't want to hear any excuses. You broke my merchandise, and you'll pay for it one way or another. So if you really want to talk to me, you can talk while you're cleaning. And if you don't work long enough tonight to pay for those vases, you'll come back and work again until I'm satisfied. Or I'll find you and take it out of your hide. Got me?"

Lily frowned, but she nodded.

"Good," Carolyn said. "Now put your shirt back on. I haven't been impressed by tits since I got my own, and that was twenty-three years ago. Besides which, you're shedding feathers all over the place."

Lily's wings folded, and she pulled her shirt back on. Then she got down on her knees and began picking up the cards and feathers. She looked up at Carolyn with a puzzled expression.

"Aren't you the slightest bit intimidated?" Lily asked. "After all, I just proved to you that I'm a goddess."

Carolyn shrugged. "Yeah, well, so am I. At least, that's what numerous men have said whenever I took off *my* shirt. Including, I might add, Jack."

Lily's eyes narrowed. "You said that because you want to be sure that I know you had him first."

"In more ways than one." Carolyn squatted and began helping gather up the cards. "I had him first in the sense that I had him before you did, and I also had him first in the sense that I had him before anyone else did, either. Maybe I don't have wings—but I got his cherry."

"Then you threw him over for someone else," Lily said. "And you aborted his baby without telling him."

Carolyn gave Lily a sharp look. "Fuck you three times. I don't know how you found that out, but it doesn't matter, because it doesn't bother me. Leaving Jack for David McIlhenney was what I wanted to do, so I did it. And if it'll make you happy, I'll admit that McIlhenney turned out to be a big mistake. Ending my pregnancy, on the other hand, was absolutely the right thing to do. Neither Jack nor I could have been parents back then, not even if we'd stayed together. And there was no point in telling him about it. He had enough on his mind. It was my problem and my decision." She rapped the edges of a handful of cards against the floor. "So you see, Miss Lily the High-and-Mighty, even if you are a goddess, you're not a goddess I'm going to worship. You don't have the power to pass judgment on me."

Lily stood with a stack of cards in her hands and went to the rack by the register. "I wasn't passing judgment," she said. "I was stating facts. Just as I'm stating a fact when I say that you took Stephen Corman into your bed this morning after Artie left for the restaurant."

Carolyn's spine stiffened. Lily had no right to that information. It was her own business and nobody else's. Except Stephen's. And maybe not even his.

"So you *have* been spying on me," Carolyn said.

Lily replaced the cards in the rack. "I don't have to spy when it comes to sexual matters. Do you have a broom and dustpan?"

"Excuse me?"

"So I can sweep up the broken vases."

Carolyn stood and headed past Lily to the workroom. On the way, she slapped the cards she had picked up onto the counter. "I'll be right back," she said. "Put those in the rack."

"Yes, ma'am," Lily said. Carolyn couldn't tell whether she was being sarcastic or not.

The workroom was cool even though it wasn't air-conditioned. The day had been hot, but the pecan trees lining the alley behind the building had kept the room shaded, and the smooth cement floor seemed to suck up a chill from an underground river. Carolyn shut the door to the shop, sat down on that cool cement, and cried.

She had used Stephen. She had used him to make her feel that she was still in control. He was her friend, and she liked him, and he didn't excite her in the least. But despite that, she had set about getting him into bed once she had realized what was going on between Artie and Katy. And this morning she had succeeded.

She had left her car's headlights on all last night, and since it had been parked in the garage, no one had noticed. Then this morning, after Artie had roared off on his motorcycle for a rare breakfast shift, she had called Stephen and asked him to bring over his jumper cables.

The rest had been easy. Easier, even, than she had thought it would be.

But afterward he had said he loved her, and that was worrisome. She had assumed that he was having sex with her for the same reason that she was having sex with him.

It was possible, though, that he didn't even know about Artie and Katy. He hadn't said anything about it, and she hadn't told him. So he might have gone to bed with her for some other reason entirely.

He might actually have feelings for her.

Except that Halle had said that Stephen was smitten with *her*.

So Carolyn didn't know what to think.

That sort of confusion was unacceptable. Carolyn began to feel a little scared—but then she got hold of herself and decided that whatever Stephen's feelings were, she wasn't responsible for them. His motivations were his own.

Besides, it wasn't as if she had held a gun to his head. He had been willing. Enthusiastic, even. And she hadn't told him any lies.

No. She had just used him in order to get back at his wife for screwing Artie. To get back in control.

And now some bitch with wings was getting in her face and tearing up her shop. As if she didn't have enough problems.

Goddess, schmoddess. Lily was a pain in the ass.

A pair of cross-training sneakers appeared on the floor beside Carolyn's knee. Carolyn looked up and saw Lily regarding her with an expression of intense sympathy. It was infuriating.

"Are you worried that your encounter with Stephen might have meant more to him than it did to you?" Lily asked. "Or are you worried that he might have thought it meant more to you, too?"

Carolyn wiped her face on her sleeve, pushing away the tears. She would not cry in front of Lily. "No. I didn't misrepresent myself. I didn't tell him that I loved him or that I wanted a relationship with him, or any of that bullshit. It was sex. It was just sex. He can't possibly expect anything more from it."

Lily made a clicking noise with her tongue. "Perhaps not," she said. "Although I understand that some men do consider a blow job to be a bit of a come-on."

Carolyn stood. "I don't suppose it would do any good for me to say, 'Fuck you four times,' would it?"

Lily smiled. "I don't know. What good did you expect it to do the first three times?"

"Make you leave," Carolyn said.

"I thought you wanted me to stay and clean up the mess I made."

Carolyn went to the utility closet. "Do I contradict myself?" she asked. "Very well, then, I contradict myself. I am vast; I contain Walt Whitman." She opened the closet and brought out a broom and dustpan. "Here," she said, thrusting them toward Lily. "Go wild."

Lily took them from her. "I don't think you really want me to do that. When I go wild, the earth shudders and men fall to their knees bleeding."

Carolyn sneered. "How nice. You sweep in here, and I'll straighten up the other room."

"I fear that you don't want to be near me," Lily said.

"Good guess." Carolyn started for the door to the shop.

"And I also fear," Lily said, "that you hate me."

Carolyn stopped at the door and turned around. She and Lily stared at each other as if it were a contest to see who would blink first.

"Why shouldn't I hate you?" Carolyn asked. "You're superhuman, right? I mean, when you took off your shirt, I saw that your breasts are perfect. Well, mine aren't bad—but I'm thirty-seven years old, and I can tell they're starting to head south. I'm also getting lines at the corners of my eyes and mouth, and it's getting harder and harder to exercise enough to keep from getting fat. So I'm guessing that a few years from now, my breasts will be obscuring my belly button, my face will look like a road map, and my ass will show up on satellite photos. And a few years after that, I'll die."

She sneered again. "But you? You'll always look just as good as you do now, won't you? Ten or fifty or a thousand years from now, you'll still be flying down from Bumfuck, Jupiter, and taking any man you want, won't you?"

Lily stood with the broom in one hand and the dustpan in the other. She looked almost vulnerable. "I don't know," she said. "I've been the way I am for as long as I can remember, but I don't know whether it will last forever. I used to think it would. But now I'm not so sure."

Carolyn wasn't going to let herself be suckered into feeling sorry for Lily. She gestured at the floor. "Look, this place isn't going to sweep itself. If you insist, I'll force myself to stay in the same room. But get to work."

Lily set the dustpan on the floor and began sweeping. She was awkward at the chore, and Carolyn could tell that it was a new thing for her. Good. Maybe it would give her a backache, and she wouldn't be so quick to flap those wings around.

"That's more like it," Carolyn said, sitting down on the stool at her potter's wheel. "Now, what do you mean you don't know whether you'll stay the same forever? Are you a goddess or aren't you?"

Lily looked miserable. "Yes, but I don't feel the way I used to. You see, these days I find myself worrying about Jack and the people who matter to him. I never used to worry at all. And sometimes I don't like my body. I hate my wings and my feet."

Carolyn looked at Lily's sneakers. "What's wrong with your feet?"

"Never mind," Lily said. "I showed them to Halle last month, and she freaked out."

Carolyn grimaced. So Lily had gone to talk with Halle first. Just as Jack had called Halle first when he'd landed in jail. Just as Stephen had wanted to sleep with Halle first . . . but then, when he couldn't get her, he had settled for oral sex with Carolyn.

Everyone thought of someone else before thinking of her. Even

Artie was thinking of Katy before he thought of her.

"What am I, anyway?" Carolyn muttered. "Chopped liver?"

Lily swept a pile of dirt and trash into the dustpan. "And I don't understand the things people say," she said. "For example: What does chopping a liver have to do with anything? Is it a reference to Prometheus having his liver eaten? And even if it is, what does that have to do with making love?"

Carolyn was exasperated. "Why do you assume that everything a person says has to do with sex?"

"Because it always has," Lily said. She sounded petulant. "And it always should."

"I see," Carolyn said. "You're saying that because sex is what *you've* always been about, it's what *everything* should be about. It should be the most important thing in the world."

Lily's eyes brightened. "Yes," she said.

Carolyn opened her mouth to say something sharp to burst Lily's bubble. She had just counted the receipts for a lousy day. On a day like today she worried about whether she could keep the shop or pay the mortgage on her house, not about whether she would have an orgasm that evening. Maybe a goddess who showed up on the planet only once a month could afford to think that everything in life was about sex, but that wasn't true of someone who had to deal with car payments, dental bills, and a next-door neighbor who stole her newspaper every morning. Carolyn had a lot more than just sex on her mind, and so did everyone else. Lily ought to be told that.

But Carolyn closed her mouth and said nothing.

After all, despite everything else, she had managed to find time to suck off a friend's husband that morning. It would be hard to argue with Lily's assessment of human concerns with that particular fact still fresh and throbbing in her forebrain.

Lily picked up the overflowing dustpan. "Where should I put this?"

"Wastebasket by the back door," Carolyn said, but even as she spoke, she looked at the wastebasket and saw that it was overflowing too. She was lousy at cleaning up after herself. For a while she'd had a part-time employee who had done the cleaning up . . . but he had quit two weeks ago to take a higher-paying job as a busboy.

Carolyn groaned and stood. "Come on," she said. She went past

Lily to the back door, unlocked it, and took the wastebasket into the alley. Lily followed her. The Moon hadn't yet risen above the buildings lining the alley, so a single sodium lamp on a pole provided the only direct light. It cast a yellow glare over everything and made even Lily's complexion look bad.

There was a trash Dumpster at the end of the alley behind a Chinese restaurant. Carolyn gave the restaurant owner thirty dollars a month to use the Dumpster, and it wasn't worth it. But it was either that or take her trash home with her.

Yeah, sure, she thought. Everything was about sex. Thirty bucks a month to toss floor sweepings into a Dumpster. Sales tax statements and shoplifters. Perpetually clogged drains at home because of that long blond hair of Artie's. Plus laundry, plus bills, plus the fact that Artie never cleaned out the litter box even though he was the one who brought those two goddamn kittens home in the first place. Yeah, they were cute, and yeah, Carolyn would fight to keep them when she and Artie split up . . . but since it had been his idea, he ought to at least be willing to scoop a turd now and then.

Yet despite all of that, she realized, the one thing that bothered her most . . . the one thing that made her temporarily forget everything else . . . was the knowledge that her beautiful golden lover was giving himself to someone else.

So Lily was right. And wrong. And right.

Carolyn emptied the basket into the Dumpster, which smelled of rotten shrimp and moldy wontons, then stepped aside so Lily could empty the dustpan. Lily made a face as she held the dustpan at arm's length over the Dumpster and shook it hard. Dust and crud flew everywhere, most of it missing the Dumpster, and both Carolyn and Lily backed away coughing.

"Why'd you do that?" Carolyn snapped.

"I couldn't help it," Lily said, retching. "That was horrible."

Carolyn gave a short, sardonic laugh. "What, the smell? Of course it was horrible. That's what garbage smells like."

Lily put a hand to her mouth. She really looked sick. "I've never smelled anything like that before."

"Well, then," Carolyn said, "you've just learned a lesson that we mere mortals have to deal with on a daily basis: Life stinks."

Lily lowered her hand. She still looked sick, but there was something else in her eyes too. "Carolyn," she said, "I can only visit you people once a month, and even I know that what you just said was stupid."

Carolyn didn't care. "Doesn't mean it isn't true," she said. She started walking back up the alley toward the shop.

Lily walked beside her. "Perhaps you're right. In recent months I've been wishing that I could visit more often and stay longer, but that awful stink has cleared my head. I see now that I'm lucky to be here so little, and to be able to spend what time I do have on ravishing the one I choose."

Carolyn gave Lily a sidelong glance. In just three sentences, Lily had revealed herself.

"You're doomed," Carolyn said.

Lily looked perplexed. "What do you mean?"

Carolyn stopped at the workroom door and leaned against the wall. A breeze came down the alley and rustled the leaves on the pecan trees. It was the only sound in the world. Even the traffic noise from Burnet was gone. Carolyn and Lily were alone on earth, and Carolyn wondered if that made them both goddesses.

No. Even if they were alone, they were still just people. Both of them. Lily had wings and secret knowledge, but so what? Carolyn could take up hang gliding and gossiping, if she wanted.

"I mean," she said, "that it sounds as if you're trying to convince yourself that what you have is all you really want. But if that was true, you wouldn't have to convince yourself. So it seems that despite the fact that you're a goddess, you've become dissatisfied. And you can trust the voice of experience on this: Once dissatisfaction sets in, you never get rid of it. Because there's always something better than what you've got."

Lily shuddered. "That sounds awful."

"Oh, it is," Carolyn said. "And believe it or not, it's not only sex that does it to us. We want not only our ideal lover, but our ideal house, our ideal automobile, our ideal dining experience, our ideal big-screen TVs, and our ideal bathroom fixtures. Not to mention the respect and admiration of every single person we meet. We mortals are, each and every one of us, selfish and greedy fucks."

"Jack isn't," Lily said.

Carolyn chuckled. "Okay, but that's only because Jack's insane.

In fact, that's probably why he's affected you the way he has. I'll bet every other guy you've put under your spell has been a self-centered asshole with all of his marbles in their usual Chinese-checker holes. Jack, however, is all sweet and vulnerable and crazy, and it's gotten under your flawless milk-white skin. That's why you're talking to me, and to Halle, and to whoever else you're talking to: because you can't figure out what's happened to you without figuring out Jack, and since we're his de facto family, we might give you some clues."

Lily's eyes widened. "Precisely."

Carolyn turned the wastebasket upside down and sat on it. "Well, forget it. The fact that we're his friends doesn't mean we understand him. See, as a supernatural being you may not know this, but we humans are all mysteries to each other. We're alone in our own heads, sentenced to solitary confinement for life. We can pretend to care about those people in Waco getting burned alive, or about the U.S. role in Somalia, or about the destruction of the rain forest, or whatever . . . but when you come right down to it, all that really matters to individual human beings is what affects *them* personally. So we want what we don't have—and we don't want anyone else to take away what we *already* have."

She stopped and took a deep breath. She felt tired now, and a little stupid for having given Lily a lecture. She felt tired, stupid, and old. Sitting on the wastebasket was uncomfortable, and her lower back hurt. She would be thirty-eight next month. Was thirty-eight supposed to feel this creaky and ancient?

"I see," Lily said. She looked tired too. "That explains why you had sexual relations with Stephen even though you had no particular desire for him."

Carolyn found this annoying. Just because Lily was a goddess devoted to sex didn't mean she knew anything about what Carolyn desired or didn't. In this case, she did happen to be right . . . but she might just as easily have been wrong.

"What I do," Carolyn said, "and why I do it—as well as with whom I do it—is none of your business."

Lily gave her a weak smile. "Actually, I think it is. I think I'm responsible for what's happened between you and Stephen. And for whatever else is going to happen as a result. My presence has made you do things that you would not have done if left alone."

Carolyn was beyond annoyed now. She was once again pissed off. Anger—her companion, her weapon, her shield—was back.

"Let's get this one thing straight, Lily," she said, standing. "You don't control me. That's *my* job. It may be a job that I screw up on a regular basis, but it's still not a job that I'll relinquish to you or anyone else. I jumped Stephen because I felt like jumping Stephen. And the reasons why I felt like it are mine and mine alone. You had nothing to do with it."

Lily didn't flinch. "I'm sure that Artie and Katy believe that too."

Carolyn turned her back on Lily then and picked up the wastebasket. Hearing Lily mention Artie's and Katy's names together made her want to die.

"Fuck you four times," she said. "Fuck you four times and get away from me."

"But I haven't finished cleaning your shop," Lily said.

Carolyn opened the door and stepped into the workroom. "I don't care. Go away. Go straight to hell."

Something clattered on the pavement behind her. The noise gave her a jolt, and she dropped the wastebasket and turned back to see what had happened.

The dustpan and Lily's purple blouse lay in the center of the alley. Lily was gone. The pecan trees rustled in the breeze again.

Carolyn stood there a moment, shaken. But she never allowed herself to stay shaken for long.

"Good riddance," she said.

She went back into the alley and picked up the dustpan and blouse. Then, as she started back to the building, she looked up and saw that the full Moon had risen over the roof.

"Just go back where you came from!" she yelled.

Then she went inside to deal with the mess that the goddess had left her.

17

◆

Below the Cliff,
the River Was Black

Below the cliff, the river was black. Jack could see the Moon, the stars, and the rich people's houses shimmering from its surface. Here the river was called Lake Austin, and the wealthy had built fine homes on its banks. Now and then Lake Austin rose and flooded those homes, but Jack doubted that their owners minded too much. The rich didn't mind much of anything, because if anything went wrong, they could pay someone to put it right again. That was the point of being rich.

But up on the bluff called Mount Bonnell, even the commonest man could look down upon those fine homes and contemplate pissing on them. It was unavoidable. Pissing down onto the rich was just one of those thoughts that everyone had and no one could help. Jack was sure of it. It was the first thing he had thought of the first time he had come up here, and he doubted that he was unusual. Anyone would be tempted by the promise of such power, such a lifelong victory. If you pissed on a rich man's roof, he could pay someone to wash it—but he would always know that his roof had been pissed on.

Some of those who climbed Mount Bonnell had probably even tried it, but Jack supposed that they had failed. The height of the cliff made the houses along the water look as if they were just below, just within pissing range . . . but in fact they and the riverbank were at a horizontal distance of forty yards or more. And while Jack had witnessed some prodigious pissing feats in high school and college, he had yet to meet the man who could piss a horizontal distance of forty yards, even if the wind was with him.

Throwing rocks, however, was another matter. It might be possible, with good aim, to chuck a stone that would bounce off or punch through some rich guy's shingles. Jack seemed to remember that several people had done so and had gotten arrested for it. And he was glad that they had. Piss would be memorable but harmless. Rocks, on the other hand, might hurt someone so they couldn't remember anything at all. Jack preferred being memorable, and he thought that everyone else should too.

There were also, he recalled, a number of drunken fraternity pledges who plunged to their deaths here every year or two during some sort of hazing ritual. But they never flew out very far from the cliff face, and had never hurt anyone. Usually they just impaled themselves on a cedar. The worst that one had ever done was crash through the roof of a camper trailer. But no one had been in the trailer at the time, so that had been no big deal, either.

Jack was neither pissing nor chucking rocks tonight—and he had never been drunk enough to join a fraternity—but if the cops happened to find him up here, they would no doubt arrest him anyway. He was sitting on the stone wall at the bluff's highest point, and he was stark naked.

It was, after all, the night of a full Moon. And since he and Lily had agreed to meet in Austin this time, Mount Bonnell had seemed the best choice. He had already discovered that sitting naked on the curb outside his apartment was a bad idea. But the gate to Mount Bonnell Municipal Park was shut at ten o'clock, and the park was patrolled only sporadically after that time. So the odds that he would be arrested here were slimmer than they were down in the city, and the additional height and exposure should make him more visible from above.

But he was sitting in the wrong place, he decided. There was a small shelter house just behind him, and he might be obscured by its roof, since Lily would fly in from the east. He wanted to be sure that he was completely bathed in the light of the Moon for her, and that she would have no trouble spotting him.

So Jack turned away from the river and the rich people's homes, hopped off the wall, and began making his way down the rocky slope to the south. It had been a while since he had been up here, but he remembered a spot on the bluff that was not unlike the Moon itself. It was a barren, exposed slab of limestone above a water treatment plant. He only wished that he could wear his shoes to get there. The slope was treacherous, and the rocks were sharp. But the rules of Lilith-attraction were clear: Nude meant nude. And if you were wearing shoes, you weren't nude. So he left his shoes, along with the rest of his clothes, beside the wall.

He slipped once going down the slope, but managed to grab a spur on a boulder and keep himself from falling. He stayed there for a few moments then, clinging to the rock and breathing hard. He marveled. It was the end of August. He had met Lily at the full Moon the previous November, so this had been the tenth month that he had been smitten with her to the extent that he would climb mountains naked. She could give herself to him only once every lunar cycle . . . yet he was still willing to do anything to make that happen. And the impulse showed no sign of abating.

He understood that this made the rest of the world, his friends included, think he was crazy. And if he had been doing things like this for no reward, he would be able to understand why they felt that way. But to do it for Lily—why, that wasn't crazy.

It was just being in love.

So if no one else could see why he behaved the way he did, that was their problem. He felt sorry for those people, really. Because if they couldn't even imagine themselves behaving likewise, then they would never know what he knew, never feel what he felt. And that meant that a great joy was missing from their lives.

A cool wind blew up the face of the cliff, rushing over Jack and drying the sweat from his skin. August in Austin had been brutal, and September would be just as humid and hot. In Jack's opinion, instead of laws that punished public nudity, there ought to be a law *requiring* people to walk around naked in this kind of weather.

The wind died down, and Jack continued his descent to the limestone plateau at the southern end of the bluff. Once there, he sat down cross-legged and waited. He couldn't help grinning. It was wonderful here. Only a single rusty cable marked the western edge of the plateau, where the cliff dropped down to the rich people. But from his seated position, Jack couldn't see those houses or even the river. He was alone in the center of the sky.

A few miles to the southeast, the electric skyline of Austin cast a golden aura into the hazy night—but even this evidence of civilization didn't make Jack feel less isolated, less free. The buildings and their lights seemed to have nothing to do with the presence of human beings. They were merely part of the natural landscape, thrust up from the earth like Mount Bonnell itself.

Jack was naked, alone, and happy. He knew that Lily would find him.

And so she did. But Jack could tell that something was wrong. He saw her spiraling down from high above, wobbling in flight as if she were exhausted or wounded. He stood, frightened, thinking that she might fall and he might have to catch her. And when she landed on the rock before him, she stumbled and collapsed into his arms. Jack was so stunned that he couldn't even ask her why she was dressed so strangely. Her breasts were bare, and that made sense—but she was also wearing black jeans and sneakers, which made no sense at all.

Lily pressed her face against his chest, and he held her tight. A few feathers drifted down from the sky, and Jack saw then that Lily's wings looked as if they were molting.

"I feel like shit," Lily said.

Jack was so worried and afraid for her that he wasn't even aroused.

"What's happened?" he asked, caressing her left wing. But the caress brushed off two more feathers, so he jerked his hand away.

"Put it back," Lily said, clutching his shoulders. "Put your hand on my wing again."

Jack tried to, but found that he couldn't. "I'm afraid to," he said. "I'm afraid that I'll hurt you."

Lily looked up at him. He could see the Moon in each of her eyes.

"I don't care," she said.

Jack had never seen Lily like this, and he didn't know what to do about it. He didn't think he *could* do anything about it. How could a man save a goddess?

"But I do care," he said. "I wouldn't hurt you for the world."

She gave him a thin smile. "How about for the Moon?"

He touched her lips with his fingers. "You're the Moon," he said. "You're the Moon and the Earth and the stars."

Lily made a gagging noise and pushed away from him. "Please," she said. "I've heard that same crap from mortal men century after century. You ought to be more original."

For the second time, Jack felt himself getting angry at Lily. What was he supposed to be—more clever than any other man since the dawn of time? He couldn't even keep his socks matched, and Lily ought to know it by now.

"Sorry," he said. But he wasn't, and he knew it was obvious.

Lily's face crumpled. "No," she said. Her wings unfolded and wrapped around her torso, hiding her breasts and arms. More feathers dropped away. "I'm the one who should be sorry. That was stupid of me. That was cruel." She hid her face in the V her wings made below her throat.

Jack's anger vanished like smoke, and he pulled Lily close again and began stroking her wings where they sprouted from her back muscles. This time he didn't stop when more feathers fell.

"It's all right," he said, but he knew as he spoke that it wasn't true. Of course it wasn't all right. Whatever it was, it had gone all wrong.

"My fault," Lily said, her voice muffled.

"What is?" Jack asked. "What could possibly be your fault? You're a goddess, remember?"

But she felt vulnerable in his arms, and she had never felt that way to him before. Jack was shocked to realize that at this moment, he seemed to be physically stronger than she was.

"Artie and Katy are my fault," Lily said. "And Carolyn and Stephen. And the fact that Stephen wants Halle. And you're going to hate me for all of it."

Jack was confused. He knew that Stephen had a crush on Halle, but the rest made no sense. "What are you talking about?"

Lily looked up at him again, but this time all he could see in her eyes was darkness. "Your friends are doing things that will hurt them, and it's because of me. So you're going to hate me."

Jack had never heard Lily talk this way before. It just wasn't in the nature of the goddess as he knew her. It was almost as if . . . as if she were only a woman, just as he was only a man.

With that thought, he felt something toward Lily that he had never felt before. Until now, he had desired and worshiped her. And he still did . . . but now there was something else, too:

He wanted to protect her.

Such a thought, such an emotion, had never occurred to him with regard to Lily. Protect a goddess? From what?

But now she seemed different. She *was* different.

"Listen," he said. "In the first place, even if my friends are having problems, it's not the end of the world. It's not as if they haven't dipped their asses in batter and fried themselves up before."

Lily was trembling. "But not because of me."

"You don't know it's because of you," Jack said. "People are perfectly capable of doing stupid things without any help from outside forces. I mean, you can't figure out what they're doing or why from one goddamn minute to the next. One minute they're whispering prayers to the Prince of Peace, the next they're cutting off a nun's fingers and screaming, 'Tell us where the rebels are hiding!' Or one minute they're sure that they'll be happy with one person forever and always, and the next they're off porking someone they just shared a dryer with at the Laundromat. And no matter how many centuries you've been coming down to watch us, I don't think that even you can know what makes us behave that way."

"But that's what I do," Lily said, her voice quavering. "I'm a goddess, Jack."

Jack touched her cheek, and to his surprise it was moist. "I know you are," he said. "But that doesn't mean you can't be wrong."

"No," Lily said, "that's exactly what it means. I admitted to you two months ago that there are things about mortals that I don't understand—but about the things I do understand, I'm always right." She sighed. "I used to think of that as just part of what I am. But now I think maybe it's a curse. Because if I wasn't always right, I might have some hope that . . . that you wouldn't hate me."

"Now, see," Jack said, "that's how I know you're wrong. Because even if you did ruin the lives of people I cared about, I would never hate you." He paused, shaking his head. "Don't you get it, Lily? I'm ass-over-head crazy about you. There's nothing you could ever do that would change that. Once I've started something that big, I can't stop."

"You've stopped before," Lily said.

Jack began to feel a little angry again. "That's not true. I still care for everyone I've ever begun to care for. The relationships may have changed or even ended, but that was always the other person's choice, not mine. And I still feel the same way about them. I could never hate them."

Lily looked away from him. "You hate Natalie," she whispered.

A rod of ice stabbed into Jack's skull and down his spine, freezing him for what might have been an instant or an hour.

Then he broke away from Lily and ran for the river. He had no thought of anything except diving into the water. He would leap out as far as he could so that he would clear the cliff face, the trees, and the rich people's houses, and then he would fall and sink down down down into the cool, slick dark of Lake Austin, far down where he couldn't see anything or touch anything or hear anything and he wouldn't have to worry about anything or anyone ever again.

Instead, he tripped over the rusty cable at the edge of the plateau and tumbled from the cliff, falling toward the tangled branches below. He would be impaled like a drunken frat rat.

But then he was soaring upside down out over the water. He saw the reflections of the Moon and stars, and of his own pale body suspended in the sky. A feather whirled past his face, tickling his cheek, and as he watched it spiral down to the river, he knew that he had done something stupid, and that Lily had saved him. He knew that she had kicked off her shoes and caught him as he fell, because he could feel her talons around his right ankle. His left leg—and everything else—dangled free.

He was chilled now, chilled despite the muggy Texas night, and the last thing he wanted was to be down in that water that looked so dark and cold.

He was grateful to Lily. More so than ever.

She took him back to the wall where he had begun his vigil. She set him down gently, but he was upside down, so the landing was awkward anyway. Jack wound up sprawled on his back looking up at Lily as she sat down on the wall.

He was astonished to see crystal droplets glistening at the corners of her eyes and on her face. He had felt moisture on her cheek a short while ago, but he hadn't understood what that meant until just now.

His goddess was crying. Because of him.

"I'm sorry," he said, getting up to his knees and grasping Lily's hands. "I'm so sorry."

Lily shook her head. Her glossy hair was tangled, and it didn't swirl across her shoulders the way it usually did. Jack had never seen it like this before, and it scared him.

"I'm the one who should be sorry," Lily said.

Jack kissed her talons and ankles. "No," he whispered.

Lily stroked his hair. "Yes," she said.

He looked up at her face. She looked so sad. It was awful.

"A goddess should never be sorry," he said, "because almost by definition, she can do no wrong. That's the point of being a goddess, isn't it?"

She smiled at him then, but he could tell that it wasn't a smile she really felt.

"I used to think so," she said. "Until—"

She cut herself off then, but Jack knew what she had been about to say: "Until I met you."

That knowledge made him feel rotten, guilty . . . and powerful. He didn't want Lily to feel any kind of sadness, yet the realization that he had made her feel that way when no one else ever had was wonderful.

And that in turn made him feel even more rotten and guilty.

When he and Lily had first met, everything in his life had suddenly made sense. But now a terrifying confusion seemed to be trying to return.

And if it did, he might wind up not caring about anything again.

So to keep that from happening, he told Lily the one thing that he knew was true—the one thing that no matter what happened to him, or to his friends, or to the rest of the world, would remain true as long as his brain had enough spark to form a thought.

"I love you," he said.

She nodded, sniffed, and then smiled again. This time, he saw that it was real.

"That's really stupid of you," Lily said.

They stayed there for a few minutes then, Lily on the wall, Jack on his knees before her, and said nothing.

Finally Lily shivered and said, "Could we go to your apartment? Somehow I don't feel like being outside anymore tonight."

Jack stood. "Sure. I'm ready for takeoff when you are."

Lily frowned. "Would it be all right if you drove us? I'd . . . just as soon not fly again until I have to."

"Is it because you're losing some feathers?" Jack asked.

Lily shrugged, and a few more feathers fell away.

Jack picked one up. It was soft and beautiful. "It's natural for you to molt now and then, isn't it?"

"I don't know," Lily said, scooting from the wall to stand beside Jack. "It's never happened before." She shivered again. "Let's go now, okay?"

"You want to get your shoes?"

"No. They're in the river, thanks to you."

So Jack dropped the feather and put his clothes on, and then they walked down the steep concrete stairway to the park entrance. But just as Jack was stepping over the chain that had been strung across the entrance at closing time, a flashlight beam caught him in the face.

"Hold it a minute, sir," a voice behind the flashlight said.

Jack turned to tell Lily that it might be a good idea for her to vanish, she being topless and all. But she had already done so.

The cop came up from the street and said, "You can go ahead and step over the chain, sir."

Jack realized then that his left foot had been suspended above the chain since he had heard the words "Hold it." So now he stepped on over and gave the cop what he hoped was a disarming grin.

"Are you aware that the park closes at ten P.M., sir?" the cop asked.

Jack squinted in the glare of the flashlight. "Yes," he said. "I lost track of time." That was true enough. Once the full Moon rose, he never paid attention to anything but Lily.

Just then, something flew from the trees and flapped away, passing right over the cop's head. The rush of air blew the cop's hat off, and Jack caught it.

"Mary Mother of— Jeez!" the cop yelled, spinning around and searching the night with his flashlight. "What in hell was that?"

Jack stepped up to the cop and held out the hat. "I think it was an owl," he said.

The cop swept the flashlight beam back and forth, but found nothing. "An owl? I've never seen any owls around here. And owls don't get that damn big anyway."

Jack almost laughed. This guy didn't know shit from Shinola about nocturnal birds of prey.

"There are owls everywhere, Officer," Jack said. "We don't often see them because they're only active at night. But they're big and powerful. Bigger and more powerful than people think. And they're here all the time."

The cop lowered his flashlight and took his hat back. "Park closes at ten," he said. "Just a warning this time. But if I catch you again, you'll have to pay a fine."

Jack nodded. "I understand. Thank you, Officer."

The cop grunted. "Now get on about your business."

Jack went on about his business, walking down the street a few dozen yards to where his postal jeep was parked. He glanced back when he reached it and saw the cop's flashlight beam heading up the steps and into the trees.

"Close call?" Lily asked.

Jack jumped, startled. Lily grinned down at him from the roof of the jeep.

"You scared the crap out of me," he said.

"Ah," Lily said. "That would explain the smell."

They got into the jeep then, and Jack fastened Lily's seat belt around her hips.

"What's this for?" she asked.

Jack gave her a sidelong look. His heart was still pounding from the start she'd given him.

"You've never ridden with me before, have you?" he asked.

"I've never ridden with anyone before," she said.

Jack started the jeep, which chugged and clattered to semi-life. "Hang on, then," he said.

When they got to Jack's apartment, Lily went to the bathroom and threw up. It was, she told him afterward, yet one more thing that she had never experienced before getting involved with him.

Then Jack took off his clothes, and they discovered that he'd gotten a few scrapes and bruises when he'd tripped over the cable and fallen off Mount Bonnell. So Lily kissed his wounds, and by morning he was healed.

PART X

HARVEST MOON

Thursday, September 30, 1993

◆

18

◆

"He's Naked Again"

He's naked again," Katy called out as she hung up the kitchen phone.

Stephen didn't respond, so she went looking for him and found him slumped on the couch in the living room, watching *Seinfeld*. His posture was troubling. Stephen was not a slumper. Right now, though, he looked as if he were paralyzed in that position.

"Uh?" he said without looking away from the tube.

It was a grunt. A groan. Not even a complete "Huh?" Just half a guttural syllable to acknowledge the fact that his wife had spoken.

Katy pressed her fingertips against her forehead. "I said, Jack's naked again. He's been arrested."

Stephen looked up at her now. His eyes were as dull as an old dog's.

"Bummer," he said. *Seinfeld*'s laugh track blared.

Katy was lost. She had feared for weeks now that Stephen knew about Artie . . . or at least that she was having an affair. Now she was almost sure of it. He was punishing her for something, anyway.

More than once, she had told herself that by sleeping with Artie, she might actually be doing Stephen and their marriage some good. If Stephen realized what was happening, she had reasoned, it might shock him into better behavior. It might make him fight for her.

What a stupid excuse. If Stephen did know, the knowledge had done nothing like make him fight for her. Instead, it had made him give up. It had made him drown her out with the television.

"Could you turn that down, please?" she asked.

He looked back at the tube and pointed the remote control at it. The laugh track grew louder.

"Why?" Stephen asked.

Katy glared at him. He was supposed to love her. He was supposed to want her. He was supposed to go out of his mind with rage if he thought she was doing it with someone else.

"Because it's bothering me," she said. "If it wasn't bothering me, I wouldn't ask you to turn it down." She closed her eyes and took a deep breath. She couldn't fix her marriage right now. She had to deal with the problem at hand. "But it's not so much that it's bothering me. It's that Jack's in jail, and we don't have time to watch TV."

Stephen grimaced and pointed the remote control again. The TV shut off with a snap of static, and the air in the living room fell so dead that Katy almost wanted the laugh track to return. In the silence, Stephen was regarding her with an indifferent stare.

"I'm sorry," she said, trying to get through to him from another angle. "I know you're having a rough week, but we've got a crisis. Jack needs us."

Stephen gave a short laugh. "What you mean we, paleface? Maybe he needs *you*, but I don't see what that has to do with me."

Katy was taken aback. Even if Stephen did suspect that she was having an affair, he had to know that it wasn't with Jack. Jack made love only to goddesses these days.

"It has to do with both of us," Katy said, "because we're both his friends."

Stephen seemed to sink deeper into the couch. He was slumped so far now that his neck was at right angles to the rest of his spine. It looked painful.

"I'm not his friend," Stephen said. His voice was bitter. "I'm just the husband of one of his former lovers."

It was as if he had slugged Katy with a wet sandbag.

In a dizzying flash, she saw herself in a ramshackle house on Avenue F, living in the back bedroom with Jack.

She saw herself killing hundreds of cockroaches.

She saw herself laughing a lot.

She saw herself cheating on Jack with David McIlhenney, then sticking her finger down her throat afterward.

But all of that had been dead and gone before she'd ever met Stephen. None of it had anything to do with him, or with their relationship, or with whether or not he ought to be Jack's friend.

Which was why she had never told him about any of it.

Or at least that was why she had told herself that she'd never told him about any of it.

Katy tried to compose herself. This was no time to get emotional over the past. This was no time to get emotional over anything. She was facing an immediate problem, and problems were never solved by knee-jerk emotions. Problems were solved by maintaining composure, breaking the problems into their component pieces, and then dealing with each piece in turn.

Piece one was to get Stephen off the couch.

So Katy sat down cross-legged on the floor in preparation for a brief siege. The brown carpet felt grungy under her bare legs—she had changed into shorts and a T-shirt when she'd gotten home—and she wished that Stephen would run the vacuum cleaner now and then. He had a more flexible schedule than she did, so why was she always the one who did the cleaning?

But that, she reminded herself, wasn't the problem she was supposed to be dealing with right now.

"All right, then," she said. "We don't have time for this, but—all right. Who told you about me and Jack?"

Stephen turned toward the TV and stared at the blank screen. "The point is that it should have been you."

"And just when should I have done this?" Katy asked. "Before you met Jack? Should I have said, 'By the way, honey, this guy I'm going to introduce you to—I used to live with him. Is that okay with you?' "

Stephen kept his eyes focused on the TV. "Something like that. That's the sort of thing that someone you're going to marry has a right to know, don't you think? Particularly if the former lover in question is going to require as much babysitting as Jack does."

Katy tried not to get angry. Anger, after all, was a knee-jerk emotion. But that was a difficult fact to remember when Stephen was behaving like a prick.

"I'm sorry that I couldn't see the future," she said. "But I had no way of knowing that Jack would lose Natalie, or that we would wind up 'babysitting' him. But what else can we do? After all, he would still be my friend regardless of whether anything else had ever happened between us."

"Well," Stephen muttered, "he wouldn't necessarily be mine."

Katy fired right back. "Then perhaps that's why I've never told you about my brief time with him. I couldn't kick him out of my life, yet I wanted you in it. So perhaps I feared that if I told you, I might lose you. Besides, what did it matter? It was in the past. The present and future are all I care about."

Stephen looked at her again, and this time his eyes weren't just dull. This time they looked small, hard, and hateful.

Katy shuddered. She had never seen an expression on Stephen's face that looked anything like this. She wanted to get up and run out of the house, but she couldn't move.

"The present and future," Stephen said in a cold voice that mocked Katy's, "are built on the foundation of the past. So perhaps the reason our present is so difficult, and our future so dubious, is because I didn't know enough about the foundation I was trying to build on."

Katy was terrified. She tried to control that sensation, to keep it at a distance where she could analyze it and plan a course of action—but it was too powerful.

"Is our future dubious?" she asked. She couldn't keep her voice from quavering, and she hated herself for that weakness.

But as she spoke, the hardness in Stephen's eyes cracked, melted, and was gone. He still looked unhappy, but at least he resembled himself again. He didn't look like a hateful stranger anymore.

"I don't know," he said. "The way things have been lately . . ."

His voice trailed off. He didn't explain what he meant. But he didn't have to.

He knew, Katy thought. He knew what she had been doing, and he believed it meant that she wanted to leave him.

Except that it didn't. Katy wasn't at all sure what it did mean, but it didn't mean that.

"We're just going through a rough patch," she said. "Everyone goes through those." She hesitated. "At any rate, I'm sorry I've never told you about me and Jack. But I really didn't think it mattered."

Stephen pushed himself up to a sitting position and rubbed the back of his neck. "Forget it. Come to think of it, I haven't told you everything about my past, either."

Katy began to breathe easier. She was beginning to think that she and Stephen might survive as a married couple for another day or two. Maybe.

"So," she asked, trying to lighten the mood, "what old lovers have *you* failed to mention?"

Stephen's face reddened, and Katy was delighted. She hadn't seen him blush in a long time.

"I didn't have anyone before you," he said. "You know that." He sounded bitter again.

So Katy tried to tease him past the moment. "But dear, you just hinted at dark secrets," she said, extending a foot and nudging his. "What else could they be?"

Stephen pulled his foot away. "Only one comes to mind. When I was ten years old, a girl was pestering me, so I picked up a river rock and told her that if she didn't go away, I'd hit her with it. She didn't believe me, so I took a swing at her. I meant to miss, of course, but I didn't. Instead, I conked her in the forehead and gave her a lump the size of a Ping-Pong ball. I've felt awful about it ever since."

"Oh my!" Katy said, feigning shock. "Childhood mayhem. Dark secrets, indeed. Just what did the poor knot-headed girl do to pester you, anyway?"

Stephen made a wry face.

"Basically," he said, "what you've been doing every minute since I met you."

Katy bit her lip and stood. "Well then," she said, "I shall endeavor to stay out of range."

Stephen stood as well. "You seem to have managed so far. Which car are we taking?"

❖

They reached the Municipal Court building a few minutes after nine. The Moon hung low over the I-35 overpass, and the sight of it gave Katy a chill. Yesterday evening she had seen that Moon over Artie's shoulder as he had made love to her in the backseat of her Toyota.

Things had been exciting at first but had ended uncomfortably as they bumped their heads, knees, and elbows against the windows and door handles. The Toyota wasn't built for sex. Artie hadn't seemed to mind, but Katy had wished that she'd just done as he'd asked and gone to a motel with him. As it was, she would have to wear long-sleeved blouses for at least a week so no one at work would notice the bruises on her arms.

Keeping those bruises hidden from Stephen didn't seem to present much of a problem, though. He had hardly been looking at her these days, much less touching her.

Stephen had been watching TV—of course—when Artie had called her to say that he wanted to see her. Carolyn was working late at her shop, so . . .

Katy had been furious that Artie had called her at home while Stephen was there, but even within that fury, she had known that she would go to him. After hanging up, she had told Stephen that she was going out to gas up the car so she wouldn't have to do it in the morning.

Stephen hadn't even acknowledged that she had spoken to him.

She had gone to Artie then, and they had driven to a secluded road south of the city and done it fast and cramped. Artie had wanted to either stay at his and Carolyn's place or go to a motel, but Katy had vetoed both suggestions. Carolyn might come home unexpectedly. And going to a motel seemed sleazy.

Not that doing it in a Toyota on a dirt road *wasn't* sleazy. But at least it hadn't cost anything. And on the way home, she really had filled the tank with gas. So technically she hadn't lied to Stephen.

It wasn't much of a moral victory, but it was all she had. And it was enough. Stephen would deserve better only when he began behaving as if he gave a damn about her.

In the meantime, she had someone young and beautiful who gave her terrific pleasure. Sometimes. For brief moments. But wasn't that the best that anyone ever had?

It was certainly better than what she'd been getting from her husband.

But as Katy and Stephen left the parking lot under the overpass and crossed the I-35 access road to the Municipal Court, Stephen did something unexpected:

He took her hand.

Katy was astonished. She couldn't remember the last time Stephen had held her hand in public. Or in private, for that matter.

His hand was moist. Austin hadn't yet escaped its summer heat and humidity, and even now that the sun had set, Stephen was perspiring. That had been one of the first things Katy had noticed when they'd started dating: He sweated a lot. The first time they'd gone to bed together, his skin had been slick, and she had tasted salt for hours afterward. To her surprise, she had liked it.

All of that came back to her now as he took her hand, lacing his fingers in between hers, pressing his damp skin against her own dry palm. Squeezing.

The pressure was slight. But it rippled into Katy's wrist and arm, the wave growing as it flowed upward through bone and blood. And then it washed into her shoulders and chest, and she trembled.

"You okay?" Stephen asked as they stepped onto the curb.

Katy looked up at his pale, sweat-pimpled face, at his thick glasses, receding hairline, and almost nonexistent chin. At the odd angle his neck and throat made. At his Adam's apple rising and falling.

He looked back down at her, and his eyes were a pale, watery blue behind his glasses. They were huge.

Katy nodded, giving him a silent answer. Yes, of course I'm okay, the nod said. Why wouldn't I be?

She didn't want to speak because she was afraid of what she might blurt out. She was afraid she might spontaneously confess. Because when he had taken her hand, and she had looked at his face, she had realized that she loved him.

It was not what Katy wanted to realize just now.

She was still bruised and sore from her tryst with Artie the night before. And right now there was the problem of Jack to deal with. The last thing she needed to be reminded of was that Stephen was the most important thing in the world to her.

Keeping her mouth shut wasn't like her, and she was afraid that Stephen would notice—but it was better than bursting into tears and begging forgiveness. Besides, she had burst into tears only once or twice in her entire life, and she had never begged forgiveness. This was no time to start.

So she just nodded, and Stephen didn't ask why she didn't speak. He seemed about to, but then the sound of squealing children took his attention away from her, and Katy was glad.

Except that he also pulled his hand away.

Then Katy saw Cleo and Tony come bounding down the Municipal Court building's steps so fast that she was afraid they would fall and break their teeth on the sidewalk. Halle was nowhere in sight.

"Aunt Katy!" Cleo screamed happily.

It gave Katy a thrill, and she squatted to catch Cleo in a hug. Holding that tight little body made her feel fierce and strong. "Hey, you!" she said, breathing in the scent of Cleo's hair. It smelled of baby shampoo. "What's it like to be nine years old?"

Cleo pushed away from Katy and rolled her eyes. "Everybody asks that," she said. "But it's just like being eight. And I'm still in the stupid fourth grade, so what good was having a birthday?"

Tony grabbed Katy's hand. "I'm going to be seven in November," he said, "and then I'm going to change my name to Barney and move to San Francesca, California, to be a professional dinosaur in the movies."

Cleo rolled her eyes again. "It's called San Francisco, retard. And you can't change your name unless Mom says you can. But even if you do, you'll still be a moron and you'll still only be in second grade."

Katy stood, taking Cleo's hand in her free one. "Where is your mom, by the way?"

Tony pointed back at the building's doors. "She's talking to the cops and to some guy who knows Jesus."

Cleo frowned. Katy could see that the girl was trying to look grown-up, and she wanted to tell her not to be in such a hurry. Growing up did get one out of the fourth grade, but that was all that it had to recommend it. At least that was all that Katy could think of right now.

"Mom doesn't like the Jesus guy," Cleo said. "She called him some of the words I'm not allowed to say."

"She called him a limp dick," Tony said.

Cleo sneered at her brother. "I'm telling Mom you said that."

Tony looked indignant. "But Mom said it first!"

Katy was exhilarated. She loved the energy that crackled between the kids. She wanted to scoop them up and take them home with her. Halle was no doubt an adequate mother . . . but Katy would be a better one. For one thing, she wouldn't let any children of hers run out into the night by themselves.

Stephen coughed and took a step toward the building. "Um, Katy, maybe you could stay out here with these guys," he said. "It can't be much fun for them inside. That's probably why Halle sent them out. She must have seen us coming. I'll go see what's happening."

Katy had an immediate reaction against that idea. She didn't want Stephen going into the building without her. But she didn't know why, and she couldn't think of any legitimate reason why she shouldn't wait here with the kids.

"All right, fine," Katy said, trying to make it clear with her tone of voice that it wasn't fine at all.

"Good," Cleo said. "It smells bad in there."

"Only because somebody puked," Tony explained.

Stephen gave a polite chuckle, as if he were responding to a bad joke at a cocktail party. It annoyed Katy.

Tony seemed puzzled. "They really did," he said. "The puke was right there on the floor. Mom kept telling me not to step in it."

"But you did anyway," Cleo said. "You have puke on your shoes. I'm going to call you Pukefoot."

"You better not!" Tony hollered.

Katy decided it was time for tactful intervention. "Actually, Cleo, *puke* isn't a very nice word."

Cleo frowned again. "Well, what is, then?"

"How about *barf?*" Stephen suggested, smiling.

Katy gave him a sharp glance. "I thought you were going inside."

Stephen's smile faded. "So I was." He turned away and went up the steps.

"Don't step in the barf!" Tony called after him.

Stephen pulled open one of the smoked glass doors and went inside without looking back.

Katy tried to be glad that he was gone. "So, you two," she said, "what shall we do while we're waiting?"

Cleo let go of Katy's hand, reached into her jeans pocket, and pulled out a red rubber ball along with a number of six-pointed red, blue, gold, and silver metallic stars. They gleamed in the mingled bluish and white glows of the mercury-vapor streetlamps and the Moon.

"We can play jacks," Cleo said. "Mom taught me how."

Katy had a pang of jealousy, and she hated it. "Jacks sound like fun," she said, trying to sound anything but jealous. Jealousy was not one of the states of mind she allowed herself. "We can sit here on the bottom step and play on the next step up."

Tony pulled his hand from Katy's, crossed his arms, and scowled. "Jacks are stupid," he said. "I want to play Nintendo. Or Sega."

Katy sat down on the bottom step. "I'm sorry, Tony," she said, "but I can't think of a way we can play video games out here."

"Yeah, dip," Cleo said, sitting down beside Katy and spilling the jacks from her hand onto the second step.

"Well, if I can't play Sega," Tony said, "then I want to roll drunks."

Katy stared at him. "Where on earth did you get such an awful idea?"

Tony looked wounded. "From Uncle Artie. He says that a bunch of drunks live near the jail, and that you can roll them."

Something tightened inside Katy's chest. She hadn't expected to hear Artie's name. And she didn't like knowing that he was telling children it was fun to assault derelicts. He was her lover, and he wasn't supposed to do things like that.

Even as she had that thought, she chastised herself for it. She knew perfectly well that she wasn't having an affair with Artie because he was a good person. She was having an affair with Artie because he was good at it.

"Tony," she said, "do you know what rolling a drunk really means?"

Tony nodded. "You give them a push and they go like Sonic the Hedgehog."

"I'll start," Cleo said, ignoring the whole conversation about rolling drunks. "First you bounce the ball and pick up one jack, then catch the ball in the same hand before it bounces again. That's called onesies." She bounced the ball, scooped up a jack, caught the ball, and then handed it to Katy.

Katy played onesies successfully and returned the ball to Cleo before speaking to Tony again. "They don't really go like Sonic," she said. "They're just people, not video games, and if you push them, they can get hurt. Now, does that still sound like fun?"

Tony squinched up his face. He was clearly thinking hard. "Not so much, I guess," he said after a few moments.

"Twosies," Cleo said, and did it. "Hah! Eat hot six-pointed death, Aunt Katy." She handed the ball to Katy again.

Katy was feeling a bit flummoxed. Cleo and Tony were revealing violent streaks that she found disturbing. She would have to have a stern talk with Artie . . . and with Halle, too, perhaps.

"Come on," Cleo said. "You're not chicken to do twosies, are you?"

So Katy bounced the ball and scooped up two jacks—but one of them popped out between her thumb and forefinger and went skittering off the steps, across the sidewalk, and into Seventh Street. A taxicab heading toward the interstate access road ran over it, and it disappeared.

"Where'd it go?" Cleo asked, staring at the spot where the jack had vanished.

"It must have gotten caught in the tire tread," Katy said, watching the taxi as it turned onto the access road and headed south. A blue spark flashed from its right rear tire, and then it was gone.

"I want it back!" Cleo yelled, standing up as if to chase after the car.

Katy caught her arm. "I'm sorry, honey. It's lost. But we can still play. You have plenty left."

Cleo pulled her arm away, sat back down, and put her face between her fists. "It's not the same," she said.

Tony stuck out his tongue and made a wet, flatulent-sounding noise. "What a big sissy barf," he said.

Cleo drew a fist back as if she was about to punch him, so Katy put a hand on each child's head to hold them apart. But just as she did so, the children forgot about each other and looked up at the building's doors. Katy hadn't heard a thing, but she turned to look too.

A dark-haired man in a business suit came outside and stomped down the steps. He had a foul look in his eyes, and his mouth was twisted as if he had been eating dairy products past their expiration dates. He came down past Katy and the children without looking at them, and he almost stepped on Tony.

"Excuse us," Katy said icily. But the man ignored her. He continued stomping eastward up the sidewalk, then crossed the I-35 access road to the city parking lot.

Cleo pointed after him. "That's the man Mom called a limp dick."

"I'm gonna tell her you said that," Tony said.

"Shut up, Pukefoot."

Katy shushed them. "You should be nicer to each other," she said, but without much conviction. She was still watching the man in the business suit.

Then she remembered that Tony had said Halle had been talking to "some guy who knows Jesus." And she realized who the man was. His name was Leonard Deacon, and for several years he had been in and out of the local news because of his ongoing crusade to rid Austin of pornography—or for that matter, of any films, videos, signs, commercials, comics, matchbooks, and mud flaps that contained any hint of anything that smacked of sex. To this end, Deacon kept notebooks and tapes of all such material that he discovered, and he brought them out to show to reporters and city officials whenever possible.

It had always struck Katy as ironic that the most adamant antipornographer in town owned what was probably the largest collection of smut in Texas.

As Katy watched, Leonard Deacon stomped to a beige Lincoln Town Car and unlocked the driver's-side door. But before he could get inside, a figure emerged from the shadow of the nearest overpass pillar and spoke to him.

Katy was too far away to hear what the figure said. And because Deacon was partly in the way, she couldn't see the figure clearly enough to know whether it was a man or a woman. Whoever it was, though, seemed to be wearing a long coat despite the fact that the night was warm and muggy.

Then Deacon took a few steps backward, and the figure's coat opened. Katy saw now that the figure was a slender woman with long dark hair and impressive breasts. Katy could tell that her breasts were impressive because except for the coat, the woman was naked.

"Look!" Katy said, pointing to the sky in an attempt to distract the children. "A shooting star!"

"Look!" Tony said. "Boobs!"

"Mom's are bigger," Cleo said. She sounded bored.

The bare-breasted woman in the parking lot took a step toward Leonard Deacon, and as her face caught more moonlight, Katy remembered her. She was the woman who had come to Jack's Zilker Clubhouse "lecture" in February.

She was Lilith. Or, as Jack called her, Lily.

Leonard Deacon moved into the shadow of the overpass pillar then, and Lily went with him. As she did so, her "coat" spread out from her shoulders and became two black-and-white wings. And then she became invisible, swallowed up by the shadow.

Katy heard a buzzing noise inside her skull. It was as if she'd been dropped on her head.

"It was the where-bird!" Tony exclaimed.

"She wasn't wearing anything on the bottom, either," Cleo said. "Did you see the size of her butt?"

Katy was dry-mouthed and shaky. She had seen the wings. There was no way around it:

Jack was not crazy.

Or if he was, then so were Cleo and Tony.

And so was she.

But considering the kind of life she had been living since June, should that be any big surprise?

Traffic whizzed by on the overpass, the access road, and Seventh Street. Stoplights changed from green to amber to red. A few blocks away, a siren shrieked, and as it faded away, Katy could hear hints of the drums and guitars that were blasting away in the clubs on Sixth Street. The air was soupy, and the concrete was hard and gritty under her rump. Everything around her indicated that the world was exactly as she knew it to be. She hadn't fallen down a rabbit hole, stepped through a mirror, or ingested a psychedelic drug. She wasn't crazy. Everything was real and right.

So that meant that the woman with wings must be real and right too.

A hand closed on her shoulder, and she yelped.

"I'm sorry," Stephen said. He was standing above and behind her. "Didn't you hear me?"

Katy tried to calm her hammering heart. "No, I, I—" She shook herself and stood, turning to face Stephen. "I was distracted. There was quite a display under the overpass just now."

"A naked lady and a limp dick," Tony said.

Stephen looked as if he'd just been smacked across the bridge of his nose with a crowbar. His mouth opened, but he didn't say anything. He stared at Tony.

At that moment, one of the doors behind him opened, and Halle came outside. She was stomping almost as angrily as Leonard Deacon had. Cleo and Tony ran up to meet her and then came down with her, holding her hands.

Halle was so lucky, Katy thought. Halle always knew that there were at least two people in the world who loved her every minute of every day.

"I swear to God," Halle said as she came to a stop beside Stephen. "The world is full of schmucks and cops. Those are the only two kinds of people there are, I'm telling you. Schmucks who complain to cops, and cops who fall all over themselves to do what the schmucks tell them. Somebody please tell me there's a country somewhere that isn't run by schmucks and cops, and I will stuff my kids and my computer into the Plymouth and get the fuck out of here."

"I take it that things aren't going well," Katy said.

Stephen shook his head. "Not for Jack. As I understand it, he was caught up on Mount Bonnell doing what he tends to do at the full Moon. The bad news is that the person who spotted him and made the complaint was Leonard Deacon. And he won't back off from it." Stephen glanced at the kids, then stepped down and whispered in Katy's ear. "He claims that Jack was masturbating."

Katy was immediately angry. "That's got to be a lie," she said. "Jack doesn't do that. He doesn't like it. I remember one time he—"

She stopped herself. The expression on Stephen's face might have been shock, disappointment, misery, or all three. Katy had spoken without thinking. The scene between Lily and Deacon had rattled her.

"This is all my fault," Halle said. "I've been so preoccupied with my own personal crap these past few months that I just gave Jack a key to the cabin and told him he could go there on his own. But apparently he decided to stay in town instead. I should have made sure he went."

"It's not just your fault," Stephen said. "The rest of us haven't been keeping a constant eye on Jack, either." He paused, taking an audible breath. "Look, I know he had some counseling after he was arrested last winter, but it's clear that he needs more. Something long-term. And if we keep on trying to babysit him ourselves, we might actually be preventing him from getting the care he really needs."

Katy wanted to slap Stephen. What he was suggesting was rotten, all the more so because Katy didn't think for a second that he really meant it. He was speaking out of pettiness, not genuine concern.

"And where has his family been while all this has been going on?" Stephen asked. "Jack does have relatives somewhere, doesn't he?"

In that moment, Katy decided that she was glad she was cheating on Stephen. He deserved it.

"His mother's dead," Halle said. She sounded a little pissed off herself. "His father's still alive, but he lives in South America. Venezuela, I think. He went down there for some oil company, got married, and has a whole new family. Jack invited him to his and Natalie's wedding, but the guy just sent a card. No letter or gift, just a cheesy card with a squiggle that might have been a signature."

"There was also a brother," Katy said. "But I don't know where. Do you, Halle?"

Halle shook her head. "Nope. So as far as genuine family goes, Natalie was it. And now that she's gone, I guess that leaves us."

Katy gave Stephen a cold stare. "Sorry if that's a burden, honey."

Stephen's lips twitched. "That's not what I meant. I only meant that if Jack needs serious therapy, maybe we're not the best people in the world to be giving it."

Katy didn't like the implications of that. It was the sort of thing someone might say as a joke, but Stephen's tone made it clear that he wasn't joking at all. It demanded a response, but Katy refrained for the time being. She didn't want to make a scene in front of Cleo and Tony.

Halle, however, didn't seem to have any such concern. "Jesus, Steve," she said. "Are you saying that all of Jack's friends are as fucked up as he is? Or that we'll fuck him up even more?"

"Mom!" Cleo said, tugging on Halle's arm. "Language."

Halle smiled at Cleo. "Sorry, sweetie. Mom forgets herself sometimes." Then she looked at Stephen, and the smile vanished. "So which is it?"

Stephen didn't reply right away, and Katy studied his face as he looked at Halle. And she saw something there she didn't understand. It was something about the way the lines at the corners of his eyes seemed to deepen. She couldn't even see the eyes themselves, because a streetlight was being reflected in Stephen's glasses. But the lines around his eyes, and the muscles in his cheeks—she could see those. The muscles were tight, but not the way they were when he was angry.

Katy didn't know what it meant. But she didn't like it. It made her feel the way she had felt a few moments before when Cleo and Tony had run up to Halle and taken her hands in theirs.

"I think that in some ways," Stephen said then, his voice quiet, "the rest of us are *more* psychologically confused than Jack is. After all—" Stephen looked eastward, and now it was the full Moon that was reflected in his glasses. "—at least Jack knows what he wants."

Halle made a snorting noise. "And the rest of us don't? Speak for yourself, Steve."

"I am," he said.

Those two words and the way he said them made everything clear. Katy knew now why Stephen looked the way he did. She knew what he wanted.

He wanted Halle.

And that was wrong. That was so wrong. Halle wasn't better than she was, not in any respect. She wasn't smarter. She wasn't prettier, kinder, or wiser. She wasn't even as good a mother as Katy would be, given the chance.

If Stephen were going to want someone else, why couldn't he at least want someone who was her superior in some way? Someone like Carolyn, for example. She could deal with that. Sympathize, even. Physical desire was something she could understand.

She wanted nothing more right now than to go find Artie and let him have her in the backseat of her Toyota again. She wouldn't mind the bruises.

"Look!" Tony said, pointing toward I-35. "The limp dick's coming back!"

Katy looked, thankful for a reason to turn away from Stephen and

Halle, and saw that Tony was right. Leonard Deacon was crossing the access road and coming toward them. His hair had gone wild, and he was chewing on the end of his necktie. He was walking as if he had been riding a bicycle for twelve hours.

Halle whistled. "Boy, Lenny looks like shit."

"Mom!" Cleo said, stamping her foot.

"Well, sorry, sweetie," Halle said. "But he does."

Leonard Deacon stopped in front of them and wobbled. His eyes looked like hard-boiled eggs.

"I must offer an apology," he said to Halle. His words were muffled because he was still chewing on his necktie. "I was mistaken in what I thought I saw on Mount Bonnell tonight. It must have been a trick of the moonlight. I am therefore going inside to withdraw my complaint and to beg the forgiveness of the good people of Austin. Praise the Lord."

With that, he stumbled around Katy, Stephen, Halle, and the children, climbed the steps in an uncertain zigzag, and went into the Municipal Court building.

Katy stared after him. She wanted to believe that he was drunk or stoned, but she knew better.

Lily had done something to him.

And that was good, because if Leonard Deacon really did withdraw his complaint, Jack would be released. But it was unsettling too. Because now Katy remembered the odd telephone call she had gotten in June, on the day that she had started her affair with Artie . . .

Lily had the power to make people do what they would not do otherwise. Leonard Deacon's about-face had just now proven that.

And if Lily could do it to him, why not to Katy? Or Artie? Or any of them?

Katy was glad that Lily was helping Jack, but despite that, she decided that she didn't like her at all.

This time she and Stephen went inside while Halle and the kids waited outside, and after a confusing half hour during which Leonard Deacon not only withdrew his complaint but also sang "Bess, You Is My Woman Now" in its entirety, Jack was released. Katy was relieved to see that he was fully dressed.

"I was afraid you'd strip in your cell," she whispered to him as they went outside.

Jack looked at her as if she were nuts. "What good would that have done?" he asked. "There's no moonlight back there."

Then, as Katy, Stephen, and Jack joined Halle and the kids, Carolyn's Honda came up Seventh Street and stopped at the curb in front of them. Artie waved from the passenger seat while Carolyn got out and smacked the car roof with an open hand.

"Goddamn it!" she said. "Did I miss everything again?"

"I called you first this time," Jack said. "Really, I did. But you weren't home."

Carolyn gave an exasperated growl. "The first time in ages that Artie and I go out for dinner, and of course that's the night that more poop hits the fan."

Despite herself, Katy experienced another stab of jealousy. It was ironic that it should happen just as Carolyn arrived, because jealousy was one of the hallmarks of Carolyn's character, not hers. But for now, Katy couldn't escape it. Halle's kids liked Halle better than they liked her; Stephen liked Halle better than he liked her, too; and Artie had just gone out to dinner with Carolyn instead of with her.

She was sick of it all. She'd had enough.

"Well, of course more poop hit the fan tonight!" she yelled. "It's a full Moon tonight! When *else* would more poop hit the fan? Where have you been since January?"

And then there was silence. No one said a thing. Carolyn stared at Katy, and Katy glared back. She didn't care. She really didn't care.

Then she heard a door open behind her, and she looked back to see Leonard Deacon come tottering down the steps. The police had apparently decided that he wasn't worth keeping. He staggered past Katy, bounced off the fender of Carolyn's car, and then stumbled toward the overpass again.

"Cock suck," he yelped. "Mother fuck. Nipple, nipple, nipple."

Katy and everyone else stared after him.

Cleo sighed. "Everybody keeps using naughty words," she said. She sounded as jaded and world-weary as a nine-year-old could sound.

"Maybe everybody's a limp dick," Tony said.

"I'll second that," Stephen muttered.

Katy didn't think that Stephen had really meant that to be audible, but she was sure that everyone had heard it.

"Okay, we've had enough entertainment for one night," Halle said. "Cleo, pick up your jacks. Tony, stop saying limp dick. And Jack—who are you riding with? You don't have your jeep, do you?"

"Nope," Jack said. "I arrived via squad car. They wouldn't let me blow the siren, though." He crossed the sidewalk to Carolyn. "I'm more on your way than anyone else's, if that's okay. Lily will be waiting for me."

Katy couldn't stand it. Carolyn had shown up late, yet Jack had picked Carolyn to take him home. And even as she had the thought, Katy felt ridiculous for thinking it. But there it was, ridiculous or not.

As the Honda pulled away, she let herself look in at Artie and saw that he was looking at her, too. She saw that he wanted her.

That made things better.

She and Stephen walked Halle, Cleo, and Tony to Halle's Plymouth, which was parked at the near edge of the city lot. Then, as the Plymouth chugged off in a cloud of blue smoke, they continued to their Toyota, which was parked under the overpass. Katy went to the driver's side, Stephen to the passenger side. They each got out their own keys and unlocked their own doors. Neither of them spoke as they got inside.

Then, as Katy started driving out of the lot, her headlight beams caught a figure sitting at the base of a support pillar. It was Leonard Deacon. He was masturbating.

Katy and Stephen gave simultaneous cries of shock and disgust, and Katy hit the accelerator and sped out onto the northbound access ramp.

"Yecchh!" she said as she pulled onto the interstate. "Yecchh, yecchh, yecchh!"

"Enough to make you puke, ain't it?" Stephen said.

"Barf, even." Katy shuddered. "Yecchh!"

"You want to go back and file a complaint?" Stephen asked.

"Good God, no, I—" Katy began, and then she glanced at Stephen and saw that he was grinning at her.

She couldn't help grinning back, and before she knew it, they were both laughing.

It felt good.

PART XI

HUNTER'S MOON

Saturday, October 30, 1993

19

◆

He Longed to Be Truly Stupid

He longed to be truly stupid, as stupid as Carolyn and everyone else seemed to think he was. If he really had been that stupid, Artie thought, then it wouldn't bother him that his father was lying in a hospital bed with a tube in his mouth and his face all twisted up like a melted rubber mask. It wouldn't bother him that he had been sitting next to that bed for forty-five minutes, listening to the rhythmic hissing of the machine that the tube led to.

"You goddamn old man," Artie whispered. "Halloween's not until tomorrow."

A nurse came in, smiled at Artie, and took the old man's blood pressure. Old man. Artie made a face. The guy was only fifty-three. You weren't supposed to have a stroke when you were only fifty-three. Not even a little one. Much less one that was like a hand grenade going off in your skull.

But then, the old man's old man had kicked off from heart failure at forty-nine. And Artie's mother's father had died before sixty. Artie wasn't sure just when, but that didn't matter. The point was that men on both sides of Artie's family had a tendency to keel over before they got old. Artie had the feeling that this did not bode well for his own future.

He had turned twenty-four in August. His life was probably half over.

That realization made him think of how some of his friends gave him shit for living with Carolyn, who was so much older than he was. And he supposed that if they knew he was sleeping with Katy, they'd give him shit about her too. What are you doing with that old lady? some of them had asked when he'd moved in with Carolyn. Yeah, she's good-looking—but with so many nubile babes in the world, why are you shutting yourself up with a middle-aged woman?

Artie's standard response was that Carolyn really knew what she was doing, if you got his drift, but the truth was that he didn't understand it himself. Carolyn was gorgeous and skilled, but so were a lot of women a whole lot younger. And they would stay that way longer. He didn't know why he had decided to live with her, other than the fact that he liked her. But that raised the question of why he liked her, and he couldn't answer that one, either. She was in a lousy mood most of the time, and she put him down or told him to shut up on a daily basis.

That, at least, explained why he wanted to screw around on her. But it didn't explain why he had chosen to do so with yet another woman who was more than a decade older than he was.

Now, though, as he watched the nurse adjust the IV in his father's arm, Artie thought he might have a glimmer of an idea about why he wanted women who were older.

And it had nothing to do with that psychological bullshit about wanting to sleep with your mother. One of the other waiters at the restaurant had suggested that, and Artie had responded by asking, "Why should I want to sleep with *my* mother when I've already slept with *yours?*" The other waiter had then taken a swing at him, so Artie had knocked him on his ass.

The other waiter hadn't given him any more trouble after that, but Artie guessed that might change if the guy ever realized that Artie really had slept with the guy's mother.

There hadn't been anything psychological about that, though. Certainly nothing about his own mother. Wherever she was.

Besides, now he had a better explanation:

It was because he was going to die young.

Using his immediate male predecessors as indicators, Artie guessed that he was about twelve to fifteen years closer to death than his calendar age suggested. So by living with Carolyn, a woman who had just turned thirty-eight, he was in fact living with a woman who was more or less the same age that he was. If they stayed together, the odds were good that they would croak at about the same time.

Artie was pleased with himself for figuring that out. But then he looked at his father's face again, and he stopped being pleased. The old man's brain had blown out, but he hadn't died. And Artie might not either. Dying before he got old would be bad enough. But not dying, like his father had not died, would be worse.

"How's he doing?" Artie asked.

The nurse, a woman about Carolyn's age, but heavier and not as pretty, made some marks on a clipboard and then gave Artie another smile. She had nice lips. Artie decided that even if she was a little chunky, he might not mind kissing her.

Her skin would probably smell like disinfectant, though, and he wasn't sure he could deal with that.

"Well, his vitals are about the same," the nurse said.

Artie looked at her left hand. She wasn't wearing a ring. He wondered what would happen if he asked her to go somewhere with him for a few minutes. Would she get angry, or would she be flattered? What were the odds that she might really lead him to a closet or something?

He considered taking the risk. It would be worth it just for the chance of getting out of this room for a little while. What was he supposed to do here, anyway? Even if the doctor showed up—he was half an hour late already—what possible use could Artie make of any information the bloodsucking son of a bitch would give him?

He looked at the nurse's hair, breasts, and hands. He imagined holding her hands clamped together in one of his, then sliding his other hand inside her soft blue scrubs.

Just then his father made a gurgling noise, and Artie jumped up from his chair and leaned over the bed. Miraculously, the old man's eyes were open. But they weren't moving. And his face was still twisted, his mouth still half open. There was saliva on his salt-and-pepper cheek and on his pillow. Artie pulled a wad of tissues from the box on the little wheeled table beside the bed and wiped the saliva away. The tissues caught on the old man's stubble and made a sound like Velcro ripping apart.

"He opened his eyes," Artie said. "That means something, doesn't it?"

The nurse came close to Artie and leaned over the old man, too. Her left breast touched Artie's right shoulder.

"I couldn't say," the nurse said, touching the old man's temple with her fingertips. The old man didn't react. "You'll have to ask Dr. Lawrence."

Artie was feeling aroused at her proximity, but he was also a little pissed off. She wasn't giving him any straight answers. So he turned and looked into her eyes. That always got them.

"The doctors go in and out like this was McDonald's," he said. "But you nurses are here all the time. I'll bet you know more than Lawrence does."

The nurse blushed, but she didn't back away. "I wouldn't say that," she murmured.

There it was. She was attracted to him. He could hear it in the breathiness of her voice. If he just talked nice to her now, he could get anything he wanted.

"Come on," he said. "You take care of more people than ten doctors do." He glanced at his father. "Is he going to get any better?"

The nurse didn't answer right away, so Artie stared deep into her pupils.

"I—" the nurse began. Then she took a shaky breath. "I can't say for certain. But the MRI scan indicated massive brain damage, and, well . . . no. I don't think he's going to get any better."

Artie gave her a smile. He doubted that it was much of a smile, but thought that he owed her something.

He also thought that he might as well go ahead and kiss her, so he leaned forward to do it.

Then Carolyn walked into the room. Artie spotted her and was just able to turn the potential kiss into a whisper that the nurse would feel as a puff of air on her cheek.

"Thank you," he said.

The nurse blinked, stepped back, and said, "You're very welcome." Then she clutched her clipboard to her chest, brushed past Carolyn, and left the room.

Carolyn gave Artie the narrow-eyed glare she always used when she was about to ream him for something.

He tried to head it off. "You must have closed the shop early," he said.

She scowled. "I told you I would." Then she jerked a thumb after the nurse. "What was that all about?"

Artie tossed the wet tissues into the wastebasket in the corner. "She's taking good care of him, so I was saying thank you."

"It looked like you were about to stick your tongue down her throat."

Artie didn't respond to that. Instead, he turned toward the old man and asked, "Does he look any different than he did yesterday?"

Carolyn came up beside Artie, put her arm around his waist, and looked down at the old man with him. "His color might be a little better," she said. "Maybe."

Artie put his arm around Carolyn's waist too. He kept on staring at his father.

"Well, fuck," he said.

❖

After leaving the hospital, they took off for Halle's cabin, stopping by home just long enough for Artie to park his motorcycle and jump into the Accord's passenger seat. Carolyn had already packed clothes and toiletries for both of them, so they didn't even go into the house.

Artie wished he could go inside to grab a few condoms, but he couldn't think of a way to do it since Carolyn didn't even know that he had them. Carolyn was on the pill, and ever since their HIV tests had come back negative, they hadn't used anything else. But Katy always insisted on condoms. And that was fine with him. He lasted longer that way.

Now, though, there might be a problem. He wanted to find a few moments to be with Katy this weekend, but if he didn't have any condoms— Well, there were other things they could do.

Carolyn drove fast through the Hill Country. The Honda's headlight beams swept around the curves so fast that Artie could hardly make out individual trees. He guessed that Carolyn was driving this way because she was mad that they had gotten away so late. It was after eight o'clock on Saturday night, and everyone else had been at the cabin for a whole day already. Carolyn hated feeling left out, and she no doubt blamed Artie for it.

But was it his fault that the old man's brain had popped like a water balloon? Or that the doctor hadn't shown up tonight until after seven?

"Hey," Artie said after they'd been driving an hour. "Could you answer a question?"

Carolyn nodded. "I'll try."

Her face glowed green in the dim light from the instrument panel. She really was the most beautiful woman that Artie had ever met. Smart, too.

"What does *intubate* mean?" he asked.

Carolyn flashed her brights at an oncoming pickup truck. "Christ on a crutch!" she yelled as the truck blasted by with its lights still on high beam. "You idiot bastard putz!" Then she answered Artie. "I think that's when they insert a breathing tube into the trachea."

That didn't make sense to Artie. "But Dad's already got a breathing tube. That's the thing in his mouth. It goes all the way down his windpipe."

Carolyn glanced at him. She didn't look pissed off, exactly. In fact, she looked kind of worried. Artie didn't think he had ever seen Carolyn look worried before.

"Yes," she said, looking back at the road as she whipped another curve. "But I think *intubate* means a tracheostomy. That's when they cut a hole in the trachea and insert the tube there instead of going in through the mouth."

She was talking down to him, and he didn't like it. "I know that," he said. "I know what a tracheostomy is."

"Okay," Carolyn said. "Sorry."

Artie didn't think he'd ever heard her say she was sorry before, either. Not like she meant it, anyway. And he was a little bugged that she was doing it now. What, because his old man was in the hospital, she was going to try to be sweet to him? Did his old man being in the hospital mean that he had become a different guy? Or that she had become a different woman?

He stared ahead at a yellow-orange glow that had just appeared between the hills. Kerrville was coming up. And after Kerrville, he would only have to wait another half hour or so before he was at the cabin with Katy . . . assuming that Carolyn and her wild-ass driving didn't put him into a hospital bed alongside the old man.

Carolyn was silent as they drove through Kerrville, but it was the kind of silence that meant she was building up to something. There was a weird kind of energy that seemed to pulse around her. Artie could feel it. And when he looked at her, he could see her lips pursing, building up tension.

As they left Kerrville behind, she let it out. "Is that what the doctor said? That he was going to give your father a tracheostomy?"

Artie was perturbed. He'd asked a question, and she'd answered it. Now he didn't want to talk anymore. But Carolyn never gave him a choice.

"No," he said. "What the doctor said was, if there's no change for the better by Monday, he might intubate."

"Oh. Then that's what he meant. He's going to give him a tracheostomy."

Artie tried not to get angry. Anger was Carolyn's scene, not his. But he couldn't help it. Her and her know-it-all tone. So she knew what intubate meant. That made her a medical expert?

"Maybe if you'd stayed with me when the doctor showed up," Artie said, "you could have explained that to me then. But you took off as soon as he stuck his head in the door."

Carolyn glanced at him again. She still looked worried. "I had to go to the bathroom. Besides, I didn't think you wanted me there."

"Why'd you think I was holding your hand?" Artie asked. "I was holding your hand, and when he showed up, you yanked your hand away and took off." He glared at her, hating that her skin was so smooth and delicious despite the fact that she was fifteen years older than the women he ought to be sleeping with. "You left me alone with that—that—" He ran out of words. "—that doctor dude."

Carolyn accelerated down a hill, passed a minivan, and pulled back into the right lane two seconds before the Honda would have slammed head-on into a propane truck. Artie gritted his teeth and wished he was on his motorcycle. It was only a Kawasaki, so it wasn't like tooling around on something cool like a Harley. But it was better than riding shotgun for a batshit-crazy driver who was old enough to be his mother. Assuming she had gotten pregnant when she was thirteen.

"I'm sorry," she said again.

That made two sorries in less than thirty minutes. Artie was stunned. He wanted to shake his head and make a flapping-lipped, astonished-cartoon-character noise. But as he started to do so, Carolyn took a 45-mph left-hand curve at 60, and he banged his head on the passenger window. So instead of making his cartoon noise, Artie rubbed his head and glowered.

"I just didn't think it would be appropriate for me to be there while the doctor was discussing your father with you," Carolyn said then. "It was a family matter. It felt wrong for me to be part of something that intimate."

Artie didn't get it. "You mean we sleep together every night, but we're not intimate?"

"Well, we're not family." Carolyn sounded annoyed now, more like herself. "I'm not your wife."

"I never said you were, babe."

"All right, then. And don't call me babe."

They didn't talk for a while after that. Artie looked out the window part of the time and closed his eyes the rest of the time, especially when Carolyn passed cars by crossing a solid yellow line in the glare of oncoming headlights. But every time he closed his eyes, he saw the old man's twisted Halloween-mask face and empty eyes again. He wished he could shake it. There wasn't anything he could do, anyway, other than just going in and sitting beside the bed. The old man had good insurance, so the money part was taken care of. At least, that was what Carolyn had said when he'd showed her the papers.

Still, he felt as if he ought to be doing something. He had called his tight-assed sister Anne in Michigan because Carolyn had said he ought to, so it wasn't as if he had done absolutely nothing. And Anne had their mother's address and phone number, so that part was up to her. Not that Mom would care.

So Artie had done his duty, and there was nothing more to do. The old man had stroked out on Wednesday morning, and now it was Saturday night. Artie had been dealing with nothing else for four days, and until Monday, there would be nothing more to deal with. Then the doctor would decide whether or not to intubate, and he would also recommend a permanent care facility. Artie was supposed to sign some more papers then, and that would be that.

There was one other thing, but Artie wasn't sure about it. He thought that maybe the doctor had hinted that Artie could choose not to have the old man intubated. The doctor would then just remove the breathing tube that was already there . . .

Artie had really wanted Carolyn with him during that part of the conversation. She would have known how to respond. She would have known whether to thank the doctor or to tell him to intubate himself straight up his own rectum.

As Artie was having that thought, Carolyn reached across and put her hand on his thigh. It startled him, and he banged his head on the window again. Carolyn was not one for small gestures of affection. She would do almost anything during lovemaking, but almost nothing at any other time. Her deliberate niceness to him now was starting to rattle him.

"Are you okay?" she asked, putting her hand back on the wheel again.

"Yeah, sure," Artie said, trying not to wince. "Why wouldn't I be?"

"You just bumped your head."

Artie didn't acknowledge that, but instead leaned forward and turned on the radio. He wished that Carolyn would spring for a car CD player, or at least a tape deck.

"You're not going to find any alternative stations out here," Carolyn said.

She was right. She was always right. There was nothing but country, classic rock, and static. Artie snapped off the radio and wished they would hurry up and get to the cabin. He needed to get laid. Carolyn or Katy, he didn't care. He just needed to get laid.

"Ten more miles," Carolyn said, as if reading his mind.

He watched her drive for a few minutes then, waiting to see how long it would take her to react. It took more time than usual for her to say "What? What?"—but he had seen the tension start to build as quickly as ever. She had just held it back a little longer.

"I was wondering," he said, "if you think I'm an asshole for going to the cabin with you while my old man's in the hospital."

Carolyn blared the Honda's horn at a Buick that had pulled onto the highway from a side road.

"Did you see that?" she shouted. "That motherfucking jerk-off pulled out right in front of us. There was a stop sign, but he didn't even slow down. He's a goddamn menace. He shouldn't be allowed on the fucking road." She took a deep breath and let it out slowly. "No, I don't think you're an asshole for going on this trip. It's pretty clear there's nothing you can do for him." She paused. "In fact, I don't think he even knew you were there."

Artie fiddled with his seat-belt buckle. "Me neither."

"What's odd, though," Carolyn said, "is that until Wednesday, I didn't even know your father lived in Austin." She gave Artie one of her narrow-eyed looks. "We've been together a year now, and you've never mentioned it. Not even when I've asked about your family."

Artie couldn't believe they hadn't reached the cabin yet. "Well, you never asked where my dad lived."

"Yes, I did. You said Oklahoma City."

Artie tried to remember that conversation and couldn't. But of course it had happened. Carolyn's memory was flawless. He hated that about her. She always remembered everything they said or did together, and then threw it up in his face weeks or months later, expecting him to know what the hell she was talking about. And considering it an insult when he didn't.

"I grew up in Oklahoma City," he said. "But Dad moved down here after Mom took off for the last time. That was, like, five years ago. Right after I dropped out of UT."

Mentioning the fact that he'd bailed out of college reminded Artie of why he'd done it. For one thing, his grades had been for shit, and he'd hated going to class. For another, he'd been playing drums in a band called Stigmata Breath, and it had looked like they were going to get an indie recording deal. But the label had wanted them to shorten the band's name to just Stigmata. The lead guitarist and Artie had rebelled at that, insisting that if the band was going to shorten its name at all, they should drop the Stigmata and just call themselves Breath.

The label had folded before the controversy could be resolved, and the band had disintegrated soon afterward due to lack of gigs. Artie had hocked his drums and had never gotten them back. But now he wondered if he should have. He was tired of being a waiter. And it wasn't as if he couldn't still play. Once you learned how to hit things with sticks, you never forgot.

"So your dad moved to Austin to be closer to you?" Carolyn asked.

Artie laughed. "Yeah, right. When I was sixteen, he rapped me in the mouth for taking too long in the bathroom and told me that he couldn't wait until I got out of his house. So I kind of doubt he came down here to be closer to me." In fact, Artie hadn't even known that his father wasn't still in Oklahoma City until he'd tried to call one day and had gotten a recording that said the number had been disconnected. He had then called his sister, and she had known where the old man was.

"Why'd he come down here, then?" Carolyn asked. "You said once that he was a janitor at the Oklahoma state capitol, and that's not the kind of job that gets you transferred to Austin. So it wasn't for work, was it?"

Artie shrugged. "Sort of. He plays the accordion. Or did until Wednesday."

He looked out the windshield and saw moonlight shining from a river that ran alongside the highway. He thought he knew where they were now. Halle's cabin was close. That meant Katy was close, too.

"Why would a middle-aged accordion player move to Austin?" Carolyn asked. "It's not exactly one of your hipper instruments to sling down on Sixth Street."

"Depends," Artie said. "You ever spend much time east of I-35?"

"No."

This didn't surprise Artie. "Well, my old man did. He played accordion for three or four *conjunto* bands. Had gigs at bars along East Sixth almost every night of the week. I doubt he made much money, but I don't think he cared. He had the whole pile from selling the house in Oklahoma City, plus his retirement fund. And he lived cheap. Cheap apartment, cheap food." Artie shifted in his seat. His butt cheeks were getting numb. "I guess he kept up his health insurance, though."

Carolyn made a clicking noise with her tongue. "He probably knew what was coming." She touched Artie's thigh again, nearly swerving across the left lane and into the river as she did so. "Did you ever hear him play? In Austin, I mean."

Artie wished she hadn't made him remember that. "Once. It was before you and I got together."

"So why didn't you go again? Was it because of me?"

That, Artie thought, was typical Carolyn. Everything had to have something to do with her, didn't it?

"No," he said. "It was because I was going to sit in on drums that first time, but the band's regular drummer said that if I touched his kit, he'd kick my Anglo ass. And everyone else in the bar kept calling me Blondie."

Carolyn frowned. "I call you Blondie sometimes."

"It's not the same thing," Artie said. "Trust me. See, I just wasn't supposed to be in their bar, and they wanted to be sure I knew it."

"That sounds racist."

"Well, duh. Fucking-A right it was racist."

"No," Carolyn said, "I mean that *you* sound racist. After all, your dad's Anglo, and they didn't have a problem with him."

Artie grimaced. If he was the stupid one here, how come Carolyn was the one talking about something she didn't know the first thing about?

"Okay, my old man's Anglo," Artie said. "But he's almost bald, and the hair he's got left is gray. And his eyes are brown, and he speaks Spanish and plays the accordion. But I take after my mom. She has blond hair and blue eyes, and those guys wouldn't have liked her, either." Or you, he thought.

Carolyn made a noise in her throat, but she didn't say anything. Artie didn't know whether that meant he had won the argument or not. For one thing, he wasn't sure whether what they'd just had was an argument. He never knew until it was too late and Carolyn was furious. But she didn't seem furious now. Just quiet. And that didn't seem right. If he really had won an argument with her—which would be a first—he was pretty sure she would never let him get away with it. But that was what she seemed to be doing.

No, there was something else going on. Maybe he had been right earlier, and she was cutting him some slack because of his old man. Maybe she thought he was ripped up over it, and she didn't want to rag on him while he was all grievous. If that was the case, Artie figured there would be hell to pay once she decided that he'd grieved enough.

He was really looking forward to seeing Katy. Even if she couldn't get away from Stephen and he couldn't get away from Carolyn, at least they could exchange a few surreptitious glances. Artie liked doing that. He liked getting away with something right under people's noses.

Carolyn hit the Honda's brakes, and the car decelerated hard, throwing Artie forward so that the shoulder belt slammed him back into the seat as Carolyn made the turn onto the gravel drive. They had arrived at what Artie had come to think of as Magic Mountain, or Weird-Ass Hill. He and Carolyn hadn't been here since the Fourth of July weekend, which had been pretty fucked up what with the fire and Lily freaking him out and all—but despite that, he was glad to be here again.

For one thing, it was getting him away from the old man for a little while. For another, he was going to be here with two women he was sleeping with. And unlike last time, he was going to have some fun with it. He wouldn't let anything spoil that. Not even Lily. If she showed up and tried to mess with his head again, he would ignore her. He was pretty much convinced that all those feathers were fake anyhow, and that she had hooked up wires to make it look like she could fly. That was all there was to it. Lily was just an ordinary babe who thought she was a goddess, and Artie had met plenty of those. He was riding with one right now.

Carolyn brought the Honda to a stop in front of the cabin. Halle's Plymouth and the Cormans' Toyota were parked just inside the gravel circle next to the trees, and when Artie saw the Toyota his heart jumped. Katy was here. Was she waiting for him? Was she thinking about him the way he was thinking about her?

"I don't see Jack's jeep," Carolyn said, shutting off the Honda's engine and lights. "He must have caught a ride with Katy and Stephen."

"They probably wanted to make sure the dude got here," Artie said. "Otherwise he might prance around bare-assed on Mount Bonnell again." He reached for his door handle.

But Carolyn grasped his wrist. "Wait a minute," she said. "There's something we have to talk about before we go inside."

Artie couldn't suppress his groan. He was sick of talking.

"Don't you make a disgusted noise at me," Carolyn said. "You don't have the right."

Artie froze, scarcely breathing.

Oh-oh.

Carolyn's voice had been dead calm. That was when it was the worst: when she was dead calm. And just now she had sounded deader and calmer than he had ever heard her sound before.

"Okay," he whispered. He was racking his weak memory, trying to think of what he had done in the past few minutes that could have gotten him into such trouble.

She was still holding his wrist, but as he made himself turn to face her, he saw that she wasn't looking at him. She was staring out the windshield at the full Moon. Her eyes glistened with white light.

Artie tried to wait for her to speak again, but it took so long that he couldn't stand it.

"Babe," he said. "What's wrong?"

Carolyn's nostrils flared, and she let out a breath that Artie hadn't even known she was holding.

"I know you're fucking Katy," she said.

Artie felt as if his head had been dunked in a bucket of molten lead. His skin burned, and his blood screamed in his ears. He couldn't hear himself think.

"No, I'm not," he said.

Now Carolyn turned toward him, and to his amazement, she still didn't look pissed off. But then he realized that how she did look was worse.

She looked sad.

Artie had never seen Carolyn look sad before, and it was awful.

"Shut up," she said. "Don't say anything. If you deny it, we'll just wind up fighting about the fact that you're lying, and we don't have time for that."

Artie opened his mouth again, but he couldn't think of anything to say. His brain was boiling away.

"I'm not telling you this because I want you to feel guilty," Carolyn said. "I don't think you're capable of that. But I want you to know that if you do anything with her this weekend, I'll make you sorry. Do you understand?" The reflected moonlight from her eyes burned into his. "Nod if you understand."

Artie managed to nod. He suddenly had to pee so badly that he thought he might wet his pants.

"Good," Carolyn said. "Because if you did anything with her here, Stephen would know it. The quarters are too close."

Carolyn squeezed Artie's wrist so hard now that her fingernails dug into his skin. Artie sucked in air through his teeth, but he still didn't say anything. The only thing he was sure of right now was that even if he could manage to speak, he had better not.

"You see, Stephen is my friend," Carolyn continued, keeping up the pressure on Artie's wrist, "and I won't let you hurt him. I don't think he knows about the two of you, and we're going to keep it that way. Right?"

Artie managed to nod again. He wished he were back in his old man's hospital room.

Carolyn released his wrist. "All right, then." She opened her door, and the shoulder belt whirred away. "As for you and me . . . we'll talk about that after we get your dad squared away. I don't want to put too much on you at once." She stepped out of the car. "After all, I'm not your wife."

She closed the door without slamming it, then walked to the cabin and went inside.

Artie sat there looking at the yellow light spilling from the cabin windows until the screaming in his ears subsided a bit. Then he got out of the car and walked into the woods to the north. He would take a leak before going inside. No one would miss him. And if anyone did ask where he was, Carolyn would just say that he was being a jerk. They would believe that. He was an outsider, and none of them liked him. Not even Katy. She just liked that he was better in bed than Steve was. She sure as shit would never consider leaving Steve for him.

Not that he wanted her to.

He whizzed against a tree trunk. There was still a low throb in his ears, but he didn't mind that. At least it covered up the night sounds that always bothered him out here. In fact, maybe he would sleep outside tonight. If he could get into the cabin and grab a few blankets before anyone noticed him, that was just what he would do.

As he zipped up, something brushed his cheek. He jumped and looked around, but saw nothing. Then something tickled his scalp. He reached up to swat it away and wound up with a feather caught between his fingers. As he stared at it, another feather, and then another, drifted down before his eyes.

He looked up. Lily was sitting in a shaft of moonlight on a branch a dozen feet above him, her legs and feet tucked up under her ass. Her wings, which were wrapped around her body, looked awful. There were feathers missing everywhere.

She looked down at him and shivered, but Artie didn't feel much sympathy.

"Halloween's not until tomorrow," he said for the second time that day. "And your costume looks crappy."

Lily blinked, and something else touched Artie's cheek. He reached up to brush that away too, and his fingertips came away wet. Lily was crying.

Now Artie felt bad. He hated seeing anybody cry.

"You need help getting down?" he asked.

"No." Lily's voice still sounded like music that came from everywhere, but there was a quaver to it that Artie hadn't heard before. "I'm just waiting for Jack. Have you seen him?"

Artie shook his head. "I haven't been inside yet. But if you want, I'll tell him you're here."

"Thank you."

Artie took a step away, then looked back up at Lily again. "Are you okay?" he asked.

Lily gave him a weak smile. "I'm sick, Artie."

Artie wasn't surprised. "Yeah," he said. "There's a lot of that going around."

As he headed back to the cabin then, he passed Jack going the other way. Jack was shedding his clothes behind him as he walked.

"Artie!" Jack said, grinning. He sounded glad to see him. "Hey, have you seen Lily?"

Artie pointed back the way he had come. "Forty, fifty feet in that direction. Stuck up a tree like a scared cat." He put a hand on Jack's bare shoulder. "She needs you, man."

Jack's grin disappeared. "Thanks, Artie," he said, and broke into a run.

Artie continued on to the cabin. When he went inside, Carolyn and Katy were playing Scrabble, and neither of them so much as glanced at him. Neither did the other adults. Halle had a new boyfriend with her, and Stephen was reading a book and looking morose.

But Cleo and Tony were making caramel apples and popcorn balls in the kitchen, and they were willing to let Artie help. He was grateful.

Afterward, by the light of the marshmallow-roasting fire in the living room, he told the kids the stories of the Hook-Armed Maniac and the Choking Doberman, scaring the living shit out of them. Or out of Tony, anyway. Cleo was copping an attitude.

But Artie still liked telling the stories, so the day wasn't a total loss. He wasn't sure he would ever come up to Halle's cabin again, though. Now that he thought about it, he realized that he had never really had much fun there.

PART XII

BEAVER MOON

Monday, November 29, 1993

◆

20

❖

What's-His-Face Had Been Like Mouthwash

What's-His-Face had been like mouthwash, Halle realized as she walked out of the Austin Public Library. He had washed away the taste of everyone and everything else. After the murky confusion of a three-month semi-relationship with her semi-colleague Carl Sugarman, What's-His-Face—a lawyer, of all things—had come along this past Friday and made her feel as sharp and clear as cut glass.

Just now, she had gone into the library to return seven overdue books (four of them Cleo's, two of them Tony's, and one hers), but as she'd tried to browse the shelves for replacements, she had found herself thinking only of the weekend she'd just had and of the man she'd had it with. So she had left the library empty-handed and discovered that the sun had set while she'd been inside. Clouds had moved in, too, and the temperature had dropped. She took a deep breath and smelled rain coming.

It was almost seven-thirty, so she had just over an hour before her ex-mother-in-law would drop off Cleo and Tony at the duplex. The kids had been staying in Round Rock since Thanksgiving, and their grandmother had promised to take them to school today and pick them up afterward. Then Grandma was to take them to the Children's

Museum and to dinner at an animated-animal pizza joint before bringing them home.

Halle would be glad to see them again, but she was also sorry that her long weekend of non-motherhood and non-work was coming to an end. There was no way to extend it further, though. She had already given herself part of today off, sleeping late on a Monday for the first time in she didn't know how long. What's-His-Face had awakened her briefly at eight A.M. to tell her that he had to leave, so she had kissed him and then fallen back asleep until eleven. Then she had gotten up and made a halfhearted attempt at debugging a client's accounting software, but had soon abandoned that. Instead, she had chosen to watch soap operas and talk shows until early evening, when she'd remembered the library books. It was only then that she'd taken a shower and gotten dressed.

Pausing just north of the library, on the sidewalk in front of the Austin History Center, Halle looked across Guadalupe Street at one of the city's Moonlight Towers. This one stood at the southeastern corner of Guadalupe and Ninth, but it was identical to the one that she and What's-His-Face had tried to climb on Saturday evening in the West Campus neighborhood. After several attempts, they had been forced to give up and fall to the ground laughing. Each tower was a hundred and sixty-five feet high, the first fifteen feet of which was a smooth steel pole. On their last attempt, What's-His-Face had tried to shimmy up that pole, and Halle had assisted by jamming her head into his butt. It hadn't worked. Not in terms of getting them up the tower, anyway.

That Saturday night, and the night before, and the night after, had each been a blast . . . all the more so because the weekend hadn't started off well at all. She and the kids had gone to her ex-mother-in-law's on Thursday for Thanksgiving dinner, and to her horror, her ex-husband, Bill, had emerged from whatever rock he had been hiding under for the past three years. He had just shown up out of the blue expecting dinner and affection, as if he deserved either one. Even Bill's mother had seemed less than thrilled to see him, but she had gone ahead and set a place for him anyway. So for the next four hours Halle had suffered the torments of the damned.

Cleo and Tony, however, had enjoyed themselves, treating Bill with the same courtesy that they would have shown to any strange man who kept trying to touch their mother. In short, they had made fart noises in his face and spilled gravy in his lap. Halle's heart had swelled with pride, and she had granted their request to spend the weekend with Grandma.

So after making sure that Bill was gone and wasn't coming back, Halle had kissed the kids good-bye, warned their grandmother not to fill their heads with Baptist propaganda, and taken off for four days of freedom. She had spent Thursday evening at home, gloriously alone, but on Friday she had decided to treat herself to a movie.

The movie she had gone to see was *The Piano,* and when Harvey Keitel had gotten naked, she had let out a hoot of appreciation. A few people in the theater had made shushing noises, but the guy sitting just behind her had leaned forward and whispered, "It's only a special effect."

They had wound up talking in the parking lot after the movie, and then had gone to dinner together, and then had gone to bed. Somewhere in there, he had admitted to being an attorney, and had revealed that his name was Duane. Halle had then told him that while she could forgive his occupation, she didn't much care for the name "Duane."

"So I'll just call you What's-Your-Face, if that's okay," she'd said, thinking that his face was really pretty darn nice, if a bit too round and a bit too balding on top.

"That's fine," he'd replied. "And I'll just call you Holly."

She had tried to correct him. "Your pronunciation's off," she'd explained. "It's Hal-ley, not Hol-ly."

He'd grinned and kissed her. She had noticed at that point that he'd still smelled of movie-theater popcorn.

"If you can call me What's-Your-Face," he'd said, "I can call you Holly. See, you may recall that Harvey Keitel wasn't the only one naked in that movie."

Halle had pretended to be offended. "I'm not sure I appreciate being called by the name of an actress that much shorter than I am. But, hey, whatever turns your crank." She'd considered for a moment. "And I suppose I could call you Harvey, but that's almost as bad as Duane."

He had held her tighter. "Aren't you supposed to be mute?"

So then they hadn't talked for a while.

They had spent the rest of the weekend together, and Halle had enjoyed every second of it. She thought that What's-His-Face had liked it too. She even thought that they might decide to see each other again.

But as she looked up at the six mercury-vapor floodlights casting their artificial moonglow down onto the intersection—the only moonlight visible right now, what with the cloud cover—Halle knew that she and What's-His-Face would never be more than friends and perhaps occasional lovers. There would never be any talk of marriage, or even of moving in together. She even doubted that there would be weekly dinners or sleepovers. Because no matter how good they were together, they would turn into something else if they were together with Cleo and Tony.

That had been part of the problem with Carl Sugarman. Halle had thought that she might be falling in love with him, but then one evening he had spoken to Tony in a tone of voice that could only be described as fatherly. It hadn't been mean or even commanding, but it had carried with it a subtle implication of ownership. And that had been that.

Halle's children were hers. Nobody else's.

And knowing that she felt that way led to the further knowledge that until both Cleo and Tony were grown and on their own, she would be unable to bring a man into the family. Trying to do so would put both her and the man into a rock-and-hard-place dilemma. Carl Sugarman had blown their relationship when his voice had betrayed fatherliness, but What's-His-Face—or someone else—could blow it just as easily should his voice betray indifference. There might be an ideal balance between the two where a man might teeter for a while, but Halle doubted that anyone, no matter how viable a candidate for sainthood, could last there for long. Tommy hadn't been able to, and Carl Sugarman hadn't been able to, and What's-His-Face wouldn't be able to either.

The one man Halle could think of who might be able to do it was Stephen Corman. But a relationship with Stephen wasn't even a remote possibility. For one thing, while she was flattered by his attraction to her, she felt no attraction to him in return. She didn't know why, because there wasn't a thing wrong with him. In fact, she thought he was terrific. But he just didn't do it for her.

Besides, he was married to Katy. And Halle had rules about things like that.

So there it was. No man could meet her requirements. As long as her children were *her children,* Halle was doomed to nothing more than casual relationships. It was kind of a drag, but if that was the price she paid for having Cleo and Tony . . . well, she couldn't very well drive them into the country and leave them by the side of the road.

The upshot was that playing house with What's-His-Face had been fun, but now it was over. In a few minutes it would be time to head home and start living on the planet Earth again.

Halle smiled, her eyes watering as she gazed up at the Moonlight Tower. There were sixteen more of the towers scattered around town, left over from the thirty-one that had been put up in 1895. Back then, the six lights at the top of each tower had been carbon-arc lamps powered by electricity from a dam on the Colorado. The lighting system had been so successful that Austin had become known far and wide as a city of eternal moonlight—and consequently, Halle supposed, as a city of eternal lunacy. The modern switch to mercury-vapor lamps didn't seem to have changed that.

She wished now that she and What's-His-Face had managed to climb the West Campus tower on Saturday. If they had made it to the top, she might have been able to unscrew one of the lamps. Then she could have taken it to Jack so that he could keep a piece of the Moon in his apartment. That way he could go crazy and get naked any old time, indoors, instead of just once a month out in the open.

"You'd better be at the cabin," Halle murmured. Jack had promised her that he would drive his postal jeep to her Hill Country property today even though he had to go there alone. The trouble on Mount Bonnell two months ago had been an aberration, he'd sworn. He was doing much better now, and would be sure to get out of town before exposing himself.

Halle hoped so. No one else among the usual gang of suspects had been able to go with him this month because the full Moon fell on a post-holiday Monday, and they all had too much work piled up. Even Stephen, usually Mr. Helpful, had begged off because of a stack of term papers.

But Halle had spoken to Tommy Morrison last week, and he had told her that he would be at his own Hill Country cabin from Thanksgiving until New Year's. So she had asked him to go over and check on Jack this evening. He had said that he would. And since he had a telephone at his place, he had also promised to call her around ten o'clock to put her mind at ease.

A white flash rippled through the clouds over the Moonlight Tower, and there was a rumble of thunder. Halle smelled the sharp stink of ozone and was surprised at it. Lightning should have struck nearby for that smell to be as strong as it was, but the only lightning she had seen had been up in the clouds.

As she had that thought, the lamps atop the Moonlight Tower flickered and dimmed. But they brightened again in seconds, and continued to become brighter and brighter until Halle's eyes stung and she had to look down.

She saw six shadows of herself on the sidewalk. The shadows were so dark, and the light surrounding them so bright and blue-white, that Halle was sure the Moonlight Tower's bulbs were about to explode and shower her with slivers of glass.

She started to run northward, thinking that she would try to sprint across Ninth and into Wooldridge Park before the lamps burst, but she had gone only a few steps when the light dimmed to its normal intensity. So Halle stopped and stood looking down at the sidewalk, hoping to give her eyes a chance to readjust. She could see bright blue spots swirling in the concrete. It reminded her of some LSD she had taken in 1982.

Then a gust of wind ruffled Halle's hair and cut through her sweatshirt, and a huge shadow swept across the sidewalk and set the swirling blue images spinning like fireworks pinwheels.

Halle had to look up at the tower again.

For a moment, looking through the pinwheels, she thought she was seeing an enormous owl that had become mesmerized by the tower lamps and was now flying around them like a moth around a porch light. But then, squinting as the pinwheels faded in the glare of the lamps, she was able to see that the thing flying around the top of the Moonlight Tower had feathers only on its wings—and that some of those feathers were falling away and drifting down to the street. As Halle realized that, she was also able to make out long black hair and skin the color of milk.

This wasn't an owl. It was Lily.

And even though Halle had seen Lily rise into the sky from her own front walk in August, it was still a shock to see her now, flying in circles more than a hundred and fifty feet over downtown Austin. For twenty or thirty seconds, Halle could only stare up, speechless.

Then, just as she was about to call to Lily to ask what the hell was going on, she heard people coming up the sidewalk from the library. So she looked down quickly, fearful that if they saw her staring up at the tower, they would look up too. She had no idea what might happen if they did, and she didn't want to find out.

Two women and a man walked by her then, talking, and ignored her. And they didn't look up even though Lily's wings passing before the lamps made the light flicker.

After the people had turned westward along Ninth Street and disappeared down the hill, Halle looked northward on Guadalupe. The street was unusually quiet. There were only four cars coming toward her down the one-way street, but a few seconds later they had passed her and disappeared as well. The coast was clear.

Halle ran across to the base of the tower and craned her neck, staring up along the tower's triangular steel skeleton. It seemed to her that Lily's wings were flapping dangerously close to the tower's support cables. Lily's flight looked wobbly anyway, and Halle was afraid that if a wing hit one of the cables, Lily would fall.

"Lily?" she called. She was careful not to be too loud; she didn't want to startle the goddess. "Is that you?"

Lily didn't respond, but kept flying around the top of the tower.

Halle tried calling a little louder. "Lily, it's Halle! Are you all right?"

This time Lily flew a little way out from the tower, hovered for a split second—and then dove back in between two of the support cables, colliding with the tower a dozen feet below the lights.

Halle yelped and jumped back, sure that Lily was going to plunge to the ground. But then she saw that Lily had managed to grasp the tower with her hands and feet. Lily's talons scratched against the steel, and she clung to the tower with her wings moving feebly. Fifteen or twenty feathers fluttered down, dancing in the bluish light.

"Hang on!" Halle yelled, not even trying to sound calm now. "I'll get help!"

Even as she said it, though, she realized that she had no idea of what kind of help to get. Whom did one call to get a naked goddess off a Moonlight Tower, anyway? Emergency Medical Services? City of Austin Utilities? The Fire Department? Or just 911 so the dispatcher could make a judgment call?

She looked northward up Guadalupe and westward down Ninth, hoping to flag down someone who might have a better clue than she did. But the streets and sidewalks were weirdly empty.

Then she heard Lily's voice, soft and tremulous. It sounded as if it were coming from a vibrating button inside a tin-can telephone.

"Halle, don't leave me alone," Lily said. "I've gone blind. I can't find Jack. I don't know where I am. I don't know how to get down."

Halle was in a quandary. "Well, I don't know how to get you down either, so I'm going to have to find someone who does. And you're going to have to hang on until I do."

Lily shook her head. Her hair brushed across her wings, and more feathers fell.

"I want Jack," she said. "Jack will know what to do."

Halle groaned. Talk about the blind leading the blind. "Jack's not in town. He went out to my cabin."

"I know," Lily said. Her voice was plaintive. "That's where I thought I was going too. But then the clouds covered the hills, and I could hardly see, so I looked for the Moon. And I thought I'd found her, and was trying to go to her and start over again—but then the light was too bright, and I couldn't see at all. Where am I?"

"You're more than a hundred feet up a hundred-year-old light tower in downtown Austin," Halle said. "So don't move. Or can a goddess like you fall a hundred feet and not get hurt?"

Lily was trembling. "I don't know. I've never fallen before."

Halle groaned again. "Better stay put, then. Jesus."

Lily gave a weak but musical laugh. "I thought I asked you not to mention that name in my presence."

"Sorry."

"I just don't like rejection, that's all."

They were both quiet for a few moments then, Lily clinging to the tower, Halle staring up and getting a crick in her neck.

"Look," Halle said at last, "we've got to do something. I have to get home pretty soon or my kids and their grandma, better known as the Wicked Witch of the North, will be stuck outside waiting for me. The old bat already thinks I'm a crappy mother, but I'd just as soon not give her more ammo."

"All right," Lily said. "What do you want to do?"

Halle tried to think of a plan and wound up feeling like Pooh trying to get Tigger down from a tree. "Well," she said, studying the tower, "there's some kind of platform inside the skeleton that looks like it might be a manual elevator. But I don't know how it works, and there's a padlock on it anyway. And there are footholds down the southern edge of the triangle, but since you're blind and have, um, odd feet, I wouldn't recommend trying that, either. So I say we bring in the Fire Department."

"No," Lily said. "No man sees me except when I choose."

Halle thought this might not be the best time for Lily to indulge in an imperious attitude, but at the same time she had to sympathize. There was a privacy issue here. So she tried to think of something else. "Try keeping your eyes closed for a minute," she said. "Maybe you're blind because you're just too close to those bright lights."

"All right," Lily said. "But I still wish Jack were here."

Halle felt snubbed. "Hey, I'm doing the best I can without a cherry picker, you know?"

"My eyes are closed now," Lily said. Her talons scratched along the steel again, and the sound reverberated down the tower. "But what does picking cherries have to do with anything?"

Halle didn't respond to that. Instead, she looked across the street and down the block at the library. More people had just come outside, laden with books and videotapes. But like the others, they just walked up the sidewalk to Ninth, failing to notice that a naked woman with wings was clinging to the Moonlight Tower on the opposite corner. A few moments later, they were gone.

Halle wondered if maybe this explained why gods and goddesses had fallen out of fashion in recent centuries. Maybe people had just stopped *noticing* them.

The thought occurred to her then that Jack wasn't at all crazy and never had been. He had just started paying attention, that was all. And now Halle was paying attention too. That probably meant that the rest of the world would consider her insane . . . but unlike Jack, she would be smart enough never to let the rest of the world know.

"Oh!" Lily cried. "You were right. I can see again, a little. I think I might be able to fly down now."

Halle was dubious. Lily still seemed to be trembling, and her wings were still losing a few feathers.

"What do you mean you *think* you *might* be able to fly down?" Halle asked.

Lily shifted position, slipped, and clutched at the tower. Halle cringed.

"I, uh, I mean," Lily began. Her voice cracked. "My vision's fuzzy. And I'll have to take off backwards. And the cables are close together up here. I might hit them."

"All right, then, forget it," Halle said. "The Fire Department it is. Hang on, and I'll—"

"No!" Lily shouted.

And she plunged backward off the tower with her wings pulled in close, falling headfirst and twisting a hundred and eighty degrees. She just missed one of the cables.

Halle gave a yelp and moved under Lily to try to catch her even as she realized that they would both be flattened.

But less than thirty feet from the ground, Lily spread her wings. Her fall turned into a dive, and she swooped away from the tower. Her talons brushed Halle's hair, and then she glided out over Guadalupe Street and made an awkward landing on the steps of the Austin History Center.

Halle ran into the street after her and was nearly run over by a silver Lexus whose driver leaned out his window and called her a stupid cunt. She ignored him and ran on to where Lily sat on the steps, looking dazed.

"Jes—I mean, cripes, are you hurt?" Halle asked.

Lily pointed a wobbly finger at the Lexus, which had stopped for a red light at the Eighth Street intersection. "Why did he say cunt as if it were a bad thing?" she asked. She sounded shaken.

"Because he meant it as a bad thing," Halle said. She held out her hands. "We should get out of here. I'll help you up."

But Lily was still looking at the Lexus. She scowled, and it gave Halle a chill.

"Nobody should say cunt as if it were a bad thing," Lily said.

She wiggled her finger at the Lexus as the light turned green, and when the car began to accelerate, both of its rear tires exploded. The Lexus ground to a halt in the middle of Eighth Street, and then the front tires exploded as well.

Halle stared as a flatbed truck came roaring along Eighth Street, ran its red light, and hit the right rear fender of the Lexus. The car spun around with a shriek of metal on asphalt, and the truck continued through the intersection without slowing.

The driver of the Lexus emerged just as one of Lily's loose feathers wafted onto the windshield. When the feather touched the glass, the car's antitheft alarm began whooping. The driver stood there looking at his wrecked automobile as if it were a beached whale.

"I've given him scrotum boils, too," Lily said.

Halle took Lily's hands. "That was really a little extreme," she said, shouting to be heard over the alarm.

The pupils of Lily's eyes dilated, then shrank, then dilated again.

"I'm in a mood," she said.

Halle decided not to question that. "I understand. But we really ought to get you away from here now. After all, you're naked, and since you're at ground level, someone might actually notice. And that can be trouble, as we've learned from Jack's example."

"I've visited this town a number of times in the past century," Lily said as Halle pulled her to her feet, "and public nudity hasn't usually been a serious cause for alarm here. So I doubt that Jack would have even been arrested if he hadn't had an erection. And that was my fault, so please don't blame him."

"I'm not blaming anybody," Halle said, grasping Lily's arm and steering her to the sidewalk. "Nevertheless, I'd like to get you to my car. I have a blanket in the trunk, and we can cover you with that until we get you to my place." She looked around at the feathers scattered on the sidewalk and street. "You don't seem to be too healthy right now. Do you need a doctor or . . . something?"

Lily gave her a wan smile. "I have no idea. I would like to go to your house until I get my bearings, though. And if you'll release my arm, we won't need your blanket."

Halle released Lily's arm. "You still seem shaky. Can you stand on your own?"

"I think so," Lily said. "I can even clothe myself." She stood still then, held her arms out straight, and put her legs together so her body formed a T. Then her wings swept down from her shoulder blades, came up under her armpits, crossed in front of her torso, and wrapped around her buttocks and thighs.

Her feathers all seemed to flow together then, and at some point—Halle thought it must have happened as she blinked—Lily's wings became a sleeveless black-and-white dress.

Halle gave a whistle. "I'm impressed. Now pull a quarter from my ear."

Lily looked puzzled, but shrugged and pulled a quarter from Halle's ear.

Halle gaped for a moment, then snapped out of it. "I deserved that," she said, taking the quarter from Lily and putting it into her jeans pocket. "What I really meant to say was nice 'dress.'"

Lily looked down at the dress and ran her hands over it. "Thank you," she said. Then she leaned forward and looked at her talons, which flexed against the concrete. "I can never seem to do anything about those, though. I always have to steal shoes so I can hide them."

"You look fine without shoes," Halle said, glancing down the street at the whooping Lexus and its shell-shocked driver. He was being joined by a number of people who were coming out of the library. "Now let's go before the villagers come after us with pitchforks and torches."

Halle led Lily across Ninth Street and down into the green bowl of Wooldridge Park. Lily's talons scritched on the pavement, making Halle think of the deep scratches that still marred her living room floor. And that in turn made her feel a little perturbed. But then she took a look at Lily's face, and her heart softened. Lily looked sad. Sad and tired. And then she looked even worse as raindrops began spattering on her cheeks and flattening her hair.

"Come on," Halle said, taking Lily's arm again and guiding her onto a sidewalk that cut diagonally across the park. "My car's parked on Tenth near the courthouse, and if we run we might make it before getting soaked."

Lily nodded, so Halle started running with the goddess in tow. It didn't work too well. Lily's feet weren't made for running. Before they were halfway across the park, the sky thundered, and the spattering raindrops became a gullywasher. So Halle gave up and slowed to a walk. She and Lily were drenched, so there was no use in hurrying now.

"I'm sorry," Lily said.

Halle gave her a look. "For what? The weather?"

Lily's shoulders were hunched, and her hair hung down in thick black ropes. "That and everything else," she said.

Halle made a sputtering noise. "I should lock you and Carolyn in a room together to see how long it would take for your egos to cancel each other out. I mean, really. You both seem to think that the sun rises and sets in your butthole, and that anything that happens in your vicinity is because of you. Your responsibility, your fault. Well, get set for a shocker, kid." She leaned close to Lily and spoke into her ear. *"It's not."*

Lily blinked away rainwater. Or tears. Halle couldn't tell which.

"It used to be," Lily said.

Neither of them spoke again until Halle had driven them south of the river to her duplex in Zilker Gardens. As they started to turn onto Halle's street and came in sight of the duplex, Halle saw that her ex-mother-in-law's minivan was already parked at the curb.

"Shit!" Halle said. She pulled her Plymouth out of the turn and accelerated back onto the cross street, then checked her watch. "I'm still five minutes early, but I forgot that Cruella always has her clocks set ten minutes fast. That way she gets to pretend that everyone else is just a smidgen less responsible than she is." She touched Lily's wrist and found that it was cool and dry despite the fact that they'd just been out in the rain. "Listen, I'm going to ask you to duck down while I go around the block and pull into my garage. I don't know how I'd explain you to the Wicked Witch, and I'm not up to dealing with the state you'd put the kids into, either."

Lily looked out the passenger window and up at the sky. The rain had slacked off, but the clouds were still thick and low.

"I don't mind," Lily said. "I can stay in your garage while you deal with your family. Until the Moon shows herself again, I have nowhere to go anyway."

She turned toward Halle then, gave her a pitiful smile, and scrunched down below dashboard level.

Halle let out a sigh. It was a good thing she'd had a fortifying weekend. Between the Wicked Witch, two kids who were sure to be hyperkinetic, and a despondent goddess who was losing her feathers, the post-holiday week was already getting to be a grind.

❖

At nine o'clock, while Cleo and Tony were playing Nintendo in the living room, Halle was able to sneak Lily in from the garage and take her down the hall to her bedroom.

She closed the door behind them. "The kids don't have any homework tonight," she said. "Or at least they claim they don't. So I'm letting them play video games in the living room until nine-thirty. Then we'll go to war for thirty minutes, and I'll get them into bed by ten. You can come out after that if you like."

Halle remembered then that Tommy was supposed to call at ten with news of Jack, and she considered telling Lily that. But she decided against it. Lily still seemed unhappy and bedraggled, and mentioning Jack might not be helpful.

"You're kind," Lily said. "Your children, friends, and lovers are lucky."

Halle couldn't help grinning. "Yeah, I've always thought so. Even when they didn't. Would you like a towel, by the way? Your hair's still wet. It smells good, but I'll bet it's uncomfortable."

"A towel would be nice. Thank you."

Halle left, closing the door again, and went to check on the kids. To her relief, Cleo and Tony both seemed to be getting sleepy, although they weren't ready to give up their video game just yet. So she let them be and headed back to her bedroom, stopping for a towel on the way.

When she reentered the bedroom, she found Lily seated in the worn office chair at her desk, staring at the blank grayness of the computer monitor.

"Ever done any programming?" Halle asked, coming up behind Lily and rubbing the towel over her hair. "I've been thinking of hiring a subcontractor to do some of the boring shit work."

Lily continued staring into the monitor. "I wouldn't know where to begin." Her eyes narrowed in the reflection in the glass. "It's a god, isn't it?"

Halle almost laughed, but suppressed it when she saw that Lily was

276

serious. She gave Lily's hair a final fluff and then tossed the towel onto the bed.

"No," she said. "It's just a tool."

"But you keep it beside your bed," Lily said. "And you depend on it for your life and livelihood. And it is never far from your thoughts. Yes?"

"Well, I guess that's true," Halle admitted.

Lily stood and faced her. "Then it's a god."

Halle made a face. "But I don't worship it."

Lily smiled again, and for the first time all evening, she looked like she meant it.

"Do you bring it offerings?" she asked.

"In a sense," Halle said. "It's called software. But that isn't—"

"Do you visit it at regular intervals and suffer from guilt when you fail to do so?"

"Yeah, but—"

"And do you pray for it to give you the things you desire, and curse when it fails to do so?"

Halle gave up. "Okay. Yes."

"Sounds like worship to me," Lily said, and then cast a rueful glance back at the monitor. "I never guessed I'd have to compete with things like that. No wonder I'm ill. I lose more of my nature every time I come near you contemporary people and your bloodless, soulless, *sexless* deities." She bit her lip. "I won't deny that I have affected some of you to your detriment, and I feel ashamed of that. But you and your things have done even greater harm to me."

Halle wasn't about to take that without responding, but to do so she was going to have to mention what she wasn't sure she should. So she sat down on the edge of her bed and patted the mattress beside her. For a few seconds Lily seemed not to know what she meant, but then she sat down, too.

"Look, honey," Halle said, taking Lily's hand, "we both know that's a crock of shit. Your problem isn't computers or telephones or microwave ovens or anything else we contemporary people use to complicate our lives. In fact, we've already talked about what your problem really is, and I know from personal experience that he's in full possession of blood, soul, *and* sex." She squeezed Lily's fingers.

"And right now he's up at my place in the Hill Country, no doubt wondering where the hell you are."

Lily looked at the floor and said nothing. But she squeezed Halle's fingers in return.

They sat there for a while until Halle saw that the clock on her nightstand said 9:35. Then she released Lily's hand and stood.

"Time to fight the kids upstairs and into bed," she said. "And you look like you could use some sleep, too."

"I don't sleep," Lily said. She was still looking at the floor. "The men do. That's when they call to me. If I slept too, I couldn't hear them."

Lily sounded miserable, and Halle wished there were something she could do that would make her feel better.

"Well, even if you don't sleep," she said, "maybe you should at least lie down and rest."

In response, Lily lay down on her back across the bed. As she did so, her black-and-white dress shifted, split, and became wings again. And then Lily, naked, stared up at the ceiling with her arms and wings at her sides. She didn't speak.

This is one bizarre chick, Halle thought. But she kept that to herself and went to put her children to bed.

A few minutes before ten, when both Cleo and Tony were settled in their beds, Halle came back downstairs to find Lily standing in the entryway with the front door open.

"The rain has stopped," Lily said as Halle came up beside her.

Halle looked out. Not only had the rain stopped, but the clouds were breaking up as well. The Moon was sliding into view in one of the gaps, its light so pure and intense that it made Halle's eyes sting.

"Good," Halle said. "You'll be going to Jack now, I assume?"

Lily gave her an unblinking gaze. "No," she said, "I'm going home."

Halle didn't understand at first, but then she realized from Lily's tone as much as from her words just what she meant.

"You mean you're not coming back, don't you?" Halle said.

Lily looked up toward the Moon. "Yes. Each time I do, each time I'm with him, I find it harder to leave. Each time I lose more feathers. Each time I feel more and more as if I'm becoming something else." She began to tremble again. "My difficulties tonight were a final warning. I must return to where I can be what I've always been. And I must remain there."

Halle reached out and touched Lily's quivering right wing. "But, Lilith," she said. "If you do that, you *can't* be what you've always been. To be a true goddess, you have to come to Earth and touch the lives of human beings." She moved her fingertips up to Lily's cheek and found that it was as cool and dry as her wrist had been. "And if those human beings happen to touch you in return, then it seems to me that's the price you pay for your divinity."

Lily stepped outside, away from Halle's fingertips.

"It's too high," she said, and then turned back toward Halle. "I know that your friend Tommy is about to telephone you. Please ask him to tell . . . the other one . . . that he won't see me again."

Halle crossed her arms and glared. "The bleeding fuck I will," she said. "If you're going to dump a guy, have the guts to do it yourself."

Lily closed her eyes, as if she were clinging to the Moonlight Tower and the light was too bright. "I can't."

"Yes, you can," Halle said. "If you ever loved him at all, you owe him that much. I mean, hell, I've managed to do it any number of times. And I won't deny that it's rotten and awful and hard, but if I can do it, so can you." She paused, letting the weight of her next words build up. "Otherwise, I'm more of a goddess than you are."

Lily turned away. Her black hair swirled.

"In this world, in this life," Lily said, "I believe that's true."

Then she spread her wings and rose up to the gap in the clouds. Halle tried to watch her go, but lost her in the blue-white disk of the Moon.

"Well, goddamn," Halle muttered. "Don't let the door hit you in the ass on your way out."

Then the phone rang, so she closed the door and went to answer the call.

It was Tommy. He said that he'd gone to check on Jack and that Jack was fine, albeit naked and chilly and sitting near the top of a live oak tree in front of Halle's cabin.

Halle thought for a few seconds and then asked Tommy to take a blanket to Jack and give him a message from Lily: "Got lost. Got tired. Can't make it this month."

Tommy promised to relay the message, and Halle thanked him for being a great ex-boyfriend. He grunted something about how that made his life complete and then hung up.

Halle replaced the receiver in its cradle and went to the refrigerator. She made herself a turkey sandwich and took it back to her bedroom, where she turned on her computer and got online to check her E-mail.

She had a few queries from clients, but the note that interested her most was personal:

Dear Holly—

Had to get on a plane to Washington today on short notice. Lawyer stuff; you'd commit seppuku before I could finish describing it. But thought I should let you know I was out of town.

Am hoping you wanted to know where I am. Am also hoping you'll be where I left you when I get back.

Yours,

What's-His-Face

Halle read the message twice, then thought she heard one of the children cough. So she got up and stepped into the hall to listen. She could hear Tony and Cleo sleeping upstairs, and both of them sounded fine. They sounded strong and healthy.

She went back to the computer and began writing an answer to the personal note:

Dear Duane—

It's Halle, not Holly. But thank you. I did want to know.

And yes, I'll be here. I'm always here.

She paused for a moment, listening again. She heard the hum of her computer, and she heard her own breathing and the breathing of her children. All else was quiet.

She finished the note:

This is where I live.

21

◆

The Shadows of Earth
Were to Blame

The shadows of Earth were to blame, Jack thought. That included the shadow she cast into space, and the shadows she contained within herself.

Last night, the shadow she cast into space had fallen over the Moon, eclipsing her, and Jack had wondered how that might make Lily feel. Would she miss the light of the sun, or would she enjoy the cool darkness?

And what effect would it have on the journey she would make tonight?

Jack hadn't thought it would matter much. After all, the eclipse would have been over for fourteen hours by the time the full Moon rose over Texas on Monday evening. But Jack had been uneasy, because he still didn't know how long it took Lily to make the trip. If it took more than fourteen hours, the shadow might interfere with her navigation. It had delayed her for only a few minutes during June's eclipse—but then, that eclipse hadn't even been visible in the skies over the Hill Country.

Even if last night's eclipse hadn't mattered, though, there were still the shadows of the clouds that were moving across the face of the

Moon right now. How could Jack keep her light shining on his skin if the clouds kept hiding her?

He pushed his wet hair back from his forehead and brushed droplets from his beard. He didn't mind that the clouds had rained on him, but if they kept Lily away, he was going to be angry. They had better clear off and let her through. She was already later than she had ever been before, and he was scared. Moonrise had been four and a half hours ago. Something was wrong. Lily had seemed increasingly upset these past few months, and she'd been losing feathers.

Last month, when he had found her in the tree that Artie had directed him to, Lily hadn't even wanted to talk. She hadn't wanted to do anything but possess and consume him the way that she had the first time they'd met. As she'd touched him, though, he had known that she wasn't herself. He had felt that her trembling was as much from fear as from passion. So he had asked her to tell him what was wrong, but she had hushed his questions with kisses.

And Jack, weak and selfish mortal that he was, had let her. There were shadows in him, too.

"Hey, buddy," a voice called from below. "You still up there?"

Jack recognized the voice. It was Halle's friend Tommy Morrison, who had already come by once tonight. Jack peered through the dripping jumble of live-oak leaves below him and saw Tommy standing between the tree and the driveway.

"Sure am," Jack called back. "And I'll be here until my date arrives."

Tommy coughed. "Thing is, I've got some unfortunate news about that. I just called Halle, and she said Lily isn't going to make it tonight. So I thought I'd better tell you so you don't stay out here and freeze your ass off."

Jack hadn't felt cold at all until Tommy had said that. But now he hugged his chest, teetering on the branch, and shivered. His skin goose-pimpled.

"How does Halle know Lily isn't coming?" he asked.

"She didn't say," Tommy said. "All she told me was that Lily got lost, got tuckered out in the process, and won't be here this month."

Jack felt petulant. He couldn't help it. "Did she talk to Lily directly? Did Lily really say that?"

Tommy gave an exasperated sigh. "Come on, Jack. Have you ever known Halle to bullshit?"

Jack had to admit that he hadn't.

"Me neither," Tommy said. "Halle's as straightforward a woman as I've ever been shat on by." He coughed again. "Look, I'm gettin' me a hellacious chest cold, and this weather ain't doin' it much good. What say you come down so we can both get indoors and call it a night?"

Jack considered. It was true that Halle didn't bullshit. If Halle said that Lily wasn't coming, then Lily wasn't coming.

But how did he know that Halle had said that? How did he know that Tommy wasn't lying just to get him down from the tree?

"I don't know," Jack called down. "I think maybe I'll stay here just in case. Maybe Lily will change her mind."

Tommy groaned. "Aw, shit," he said. "I guess I have to come up and get you, then. Halle'd tear me a new asshole if I let you stay out here all night."

He came across to the tree and began to climb. But he was wearing cowboy boots, and Jack knew what would happen.

"Better be careful," Jack said. "You're going to—"

But the warning was too late. Tommy slipped on the wet bark, fell, and landed on his back on the ground. Jack could hear the air in his lungs blow out through his mouth with a whuff. Tommy winced, cursed, and then just lay there staring up at Jack.

"Are you hurt?" Jack asked.

"I ain't remaining in the supine position 'cause I enjoy wallowing in wet mulch," Tommy replied.

He sounded annoyed, but Jack supposed that was understandable. Tommy had fallen only five or six feet and had landed on rain-softened soil . . . but even so, it had probably hurt.

Jack hated the thought of anyone getting hurt because of him, so he climbed down to make sure that Tommy was okay. He jumped the last several feet, and his landing splashed Tommy in the face.

"I have a recurring nightmare like this," Tommy said, sitting up and wiping his eyes. "A naked monkey-man jumps down from a tree and takes me off into the jungle, where he forces me to marry his ugly monkey-daughter. Then I have to raise a whole passel of butt-faced monkey-kids, plus eat bugs for the rest of my life."

Jack nodded. "Most of my dreams are about sex, too," he said. "By the way, are you all right?"

Tommy squinted at him. "I think my lower back's fucked up. Maybe my right leg, too. And excuse me, bubba, but that dream of mine isn't about sex."

"Sure it is," Jack said. "First of all, the monkey-man is wild and naked, right? That's sexual. Then you make love to the monkey-girl—sex itself—the result of which is monkey-children with faces like buttocks. And buttocks, obviously, are sexual too."

Tommy seemed agitated. "I did *not* make love to the monkey-girl."

"Then how'd you have all those monkey-kids with her?"

"I didn't," Tommy said. "She already *had* the monkey-kids. I just had to *raise* them."

"Plus eat bugs," Jack reminded him.

"Stink bugs, to be specific."

"Whoa," Jack said. "You can't tell me *that's* not sexual."

It was starting to rain again, a fine drizzle. Tommy scowled up at the sky, and then at Jack. "I can tell you whatever I damn well please," he said, "and I'm telling you that I don't find stink bugs sexy in even the slightest degree." He held out his right hand. "Now help me up, willya?"

Jack helped him up, and then they started toward Halle's cabin. Tommy was limping, so Jack tried to hold his arm to help. But Tommy brushed him off.

"I needed a hand to get to my feet," Tommy said, "but I'd just as soon not make any other sort of physical contact with you. It's nothing personal, you understand. I'd feel the same way about any guy who happened to be naked."

They reached the cabin then and went into the west wing. Jack had left a lamp on in the living room, and there were coals smoldering in the fireplace.

"I have to say that I still think your dream is sexual," Jack said as he closed the door behind them. "But if you want to hide from your own psyche, that's your business. Would you like a towel?"

Tommy gave him a short nod, then sat down on the couch with a grunt.

Jack went to the bathroom, took two towels from the cabinet, and returned to the living room. He tossed one of the towels to Tommy and then began drying himself, rubbing hard. He was still cold, and he hoped the friction would help.

"You know," Tommy said, wiping his towel over his face, "not everything in this life has to do with sex. Especially not that dream."

Jack finished drying off, then grabbed his underwear and jeans from where he'd left them on the card table. "What else could it be about?" he asked.

Tommy glared at him. "It just so happens that I have an unresolved childhood fear of monkeys."

Jack pulled on his jockey shorts and jeans, then scooped up his shoes, socks, and sweatshirt and went over to finish dressing by the fireplace. The heat coming off the coals wasn't much, but it was something.

"Well, Tommy," he said, pulling on his Albert-Einstein-riding-an-invisible-bicycle sweatshirt, "the fact is that most childhood fears that carry over into adulthood tend to be sexual in nature. Particularly, I would think, if they have to do with monkeys."

Tommy dropped his towel onto the floor. "You're full of warm, soupy shit. What the real fact is, is that when I was five or six, my mother took me to a zoo, and the monkeys scared the bejeezus out of me. Okay?"

"Okay," Jack said. He could tell that Tommy wanted to drop the topic—but if Lily really wasn't coming, Jack needed to keep talking so he didn't think about it. And if she really *was* coming, then Tommy had lied to him and deserved to be tortured. "But what did they do that scared you so much?"

Tommy rolled his eyes. "Judas Priest suckin' a tailpipe, how should I know? I was five, and they were *monkeys.* They didn't have to *do* anything." He frowned. "Although I do remember that two of them threw their nasty little monkey-turds at me."

Jack took a poker from beside the fireplace and scrambled the coals, trying to get them excited. It didn't work.

"Monkeys will do that," he said. "As with all primates, they're intrigued with their bodily functions and the products thereof. They're also extremely sexual, but because the females have estrus cycles, the males have to do without intercourse for long periods of time. So among the males, at least, masturbation and homosexual behavior occur frequently." He gave Tommy a sidelong glance. "Now, what was that nightmare about? And why do you have such an aversion to physical contact with naked men?"

Tommy glared at Jack again, but after a few seconds the expression dissolved, and he laughed.

"How do you know so much about monkeys, anyway?" he asked then.

Jack didn't answer for a few moments because he was looking around for a stick or two to throw on the fire. But there was nothing. And everything outside would be wet. He had thought that he would be with Lily tonight, so after building a fire upon his arrival— just to keep busy while waiting for the Moon to rise—he hadn't worried about keeping warm.

"Actually, I don't know a thing about monkeys," Jack said, giving up his search for firewood. "But I do know that you're wrong when you say that not everything in life has to do with sex. My relationship with Lily has shown me that sex is the most important thing in the world."

Tommy shrugged. "I'll admit that it always seems like it at the time. But then it's over, and you move on."

Jack squatted in front of the fireplace, trying to get warmer. "That's just what makes it so precious," he said. "Getting to see Lily only once a month has made that clear. It's made me realize that most people's lives—"

He hesitated, thinking of what his own life had been like after losing Natalie. Of being empty and dry.

"Most people's lives," he said then, "are like deserts. And in a desert, no matter how much water you have, it's never enough. So it's too valuable to waste."

Tommy's eyes narrowed. "This is a metaphor, right?"

"Right."

"Okay, good. Last time I thought something was a metaphor, I was wrong, and your pal Steve tried to kick my ass for being ignorant."

Jack was surprised. "That doesn't sound like him," he said. But then he remembered that until a few months ago, Tommy had been sleeping with Halle. "Unless he was acting out of jealousy."

"I believe he was," Tommy said. "Also out of being shit-faced drunk. However, having been the victim of unrequited desire my-self, I can't say as I blame him. But I still would've busted his jaw if he'd laid a hand on me."

"Then I'm glad he didn't."

"You and me both." Tommy shifted on the couch. "Damn, my jeans are damp, and it's causing some serious discomfort. Water ain't so precious at the moment, if you ask me."

"But it is in the desert," Jack said. "Just as sex is in life."

Tommy shook his head. "Except that ain't a universal truth. I mean, it *is* possible to live without it. Some folks do, and don't seem to mind." He grinned. "Although I confess that I don't happen to be one of them. I may be lost in that desert of yours at the moment, but I expect to find a girl skinny-dipping at an oasis before too awful long."

Jack was amused at Tommy's effort to participate in his metaphor, but he didn't let his amusement show. Instead, he said, "Just be sure that she's someone who'll stick by you when you get caught in a sand-storm."

Tommy looked horrified. "Hey, I ain't gettin' married."

Jack stood up again. His knees were hurting, and the coals in the fireplace had almost died out anyway. He would have to get used to being cold.

"I know you're not," he said. "After all, you think of marriage as enslavement to the monkey-girl and her brood. Consider this, though: You and Halle aren't involved anymore, but aren't you glad she's still a friend in the desert?"

Tommy pushed himself up from the couch with a grimace. "This conversation has gotten too goddamn personal," he said. "Besides, it sounds like the rain's stopped, so I think I'll hike back to my place now. If I don't get outta these wet jeans pretty soon, my crack's gonna chafe and put me in an unpleasant mood." He took a few limping steps toward the door, then paused and gave Jack a don't-shit-me stare. "You gonna be all right here? You need anything?"

Jack returned the stare. "Yes. I need to know if you've told me the truth about Lily."

Tommy didn't blink. "So far as I know it."

Jack believed him and wished that he didn't. "But what about next month?" he asked. "Will she come then?"

Tommy spread his hands. "I got no idea."

Jack looked down at the rag rug where he and Lily had lain together. His clothes itched. He wasn't used to wearing them on the night of a full Moon, but now he was too cold to take them off again. He felt like a six-year-old. He felt like crying.

"Wish I could be more help," Tommy said, going to the door. "But all I can offer is assistance of a practical nature. For example: There's an electric heater in the big bedroom in the east wing. I assume that it works, but I don't know for sure. I was only there in warm weather."

"Okay. Thanks."

Tommy opened the door and stepped outside. "You're welcome. And I hope you don't take this as an insult, but I have to express the opinion that you're the most pussy-whipped man I've ever met in my life."

Jack wasn't sure, but he thought that Tommy sounded envious.

Tommy closed the door then, and Jack was alone. He turned, forced one foot in front of the other, and went into the kitchen. It had occurred to him that eating the submarine sandwich he had brought from Austin might warm him up and kill some time. But he was only able to swallow three bites before having to put the sandwich back into the refrigerator.

He returned to the living room, picked up his bathroom kit from the card table, and went outside.

The night was dark and cold. It wasn't raining right now, but the clouds had thickened again. Jack couldn't see the Moon at all. He could look up at the empty bowl at exactly the point where she should be, but she wasn't there. It was as if the world had become a cave, and there was nothing beyond it.

Jack shivered. He felt just as he had on the night that Natalie had died. It had rained then, too.

She had been working late—working late on Valentine's Day, when they were supposed to go out to dinner—and had never made it home. And while he had been waiting for her, watching TV, his skin had gone cold, and he had shivered. He had wrapped himself in the rust-colored afghan that she had made before they were married, but it hadn't helped. So he had sat wrapped in the afghan with his knees pulled to his chest, not knowing why he was so cold, until the telephone rang and a disembodied voice told him that there had been an accident.

In the weeks that had followed, he had done the things he had to do with the police and the funeral home and the insurance companies, vaguely aware that his friends were trying to help him do them. And then afterward, he had quit his job, sold his and Natalie's house, and moved into a tiny apartment in Hyde Park to wait for death.

But then, on the night of the first full Moon after Halloween, he had met Lily at the Avenue B Grocery.

So he had stopped waiting for death . . . and started waiting for Lily instead.

In return, she had come to him on the night of every full Moon since.

Except tonight's.

Tonight he was cold and alone. Lost in the desert with no water. And he was afraid.

But he wasn't afraid only for himself. He was afraid for Lily, too. He had known last month that she was frightened, that something wasn't right—but then he had let her distract him. Because he had wanted to.

They had laughed, made love, and soared high over the Hill Country. And Jack had been sure that the pinpoint lights both above and below had been winking at them.

Now he didn't think that he would ever see them that way again.

"I miss you," he whispered.

He knew she wasn't coming back. Once a goddess decided to forsake a mortal, for whatever reason, the mortal was shit out of luck.

If the human brain had been designed properly, Jack thought, a man's consciousness would cease to exist when that happened. All thoughts would just stop dead, and all connections to the senses would be severed. That way the man wouldn't be aware of his loss.

Maybe there could even be a pleasant sort of numbness, like when you were so drunk you couldn't move.

But the human brain hadn't been designed properly at all. Right now, it was telling him that the world was bleak and black and smelled of leaf mold.

Lightning spiderwebbed through the clouds overhead, and the clouds groaned with thunder. Jack ducked into the cabin's breezeway and entered the east wing just as the rain started coming down again. It came down hard.

He found that the space heater in the big bedroom did work. It filled the room with a weak orange light and the acrid stink of burnt dust. Jack's shivering subsided, but even after stripping naked again, he couldn't sleep. He sat up in bed all night, listening to the storm outside, his skin reflecting the dull glow from the heater.

He was still waiting for her. He couldn't help it.

On the night of a full Moon, that was all he could think of to do.

PART XIII

COLD MOON

Tuesday, December 28, 1993

❖

22

❖

She Drove Faster Alone

She drove faster alone, Carolyn had discovered yesterday. The miles between her house in Austin and Halle's cabin in the Hill Country had flown by in a fast-forward blur, and it had been a hell of a lot of fun.

Carolyn was thinking about that again as she hiked through the woods north of the cabin. The weather was unusually chilly, even for December, and her breath puffed out as crystal vapor. But she was dressed in jeans, a heavy sweater, a jacket, and gloves, and she was warm. Her black sneakers crunched on the dry mulch, and it seemed as if that crunch were the only sound in the world. She liked being the only one there to hear it. Not that she wanted to be a hermit. But everything seemed clearer when there was no one else around.

The drive yesterday had emphasized that. Whenever Artie had been along, she had never made the trip to the cabin in less than two hours. But this time, she had cut that to one hour and forty-two minutes.

At first she hadn't been able to figure out what accounted for the difference. But this morning, after having had a bed all to herself for the first night in more than a year, she had known what it was. It was because whenever anyone rode with her, she was always aware that she was responsible for the other person's safety and comfort. That made her tense, because she didn't like being responsible for anyone but herself. And she couldn't drive or do anything else well when she was tense.

But when she was alone, she could relax a little. Yesterday, she had felt the texture of the road through the steering wheel and pedals, and she had known exactly how fast she could drive without hurtling into the trees. She had taken the curves as if molding them to her own special trajectory.

She'd even been able to sense when there was a speed trap ahead.

The result had been that she had arrived at the cabin exhilarated. She hadn't felt that way, other than while making love, for a long time. And driving fast hadn't given her the hiccups.

So it had been a real letdown when she'd walked into the west wing's living room and discovered that everyone else was dragging ass as if they had two weeks to live. And they had also seemed disappointed that Artie hadn't come, which had confused her. She hadn't thought they liked him.

Except for Katy.

But Carolyn wasn't even sure about that. She knew all too well that it was possible not to like someone and still want him. And that it was also possible to want him so much that it turned into a heavy ache you could come to resent.

This morning at breakfast she had looked across the table at Katy and wondered why she didn't hate her guts. But she had wondered for only an instant.

For one thing, she was pretty sure that Artie and Katy's affair was over. Artie had been moping around the house ever since she'd told him that she knew about it, and when he hadn't been doing that, he'd been at the restaurant. So he hadn't had time for anything else.

For another thing, Carolyn had already gotten even with Katy, and she felt bad about it. True, she and Stephen had been together only three times, and then they'd agreed to stop. But that didn't change the fact that they'd started.

And finally, Carolyn had decided that she and Artie were splitting up. She had gotten past her ache and resentment. So why hate Katy for sleeping with Artie when she didn't even want to be with him anymore?

She had made that decision almost two months ago, but had broken the news to Artie only the day before yesterday. She had put it off because of the situation with his father, but now that they'd settled the poor guy into a nursing home, the time had come. So on Sunday—the day after Christmas—Carolyn had told Artie that she would help him look for another place to live after New Year's. And he had said that would be fine.

Then he'd said that he wouldn't go to the cabin with her this time. He wanted to work every day this week, he'd said, because people left good tips between Christmas and New Year's.

So Artie wasn't here, but the rest of the usual gang was. And Halle had brought her new boyfriend, Duane the Lawyer. Everyone had the week off work, and Halle's children were staying with their grandmother, so Carolyn had been looking forward to getting to know her friends as individual adults again. But now she wasn't so sure it was going to work out that way.

Carolyn had arrived hours after everyone else because she had decided to open her shop for regular business hours on Monday. She'd wanted to be sure that her customers had a chance to make their post-Christmas returns and exchanges before she closed for the week. And it had been the right choice, because she'd had her best day of the year. There had been plenty of exchanges and a few returns, but more than half of those transactions had been supplemented with new purchases. That had contributed to her good mood.

But that mood put her out of sync with the other Austin refugees. Even Halle and Duane the Lawyer, who still should have been new-relationship giddy, seemed sullen.

So Carolyn had spent yesterday evening and most of today reading a bodice-ripper and staying out of everyone else's way. By four o'clock this afternoon, though, the unhappiness permeating the air in the cabin had gotten to be too much. The whole idea of this week had been for everyone to decompress and help Jack get through the last full Moon of the year, but it seemed to Carolyn that they were all more pressurized than ever.

So she had decided to go for a long walk in the woods, and she was glad that she had. It was only now that she was off by herself that she was beginning to figure out just what was going on.

Some of it had to do with Stephen and Katy, for reasons that Carolyn understood better than she wanted to. And some of it had to do with the fact that Halle's old boyfriend Tommy kept coming over at mealtimes. Duane the Lawyer—who was mostly bald and not at all beefcakey, unlike Tommy—couldn't help getting surly at that, and Halle apparently couldn't help responding in kind.

Most of the problem, though, had to do with Jack.

Carolyn had telephoned him a few times in the past month and had gone to lunch with him once, and he had told her that Lily was gone for good. That in itself had been something of a relief to Carolyn, but Jack's demeanor had worried her. It would have been all right if he'd been sad or angry, but he hadn't displayed any emotion at all. Instead, he had just seemed . . . empty.

Just as he had seemed after Natalie had died.

Carolyn had been hoping that he would snap out of it this week as his friends rallied around him. But so far Jack still seemed empty, and the others were morose. And Carolyn didn't know what to do about it, so she was tempted to just take off in the Honda and have a good time by herself. But she knew she would feel guilty if she did that, and she was already managing all the guilt that she cared to.

So she had to stay. If she could just get through tonight with these people, then maybe tomorrow would be better. Tonight would be tough, though, because the Moon would be full, and Jack would be unable to think of anything other than the fact that Lily was gone. If he was able to think at all.

Carolyn stopped to rest and looked up toward the clear winter sky, watching her breath dissipate among the overhanging boughs. She had just thought of one way that she might be able to help Jack through tonight's crisis.

But as she considered it, she realized that it would wind up being even more depressing than it had been with Stephen. It would be too much like trying to revisit the past. Besides, as she had told Artie two months ago, the quarters here were too close. If she slept with Jack, everyone else would know. And someone might get hurt.

So that wasn't an option. But there ought to be *something* she could do.

There was a movement in the trees, and Carolyn jumped. She caught a glimpse of feathers and wings—and then saw an owl settle onto a cedar branch. The owl gave her a know-it-all stare.

"Bastard," Carolyn said, putting a hand over her racing heart. "You did that on purpose."

Her first thought had been that Lily had returned after all. But she should have known better. The Moon hadn't risen yet. It was too early for Lily to be here even if she was coming.

But it was also too early to be seeing owls.

Carolyn and the owl stared at each other for a while. Then, apparently bored, the owl blinked, spread its wings, and took off. It swooped low over Carolyn's head and then flew away through the woods, its wing tips brushing past leaves and branches.

It was only after the owl had disappeared that Carolyn noticed the light was starting to fade. And then she realized that her nose and cheeks were beginning to sting from the cold. It was time to head back.

She turned and took a step, then stopped and shivered.

She had no idea where the cabin was. She had been wandering this way and that for more than an hour, and now, with dusk falling, nothing looked familiar. She knew that she couldn't be too far from civilization of some sort—but for all that she could see around her, she might have been in the middle of a million-acre forest in Siberia.

This was bad. If she didn't find her way back before dusk became night, her friends would wind up searching for her as they'd searched for Jack in months past. And when they found her, she would have to admit that she had just plain gotten lost.

She couldn't stand the thought of seeming that incompetent.

So she stood still and listened. If she couldn't see the cabin, maybe she could hear it. Maybe one of her friends would go out for firewood, and she would hear the door open and close.

Minutes passed, and the sky and the woods grew darker. All Carolyn could hear were soft rustlings in the trees and brush, and the sound of her own heartbeat in her ears.

She hugged herself. She was really getting cold now, even inside her jacket and sweater. And her ears and nose were going numb. She began to think that seeming incompetent wasn't the worst thing that could happen.

Then, finally, there was a sound: a distant buzzing, like bees in a hive.

Carolyn held her breath, listening hard.

The buzzing grew louder until it sounded like a chain saw.

Carolyn didn't think that Halle even had a chain saw. But it was either head for that sound or stay out in the woods until she froze or was humiliated.

So Carolyn struck off toward the buzzing sound, and as it grew louder still, she realized that it wasn't a chain saw at all. In fact, she thought she knew just what it was, and when she saw a bright light shining ahead, she was sure.

She came out onto the gravel driveway near the highway and found Artie sitting there on his motorcycle. His helmet's faceplate was up, and he was revving the bike's throttle and fiddling with a valve under the fuel tank.

Carolyn walked over and tapped him on the shoulder of his cold-weather riding coveralls. He looked up at her with only mild surprise.

"Hey," he said, taking his hand from the throttle. The engine noise subsided to a low chug. "You didn't have to come down to meet me."

"I didn't," Carolyn said. She gestured at the motorcycle. "Problems?"

Artie shook his head. "The main tank just ran out of gas. It's running on the reserve now."

Carolyn got onto the seat behind him. "So give me a ride up the hill, okay?"

Artie drove them up to the cabin, then parked inside the gravel circle next to Carolyn's car.

Carolyn got off the bike as he killed the engine. "I thought you were going to work all week."

Artie took off his helmet, rebuckled its strap, and hung it on the handlebars. But then he just sat there and watched it swing.

Carolyn didn't like it. "Artie?"

He looked up and gave her a weak smile.

"He's gone," he said.

It took Carolyn a moment to realize what he meant. Then she leaned down and put her arms around him. But before long she could tell that Artie wanted to break the embrace, so she released him and stepped back.

"When did it happen?" she asked.

Artie got off the bike and let out a sigh that reminded Carolyn of her grandfather.

"This morning," he said. "They called me at the restaurant and said I had to take care of some stuff. So I did. And then I wanted to talk to you, but there's no phone here. So I got the neighbors to look after the cats, and I rode on down."

"I'm glad you did," Carolyn said, and she was. "We can go back tomorrow and make the funeral arrangements."

"I already did all that."

Carolyn was stunned. "You did? Yourself?"

Artie shrugged. "Yeah, but I might've messed up. See, I decided that the funeral should be this Sunday, and the mortician wanted to do it sooner, like Thursday. But I figured that if we wait until the weekend, my mom and sister could maybe come down for it. I mean, it's not like they'll show, but I figured I'd give them the choice. And I didn't want to do it on Saturday, because the guys Dad played *conjunto* with'll be too wasted from New Year's Eve gigs to go to a funeral. So I told the mortician tough titty, we're sticking with Sunday."

When Artie finished, Carolyn found herself experiencing an emotion she'd never had about him before.

She was proud of him.

"I don't think you messed up," she said. "I think you did great."

Artie made a face. "I don't know," he said. Then he looked at the ground. "And I was hoping you'd come, too."

This pissed her off. "What, did you think I wouldn't go to your father's funeral? Of course I will, you asshole."

"Well, I wasn't sure," Artie said. "I mean, since we're breaking up."

Carolyn rolled her eyes. "Christ on a crutch, Artie. That's an entirely different matter. And look, you don't even have to move out anytime soon, if you don't want. I know you've got enough to deal with right now."

Artie frowned. "Thing is, I sort of already dealt with that too. After I finished with the mortician, I called Dad's ex-landlady to see if she'd rented his old apartment yet. And she said she hadn't, so I told her I'd take it. I've got a dude with a pickup truck lined up to move me over there on Monday. Unless you'd like me to do it sooner."

"No," Carolyn said. "Monday will be fine."

She was feeling a little discombobulated, but she knew that Artie, amazingly, was right. Monday, the day after the funeral, would be the time for him to move out.

And she did still want him to move out . . . but she thought that maybe she liked him more now than when she'd wanted him to move in.

Artie seemed to relax a little. "Cool," he said. "Can we go inside now? I was okay riding the bike, but now I'm freezing my *cojones* off."

Carolyn remembered then that she was cold too, so she walked with Artie to the west wing's front door.

"I have to warn you," she said. "Everybody's in an odd mood. So don't take anything personally, all right?"

"All right," Artie said, but he sounded distracted. He was staring at the ground next to the cabin wall.

Carolyn followed his gaze and saw large white flowers shaped like trumpets on either side of the door. She could actually see the blooms opening as she watched. There were a dozen of them, and they were flawless.

"Should they be doing that in the winter?" Artie asked.

Carolyn didn't think so. These plants shouldn't even be alive, much less have perfect blooms opening. It didn't make sense.

But then, it didn't make sense that she'd ever had a conversation with a winged goddess from the Moon, either. But she had.

She opened the door, and they went inside. A stack of logs was blazing in the fireplace, and the living room was almost too warm. Carolyn could smell chili simmering in the kitchen. Halle, Duane the Lawyer, and Tommy were putting bowls and silverware on the card table, and Katy and Stephen were sitting at opposite ends of the couch, holding books that they didn't really seem to be reading.

Jack was standing in front of the fireplace watching the flames, but he looked up when Carolyn closed the door.

"Artie," Jack said. His voice was dull. "When did you get here?"

"Just now," Artie said. "Didn't you hear my motorcycle?"

"Don't think so," Jack said, and then he looked back at the fire.

Carolyn was annoyed with all of them. Being unhappy was no excuse for being rude. Someone should at least be asking Artie how he was, but Jack was the only one who had even acknowledged his presence.

Someone ought to grab them by the shoulders and shake them.

"Halle," Carolyn said sharply, "did you know you have moon-flowers blooming out front?"

Everyone stopped what they were doing and looked up at her, but no one spoke. It was as if they hadn't quite understood what she'd said.

Then Jack looked at Halle. "You planted moonflowers?" he asked.

Halle was standing at the card table with a fistful of spoons. She seemed puzzled. "Yes, but I planted them late, and they never came up. They can't have popped up now, can they? In December?"

Artie went to the fireplace and unzipped his coveralls. "Go see for yourself," he said.

For a long moment, no one budged. Then Carolyn saw Jack's expression change as if his face were being illuminated from within. He started toward the door.

"Jack?" Katy said. She sounded worried. "I think you'd better—"

But she didn't have a chance to finish, because now Jack ran to the door, flung it open, and plunged outside as if he were jumping off a cliff.

"Oh, great," Stephen said, putting down his book and standing. "I thought we weren't going to have to go through this again."

Artie shucked his coveralls, adjusted the crotch of his jeans, and gave a short laugh. "Yeah, that's life," he said. "Shit just keeps on happening whether you think it should or not."

Halle dropped her fistful of silverware and went out after Jack. Tommy and Duane the Lawyer followed her, and then Stephen went out as well.

Cold air was rushing in through the open door, so Carolyn went to stand in front of the fireplace with Artie. As she took off her gloves and jacket, she saw that Katy was regarding her with obvious suspicion.

"Do you have a comment?" Carolyn asked.

"Only that moonflowers," Katy said, "do not bloom at this time of year."

Carolyn jerked a thumb at the door. "Like Artie said, go see for yourself."

Katy's eyes narrowed. "If someone told me that a flying saucer had landed outside and that I should go see for myself, do you think I would bother?"

Artie laughed again. "Katy, if someone told *me* there was a flying saucer outside, I'd pack a bag and see if the little green fuckers took passengers."

Katy closed her book and stood. "I didn't ask for your opinion, Artie. I didn't ask you for anything."

And then Katy went outside too. She slammed the door behind her, and the cabin walls shuddered.

Carolyn gave Artie a sidelong glance. "I'm going out on a limb here," she said, "but I'm guessing you're not sleeping with her anymore."

Artie looked world-weary. It was a new expression for him, but Carolyn thought he wore it well.

"Nope," he said. "Or with you, either." He sighed like Carolyn's grandfather again. "This sure has been a bend-over-and-take-it kind of year."

"It sure has," Carolyn said.

They stood there at the fire for a minute, listening to the muffled sounds of the others marveling at the moonflowers.

But then the muffled sounds grew louder, and Carolyn heard Halle shout, "Jack, *no!*"

Carolyn and Artie looked at each other.

"You want to see what's going on?" Artie asked.

"What I want," Carolyn said, "has nothing to do with it."

So they went outside. The sun had set, and the full Moon was shining through the trees to the east. Jack's flannel shirt was unbuttoned, and his left arm and shoulder were bare. Stephen and Halle were holding him at the elbows, keeping him from running into the woods.

"Jack, she's not coming," Halle was saying. "She's *gone.*"

Jack's eyes were wild. He was staring at the Moon and straining against Halle and Stephen.

Carolyn hated seeing them hold him like that, but she knew they were right. After Jack had told her that Lily was gone for good, she had called Halle and gotten the details of Lily's last visit to Austin. And there was no other way to interpret what had happened: Jack had been dumped. So to let him go into the woods naked again would be cruel. At best, he would be disappointed. At worst, he would freeze.

"Man, what happened?" Artie asked. "The dude was fine five minutes ago."

Katy held out a half-destroyed moonflower blossom. "He tried to eat it," she said. She sounded as if she were about to cry. "And then he started tearing at his shirt."

"He's gone crazy," Duane the Lawyer said.

Carolyn glared at him. "You don't have any right to that judgment," she said. "I've seen what did this to him, and if he's crazy, then so am I. And so are the rest of us."

She stepped in front of Jack and put her hand on his chest. At her touch, he stopped straining and stood still. But he kept on staring at the Moon.

Carolyn took his face in her hands, and his beard tickled her palms. "Look at me," she said.

Then his eyes shifted toward her, and he seemed to come back from wherever he'd been.

"Oh, it's you," he said. "It's good to see you, Carolyn."

"It's good to see you too, Jack."

He gave her a shy grin. "Did I ever tell you that you were the first woman I ever fell in love with?"

"No." She grinned back. "But I already knew."

Jack chuckled and looked at the Moon again. It was rising above the trees, casting long shadows on the ground in front of the cabin. A blue-white ring was shimmering in the sky around it.

"I'll bet you did," Jack said. "And we both also know that Lily isn't coming back. Not even if I stay naked under a full Moon for the next hundred years. No one mortal can change the mind of a goddess." He closed his eyes. "But I wanted to try."

"I don't blame you," Carolyn said. Then she looked at Halle and Stephen. "You can probably let go of him now."

"Are you going to run off?" Stephen asked Jack.

Jack opened his eyes again. "Where would I go?"

So they released his arms, and everyone started heading back into the cabin.

Carolyn brought up the rear. As she reached the door, she looked down at the new flowers and was struck by how the moonlight seemed to make them glow. It gave her an image of how Jack must have appeared to anyone who had seen him waiting under all those full Moons. His skin must have glowed like this.

At that thought, something he had just said reverberated in her brain:

No one mortal can change the mind of a goddess.

Carolyn plucked a blossom and smelled it. Its scent was a mingling of honeysuckle and musk. It was the kind of scent she could imagine getting drunk on.

Then she saw a single drop of moisture quivering at the blossom's edge. And as she looked closer, she realized that she could see the entire Moon reflected in its surface.

The drop looked delicious, and she wanted to let it touch the tip of her tongue.

She resisted the urge for a moment, but then decided that she could do as she liked. What difference did it make? No one was watching. And what if they were?

"What the hell," she whispered, and brought the blossom to her mouth.

The drop was sweet and cool . . . but as the sweetness filled her mouth, it grew warmer. And then hot. And then it surged into her throat and chest and flooded her muscles and skin.

And as she felt her skin begin to glow, she finally knew what to do. She finally knew how to help Jack.

She burst into the cabin holding the moonflower high in her fist. "No one mortal!" she yelled. "No *one* mortal!"

Everyone, even Jack, stared at her as if she were a talking dog.

It made her laugh. It was hilarious.

Because she knew that she would *make* them understand.

She danced and giggled and leaped. It was too wonderful for her to stand still.

"We have to pick the moonflowers!" she cried. "And then you all have to follow me!"

For several seconds, no one else seemed to be able to make a sound.

Then Halle asked, "Uh, follow you where?"

Carolyn sprang to Halle's side, kissed her on the neck, and whispered into her ear.

"Do you remember that little clearing?" she asked. "Where we had the tent?"

Halle nodded. She looked dubious.

Carolyn danced away across the rag rug. "Then pick a moonflower and follow me there!" She stopped suddenly, crouched, and pointed her finger at each person in turn. "Or are you all chicken?"

Everyone looked uncomfortable, and Carolyn was glad to see it. This was no time for comfort. This was a time for dancing and shouting and eating moonflowers.

This was a time for these people to drop their ridiculous pretense of sanity and start acting like the lunatics they really were.

She put her hands on her hips, stuck her elbows out behind her, and began strutting around the room like a rooster. She made clucking noises. Her moonflower wobbled.

"Chicken!" she squawked, thrusting her head out at each of them. "Big—sissy—chicken!"

Almost all of them looked nonplussed. But when she got to Halle's ex-boyfriend Tommy, he glared and stuck out his jaw. "I'll be goddamned if anybody's going to call *me* chicken," he said, and headed for the door.

Then Carolyn's gaze met Jack's, and Jack's face began shining with that inner light again. He grabbed Carolyn in a bear hug.

"Thank you," he said, and then he broke away and raced Tommy outside.

Carolyn waggled her eyebrows at the rest of them.

"Come on," she said. "It's the weird-ass end of a weird-ass year. What have you got to lose?"

And then she danced backwards out the door.

Artie hurried to come with her, and then, hesitantly, everyone else followed.

Everyone except Katy.

Carolyn almost decided to go on without her. But after a moment's thought she became convinced that if Katy didn't participate, all the magic moonflowers in the world wouldn't make a difference. Not to Jack, and not to Lily. Not to any of them.

And especially not to Carolyn.

Katy was essential.

"Make them each pick a flower," Carolyn told Artie. "I'll just be a minute." She started back inside.

Stephen stepped in front of her. "Let me talk to her," he said. "After all, she's my wife."

Carolyn nodded. "And I think she'll be your wife until one of you drops dead. Even after everything that's happened, you two still know what you are to each other." She put a hand on Stephen's shoulder and gently pushed him out of her way. "But I don't know what she and *I* are anymore, and I want to find out."

Stephen opened his mouth as if to argue, but then he stepped aside to join the others.

Carolyn went into the cabin and found that Katy was once again sitting on the couch and pretending to read.

"That's the book that Steve had earlier," Carolyn said. "Yours is over there."

Katy looked up, and her eyes narrowed again. "If Stephen wants his book back, he can ask me for it."

Carolyn squatted on the rag rug in front of Katy and twirled her moonflower between her fingers. "Listen, do you remember back in May, when we looked at Halle's chart with all those numbers and lines?"

Katy didn't answer, but neither did she look away. She continued to give Carolyn her narrow-eyed stare.

"Well," Carolyn said, "I think we might as well admit that a few more numbers have been connected since then."

Katy drew in a breath, made a throat-clearing noise, and put down the book.

"Red lines or blue?" she asked.

"Red. You and Artie drew one of them, and then Stephen and I drew the other."

Katy looked away, at the fire. "I knew about the one, of course. I wasn't sure about the other."

"I didn't think you were. So I thought I should tell you." Carolyn paused, remembering their conversation in the tent. "Because back in May, you said you didn't want to be false to me. And I don't want to be false to you either."

Katy kept looking at the fire. "I'm not going to apologize, Carolyn. If I said I was sorry, it would be a lie."

"I'm not asking you to say that," Carolyn said. "Because I'm not sure that I'm sorry, either. And also because . . . those red lines are history. It's the blue ones that matter now, don't you think?"

Katy looked back at Carolyn again. Her eyes glistened, but she wasn't crying. Carolyn was glad of that.

"We'll see," Katy said. "In the meantime, what can we do to fix things?"

Carolyn stood and twirled the moonflower between her fingers again.

"We can't fix anything," she said. "Things happen, and things change, and you can't go back to redo any of them. But that doesn't mean they're broken, exactly. For example, Artie and I have split up, but I think that somehow we're better with each other than we were before we did. So maybe you and I can be better too."

Katy stood as well. "I don't know about better," she said. "Different, perhaps. You, at least, don't seem to be the same anymore."

Carolyn was pleased. "That's my plan," she said. "Keep 'em guessing."

Katy smiled the first smile that Carolyn had seen from her in months.

"Your plan," Katy said, "seems to be wildly successful so far. Now, what's this nonsense about picking moonflowers?"

"It's something to help Jack," Carolyn said. "I believe in being kind to my former lovers, you know."

"You'd better," Katy said, starting for the door.

They went outside together and found everyone else waiting with moonflowers in hand. Katy gave Carolyn a skeptical glance, but then leaned down and picked a flower of her own.

"Now what?" Stephen asked.

Carolyn's breath quickened. They were going to do it. They were really going to do it. Her eyes met Jack's, and she could see that he understood. The others didn't, yet, but they were willing to follow her lead. And that would be enough. It had to be.

"This way," she said, and struck off across the driveway and into the woods.

As she made her way among the trees, Carolyn could hear the others breathing behind her. And for the first time in her life, she thought that she not only knew the right thing to do, but that she could do it without relying on anger to sustain her. Because for the first time in her life, she knew she didn't need to be alone to feel strong.

Being alone was fine for driving. But you couldn't spend your whole life cooped up in your car. Not if you wanted to bend the gods to your will. For that, no one mortal would do.

Her moonflower began to pulse with heat, and she hoped that the others were feeling the same thing from their own flowers.

When she brought them out into the clearing, she made them stand in a circle of seven—Halle, Tommy, Katy, Stephen, Artie, herself, and Duane the Lawyer—with Jack in the circle's center.

"This is ridiculous," Stephen muttered.

But Carolyn was beyond being quashed. "You bet!" she said.

Then she brought her moonflower to her mouth so that the petals brushed her lips and the heat began to burn into her again. She stayed like that for as long as she could stand it, until she felt as if she were about to jump out of her skin and burst into flame—and then she bit into the blossom, savoring its mingled sweet and bitter tastes, relishing the sensation of tiny lightning bolts crackling across her tongue.

And when she had eaten the entire bloom, she dropped the stem and pulled her sweater off over her head.

"Carolyn!" Katy yelped.

"What?" Carolyn asked, unhooking her bra.

Artie came close to her then and gave her shoulder a quick squeeze.

"I've never turned down the opportunity to get naked with you," he murmured. "And since this might be my last chance, I'm sure not going to turn it down now."

Carolyn stopped what she was doing long enough to squeeze his shoulder in return.

"You can even call me babe if you like," she said.

Artie stepped back, grinned, and whispered, "Babe." Then he ate his flower and began taking off his clothes.

In the center, Jack did likewise.

But Carolyn saw that the others were reluctant. Duane the Lawyer looked afraid and Tommy looked baffled, while Halle seemed amused and Stephen was downright grim.

And Katy looked as skeptical as only Katy could look.

But Carolyn wasn't giving up. As she squatted to untie her shoes, she looked directly at Katy.

"Pay attention," she said. "It works like this: Moonlight. Skin. *Power.*"

Katy's eyes flickered.

"Do you really think I should trust you?" she asked.

Carolyn pulled off her shoes without breaking eye contact.

"I trust *you,*" she said.

Katy took a deep breath and let it out. "All right, then." She brought her moonflower up to her face and closed her eyes.

The tip of Katy's tongue touched the edge of the blossom, and her body went stiff for an instant. Then she opened her eyes, looked at Carolyn again, and smiled.

Stephen took a step toward her. "Honey," he said, "let's just go back inside."

But as he spoke, Katy ate her flower in one ravenous gulp, dropped the stem, and began stripping.

Carolyn knew then that they had won, and it wasn't just because she and Katy had forgiven each other. It was because Katy was the brightest and most analytical person she knew. So if Katy was doing as she asked, then it *had* to be right. If Katy had joined the effort—

Lily didn't stand a chance.

And after Katy, the others went like dominoes. Within seconds, Halle had devoured her own moonflower, and then Tommy ate his. Jeans, shirts, socks, shoes, and underwear began flying into the air all around the circle. Even Duane the Lawyer ate his flower and joined in.

But Stephen didn't. Instead, as everyone else shed their clothes, he took his moonflower and walked off into the woods.

Carolyn was sorry to see that, and she could tell that Katy was, too. But the full Moon was over the clearing now, so time was short. They would have to go ahead without Stephen.

Taking Artie's hand, Carolyn began dancing and singing a wordless song. The others picked up the melody as she invented it, and then they all joined hands and capered around Jack, who spun and whooped. The moonlight shone on their skin, and their faces and breasts and bellies glowed.

Carolyn threw back her head and howled at the Moon, and everyone else howled with her.

Then a shadow passed over them, and white flakes began to fall from the sky. From the Moon.

It was snowing. It was snowing in Central Texas, snowing big soft flakes on a clear night. Carolyn had never seen anything like it.

Then, as if at a sudden command, everyone stopped dancing and stared up at the falling snowflakes, sending clouds of hot breath up to meet them. It made Carolyn dizzy. It was as if she were weightless, flying through outer space, and the snowflakes were the stars rushing past.

And then, at last, falling with the snow . . .

. . . came Lilith.

She spiraled down in a swirl of feathers, and as her talons touched the earth beside Jack, the wind from her wings sent snowflakes spinning away in white tornadoes.

For a moment, Carolyn, Jack, and the others welcomed the goddess with awestruck silence.

Then Duane the Lawyer sat on the ground with a thump.

"Naked lady," he said, pointing. "Feathers."

Lily's wings folded, and she took Jack's hand and looked around the circle. Her hair and skin shone, and her eyes gleamed. She was trembling.

"I hate you all," she said.

But Carolyn knew better, and she thought the others did too.

She turned to Artie then and gave him a long, hard hug, crushing dozens of snowflakes into water between them. She had stopped being afraid of losing her beauty before he lost his. After tonight, they would have no choice but to see something more when they looked at each other.

As she held him, she hiccupped. Just once. And then she was fine again.

23

◆

He Wasn't Dressed
for Dancing Nude

He wasn't dressed for dancing nude, he thought as he walked away from the clearing. The others could get naked and dance around like kindergartners pretending to be witches, but Stephen wasn't playing. He wasn't naked under his clothes. Never had been.

It was galling to him that Katy was participating. He had thought she had more sense than that.

But then, if she had more sense, she wouldn't be trying to keep her pregnancy a secret from him.

She had been sick to her stomach on several mornings over the past two weeks. The first time, when he'd asked her what was wrong, she had told him that there was a twenty-four-hour bug going around at the office. And she'd stayed home from work that day. But the next time—and the time after that, and the time after that—she had kept the bathroom door closed and the shower running. But he had listened at the door and heard her being sick.

He'd wanted to do something to help, but she clearly hadn't even wanted him to know what was happening. So he'd pretended ignorance and was continuing to do so.

He didn't know whether she was still having her affair, or with whom. But he didn't think that her efforts to hide her morning sickness were a good sign.

Still, there was a slim possibility that Stephen himself was the baby's father, because he and Katy had made love about once a week since the end of September. So despite her duplicitous behavior, he would cling to that possibility until she told him otherwise.

He came across a fallen tree and sat down on it, staring at the wilting moonflower in his hand. He was in no position to condemn Katy. After all, he had secrets of his own. One was that he was in love with Halle but had never told her. Another was that he *had* told Carolyn that he loved her even though he didn't. At least, he didn't love her the same way that he loved Halle. Or Katy.

But he had slept with Carolyn anyway. And the fact that Katy had slept with someone else first was no excuse.

Especially since who he had really wanted to sleep with was Halle.

But at least he and Carolyn had remained friends after their last time together. He hadn't been sure that they would, because she was a mystery to him. Carolyn could be bitter and cutting at one moment and then warm and generous in the next. And she could be cool and aloof, but then turn around and expect everyone to eat flowers and dance naked.

Katy, on the other hand, had always been predictable. Katy was rational, articulate, and demure. To a fault.

Yet in recent months she'd had an affair and gotten pregnant. And right now she was prancing around in the nude and howling at the Moon.

It was kind of exciting, actually. It was the sort of thing that Stephen had always imagined doing with Halle.

But Halle had a new boyfriend now, and an old boyfriend as well. And that, combined with everything Stephen had been going through with Carolyn and Katy, had gotten to be too much for him. Wanting three women was wanting two too many, even when they were all naked at the same time.

So now he was sitting alone in the moonlit woods, trying not to listen to the hooting and whooping going on back at the clearing.

He clenched his moonflower in his fist and knew it was a miracle. Moonflowers didn't bloom in December, not even in Texas. Not when it was this cold.

It bugged him. His world was not a world of miracles. His world was not a world in which moonflowers could bloom in December, or in which winged goddesses could fly into the lives of mortals. His world was not a world in which a weak-chinned, four-eyed literary geek could make love to a woman who looked and felt like Carolyn. And his world was not a world in which Katy could get pregnant, because they had tried for years, and it hadn't happened.

Until now.

But there wasn't a thing he could do to put his world back the way it had been. He could try to escape into the woods, but he was still aware that the others were back there gyrating, their breasts and penises bouncing, as they wallowed in an attempt to create yet another miracle.

And he had no doubt that they would succeed. He had no doubt that their combined nudity would indeed bring Lily down from the Moon again. She would come, and they would rejoice, and then they'd have a ritual orgy or something.

He hadn't left because he'd thought they were wrong. He had left because he'd wished he could join them, but had known that he couldn't.

Because no matter whom he loved or who loved him, he was still who he was. That had been forged in psychic steel a long time ago. And even if he had slept with Carolyn or impregnated Katy, he was still the four-eyed, chinless schlub who had remained a virgin until he'd gotten engaged at the age of twenty-five. He was still the guy who wanted someone he couldn't have.

He made a gagging sound. What he still was, he thought, was the guy who liked to go off by himself and pout.

Something small, soft, and cold touched his hand, and he glanced down and saw a snowflake melting on his skin. Then he looked up and saw thousands of snowflakes falling toward him, moonlight-white against the velvet sky. It was as if the stars had come loose and were drifting to earth.

One more miracle. Terrific.

He held up his moonflower and for several minutes tried to catch snowflakes in its withering trumpet. He didn't catch even one, and that pleased him. At least some things were still happening the way they were supposed to.

313

Stephen realized then that he was chilly. He stood up, flexed his legs, and started toward the cabin.

But he had only gone about fifteen feet when Jack dropped from the sky and landed in front of him, catlike, on all fours.

Stephen stopped and stared.

"Sorry," a voice called from above. "I lost my grip."

Stephen looked up again and saw Lily hovering among the snowflakes and treetops. A few feathers were falling with the snow, and Stephen's gaze followed them down to Jack.

"That's okay," Jack called to Lily. "I'm fine." He stood up, brushed himself off, and did a quick jig. "See?"

Stephen averted his eyes. Jack was still naked.

"I'll leave you alone for a bit, then," Lily said.

She flew off in the direction of the clearing, and Jack looked at Stephen and grinned.

"She came back!" Jack said. He sounded like a kid who had just gotten a new bike.

"I see that," Stephen said. He knew that he didn't sound happy for Jack, but he didn't think he could do anything about it. "So why aren't you sticking to her like epoxy? Aren't you afraid she'll leave again?"

Jack looked at him as if he'd just asked what color an orange was.

"She won't leave until moonrise," Jack said. "That's the way it works. Of course I want to spend every minute with her that I can—but I was worried about you, so she brought me to you."

Stephen started for the cabin again. "You don't have to worry about me, Jack. I'm fine."

Jack walked with him. "Then why did you leave the clearing?"

"Because I didn't want to be there."

"Why not?"

"I don't know."

"Then how did you know you wanted to leave?"

Stephen stopped and glared at Jack, remembering another time he had encountered him naked in the woods. "I guess because I didn't want to watch all of you have sex with owls."

Jack frowned. "What's wrong with owls? Owls are wise and powerful. Owls are our friends."

Stephen couldn't stand it. "Okay, fine, owls are our friends. That doesn't mean I want to sleep with one."

"Oh, you mean an actual bird?" Jack asked. "No, of course not. That would be bestiality."

Stephen leaned back against a live oak. He was weary. Trying to have a coherent conversation with Jack was like trying to teach a hamster to play the clarinet.

"Forget the owls," he said. "The truth is, I—"

He hesitated, unwilling to reveal too much. But then he remembered that he was talking to Jack, whose perception of reality was so skewed anyway that it probably didn't matter what he told him.

"The truth is," Stephen said, "I just didn't want to see Katy naked with all of you."

Jack seemed confused by that. "But, Steve," he said. "It's just us."

Stephen could feel a pressure behind his eyes trying to push through and pour down his face. He blinked it back.

He thought of how much he loved and wanted Halle, and of how much it had thrilled him to be with Carolyn.

But mainly, he thought of how much he would miss curling up around Katy's cool rump.

"I think I've lost her," he said, turning away. "I think she's going to leave me." He drew in a shuddering breath and tried to compose himself. He hated sounding pathetic. "That's why I couldn't help you bring Lily back. Because when I saw Katy start to take off her clothes, it was like she was going away."

Jack put his hands on Stephen's shoulders. "Sit down. I've written a new lecture concerning the dynamics of the Earth-Moon system, and I want you to hear it."

Stephen tried to pull away, but Jack wouldn't let him go. So Stephen sat down among the roots of the live oak, and he listened.

"What you can't see when you look at the Moon," Jack said as he began to pace back and forth, "is that she's moving away from us. She can't help it. The very fact that she's with us at all means that she has to try to leave. Ironic, isn't it?"

"If you say so."

Jack stopped pacing. "What I say has nothing to do with it!" he yelled. "It's the nature of the relationship! It's the same thing that keeps her from showing us her dark side!"

"All right, all right," Stephen said. "I believe you."

Jack took a deep breath and then held his fists in front of his chest. "So here they are, the Earth and Moon. They've been together for four and a half billion years, and over the course of that long cohabitation, tidal friction and other unaddressed therapy issues have forced the Moon to keep her pretty side facing the Earth. Simultaneously, however, her own tidal influence and passive-aggressive manipulation have been slowing the Earth's rotation, demonstrating that this relationship is nothing if not codependent. Following so far?"

Stephen nodded. He was following. So far.

Jack moved his left fist away from his right. "So in order to conserve angular momentum and preserve her identity as an individual, the Moon has no choice but to recede from the Earth about two inches every year."

"That isn't much," Stephen said.

Jack put his fists on his hips. "It is when you're talking mumblety-mumble gazillion years, pal. But that's beside the point, which is this: *Having* her means *losing* her. It's your basic yin-yang, black-white, sweet-sour, or chocolate-and-peanut-butter dichotomy."

Stephen hugged his knees to his chest. "So you're saying that she's leaving, and there's nothing I can do about it."

"Ha!" Jack barked. "Shows what you humanities majors know. Sure, the Moon is edging away—but even as she recedes, a reconciliation is in the offing. Because the Earth's rotation is still at the mercy of the tidal force of desire, and it will continue to slow until, finally, the terrestrial day is the same length as the lunar month. And at that point, the happy couple will be perfectly in sync!"

He emphasized each of his next words by jabbing his index finger at Stephen's nose. "Then, and only then," he said, "the Moon will begin coming closer to the Earth again. In fact, she'll come closer, and closer, and closer."

"But before she can come closer," Stephen said, "she *has* to go farther away?"

Jack slapped his thighs. "Yes! It's inevitable!"

He looked up at the Moon and raised his arms over his head.

"It's fucking physics!"

Stephen stood up again. "So you're suggesting that I may seem to be losing Katy now," he said, "but that she's going to come back to me?"

Jack lowered his arms, cocked his head, and gave Stephen a quizzical stare.

"What's Katy got to do with anything?" he asked. "I've been talking about the goddamn Moon."

Stephen was nonplussed for a moment, and then he had to laugh. He had been sitting on the cold ground in the middle of the woods during a snowstorm, listening to a naked man give a lecture on orbital dynamics.

He was the one who was insane.

And he had another question.

"So what happens then?" he asked. "What happens after the Moon comes close?"

"Oh," Jack said, scratching his beard. "That's the till-death-do-us-part stage. Eventually, see, the Earth and Moon will be so close that the passion of their tidal forces will rip the Moon to pieces."

"Lovely."

Jack shrugged. "Yeah, but the Earth will be dead or senile not long after that. Which is about as close to a happy ending as cosmic marriage ever gets. You want to come back to the clearing now?"

Stephen shivered. "I would," he said, "but I need to get warm. I'd better just go inside."

Jack pointed at the moonflower in Stephen's hand.

"Taste it first," he said.

Stephen gave up. He brought the moonflower to his mouth, and as the blossom touched his lips and tongue, a jolt shot through his body as if he'd grabbed an electric fence.

"Yow," he said, and then ate the entire blossom.

It tasted fine, and he felt pretty good. His skin tingled, and he heard a buzzing in his skull.

Jack winked. "First one's free," he said. Then he raised his arms over his head again, and Lily swooped down and carried him off toward the clearing.

Stephen followed them, but he made himself walk even though his blood was urging him to run. It was a matter of pride.

Then, just before reaching the clearing, he met Tommy Morrison coming the other way.

They stopped and regarded each other warily. Their confrontation at Halle's duplex had been more than four months ago, but they hadn't said a word to each other since then.

Tommy was wearing his jeans and cowboy boots again, and he was rebuttoning his shirt. But even as he buttoned, he kept his eyes on Stephen's.

"You gonna try to kick my ass again?" he asked.

Stephen shook his head. "I'll refrain. And I want to apologize for trying to in the first place. Also for trying to pee on your truck."

Tommy seemed to be satisfied with that. "No problem, and no harm done." He started walking again. "See you at supper in an hour or two."

"You're leaving the party?" Stephen asked.

Tommy paused. "Yeah. I got some things to think about. When that goddess of y'all's showed up, I had me an epiphany and realized that I'm gay."

Stephen didn't know what to say.

"Now, don't give me that look," Tommy said. "It's merely a hitherto unexamined piece of information, is all, so I got to mull it over. Besides which, nobody turned off the stove before we all came runnin' out here, and we don't want that chili cookin' down to a brown scum at the bottom of the pot."

"Okay," Stephen said.

"Damn right," Tommy said. He started toward the cabin again. "Later."

"Later," Stephen said, and he watched Tommy disappear among the trees.

Then he went on toward the clearing, and when he was close he could see that everyone there was still naked. They were singing "The Lion Sleeps Tonight," more or less in harmony, and Lily was scooping up each of them in turn and carrying them above the trees and back. Feathers and snowflakes were swirling everywhere.

Stephen stepped into the clearing just as Katy went aloft. As she rose toward the sky, she was laughing like he'd never heard her laugh before.

Then everyone else noticed he was back, and they seemed delighted. Even Duane, whom he hardly knew. And Carolyn and Halle both kissed him, so he guessed he was glad to be there.

Then Lily brought Katy back to earth, and when Katy saw Stephen, she ran to him and threw her arms around his neck.

"I missed you," she said.

He decided there was no time like the present. "I missed you too. Are we having a baby?"

Katy's eyes became fearful.

"I think so," she said. "But—"

He didn't let her finish.

"Good," he said. "It's about time."

Then Katy looked happy, and she took his hands and spun him around.

"Take off your clothes!" she cried. "Sing with us! Dance with us!"

Stephen decided to compromise. He sang, and he danced, and he even ripped off his shirt and whirled it over his head—but he kept his pants on.

Even drunk on moonflower nectar and dancing in the snow under a full Moon, he was determined to maintain his dignity. He was going to be a father soon, and he had to set a good example.

24

◆

The Goddess Said Good-bye

The goddess said good-bye in the morning. She told Jack that this time she really couldn't come back again.

They were in the small corner bedroom in the cabin's east wing. At 4:00 A.M., when everyone else had danced and sung to exhaustion, Jack and Lily had come here and made love. Lily said now that it had been for the last time.

But at least, Jack thought, she was telling him herself. At least she had come to him once more before leaving.

"Luna is setting," Lily said. "I've already stayed too long."

Jack held her close under the covers. "All right," he said. He was trying not to be a jerk about this, but it wasn't easy.

Gently, Lily pulled away from him and got out of bed. Then, her claws clicking against the hardwood floor, she walked to the casement window in the east wall. As she pulled back the curtains and pushed the window open, the first rays of the morning sun lit her face and breasts. She arched her back and spread her wings.

Jack tried to burn this image of her into his memory. He wanted to remember her like this. He had never seen her in sunlight before.

Lily looked back at him and started to speak. But then she winced and doubled over, clutching her belly. Whatever she had been about to say was obliterated by a yelp of pain.

Jack threw off the covers and rushed to her.

He put his arms around her and was terrified at how fragile she felt. She was quivering like a frightened animal.

"What's wrong?" he asked. He held her tight against his chest and ran his hands over her back.

Then his fingers touched her wings, and Lily yelped again. She bit his shoulder as her wings shuddered and fell away.

Jack stared at the naked skin of her back and saw two pink lines on either side of her spine. He was so stunned that he let go of her, and she crumpled to the floor beside her fallen wings.

"It hurts," she said. She began to sob. "It hurts."

Jack knelt beside her, pulled her onto his lap, and stroked her hair. He didn't know what else to do.

"Where does it hurt?" he asked. "Your back?"

"Everywhere," she said. She sounded angry. "My back, my breasts, my belly, my feet—"

Jack looked at her feet and saw that the bird-claws were peeling away like snakeskin.

"Help me," Lily said. "They itch. They *burn.*"

So Jack reached down, grasped the talons on Lily's feet, and pulled. The dead claws and rough bird skin sloughed off in his hands, and underneath, Lily's ankles and feet were small and pink. Her toes wiggled.

Lily's sobs subsided then, and Jack threw the claws across the room.

"Is that better?" he asked.

Lily nodded, smearing tears into his chest. "A little," she said. "But my belly still hurts."

Jack tried to stand and pull her up with him. "I'll take you to a doctor."

But Lily held him where he was. She was still strong.

"No," she said. There was pain in her voice, but her sobbing had stopped. "I think I know what's happened."

She reached down between her thighs, and when she brought her hand up again, her fingers were red with blood.

"I've stayed too long," she said as she gazed at the blood. "I shouldn't have come back at all. But when your friends added their desire to yours, I couldn't resist." Her nostrils flared. "You ganged up on me. And now I can't go home."

Jack was torn. He hated knowing that he was the reason Lily was unhappy. But he also wanted to laugh with joy because she wasn't leaving.

He stroked her hair again. It was as thick and glossy as ever.

"Maybe," he said, "this can be your home now."

Lily pushed herself off his lap and knelt on the floor, facing him. "This cabin? Home? I thought it belonged to Halle."

Jack couldn't help smiling. "That's not what I meant. What I meant was . . . maybe your home can be on Earth now." He hesitated a moment and then decided that if he was going to take his shot, he'd better do it now. "Maybe your home can be with me."

Lily looked down at her tattered wings. A cold breeze was blowing through the open window, and the wings were disintegrating, their feathers spinning and sliding away.

After a minute, Lily looked up at Jack again. Her lips trembled.

"Okay," she said.

Jack helped her up then, and they went back to bed. They left the window open, and the sunlight that fell across them as they lay down together almost offset the chill of the winter air.

And although Lily's skin felt as smooth under Jack's hands as it always had, she *looked* different. Without her wings, and in the light of day—

She had freckles on her shoulders.

She had a mole on her right calf and another on her hip.

She had little red veins in the whites of her eyes.

Her nose had a funny bump on the bridge.

Her lower lip was twice as big as her upper lip.

Her teeth were just a bit uneven.

Her chin had a dimple.

Jack couldn't believe it.

She was more beautiful than ever.

He kissed her furiously. He wanted to devour her.

She smelled of moonflowers.

"Jack," Lily said, taking his face between her hands.

"What?" he asked.

Lily licked her lips. She looked worried.

"I want to be sure you understand," she said. "I'm not a goddess anymore."

Jack tried to nod to indicate that he did understand that, but he couldn't because she was holding his head.

"You don't need to be," he said.

She closed her eyes. "And I'm not Natalie, either."

Hearing Natalie's name made Jack remember how much he missed her. She had been something special, and he had loved her a lot. She hadn't been like anyone else he had ever known.

As he had that thought, he extended a finger and touched the funny bump on Lily's nose.

"I don't want you to be," he said.

Then he and Lily made love, and from somewhere in the cabin, Halle shouted, "Hold it down in there! Decent people are still trying to sleep!"

And as Jack held Lily, her eyes opened wide, and he saw the Moon shining in their depths.

She bit his shoulder again. The wind blew in through the open window, and feathers flew everywhere.

EPILOGUE

❖

Lily Went to the Open Window

Lily went to the open window. Her hands were shaking. Her whole body was shaking. She didn't know what to make of it.

What had that been, anyway? Nothing like it had ever happened before. Not in any century. Not even with Jack.

Not until now.

She looked out at the live oaks and cedars. They had snow on their limbs, and the light sparkling from that snow was brighter than anything she had ever seen. It stung her eyes, but she wouldn't let herself look away.

Behind her, on the bed, Jack spoke. "You know what just occurred to me? We're going to have to forge a birth certificate for you. Otherwise, you won't be able to get a social security number, or a driver's license, or any of that stuff. And you'll need those things if you ever feel like voting, or if you decide you want a job."

Lily was watching a small brown bird flit from one twig to another. And there was a squirrel, chattering, knocking clumps of snow from a branch with its tail.

"I think I do want a job," Lily said as she watched the squirrel. "I owe Carolyn a few hours of labor as it is."

"Well, there you go," Jack said. "There's a lot to arrange."

Lily took a deep breath. The air was sharp and cold. She had breathed air that was sharp and cold before, but this wasn't the same. Sunlight imparted a distinctive flavor. It made the air stronger. Heavier. More urgent.

And her skin was goose pimpled. That had never happened before, either.

Something tickled the tops of her feet, and when she looked down she discovered that it was one of her feathers. As she bent to pick it up, she again became aware of the ache in her belly and the blood on her thighs. And she noticed that she smelled different now, too.

Then, straightening up and bringing the feather to her lips, she saw that her hand was still shaking. And she knew that it had nothing to do with the cold.

She was astonished. She had known what she would lose, but she hadn't imagined that she might gain something in return.

"I'll bet you didn't know what you were getting into," Jack said.

Lily pursed her lips and blew her feather out among the trees. Then she turned toward Jack, and the sight of him made her smile.

"I had no idea," she said.

She took a step, and the wooden floor was first smooth and then rough against her newborn soles.

"I had no idea at all."

ABOUT THE AUTHOR

BRADLEY DENTON was born in Wichita, Kansas, in 1958. He attended the University of Kansas and received a bachelor's degree in Astronomy and English. Two years after receiving a master's in English, he published his first novel, *Wrack and Roll*. His second novel, *Buddy Holly Is Alive and Well on Ganymede*, was honored with the John W. Campbell Memorial Award, and his third novel, *Blackburn*, was a finalist for the Bram Stoker Award. He has published short fiction in numerous magazines and anthologies, and in 1995 he received the World Fantasy Award for his two-volume story collection. He and his wife, Barbara, live on the outskirts of Austin, Texas.